PRAISE FOR M...
ROMANCE NOVELS

THE PAGAN'S PRIZE

"Another fine example of Ms. Minger's amazing talent. I thoroughly enjoyed it."
—JOHANNA LINDSEY

"With Miriam Minger, you're assured of a good read."
—*Heartland Critiques*

"Outstanding . . . This is a well-written, moving story that shows the tremendous skill of the author . . . *Marvelous* barely describes my feelings."
—*Rendezvous*

WILD ANGEL

"Fast paced, exciting, and love scenes to curl your toes."
—*Affaire de Coeur*

"Unique . . . This non-stop, exhilarating read will capture you with its fabulous characterizations . . . lightning-fast pacing, clever plotting, and strong writing."
—*Romantic Times*

And now, enjoy her most spectacular tale of all . . .

SECRETS OF MIDNIGHT

Titles by Miriam Minger

THE PAGAN'S PRIZE
WILD ANGEL

SECRETS of MIDNIGHT

MIRIAM MINGER

JOVE BOOKS, NEW YORK

If you purchased this book without a cover you should be aware that this book is stolen property. It was reported as "unsold and destroyed" to the publisher, and neither the author nor the publisher has received any payment for this "stripped book."

SECRETS OF MIDNIGHT

A Jove Book / published by arrangement with
the author

PRINTING HISTORY
Jove edition / October 1995

All rights reserved.
Copyright © 1995 by Miriam Minger.
This book may not be reproduced in whole
or in part, by mimeograph or any other means,
without permission. For information address:
The Berkley Publishing Group, 200 Madison Avenue,
New York, New York 10016.

ISBN: 0-515-11726-9

A JOVE BOOK®
Jove Books are published by The Berkley Publishing Group,
200 Madison Avenue, New York, New York 10016.
JOVE and the "J" design are trademarks
belonging to Jove Publications, Inc.

PRINTED IN THE UNITED STATES OF AMERICA

10 9 8 7 6 5 4 3 2 1

For

Cecelia Diaz and Caryl Richards

Thank you for your encouragement, love,
and friendship.
I owe this story to you.

❧ One ❧

"Did you see the groom, Corie? His face all red and sweaty and his bulbous belly out to here? Lord, the way he was leering at Druella all through the ceremony with those little pig eyes! If I saw such a sight walking toward me on my wedding night, I'd fling myself out the nearest window!"

Fling herself Lindsay Somerset did, quite dramatically, Corisande Easton thought as her best friend tumbled to the ground in a swirl of white petticoat and silky blond hair.

Corisande's smile widened as Lindsay lay still as a corpse with her slender arms outflung and her pink-stockinged legs askew in a most unladylike fashion. Only the slight rise and fall of her breasts betrayed her. Imagining what that awful termagant Lady Somerset would say if she saw her stepdaughter behaving so wantonly, Corisande shoved away the unpleasant thought and focused again upon Lindsay as the young woman began to recite in somber dirgelike tones.

"Here lies dead a virgin bride, poor girl, wed to a man who resembled a pig. Perhaps if she'd been allowed to choose her own husband, she wouldn't be dead, she'd be dancing a jig!"

Corisande's burst of laughter was joined by Lindsay's as

she sat upright and brushed damp bits of grass from her gray merino walking dress.

It was good to hear Corisande laugh. Lately she'd been too serious by far, so many cares weighing upon her mind. So many things to do. So many local wrongs to be righted. But Lindsay was determined that their last afternoon together would be as lighthearted as possible, Corisande's responsibilities forgotten if only for a short time.

For that matter her own worries as well, Lindsay thought as she glanced out across Mount's Bay, the water's surface blinding in the brilliant sunshine that had finally broken through the fog.

No, she simply wouldn't consider the possibility that her stepmother might change her mind about allowing Lindsay to finally have her London Season. Her father's second wife, Olympia, had been nothing short of despotic these past eight years since her marriage to Sir Randolph Somerset, but she couldn't, *couldn't* be that cruel. If Lindsay was forced to wait another year, she'd be twenty-one and well on her way to spinsterhood!

"A brilliant performance, Miss Somerset, and an even more apt observation about the groom." Corisande's voice broke into her thoughts, her friend pushing a stray lock of auburn hair behind her ear as she grinned down at Lindsay. "He did have the look of a prize Truro pig, and with an unpleasant nature to boot, but you have to admit Druella Simmons seemed quite pleased with herself, no matter that the marriage was arranged."

Lindsay met Corisande's smiling dark brown eyes, which were a color that Corisande matter-of-factly considered plain as Cornish mud but that Lindsay always assured her was quite lovely, especially with those amazing green tints. "Yes, I suppose Druella would be pleased to have captured a wealthy squire. She always claimed she would make the richest catch in the parish."

"No, I believe she said something about the whole county." With the gift of a mimic, Corisande affected a lofty nasal tone that sounded just like Druella, a local girl who had long lorded it over other young women of her acquaintance just because her father was a baron, albeit an impoverished one. "And then, my dearest, *dearest* darlings, you must all come to my beautiful house in Devonshire for tea."

Lindsay gave a loud hoot of laughter, but her grin became a grimace as she shuddered, remembering how the groom had lasciviously pressed his girth to Druella's slight frame after Corisande's father, the Reverend Joseph Easton, had pronounced them man and wife at the small church wedding yesterday morning. The disgusting man had practically been drooling onto his boots!

"Druella's won herself a marvelous big house and hundreds of pounds a year, truly. Each night at bedtime she'll likely wish she'd settled for less coin when that great white whale of a husband flops under the covers with her and demands his due!"

Lindsay caught Corisande's outstretched hand, her dearest friend's own grimace melting into mirth as she pulled Lindsay to her feet. Arm in arm, they set out once more along the cliff, the strong late March breeze, laced with salt spray and smelling of the sea and the lush promise of spring, whipping their hair around their faces.

Corisande was never shocked by anything Lindsay said or did, and Lindsay loved her for it. There had been so many times she had escaped the oppressiveness of her beleaguered father's manor for the comforting chaos of the Easton parsonage where she could be herself without any fear of rebuke. Just as she had fled this morning, climbing out a dining-room window when she heard Olympia trumpeting her name from an upstairs bedroom.

Heaven help her, she'd be damned if she spent her last day at home being lectured on the proper decorum for a young lady about to embark on her first Season! Not when her father's elder sister, Winifred, Lady Penney, had no doubt been directed to torment her with the same rules and regulations once she reached London.

Sobering at the thought, Lindsay sighed as she glanced at Corisande. "I know I've nearly hounded you to death, but it's not too late for you to come with me. We'd have the most marvelous time! I'll just tell Olympia"—even saying the woman's name was distasteful to Lindsay, who had never once been able to call her father's wife "Mother"—"well, I'll tell her that you could be another chaperone for me in case Aunt Winnie grows weary of all the balls—"

"You know I can't go," Corisande interrupted gently, trying not to be affected by the disappointment shining in Lindsay's blue eyes. *Cerulean* blue, her wildly imaginative friend liked to call them, not out of vanity but simply because she enjoyed the sound of the exotic word upon her tongue.

In fact, Lindsay Somerset didn't have a vain bone in her body, an amazing thing considering she was one of the loveliest young women in Cornwall. Her flawless skin, waist-length blond hair that was practically white, and hourglass figure were the stuff of King Arthur's legends. No, if anything, her only fault lay in her being too kindhearted for her own good.

Lindsay had earned Olympia's heated censure countless times when she had been caught taking food from the Somerset pantry to feed the parish's hungry tinners and their families, or been discovered selling her own shoes to purchase coal to warm some unfortunate soul's freezing cottage.

Corisande's causes had become Lindsay's; Corisande couldn't have wished for a friend more loyal and true. Yet Lindsay's life would have been much easier under Lady Somerset's roof if she'd been less caring. For that reason, for Lindsay's sake, Corisande was almost relieved to see her go.

"If you're thinking you can't go because you haven't the money," Lindsay began, clearly making one last valiant attempt to sway her, "I already told you I would share everything I have—"

"It's not the money," Corie broke in again, though, in truth, as a vicar's daughter she had virtually no coin to her name.

"Well, don't dare tell me it's because you wouldn't fit in," Lindsay said with reproach, her beautiful sky-blue eyes flashing now. "You're so pigheaded, Corie Easton!"

"Like you," Corisande said with fondness.

"Maybe so, but you're worse. Complicated, uncompromising, and full of the silliest notions. Like only pretty girls should go to London. You're pretty, Corie, prettier than most no matter—"

"And you've always been far too generous when it comes to judging your friends," Corisande cut in, the back of her hand brushing against the pale, grooved scar bisecting her cheek as she swept windblown hair out of her eyes. Wanting to change a subject that didn't bother her nearly as much as Lindsay thought it did, she added, "London is no place for someone like me. I wouldn't know what to do with myself there."

"You could have fun. See new things, meet new people, have wonderful adventures—oh, I can't wait to get to London!"

Corisande was glad to see that excitement now lit Lindsay's lovely face, her friend's eyes dancing with anticipation. Lord help her, if Lady Somerset did anything now to thwart Lindsay's dreams, Corisande couldn't say what she might do.

At the very least, she'd give that insufferable woman a tongue-lashing sure to straighten her sausage curls, something she'd longed to do for years, although Lindsay had prevented her every time. Lindsay simply loved her father too much to make his life any more miserable than it already was, again giving little thought to herself.

Just as Lindsay was doing now, insisting that Corisande accompany her even though she knew that Lady Somerset would never approve. If Corisande stepped one foot into that coach, Lady Somerset would have just the ammunition she needed to cancel the entire journey. Corisande's friendship with Lindsay had always been a thorn in the old bat's side, Corisande's zealous determination to help the parish's poor and needy hardly a pastime Lady Somerset considered suitable for a baronet's daughter.

At least she agreed with the woman on that score, Corisande thought as she glanced at Lindsay, her friend's eyes fixed expectantly to the east, as if she could see the roofs of London all the way from Cornwall. Not because helping those less fortunate than herself wasn't suitable for Lindsay, but because she finally had the chance to do something for herself. To make her own dreams come true.

When she'd told Lindsay that only pretty girls should go to London, she had meant merely that Lindsay with her peerless blond beauty was born for such a glittering world, a fact Corisande didn't begrudge her in the least. How could she? To experience life outside of Cornwall was all her indomitable friend had ever wanted to do. Just as staying in Cornwall where she was needed was what Corisande wanted to do. God knew, she had plenty of responsibilities to keep her busy, and with times being so harsh thanks to this damned interminable war with Napoleon and now America, too—

"Don't, Corie. I know that look on your face." Lindsay's voice held fresh reproach as she squeezed Corisande's arm. "You've got that tiny little frown between your brows, and I won't have it. You're not supposed to be thinking about all the things you have to do."

"I wasn't," Corisande fibbed, although it was hard to forget that the cutter *Fair Betty* was due to drop anchor at a secluded cove near Porthleven harbor late tonight, which meant she would be busy helping to oversee the landing and dispatching of smuggled tea, silk handkerchiefs, and brandy until the wee hours of the morning—

"Yes you are! There's that frown again!" Lindsay blurted out, looking wholly exasperated. "You promised me, Corie. We were just going to enjoy ourselves this afternoon. No thinking about the villagers' problems or the tinners' problems—"

"I know, or their children's grumbling bellies."

"Or worrying about your father."

"Or wondering whether poor Frances has been chased from the house yet by one of Estelle's pranks."

"Or whether your two other sisters are behaving themselves."

"And least of all," Corisande said wryly, her temples beginning to throb, "wondering if the king's excisemen might be on the prowl tonight when we've a ship coming in from Roscoff."

"That, the very least of all!" Lindsay rolled her eyes heavenward as if realizing the impossibility of a carefree afternoon. Then, just as suddenly, a wide grin broke over her face. "I know what we'll do."

Corisande watched, bemused, as Lindsay hoisted her skirt and clambered on top of a large lichen-covered rock. Once settled, she patted the place beside her.

"I know you don't like to sit still for very long, Corie, but let's rest here a while. I want to talk about husbands."

"Husbands?"

"Exactly. And we already know what kind we don't want."

"No lecherous-eyed pigs for one," Corisande quipped as she bunched a handful of her own frayed woolen skirt and climbed up next to Lindsay.

"Or disgusting white whales." Lindsay gave a light laugh, only to become serious suddenly. "And I'll have no man, *ever,* who would allow my stepmother to govern our lives."

Corisande wasn't surprised by the steely determination in Lindsay's voice. Lady Somerset might have finally decided that it was time Lindsay found herself a husband, but Lindsay had her own ideas as to what sort of man she wanted to wed.

"Someone Olympia couldn't intimidate," Lindsay continued softly. "Someone who wouldn't hesitate to stand up to her."

"That rules out most eligible bachelors, I would imagine," Corisande said half under her breath, unfortunately voicing a sad reality for Lindsay. Her stepmother had an uncanny gift for making grown men wilt like thirsty potted plants in her presence.

"Oh, no, I'll find him," came Lindsay's fervent response, her eyes meeting Corisande's. "I damned well won't marry until I do. I swear it—in fact, we both should swear!"

"Lindsay, what . . . ?" was all Corisande managed to say as Lindsay jumped to her feet and hauled Corisande up beside her, both of them nearly toppling from the rock. Laughing, they regained their balance, Lindsay grabbing Corisande's hands as she faced her.

"Say it with me, Corie. Neither of us can wed anyone less than the man of our dreams. Ready?"

Corisande felt foolish, but she nonetheless decided to play along, never ceasing to be amazed by her more romantic-minded friend's antics. "All right. Neither—"

"You have to really *believe* it," Lindsay cut in, exasperated, as if guessing Corisande's thoughts. "Otherwise our pact won't mean a thing. You don't want to end up with a husband like Druella's, do you?"

Corisande knew she would never allow such a dreadful thing to happen, oh, no, not to herself. But for Lindsay's sake—who could say what sort of undesirable character Olympia Somerset might wish for a son-in-law?—she squeezed her friend's hands and shouted with her at the top of their lungs after Lindsay counted to three, "Neither of us can wed anyone less than the man of our dreams!"

"There, that should do it," Lindsay pronounced as the wind carried away their words. Grinning from ear to ear, she looked quite pleased with herself. "It will be our secret."

"Secret? They probably heard us all the way to Arundale's Kitchen." Thinking sourly of the tin mine that had earned such a name because of the hot, moist air at its deeper levels, Corisande turned to jump off the rock, but Lindsay caught her arm.

"Oh, no, we're not done yet. You have to close your eyes and pretend he's standing right in front of you, just as you imagine him to be—"

"Lindsay!"

"Come on, Corie, it will be fun. Here, I'll go first!"

Lindsay closed her eyes and tilted her face upward as if she were looking at someone. "Oh, Corie, he's so handsome."

"Of course he's handsome, silly." Corisande gazed wryly at her beautiful friend. "But that isn't the most important thing. What kind of man do you want him to be?"

"A valiant man, an adventurer," Lindsay murmured dreamily, making Corisande smile to herself. "Someone who'll show me new places. Grand, exciting places! There's so much more to the world than Cornwall. I want to see it all! I want to experience things I've only read about in Papa's books!"

Corisande felt a twinge of sadness, but quickly stifled it. She'd always known Lindsay might one day leave Cornwall and not return. If that meant her dear friend would be happy, she would simply have to bear it.

"He'll want me with him, of course. Always by his side." Lindsay hugged her arms to her breasts. "And we'll be hopelessly, deliriously in love. Nothing will be more important to him than our life together . . ." Sighing deeply, she opened her eyes and smiled at Corisande. "Your turn."

Corisande squeezed her eyes shut, feeling that her ideal man was going to seem bland as paste next to Lindsay's. Which in truth was fine with her. Trustworthy, dependable. A companion to help her, nothing more. She could not yet envision his face, but it mattered little if he was handsome or not—

"No fair keeping it to yourself, Corie. You have to say what you want aloud," Lindsay urged with impatience.

"Well, I'd want a man who cares about the things I do," Corisande began firmly, starting with what mattered most to her. "Someone who's willing to work side by side with me to help ease the lives of those around us." She threw a small smile in Lindsay's direction. "Now that you'll be busy traveling the world, of course. And he must care just as much as I do about righting wrongs. God knows, there's enough injustice in this parish to make the angels weep—"

"But what of love, Corie? Wouldn't you like for a man to just sweep you off your feet?"

Corisande was taken aback, but she should have expected such an unsettling question from Lindsay.

To be that much in love with someone? Her father had deeply loved her French-born mother, which was probably why he'd become an eccentric shell of a man at her death eight years ago. The same vicious fever that had claimed Adele Easton had taken Lindsay's mother as well. But while Sir Randolph had remarried, much that he must rue the day, Joseph Easton had not. No, Corisande wasn't sure at all if she wanted a love that could bring such pain. In fact, she didn't want to fall in love with anyone, something she hadn't even told Lindsay. Just thinking about her father . . .

"I'd certainly have to respect a man first before I would ever marry him," she answered, skipping over the topic of love altogether. "He would have to be honorable, selfless—"

"Sounds dull as a saint."

Corisande gave a small laugh as she opened her eyes. "Well, not so dull that he'd be afraid to take chances. Fair trading's no occupation for the faint of heart."

"And you're certainly not the woman for any fainthearted man, no matter what you say," Lindsay said with a snort. She released Corisande's hands and jumped nimbly to the ground. "You'd have suitors buzzing around you like honeybees if you'd just learn to curb your temper."

"And you might have been happily married several times over if you'd settled for a husband of good Cornish stock, but no, only a bold adventurer with a daring gleam in his eye will do!" Corisande countered, jumping down next to Lindsay. They both stared at each other for a long moment, then burst out laughing.

"I'd say we're done with making secret pacts for the day, wouldn't you?"

Corisande nodded, looping her arm through Lindsay's as they set out once more along the cliff.

"So I'll be twenty going into my first Season," Lindsay said with a jaunty toss of her head. "Better that than some foolish green goose of a girl who doesn't have a clue what she wants."

"So I'm known for my temper." Corisande gave a nonchalant shrug as she looked out across a sunlit Mount's Bay. "At least it's helped me to get things done."

Just as she'd be venting her legendary spleen first thing tomorrow morning, Corisande thought to herself. She'd already decided to ride out to Arundale's Kitchen as soon as she saw that Lindsay was happily settled in her coach and bound for London.

She doubted she would get a wink of sleep tonight with Oliver Trelawny's ship due in from Brittany and then Lindsay leaving so bright and early, but the news she'd received only a few hours ago fairly screamed for her attention. This time that damned mine captain Jack Pascoe had gone too far, cutting the tinners' wages by a full half because they'd fallen behind in their work due to bad weather. Was the man mad? How did he expect the tinners to feed their families, to clothe and shelter them on what had already been a mere pittance?

A pity it wasn't the mine owner who'd be the target of her tongue-lashing. It was clear from worsening conditions that the new Duke of Arundale possessed the same ignoble qualities as his recently deceased father.

Corisande had itched for three years to tell that miserly old bastard what she thought of a man who could pay his workers so little that they were forced to live with their families in wretched hovels . . . but the weasel had gone and died. Now she would just have to save her choice words for his son the duke—if only he'd show his face in Cornwall. In fact, she dreamed of the day—

"Corie, you're frowning again!"

⚭ *Two* ⚭

"I say, Donovan, your scowl could wake the dead. Buck up, old man! Things could be worse, you know. Father could have named a bride for you in his will rather than granting you a choice."

Nigel Trent, Duke of Arundale, realized his attempt to put a good face on the situation had failed completely as his younger brother's scowl grew blacker. So black that the owlish-looking solicitor at Donovan's right seemed to shrink in his chair, the poor man nervously adjusting his spectacles.

"Uh, perhaps, Your Grace, I should leave the library to allow you and Lord Donovan some time to discuss—"

"Good idea, Wilkins," came a low growl that seemed to make the very draperies shiver. "And you can take that damned will—"

"Yes, yes, you'd best leave us," Nigel intervened, though the slight little man was already halfway across the room, his precious documents hastily snatched from the desktop and clutched protectively to his chest. As the door closed behind Wilkins, Nigel leaned back in the polished leather chair that had been his father's until two short months ago and studied his brother, who had lunged to his feet and now stood at the wide bow window with his back to the room.

A massively broad back stiff with tension, Nigel noted, sighing to himself. In that respect, Donovan had changed little. Nigel had seen him take such a stance in nearly every encounter with their father, an iron-willed, hard-gambling, blustering titan of a man who had done his damnedest to rule every aspect of his sons' lives.

But while Nigel had succumbed to the late Duke of Arundale's domination, unashamedly taking the easier path to afford himself some peace, Donovan had confounded his father's wishes from the moment he could talk. That is, until now. The old bastard had finally won, and, at least in this matter, Nigel couldn't say he wasn't glad. The dukedom was at stake, after all.

"So I'm to bloody wed."

Nigel met Donovan's deep brown eyes—nearly black, really, depending on the light—and wondered again at the changes in his brother. Donovan was a big man, nearly a full head taller than Nigel, but his four years as an officer under Wellington had left him leaner, harder, lending him a most forbidding air, well, at least when he was angry.

And he was furious now. No wonder poor Wilkins had fled. Nigel had half a mind to retire from the library, too, until his brother had calmed himself, but he might as well be done with the unpleasant business now that it was started.

"Yes, Donovan, as the will clearly states, you must wed. *If* you want your inheritance. I had no hand in this matter, mind you, it was all Father's doing, but I think it's for the best. As you know, Charlotte and I remain childless, and if anything should happen to me—you being the heir presumptive, of course, it's damned important that the Arundale line continue—"

"Perhaps, dear brother, if you could stomach sharing your wife's bed more often, that problem could easily be remedied."

It was a cruel cut, Donovan knew as he turned back to the

window, an uncomfortable silence descending upon the room. Nigel hadn't chosen his bride, an endlessly whiny young woman of bland intellect, sour breath, and formidable fortune. Their father had chosen her seven years ago, just as he had attempted three years later to choose a "suitable" bride for Donovan once it became clear that Nigel was having difficulty producing an heir.

But Donovan had escaped that fate by taking swift leave of the country to fight against Napoleon in Portugal and Spain, the Peninsular War as good an excuse as any to keep him far away from England and Arundale Hall. Until he'd received a letter saying that the duke had died, and that Donovan must return home at once to settle important matters of the estate.

So he'd come, because he needed money. The devil take it, he needed money! If it was only himself he had to worry about, he'd leave this bloody house and never return, and on his way out the door tell Nigel, his disagreeable wife, and that damned Wilkins to hell with his inheritance if he had to wed to obtain it! But then he might never find Paloma, his personal funds nearly depleted in the search—

"I say, Donovan, that comment was uncalled for."

Forcing down his anger, Donovan glanced at Nigel—at the strained expression on his face, at the hint of jowls developing around his jawline and the noticeable paunch around his middle—his brother, only one year his senior, looking much older than his twenty-eight years. "But true. It's no secret that you've sired four bastards in Dorset County while your beloved wife remains barren as a brick—"

"All right, old man, enough! At least you have a bloody choice, which was more than I was granted! Perhaps things might have been different . . ." Nigel didn't finish, but rose abruptly from his desk to face his brother. "Father's will stipulates that your bride must be a country-bred girl of good family—"

"I heard."

"Not your sort of woman admittedly—"

"But bound to be a good breeder."

"Exactly. Now, if you're in agreement that we proceed, I'll call Wilkins."

It was all Donovan could do to force a nod, his anger rising as Nigel walked stiffly to the door.

A country-bred girl. Leave it to his father to make such a final ridiculous demand, considering that Donovan had spent many a London Season evading just that sort of marriage-hungry miss as well as any scheming provincial mother eager to make her daughter a highly placed match.

In fact, he scorned the institution of marriage. It was a farce, a sham. Why would he ever want to wed after watching his parents' marriage—another loveless arranged affair —grow colder by the year? Several of his friends had stumbled down that same wretched path while he'd been away at war, the damned fools marrying for purely mercenary reasons or caving in to family duty.

Good God, he was no blather-brained romantic, but didn't anyone of his station marry for affection? What about shared interests or a common passion? How many times over a good bottle of brandy had he sworn that he'd rather remain a bachelor than have some unwanted marriage thrust upon him and his life become a hell on earth?

A cynical bachelor to boot. He'd long been convinced that the only happiness one could hope to find was well outside the bounds of matrimony, and Nigel with his mistresses was perfect proof—along with their mother, who had created quite a scandal five years ago when she fled to Italy with the wealthy count who still shared her bed. But now Donovan was being sucked into the same miserable pit as everyone else he knew, and there didn't seem to be a damned thing he could do about it . . .

"If you're ready, Lord Donovan, we'll continue."

Donovan left the window, but he couldn't sit. He paced back and forth across the library as Wilkins in his high-pitched tenor drone began to reread the will. Nigel simply sat slumped in his fine leather chair and looked glum.

"Does he have to go over all that again?" Donovan demanded, feeling more each moment like a caged beast with not even a faint hope of freedom. He came up beside Wilkins's chair so suddenly that the little man jumped, sweat beading his pallid brow. "Show me what I have to sign, and let's be done with it!"

"But—but, my lord, there's the matter of the house in Cornwall—"

"What house in Cornwall?" Donovan looked to Nigel, who now appeared almost as uncomfortable as the solicitor.

"Father bought property in Cornwall a year or so after you left England. A tin mine there has been quite profitable for us."

"*Quite* profitable," parroted Wilkins.

Donovan glanced from one man to the other, an inkling rising like sour bile in his gut. "All right, a tin mine in Cornwall. What in blazes does this have to do with me?"

"Simple, Donovan," Nigel said with a small sigh. "The house and surrounding estate is yours outright once you've agreed to abide by Father's will, while the substantial monetary portion of your inheritance and a fifty-one percent share in the mine—the controlling share, mind you—shall be yours once we see you properly wed."

A heavy silence hung in the room once more, Donovan staring incredulously at his brother. "I'm to live in some godforsaken house on some godforsaken land in Cornwall?"

"It's a handsome house, actually, Donovan—well, in need

of a little repair, I'll admit, but not anywhere as bad as you make it out to be."

"Near the fishing village of Porthleven," Wilkins chimed in, peeping over his spectacles. "Well, a small seaport, really. Quite a charming spot—"

"It could be on the bloody moon for all I care!" Donovan roared, his fist crashing down upon the desktop. "I thought I'd be given a town house in London at the very least. That's where all those silly little country chits go to ogle prime marriage stock, isn't it? Am I to find a wife or not?"

"That's the very point of it, Donovan. Father was certain you'd be distracted in the city—all those bored Society wives looking for a discreet dalliance or some such amusement. Just the sort of woman you've always favored, and so you can see, far too much of a temptation. So Father decided that you should make your choice in Cornwall. The Season hasn't quite begun, after all. If you leave soon, you might be able to catch some willing beauty still at home packing her trunks."

"If I leave soon . . . ," Donovan muttered to himself, feeling as if he had walked straight into a great yawning trap that had been meticulously prepared for him from the moment he'd last defied his father. Meeting Nigel's eyes, he said in a dangerously low voice, "You knew I wouldn't be able to refuse, didn't you? So you've avoided your foul-smelling wife and enjoyed your damned mistresses, knowing that one day Father would have me exactly where he wanted—"

"Surely an officer's infrequent pay hasn't kept you in the style to which you're accustomed," Nigel cut in, his voice grown as low as Donovan's. "Even when combined with the paltry allowance Father's been sending you all these years. Face facts, Donovan. A man of your station needs money to live properly, or you might as well have been born a pauper.

Marrying is a small price to pay for such security, wouldn't you say?"

Donovan said nothing, thinking that his elder brother had learned well at his father's side. Too well.

But Nigel didn't know about Paloma, and Donovan planned to keep things that way. Nor did Nigel realize that Donovan cared absolutely nothing for security or the proper way in which a man of his station should live.

All he cared about was that he gained his inheritance so he could continue his search. And that somehow he would escape the trap that was fast closing in around him. He had only to think of a way—

"Father's will meets with your approval, then?"

Donovan nodded grimly.

"Good. Wilkins has the agreement fully prepared. You've only to sign."

Donovan did, then threw the pen upon the desk and strode for the door.

"I'll have a carriage brought round for you first thing in the morning." Nigel's voice carried after him. "You should arrive in Cornwall within a few days—"

"I'm leaving now," Donovan ground out without turning. "My horse suits me fine."

"As you wish. I'll send the servants I took the liberty of hiring for your household after you, then."

Donovan stopped at that, and half spun to eye his brother narrowly. "You hired servants?"

"A butler, of course. Fine fellow named Ogden. He can double as your valet until you've a chance to hire your own man. A few others too. A cook, a housekeeper, just enough to get you started. A family agent has been living in the house and seeing after our business affairs, doing book-keeping and the like, but he'll have cleared out by the time you arrive."

"Oh, yes, my lord, Henry Gilbert should have cleared out

his things several days ago. No worries there," Wilkins squeaked helpfully. "He's taken a small residence just down the road if you have need of him."

So Nigel and his bespectacled lapdog had seen to everything, Donovan thought, incensed. Even down to hiring servants—no, bloody spies. Paid to watch him. Paid to see that he honored his agreement.

Hell and damnation, he wouldn't be surprised if the whole lot of them planned to troop into the master suite on his wedding night just to observe the proceedings!

"Wedding night . . ." Donovan said through gritted teeth, deciding he'd best leave before he began throwing things—starting with Wilkins.

"What was that, Donovan?"

Glaring at his brother, Donovan said not another word as he left the room and slammed the door behind him.

∞ Three ∞

"Estelle, no feeden that mongrel under the table now! I won't have it, I tell 'ee—Linette, have 'ee a notion to eat your eggs while they're nice an' hot or is it your plan to just push them round your plate? An' where's Marguerite? Marguerite!"

"She's still sitting in front of the mirror, Frances. Where else would she be?" Corisande answered as she hurried down the stairs and into the cozily warm kitchen where the Eastons' long-suffering housekeeper stood shaking her head, her hands fisted at her thick waist.

"Front of the mirror, is she?" came the disapproving reply in a rustic Cornish accent as thick as clotted cream. Frances's wrinkled face creased into a frown. "I've never seen a young girl, comely as that one or no, spend so much time fixen herself up for the day. 'Tes wicked, I say, an' her being the good passon's daughter!"

"Well, if not wicked, at the very least it's a sorry waste of time." Thinking of how she'd bolted from bed upon waking and thrown on her clothes, barely taking a moment to run her fingers through her disheveled hair and wind it into a bun at her nape, Corisande added over her shoulder—good and loud enough for her fifteen-year-old sister to hear upstairs—"I imagine Marguerite will find herself scrubbing the breakfast dishes if she doesn't come down soon, won't she, Frances?"

"Ais, so she will, an' this evening's too," the housekeeper agreed heartily as Corisande reached across the table for a piece of barley toast. In too much of a rush to sit down, she shot a warning look at her youngest sister as the impish nine-year-old tossed a bit of fried bacon to her panting mutt, Luther, then tried to cover her action with an all too engaging grin.

"Estelle . . ."

The grin faded, big hazel eyes pleading. "But he's hungry, Corie. Just look at him, poor dog. All ribs and whiskers."

Luther was a sight, Corisande agreed, a small wiry-haired creature of indeterminate breed who peered expectantly at her toast through a spiky fringe of gray hair. "Maybe so, but you heard Frances. You're to listen to what she says—and Linette, since you've obviously no interest in your eggs, why don't you fetch Marguerite?"

"You know she won't come," Linette answered with a matter-of-fact shrug. A thin, gangly child just turned twelve with the delicate features of their mother and the auburn hair all the Easton girls shared—well, except for Marguerite, whose locks bore a deeper hint of red—Linette pushed away her plate in disinterest. "Not until she's brushed her hair two hundred strokes."

"Well, she'll find her hair's soon to fall out of her head if she keeps on." Frances shoved Linette's plate right back in front of her. "An' you eat now! Your papa will think I'm not feeden 'ee proper—"

"Corie, I miss Lindsay."

Linette's soft statement couldn't have brought the clamor in the kitchen to a more sudden halt. As Frances sighed and turned back to the hearth while Estelle's expression fell, her whining hound momentarily forgotten, Corisande gazed thoughtfully at her younger sister.

"We all miss Lindsay, sweet. I can't believe she's been gone three days. It feels like forever."

"Well, she'd be here right now, having breakfast with us and laughing and telling us wonderful stories, if only she hadn't gone to London." Linette raised her small pointed chin, her eyes filled with angry hurt. "Things will never be the same, you know. She might never come back—"

"And if she doesn't, then it will be because she's found something that makes her very, very happy. I can't believe that wouldn't please you, Linette—and you know what else I think would please you?"

Linette shook her head, her gloomy countenance clearly saying that she doubted anything would make her feel better.

"We'll read her letters together, you and I—"

"And me!" chirped Estelle.

"Yes, and Marguerite, too, if she wants to join us. Lindsay said she'd write as often as she could—so it will be almost like she's here with us, don't you think?"

Linette's nod was slow in coming, a grudging smile even slower, but Corisande could tell when she gave her a hug that Linette was somewhat mollified. Yet Linette's face broke into a full-fledged grin when Marguerite suddenly swept down the stairs, only to stop dead in her tracks beside the kitchen table when she realized everyone was staring at her.

"What are you looking at, Linette Easton?" she demanded of the sister with whom she'd once spent so much time and who now seemed more a pest than anything else since Marguerite had turned the ripe old age of fifteen. Linette merely began to giggle, pointing at Marguerite's head.

"I said what—"

" 'Tes your hair, girl," Frances interrupted, looking quite pleased with herself as if to say "I told you so." "You've brushed it so much that it's standen on end an' flying round your head! Any more an' I swear you'd have found yourself gone bald altogether!"

Her pretty face reddening at the laughter bursting around her, Marguerite's hands flew to her hair as she sought to smooth it down.

"Ais, there 'ee go, now take a seat with your sisters an' be quick! You've only got a few moments to eat before you're due at the church school."

Marguerite did as she was told, but not before yanking upon Linette's braid as she passed her sister's chair and deliberately stepping on Luther's bony tail, which set the little dog to yelping and Estelle scrambling so fast to comfort him that she knocked her plate to the floor with a crash. As the kitchen erupted in squabbling and confusion, Frances's voice rising once more above the unholy din, Corisande took a last bite of toast, downed half a cup of weak tepid tea, and fled down the hall.

Not surprisingly, the door to her father's study remained closed, Joseph Easton so far removed from the daily workings of his daughters' lives that such commotion rarely made him stir from his reading and sermon preparation. Corisande rapped on the door as she always did each morning, and had done since her mother died.

As always, there was no welcoming call for her to enter, which hurt, even if she should have long ago gotten used to her father's unintentional neglect.

Everything had changed during those wretched few days eight years ago when the fever had struck the vicarage like a heavy gale, Corisande suddenly thrust by necessity into the role of virtual head of the household at the tender age of eleven which had given her cares and responsibilities far beyond her years. Thank God Frances Hodge, a widow who'd lost her husband to a mine accident many years before, had agreed to come and help, working as their housekeeper more out of the goodness of her heart than for the paltry sum Corisande could afford to pay her.

And she'd stayed, bless her, Corisande thought as she opened the study door, Frances's stern command for Marguerite and Linette to cease their quarreling rivaling any general's as it carried down the hall. But the debacle in the kitchen was forgotten as Corisande's attention once more flew to the sole occupant of the small shuttered room, her father seated at his desk with head bent and a book spread out before him, the flickering light of a candle falling like gilt mist upon his silvery hair.

Joseph Easton's hair had turned white as Christmas snow shortly after his beloved wife's death, his once broad shoulders long since sagging under an invisible burden, and his step the slow, uncertain shuffle of a man twice his age of forty-two. But his mind had remained unclouded, at least in matters of books and the Bible, and the pulpit still rang on Sundays with the power of the Word.

If not for that, he would surely have lost his parish, for along with his white hair had come an eccentric streak that had emptied the pews as if the devil himself stood grinning at the altar with his tail twitching and fork in hand—at least until the superstitious parishioners grew accustomed to their parson's unintelligible mutterings, moonlit stints at gardening, and late-night visits to the graveyard, and other quirks of character.

Another was that Joseph Easton preferred his study to remain shuttered like a cave, Corisande forever longing to throw open the windows to fresh air and sunlight. But she never did, respecting the strange, remote existence that her father's life had become.

"Papa?"

He started, as always, her soft query jarring him out of his private world as surely as if she had shouted. For a moment, he seemed bewildered, then a fond smile came over his still handsome face.

"Ah, Corisande. Are you on your way?"

The same question, repeated too many times to remember, but even so the words warmed her heart. He uttered them so full of trust, for even in his unfortunate state did he know that Corisande had done everything she could to save his parish for him and keep a roof over their heads—paying visits to his flock as her mother had once done so selflessly, seeing that the church school and the parish poorhouse ran smoothly, attending to details of christenings, burials, and weddings and ensuring that the church register and parish accounts were properly kept.

Only within the last three years had Corisande begun to do more, involving herself in the dangerous smuggling of contraband goods for the benefit of the entire parish, and if her father had guessed her involvement, he'd given it no voice. But whenever there was boiled beef on the table, or fragrant quality tea in the pot, or a bit of brandy for him to enjoy by the fire, he'd look at her with silent knowing in his eyes and a hint of concern mixed with pride. It was all she needed to keep her going, more resolute than ever to continue doing what she believed was right.

"Yes, Papa, I'm leaving now. I've much to do today."

"Godspeed, then."

Two familiar words, and he turned away, absorbed once more in his book before Corisande had closed the door. But she, too, was already preoccupied with her own affairs, her step determined as she grabbed her cloak and left the house, Luther's high-pitched yapping and her sisters' hilarious giggling following her outside into a glorious sunlit morning.

At least they were in a better mood, she was glad to hear, wondering what silly antic Estelle had performed to make Linette and Marguerite cease their incessant warring—

maybe balancing a spoon on Luther's nose or some mischie-
vous prank concocted to torment Frances. The latest had
been a big hairy brown spider in the mixing bowl, plopped
right on top of a yeasty-smelling mound of rising dough.
How Frances had screamed . . .

"Just as I'll be screaming if I can't find that scoundrel
Jack Pascoe," Corisande muttered, walking into the small
stable that flanked the Easton parsonage. A loud nickering
greeted her; Biscuit, their hardy piebald pony, bobbed his
head eagerly as if he knew he was soon to be forging across
the heath to Arundale's Kitchen.

And why shouldn't he think they were heading to the
mine? Corisande thought irritably, hoisting the worn
leather saddle onto the pony's swayed back. She'd only gone
there three mornings in a row, looking for that damned
mine captain so she could give him a fair-sized piece of her
mind. But each time he'd been nowhere to be found, probably gone down one of the shafts to purposely avoid her, the
despicable bastard, and no doubt smug as a snake at his
cleverness.

Nor had she been able to find the Arundale family's
agent, Henry Gilbert, when she'd gone to that Tudor mon-
strosity of a house where he resided. The sullen housemaid
who answered the door had said only that Gilbert wasn't
there—hiding from her, Corisande was certain, the ferret-
faced agent as spineless as Jack Pascoe was cunning. Henry
Gilbert was the one, after all, who'd given Pascoe free rein
to run the mine as he saw fit, and *his* orders, being the
family agent, no doubt had come straight from the Duke of
Arundale.

"Yes, Biscuit, maybe we're wasting our time going to the
mine after Pascoe," Corisande contemplated aloud as she
scratched the pony's whiskered chin, his breath blowing
warm on her hand. "Maybe we should find Henry Gilbert—
before he gets a chance to hide in a wardrobe or under the

bed, and brighten his day with a show of Cornish temper. It may not help matters much, but at least I won't feel as if I'm going to explode. What do you say?"

Biscuit's obliging snort made her smile, but it faded as she mounted and kicked the animal into a trot, the pony's bumpy gait—ensuring a jarring ride at best—only adding fuel to the fire.

∽ *Four* ∽

"Is there anything else you'd like to see this morning, my lord? The rest of the grounds, perhaps? The village of Porth—"

"That bloody mine wasn't enough entertainment for one day?" Scowling, Donovan dismounted from his steel-gray stallion while Henry Gilbert slid from his sweaty mount, the rail-thin Arundale family agent nervously shifting his feet, looking as if he wanted to flee the stable at first opportunity.

And right now Donovan wholeheartedly wanted the loathsome fellow out of his sight. Ignoring Gilbert for the moment, he led the snorting animals into their stalls, the cavernous stable empty but for these two horses and a big ill-kempt gelding whose dull brown coat looked sorely in need of a good grooming. But that would have to wait as Donovan eyed again the anemic, long-nosed scarecrow who'd been attending to his family's business affairs in Cornwall.

In truth, he couldn't fully blame Gilbert for what smacked of his late father's doing; the man had been paid to follow orders after all. But for the agent to have granted such power to a mean-spirited tyrant of a mine captain because he was too lazy to attend to the day-to-day work-ings of the mine himself—good God, it sickened him!

"Get yourself something to eat at the house and then ride back and see to it that a new mine captain is hired by noon,"

Donovan grated, Henry Gilbert bobbing his head in acquiescence. "I'm giving you a chance to set things right, Gilbert, or believe me, you'll be close behind Jack Pascoe in
finding yourself without a job."

"I understand, my lord. Implicitly."

"Good. Choose a man from among the miners, someone
they respect. Be sure I don't see Pascoe on Arundale property again."

"Yes, yes, of course, my lord."

"And restore the miners' pay to its previous level until
I've a chance to go over the books thoroughly—then we'll
talk about raising it further."

"But—but, Lord Donovan, shouldn't His Grace be con-
sulted—"

"If this damned mine is half as rich as my brother said it
was, Gilbert, surely there's enough coin to properly pay the
men whose blood and sweat have made it so profitable, is
there not?"

This time the cowed agent bobbed his head in time with
his prominent Adam's apple. "Anything else, my lord?"

"Yes. Is there grain to be found in this parish?"

"Only at famine prices—but of course there's flour
aplenty at the house if that concerns you—"

"Not for me, man! The miners can't work if they have no
bread, and from the looks of some of them, I'd swear they
haven't eaten a sound meal in days." Donovan's hard gaze
bored into the agent. "No thanks to the pittance they've
been paid of late."

"And which will be righted at once, my lord, just as you've
ordered!" Henry Gilbert began walking backward to the
entrance of the stable, giving no heed to the steaming piles
of horse dung squishing under his feet. "You wish the miners to have grain, then?"

"Buy enough bushels so that every man has a decent
share to take home to his family."

"It will cost, my lord—"

Gilbert didn't finish, his eyes growing round as serving platters as Donovan tugged off his coat and threw it over a post, then grabbed a shovel from against the wall and advanced toward him. With a sharp intake of breath, the man turned on his spindly legs and fled while Donovan sank the shovel into a pile of dung and musty straw, muttering under his breath, "Blasted fool."

It appeared that the stable was as much in need of attention as everything else around this dismal place, he thought mutinously, heaving his ripe-smelling burden into an empty stall.

It might have been dusk last night when he'd arrived at his Cornwall estate, but there had still been enough light for him to see that the huge house his father had bequeathed to him was in a sorry state of disrepair. Crumbling chimneys, cracked windows, a vast overgrown lawn—and inside, enough dust to choke a man, faded furnishings fit for no more than firewood, and two slovenly housemaids who had been hired in Weymouth by Henry Gilbert before he'd taken up his employment in Cornwall. One woman was as plump as a sausage and the other was passing pretty but had a hard, calculating look and reeked of cheap cologne.

It had been disheartening and maddening, especially since Donovan had seen his welcome as a smug otherworldly message from his father—marry fast, and the quicker he'd have the funds to improve his miserable surroundings. But he didn't give a damn about the house or the surrounding estate, and he thought he'd feel the same about Arundale's Kitchen, too, as he'd been told the place was called, until he'd ridden out there with Gilbert just after sunrise, wanting to see the rest of the trap that his father had contrived for him.

Until he'd seen the careworn, expressionless faces of the tin miners as they hiked to work, some from as far as six or seven miles away, and more than he cared to remember with pallid cheeks gone hollow from sparsity of food.

When he had questioned some of the men, he'd been met with stoic tight-lipped silence, until at last a brave few came forth with the wretched truth about their mine cap'en, as they called Jack Pascoe, a pock-faced, red-haired fellow as wiry as a bantam rooster who'd cut their wages by half— only the latest of his transgressions, apparently—and who cared nothing about the wives and children starving at home. Equal parts ambitious and cruel, Pascoe had long ruled his domain by threatening life and livelihood, the miners with no choice but to shoulder their lot or face utter destitution.

So Donovan had quietly taken the bastard aside and told him to be off the property by noon, promising a full month's wage if he left the mine without saying a word. Jack Pascoe's watery blue eyes had filled with rage, but he'd nodded and stalked back into the countinghouse.

Watching him, Donovan had taken perverse pleasure in undoing a part of what his father had done; yet he knew as he sank the shovel under another pile of manure that he'd just as much been affected by the miners' misery . . .

"But don't get yourself too affected," Donovan muttered to himself, straightening just as Henry Gilbert suddenly reappeared at the entrance to the stable. Breathing hard, the agent gaped at him, then over his shoulder, and, clearly making up his mind, almost barreled straight into Donovan in his haste to reach the nearest stall—the same one where Donovan had just dumped a full shovelful of manure. "What the—?"

"She's coming right for the stable, my lord! Oh, cover me up, I'm begging you! She's seen me and she's got that look on her face—fit to kill, God help me!"

"Who's fit to kill?" Donovan demanded, but he got no

answer as Gilbert burrowed like a frightened mole into the filthy straw and horse dung.

Cursing, Donovan dropped the shovel and went to the stable doors just in time to see the most curious sight—an auburn-haired wench riding recklessly toward the entrance atop a black and white pony with the rolling gait of a foundering ship, her plain brown cloak flying like a sail behind her, her legs so long and the stout little pony so squat that the stirrups were bouncing uselessly, the irate rider's feet skimming the ground.

For Donovan could see that the young woman was furious. As if he weren't standing there, she dismounted at a run and swept past him into the stable, dark eyes ablaze, her face flushed pink with indignation.

"Where are you, Henry Gilbert? I saw you run in here, you sniveling rat! You'll not hide from me again!"

Donovan watched in bemused silence as she crisscrossed from stall to stall, kicking at the straw. A jilted mistress? Some local chit found herself in the family way and left to fend for herself? If so, Gilbert had clearly scorned the wrong woman. As she reached the last of the stalls, not having found her quarry, she lunged for a pitchfork resting in a corner.

"Come out now and face me like a man, you worm! If you can have a hand in taking the food from a babe's mouth, then you can answer for it too!" With that, she jabbed at the straw in the closest stall, then the next, drawing nearer and nearer to where poor Gilbert lay huddled.

"I'd suggest you show yourself, Gilbert," Donovan advised dryly, thinking that whatever the man had done to inspire such wrath, he probably deserved it. "She's got a pitchfork—"

"Yes, I do, and I certainly don't need your help, thank you very much!" Corisande said in exasperation, whirling upon the resonant male voice that had sounded behind her.

She could see a tall strapping shape in the shadows, but the morning sunlight was so bright coming in from the stable doors that she couldn't make out the man's face. "Just go about your work, whoever you are, and I'll tend to my own business!"

She did, too, turning back to the stalls with a vengeance and stabbing the pitchfork into another heaping pile of straw as the horses added their nervous whinnying to the fray. But just as she came to the last partition, the pitchfork poised above a suspicious-looking lump that bore the rounded leather point of a man's boot at one end, Corisande's weapon was wrested from her so suddenly that she fell backward, crying out as a steely masculine arm clamped around her waist.

"I think that's enough, Miss—"

"Easton. Corisande Easton!" came Gilbert's muffled voice. "The parson's daughter, God help us!"

"And God help *you* if you don't release me!" Corisande shouted at her assailant, wriggling and flailing her arms. But she shrieked full voice when she was swept off her feet into the air, her captor carrying her with long strides outside into the sunshine. Only then did she get a good look at his face, and his expression silenced her, the stranger scowling so deeply that she wondered with a rush of apprehension what he intended to do with her.

She'd never seen him before, of that she was certain. The man was as swarthy and dark as a Gypsy, his wildly unkempt hair long at the neck and jet-black against the white of his shirt. So was the thick springy hair beneath her splayed fingers, the man's massive chest as hard as stone and damp with sweat . . .

"Oh . . . oh, my!" In horror, Corisande snatched away her hand, her widened gaze jumping from her captor's half unbuttoned shirt to eyes even darker than her own, so dark, in fact, that they appeared almost pitch-black.

And they were trained full upon her, his quizzical scrutiny making her squirm, his scowl now but half as deep. With a near physical jolt, she realized how incredibly handsome he was, his stunning, lean-cut features the stuff of women's dreams. She began to wriggle in earnest, feeling more uncomfortable and strange and altogether unsettled than she could recall in her life. Even her skin felt odd, her cheeks blistering hot, and here it was a cool spring day!

"Please . . . let me down," she croaked, becoming even more discomfited that her voice—her voice, for heaven's sake!—had failed her.

To her utter relief, her captor obliged, and the feel of solid ground helped to calm her racing heart. At least until she realized his hands still encircled her waist, strong hands, too, and massive like the rest of the man.

She was considered tall by most standards—at five feet and nine she had Lindsay beat by three inches—and almost embarrassingly long-limbed, but now she was experiencing the rare sensation of looking up at a man instead of almost eye to eye. He was still staring at her, too, his hands a disconcerting heaviness at her waist, and . . . *and, why the devil was he still holding on to her*?

"If you don't mind, sir," she began stiffly, grateful that her normal speaking voice had returned as well as a healthy dose of indignation. "Kindly release me this very instant. I've no idea what you're thinking, but—"

"I was thinking that it's unlikely you're Gilbert's mistress as I first imagined, though if so, it wouldn't be the first time a parson's daughter has gone awry."

∞ Five ∞

Donovan wasn't surprised at the reaction his blunt comment received, the young woman's mouth falling open in shock.

A very nice mouth, too, her lips generous and full, and probably never been kissed, considering how her cheeks had flamed bright red when she realized her hand rested upon his bared chest. Probably never been this close to a man, either, which confirmed his instinct that the chit was a raw innocent. He wondered at the semicircular scar on her right cheek, though, marring what otherwise was quite a pretty face and yet which made her features oddly more interesting.

He felt an interesting womanly figure beneath his hands, too, though he'd never have guessed her waist could be so slim beneath her dowdy pea-green dress. And with her hair falling from its lopsided bun, she looked a perfect ragamuffin, this woman whom he could feel was tensing like a coiled spring.

"Henry Gilbert's mistress?" came her incredulous hiss, her lovely brown eyes—shot through with glints of bottle-green, he suddenly noticed—narrowing at him ominously. "You thought that . . . that spineless, gutless, callous-hearted, miserable—"

"Gilbert has his faults, I admit," Donovan cut in, noting as well that his infuriated captive's hands had balled into tight fists. "But that doesn't mean I want to see him pierced full of holes by some wild-tempered parson's daughter waving a pitchfork. If you've a complaint, Miss . . ."

"Easton! Didn't you hear the man? Corisande Easton!"

Donovan winced, his ears ringing at her shouting. "Very well, *Miss Easton.* As I was saying, if you've a complaint—and I've no doubt that you do—we'll settle it now and be done with the matter. That is, of course, if you promise to leave my agent in peace. He's probably suffocating under all that hay, but I don't intend to release you until I've your word—Miss Easton, did you hear me?"

Oh, yes, Corisande had heard him, but she could only stare at him in mute disbelief.

His agent? He had said that, hadn't he? Her eyes swept over him, from the fine white lawn of his shirt and the snug fit of his buckskin breeches to his dusty black riding boots. No telling white neckcloth, but a gentleman's dress all the same. And his expression reflecting pure arrogance, his overbearing tone, clearly that of a man accustomed to giving orders and having them instantly obeyed. Good God, why hadn't she noticed?

"Miss Easton." His big hands moved from her waist to her shoulders, and he gave her a firm shake as if she were a drooling idiot. "Are you listening to me, young wo—"

"You're the bloody Duke of Arundale, aren't you?" Knocking away his hands, Corisande couldn't help herself as three long years of frustration and anger burst inside her. She began to shriek like a fishwife. "You've finally come to see your precious mine, have you? To count your precious money while the poor tinners and their families are half starving around you! Well, I hope your greedy father rots in hell for all he's done, and the same goes for you and your rat of an agent!"

"Miss Easton, I'm not—"

"You're a blight on humanity, is what you are, Your

Grace." Corisande cut him off, so furious now that she shoved him with the flat of her hands, to no effect. The big lout was as solid and immovable as a boulder and scowling again, too, but by God, she would have her say!

"I suppose you're planning to give that bastard Jack Pascoe an extra month's wage for saving you so much money over the years, aren't you?" she accused, glaring at him.

"Actually—"

"Did it ever occur to you to consider the suffering that man has caused since Gilbert hired him to manage your mine? The crushed hopes? The tears? He's cut wages, a bit here and a bit there—*with* your father's blessing and now yours, no doubt—so many times that I've lost count! And the men's pay was never enough to afford them more than a dirt floor hut at the start! Now you've cut the wages so low that there's scarcely coin to keep the thatch roofs over their heads, let alone broth on the table—"

"Dammit, woman, if you don't cease your shouting, I'll soon be deaf—"

"Deaf and lucky, too, if you manage to squeak by the gates of heaven with all the terrible sins on your head! But you've a chance to make things right, if you've got a shred of decency at all, starting with dismissing Jack Pascoe this very day and raising the men's wages. I can't believe a man would want to journey through life known as a cruel, tight-fisted tyrant when instead he could earn himself some respect—"

"For the last time, Miss Easton," Donovan interrupted, having to half shout himself to be heard over her harangue, "I'm trying to tell you that I'm not the bloody Duke of Arundale, as you so delicately put it—surely language one doesn't often hear from a vicar's daughter." He gave a dry snort. "But then, I've never seen any vicar's daughter like you."

To his surprise, she had no reply to that sarcastic remark,

instead blinking at him as if he'd just knocked the wind right out of her sails.

"You—you're not the duke?"

"No. My brother, Nigel, wears the title, and he can damned well have it. I only wish he'd been here to enjoy your tirade rather than me."

She immediately bristled, and Donovan braced for the worst. "Oh, so you think I'm just airing my lungs, do you, Lord . . . ?"

"Donovan Trent."

"Well, then, Lord Donovan, everything I've said applies to you as much as your titled brother! You're all one and the same as far as I'm concerned. Blackguards, scoundrels, villains of the worst degree to deny food to hungry children and pregnant women! Despoilers, base criminals . . ."

While her vehement list grew longer, Donovan felt his own temper boiling because she'd lumped him together with his late father and Nigel. Hell and damnation, he'd been at war in Spain these past years, with no knowledge of his family's actions!

What was worse, the chit had tried, judged, and executed him before he'd been able to get in a single good word for himself. Wouldn't her face flare red if she knew he'd already called for the changes she demanded, though he'd be damned if he was going to explain himself to her now, the untidy baggage.

It was obvious she cared passionately for her cause to berate him up and down like a veritable harpy, but let her find out for herself that the Trents of Dorset weren't all cut from the same wretched cloth—yet, hell, she'd probably still distrust his motives anyway, given who he was. But what in blazes did he care what Miss Corisande Easton thought of him? As soon as he found a way out of his current predicament, he'd be gone from Cornwall so fast that . . .

Donovan didn't finish the thought, his eyes sweeping over

the incensed young woman standing before him as if seeing her for the very first time.

By God, of course! It could work, though it irritated the hell out of him that he'd have to go to such lengths to gain his inheritance, damn his father's soul. But he'd do anything if it would help him find Paloma. Why not use this situation to his benefit? This woman wasn't gentry, but a country-bred parson's daughter couldn't be said not to come from good family, oh, no, indeed.

". . . uncaring, selfish creatures who should crawl under the nearest rock for shame of everything they've done! Better yet, you deserve every curse that could befall a household. Fire, pestilence, the pox—"

"Are you betrothed, Miss Easton?"

Startled, Corisande stopped in mid-sentence and gaped at the man. She'd been expecting some reply, her heated attack clearly riling him as his swarthy face had grown darker. But this? "I—I don't see that your having the pox has anything to do with my being betrothed. Or that my personal affairs are any of your business."

"That's what we're discussing now, Miss Easton. Business. A business arrangement, to be exact." To her amazement, he took her by the elbow and half pulled her along with him until, some forty feet from the stable, he seemed satisfied and stopped beneath a tall, stately elm to face her, keeping his voice very low. "Are you betrothed or not?"

She felt her face burning as with fever, why, she wasn't sure. She really shouldn't answer—didn't *have* to answer. But for some strange reason, she slowly shook her head.

"Can't say that I'm surprised," came his wry response, which only made Corisande bristle again.

"If you mean to insult me, my lord—"

"No, I mean to ask you if you'd be my wife."

She gulped, flushing now all the way down to her toes.

But before she could say a word, he continued, his tone very matter-of-fact and more than a little brusque.

"It's merely a business arrangement, Miss Easton. Nothing more, I assure you, and one I believe you'd be a fool to refuse. A very temporary marriage in exchange for the improved well-being of the miners and their families—"

"Not miners," she interrupted stiffly, finding it difficult to believe a thing she was hearing. It was all so incredible, how could she? "We call them tinners here."

"Very well, tinners. As I was saying, a temporary marriage that will be annulled no more than a few weeks after the wedding, my father's will stipulating that I cannot receive my inheritance until I've taken a bride. But I don't want a bride, and I don't want to be married—especially if I'm being forced into it. I'm only complying because I need the money. That's why I'm here in Cornwall." Donovan waved his arm in disgust at the house and surrounding estate. "Do you think I'd have come to this ramshackle place for any other reason? Now, you want my help for the tinners, and I need a bride. You look intelligent enough to recognize a mutually profitable situation, Miss Easton. What is your answer?"

Corisande met his eyes, which had become as black as midnight in this shaded spot. "Truthfully, my lord, you're the last man on God's earth I'd consent to wed, or ever trust for that matter. Don't count on me to help you win your bloody inheritance."

With that, she wrenched away her arm and turned, gasping when she was suddenly pulled back to face him.

"So your concern for the tinners and their hungry families is merely skin-deep, I see."

"Not at all," she answered tightly, lifting her chin. "I simply don't believe that you're a man of your word. That you won't lend help simply out of charity for those less fortunate than yourself is perfect proof of your gross lack of character. How do I know that your promised support for the tinners wouldn't be just as temporary?"

"My inheritance includes the controlling share of Arundale's Kitchen, Miss Easton. Therefore anything I say to be done, *will* be done. But since you're so distrustful of my word, I'll have a legal document drawn up that would ensure that the tinners continue to be paid fairly."

"That is all well and good, sir, but as you said, your word means little to me. Perhaps if I saw that you truly intend to help the tinners . . . oh!"

Corisande's heart flew to her throat as Donovan grabbed her by the hand and began to stride toward the stable, making her run to keep up with him. But he let go of her as soon as they were inside the doors, the stable quiet but for the low nickering of the horses and a faint wheezing coming from one of the stalls. She watched wide-eyed as Donovan reached into the dirty straw and pulled Henry Gilbert out by the seat of his pants, the agent coughing and sputtering as he gulped fresh air.

"Is—is she gone, my lord? God bless me, that was a close call—" Henry Gilbert didn't finish, gaping at Corisande with teary, bloodshot eyes—the manure smell emanating from the man so ripe that she felt her own eyes begin to water. "But—but she's still here, my lord! Right there, standing right behind you!"

"Get on your horse, Gilbert," Donovan ordered, hoping that the agent wouldn't say too much and give everything away. Later he'd speak to the man about keeping his mouth shut, but right now it was impossible with Corisande only a few feet away. "Don't worry about Miss Easton or her pitchfork. I want you to ride to the mine and dismiss Jack Pascoe at once, then hire on a man the tinners trust."

The agent blinked, clearly confused. "But, my lord, you already—"

"Do as I say, man. And while you're there, tell the tinners

their wages have been doubled and that they can expect a good share of wheat for their families on Monday morning. Now, go—oh, and Gilbert, one more thing."

"Yes, my lord?" Looking thoroughly bewildered, the agent distractedly brushed some straw from his coat.

"If the men ask the reason behind their sudden change of fortune, tell them to thank Miss Corisande Easton when next they see her. The good parson's daughter's friendly visit has helped me to see the error of my family's ways."

Corisande caught the hint of sarcasm in Donovan's voice, her back stiffening when he glanced at her as Henry Gilbert mounted his horse. If she hadn't witnessed the two men's incredible exchange with her own eyes, she'd never have believed it. But it seemed Donovan was dead serious about his proposed business arrangement. As Gilbert rode from the stable, Corisande felt her stomach do a strange flip when Donovan came toward her.

"What's been done can easily be undone, Miss Easton, I think you understand," he said in a gruff half whisper that oddly enough made her stomach do another flip. "Unless, of course, you and I reach an agreement. Become my bride and see the tinners profit for years to come, or have things stay just the way they are. It's up to you."

Corisande stared at him, wanting nothing more in that moment than to tell this despicable, arrogant, condescending—and altogether too handsome for his own good—son of a duke what he could do with his accursed agreement. But the image of that vermin Jack Pascoe being banished from Arundale's Kitchen stopped her biting retort, even more so the thought of the tinners having a decent wage again and grain for flour to take home to their families.

And fair trading certainly couldn't compare with what Lord Donovan Trent was offering, no matter how much she might wish it to be so. The sale of smuggled goods had brought some relief to the parish, no one could deny, the earnings used to purchase everything from cloth to medicine. But it never seemed enough, the need so vast. Now at least the tinners would have a way to help themselves as well. How, then, could she say no?

"Very well, my lord. We have an agreement. I will become your temporary bride."

Corisande was startled by the look of relief that passed over Donovan's face, but it was gone quickly.

"For no longer than you said," she added, feeling a good measure of relief herself when he nodded. "A few weeks—"

"As soon as the inheritance is mine and transferred to my London bank where my brother and his solicitor can't touch it, our agreement will be annulled. Thus I'll have what I want, you'll have what you want, and we can go our separate ways."

It all sounded so clear-cut, really, and the fact that he hadn't said "marriage" only relieved her further. But it did little to soothe the anger she felt that he hadn't agreed to help the tinners without this damnable union.

"You know I despise you," she couldn't help telling him, just so there would be no misunderstanding. She wasn't surprised when he shrugged his massive shoulders, confirming her opinion that, indeed, all the Arundales were ruthless, coldhearted cads and only out for their own gain.

"A small price to pay." Then, just as brusquely, he warned, "Our arrangement is to be kept secret. No one must ever know the truth. No one, or you can be assured that—" He didn't finish, but Corisande knew he was referring to the tinners' wages. "Are we understood?"

She nodded, again biting her tongue.

"Good. We'll be married as soon as I secure the license."

"But—but that could be only a matter of days," Corisande blurted out, stunned. "It will seem strange . . . to the villagers, I mean, the tinners, my father, my sisters, everything happening so fast—why, we only met this morning! What will I say?"

To her astonishment he smiled, a slow, charming smile that made him look three times as handsome and sent the oddest thrill tumbling to the pit of her stomach. Until that moment, she would have doubted he was capable of such an extraordinary thing.

"Tell them . . . tell them that I simply swept you off your feet."

"Impossible! No one will believe me—at least no one who knows me well."

"Then we'll have to show them, won't we?" His smile faded as he came closer, standing so near to her now that she could feel his physical presence as surely as if they were touching, his eyes holding hers. "You may despise me, Miss Easton, but you and I now have a part to play, the happy couple eager to be wed. If I know my brother, Nigel, he's arranged for spies—"

"Spies?"

"In the guise of servants, yes, whom I imagine have been paid quite well to serve as his eyes and ears. If they suspect that things are not what they seem . . . if anyone begins to suspect . . ."

He took her hand, and she jumped, flushing hotly, but if he noticed he made no mention of it. Instead, he led her to the stall where a magnificent gray stallion swung his sculpted head to look at them. "Beautiful, isn't he? I just bought Samson in London. Come, we'll ride together."

"But Biscuit, my pony—"

"He can run alongside. How long of a ride would you say it is to your home?"

"My home?"

"Of course. A prospective groom should meet his bride's family, wouldn't you say?"

Speechless, Corisande had no answer as he shrugged into

his coat and then mounted; she numbly accepted his assistance when he hoisted her up in front of him.

In minutes they were galloping across the gorse-covered heath toward Porthleven, Donovan's arms locked around her, his incredibly hard thighs pressing against her hips, Corisande certain she might have just made the biggest mistake of her life.

❦ Six ❧

Corisande was even more certain as they reached the main road to the village, people she'd known all her life popping their heads from doorways and cottage windows or wheeling around in their gardens to stare openmouthed as she and Donovan rode by. And, as her luck would have it, one of them was Rose Polkinghorne, the plump, apple-shaped woman knocking her starched white cap askew in her haste to reach her gate and wave them down.

"Oh, Lord."

"An acquaintance, my love?"

Corisande snapped her head around to face Donovan, his pleasant expression belying the tension she suddenly felt in his body. "Don't you dare call me—"

"Keep your voice down, woman, and plant an adoring smile on your face," he interrupted her in a low growl that demanded her immediate compliance. "We're playing a bloody part, remember? Swept off your feet? Now, who is that frenzied lady?"

"Mrs. Rose Polkinghorne." Corisande forced a smile that felt more like a tight grimace. "The village's best seamstress and the most flagrant gossip this parish has ever known."

"Perfect. Just the woman to hear our happy news."

Corisande groaned to herself as Donovan veered his stallion toward the neat whitewashed cottage on the left, all the while doing her best to keep the smile pasted upon her face even when Donovan tightened his arms possessively around her waist. So possessively in fact, that even Mrs. Polkinghorne noticed, the woman's bright blue eyes bulging in surprise as she glanced from Donovan to Corisande.

"Oh, Lord—"

"Leave this to me," Donovan silenced her with a curt aside even as he nodded cordially to the gaping woman.

Leave this to him? Corisande fumed, as affronted by his tone as by his overweening confidence. Arrogant bastard! Did he think that he could just blow like a rogue sou'westerly into the parish and find himself readily accepted? He was a stranger, for heaven's sake, while she'd lived here all her life, and yet he obviously didn't think he even needed a proper introduction—

"Ah, Mrs. Polkinghorne, you're looking very well today. It is Mrs. Polkinghorne, is it not?"

Is it not? Corisande silently mimicked Donovan's gallant tone, glancing over her shoulder to glare at him. Instead, she found herself staring in awe, her breath caught, the man smiling as charmingly as he had done in the stable and looking even more handsome in the bright midday sun. But he wasn't smiling at her, she soon realized with an unexpected bit of annoyance when Mrs. Polkinghorne's flustered stuttering broke the spell, the woman fumbling in vain to right her ruffled cap.

"Why, y-yes, sir, it is, indeed, an' so nice of you to say so. Th-that I'm looking well, I mean. Oh, yes, kind of you to say, uh . . ."

"Lord Donovan Trent."

"Oh, my, Lord Donovan. Of the Arundale family?"

"The same, but I regret to say, Mrs. Polkinghorne, that my bride-to-be and I have little time right now to chat. Isn't that so, my darling?"

Stunned that such a nosy busybody as Rose Polkinghorne could be blushing as ridiculously as a green girl, Corisande wasn't aware that Donovan had addressed her until he squeezed her round the middle.

"I said, isn't that right, darling?"

"Oh, yes, of course . . . my love." Nearly choking on the words, Corisande was thankfully saved from saying anything more when Donovan continued courteously.

"My bride-to-be will be calling on you this very afternoon, Mrs. Polkinghorne. I'd like Corisande to have the finest wedding gown you can make, and as quickly as you can manage it. Ah, and she'll need some new gowns, too, the latest fashions, if you please. Send the bills to my agent, Henry Gilbert, and he'll see that they're promptly paid."

Corisande heard a strange sucking sound but no response from Rose Polkinghorne, as if the woman couldn't quite gather enough air to fill her lungs. But Donovan didn't seem to need a reply as he kicked Samson into a trot and rode on, leaving the poor seamstress to stare after them, her fleshy pink cheeks ablaze while neighbors came running from all directions to cluster around her.

"You enjoyed that, didn't you?" Corisande accused under her breath, grateful that Donovan had eased his viselike hold upon her if only a little. "The whole village will be buzzing like bumblebees in June within the hour—"

"Probably less, from the looks of it, but at least the news is out in the open."

And too bad that the wind couldn't carry the wonderful tale straight to Arundale Hall, Donovan thought surlily, wondering how Nigel would react—probably with unbridled relief—once he knew that Donovan had found a willing bride virtually overnight. Well, not exactly willing, but a bride nonetheless.

A bride with fine soft hair that smelled of fresh air and lemons, Donovan found himself musing, which made him frown. So, too, did the fact that he found Miss Corisande Easton fit quite nicely in his arms, her shape lithe and slender, the feel of her firm rounded bottom bouncing against him having jarred his senses more than a time or two during their ride to Porthleven. He'd felt her high, pert breasts, too, swelling against his arms whenever he'd shifted the reins . . .

"Which house is yours?" he barked irritably, thinking now that he should have let Corisande ride her spotted pony.

"The parsonage, of course, near the church and adjoining school," came her stiff reply. She pointed to the plain brick spire rising above the scattered rooftops that sloped all the way down to the harbor. "At the edge of the heath on the other side of the village. And if you want us to appear the happy couple, you'd best use a lighter tone. When the wind isn't blowing from the sea, every sound carries—"

"I stand corrected."

Apparently even that statement did not please her for she bristled in his arms, her spine as straight as a flagpole.

"See here, I don't like this arrangement any more than you do. But it was your brilliant idea, after all, so at the very least you could speak to me civilly, as I'm *trying* to do to you."

Donovan didn't reply, wondering if she planned as well to keep her outrageous temper in check. Given what he'd seen of her earlier, he doubted it, but he had no time to dwell on the unpleasant matter further as they approached the parsonage. An attractive two-story stone house with bright blue shutters and creeping geranium vines already halfway up the walls, the place had a warm friendly look to it that helped to ease his mood somewhat.

"Didn't you say something about having sisters?"

"I've three, all younger than I." Corisande hoped, too, that they were still hard at their studies in the more modest stone building on the other side of the church. The last thing she wanted right now was to be besieged by their wide-eyed stares and questions. Her father was foremost on her mind as Donovan drew their mount to a halt while Biscuit trotted obligingly into the tiny stable and the comforts of his stall.

What would her father say? she wondered. Might he protest the marriage? She would be twenty this September, yet still a year shy of being able to marry without his consent. Of course, she had always done exactly as she wished . . .

"By the way, you never told me how old you are."

She met Donovan's eyes, so lost in thought that she hadn't realized he had dismounted. As he reached up to help her down, his hands easily encircling her waist, she said breezily, "Twenty-one."

She held her breath as he lifted her to the ground, as much disconcerted by the strength of the man—she wasn't the daintiest of females, after all, but he handled her as if she were light as air—as the way he was studying her face. But if he thought she had just lied, he said nothing, as if mulling her response, until, an interminable moment later, he released her with a shrug.

"Then I won't bother asking your father for your hand."

She wanted to exhale with relief, nervous elation sweeping her. She really knew little about the intricacies of annulments, except that they were sometimes difficult to obtain, at least for common folk. And though she supposed enough coin could buy a man like Donovan Trent anything he desired, including an annulment, she didn't want to take any chances.

If he somehow planned to trick her, then she had already won the upper hand. She did know that marriages could be annulled if one of the parties was underage and consent wasn't obtained from the parents. Just this last winter a young heiress from Penzance had been returned to her family for that very reason, and the wily fortune hunter who'd enticed her to run away with him had fled to the Continent.

Now Corisande had her own way out of their agreement if she needed one, and, no matter if her father performed the marriage, she could always plead his state of confusion . . .

"I still intend to meet the good reverend, though. Are we going to stand here staring at each other or get on with—"

"For someone who supposedly swept me off my feet, you're an abhorrent tyrant." So said, she brushed past him, but he caught her cloak and yanked her back, pulling her into his arms.

"You're right, I'm not playing my part very well, am I?" His tone was low and mocking, but there was nothing contrived about his embrace when he drew her closer, his fingers brushing loose strands of hair from her face.

Staring up at him, Corisande gulped, his lips so close to hers that she could do nothing but focus upon them, his mouth hard-looking and yet quite appealing, and slightly opened as if he were about to speak. But he didn't speak, instead lowering his head while Corisande's heart began to beat like a snare drum, lowering, lowering, until his dark stubbled cheek was flush against hers, his day's growth of beard chafing her while his warm breath tickled her ear, a most disconcerting combination.

"There, isn't this better?"

His taunting whisper made her tense, but she gasped when she felt his lips lightly graze the sensitive spot just behind her ear, sparking delicious tremors all the way to her toes. Without thinking, she arched her neck, his lips touching her there, too, but still so lightly that his breath felt heavier than his kiss, and so hot, like nothing she had ever . . .

"You're playing your part very well, Miss Easton. So well I'd almost think you might be enjoying yourself, but of course, that can't be true. I commend you, nonethe—"

"Cad!" Mortified, her face burning, Corisande tried to push away from him, her fists balling at his chest. But he held her fast, and so tightly that she could barely move, his voice filled with caution.

"I wouldn't struggle if I were you. It will only confuse our young audience."

"Audience?" Corisande froze, craning her neck to see beyond him. To her horror, a small cluster of children were peeping curiously from around the corner of the church, a few of the older ones giggling and shoving each other. But when they realized that she had seen them, they turned and fled, squealing, in the direction of the school, while Corisande groaned.

"Must be luncheon time, since they're not at their books."

"Yes, and if my sisters hear—" Corisande didn't finish. Donovan's hold upon her loosened enough that she managed to twist free. But as she hurried toward the house, she knew he was right behind her—the man surprisingly quick and agile given his size—and he caught up with her at the front door.

"Allow me."

She merely glared as he opened the door, hating his false gallantry, hating him even more, and swept inside without a second look. But again he was close behind her, through the narrow front passage and into the formal parlor with its corner cupboard that held her mother's carefully dusted best china and glass and treasured collection of china cows, birds, and cats.

"Don't stomp so or you'll break something," Corisande warned, even though Donovan wasn't walking that heavily. But he certainly dwarfed the small room, his dark head nearly touching the ceiling, which made her think how out of place he looked in such modest surroundings.

That only made her angrier, for the tinners with their miserable one-room huts would consider the Easton parsonage a grand place, Donovan's country house a veritable palace despite its unkempt condition. She could just imagine the grandeur of his brother the duke's home, the magnificent house and gardens kept up with profits gained by shortchanging the tinners. Fuming about the injustice of it all, she headed down the hall leading to her father's study. To her surprise, the door was ajar, which was odd considering her father rarely emerged on Saturdays until his sermon was written, usually well after supper.

"I . . . I thought he'd be here," she said more to herself than Donovan as she walked into the room. It was then she noticed the candle guttering on the desk, not so odd a thing of itself, but in her father's study, a sight unseen in many years.

One of the small windows was opened slightly, a thin shaft of sunlight falling upon her father's spread papers, the blue shutter outside ajar as well. A shutter that had remained locked since her mother's death, as if her father, by keeping his study closed up, could somehow share with his wife the darkness of the tomb.

"Might your father be at the church?"

She started, whirling, having practically forgotten about Donovan. He dwarfed this room, too, standing so tall and broad-shouldered, his shadow gigantic upon the wall.

"Maybe . . . I don't know."

"Well, I hear someone humming in the kitchen. Your mother?"

His question, although innocent, made her stiffen. "My mother died eight years ago."

"I'm sorry. I suppose I should have guessed since you never mentioned her—"

"That's Frances humming, our housekeeper." Unsettled by the husky sincerity in his voice, Corisande knew she'd cut him off rudely, but she didn't want to discuss such private matters with this man. And she'd already told him so, too!

Instead, she turned back to the window, meaning to shut

it against the breeze to keep candle wax from spattering the desk. But a movement outside caught her eye, her father suddenly appearing at the edge of the garden that bordered the heath. He looked strangely distressed, pressing his hand to his chest as he leaned upon a budding apple tree.

∽ *Seven* ∽

"Papa? Papa, are you all right?"

Her heart thundering, Corisande didn't wait for an answer but fled past Donovan and down the hall into the kitchen.

"Corie? Oh, my, 'ee startled me!" Frances precariously juggled a plate of freshly baked leek tarts in one hand and a pitcher of goat's milk in the other as Corisande swept past her and lunged for the back door. "What is it? A fire?"

"It's Papa, Frances! I think something's wrong."

Corisande heard a crash of crockery, but she didn't turn around even when Frances wailed, "Lord help us, not the good passon! An' dark strangers in the house, too! Who are 'ee to be follown after Corie, eh? Eh?"

Corisande didn't have to hear Frances's indignant shouts to know that Donovan was not far behind her. She could sense him hard on her heels, which struck her as odd. What did he care for Joseph Easton's welfare? But her thoughts jumped to the crisis at hand as she raced through the garden, only to discover her father wasn't standing where she'd last seen him. Instead, he was pruning a hedge of purple veronica, already in full flower, nearer to the house. Pruning!

"Papa, didn't you hear me calling? Are you all right?"

He looked up, his hair brilliant white in the sunlight, his hazel eyes confused. "What? You were calling me?"

"Of course I was, Papa! From the window in your study. It was open, the shutter too."

He made no response, as if he hadn't heard her, taking another swipe at the rich green foliage with the pruning shears. Yet Corisande could plainly see that his face was flushed and sweaty, as if he'd recently exerted himself. She shaded her eyes and looked out over the vast heath scattered with gnarled trees bent and twisted from the wind, wondering if he might have simply gone walking and perhaps taken himself too far. He seemed all right now, though more distracted than usual . . .

"Perhaps, Corisande, this isn't a good time." Donovan's voice was surprisingly quiet as he drew alongside her, his expression somber. "We could talk to your father tomorrow."

"Yes, I . . ." Corisande stopped, shaking her head. "No, we should tell him now. I don't want Mrs. Polkinghorne to be the one to give him the news—"

"News? Is there news?"

Corisande was startled that her father seemed suddenly aware of their conversation, his eyes falling upon Donovan.

"Yes, Papa. Good news. Happy news." She swallowed, hating to lie to her father. "Lord Donovan Trent has asked me to marry him, and . . . and I've accepted. I know it's sudden, but, well . . . you'll perform the ceremony, won't you, Papa?"

For the briefest instant, she saw a flicker of such clarity in her father's face—as in those times when she sensed he knew full well about her smuggling—that she truly believed he had grasped the import of her words. And from the way he glanced back at Donovan as if taking his measure, even scrutinizing him, she began to wonder if the dark cloud that had settled over his mind years ago might be lifting.

But her shoulders fell when, a brief moment later, he merely turned back to his pruning, mumbling something to himself about how the purple blossoms were half as abundant this year as the last, their scent but half as sweet. Meanwhile Corisande felt close to tears, as close as she'd been for some time, not wanting to admit it but slowly coming to the realization that her father might very well be half mad, not just eccentric.

As he went about his business, finishing the veronica and moving across the garden to his geranium plot, where he sank to his knees in the dirt, she swallowed hard and turned away, her eyes meeting Donovan's. All this time he had said nothing, but she broke the awkward silence, waving her hand helplessly at her father.

"The Reverend Joseph Easton, my lord. Surely not a man to stand in the way of our agreement." She moved to walk past him, but Donovan caught her arm and stopped her.

"Has he been like this for long?"

Again she was struck by the stillness in his voice, but maybe he was simply unsettled or even repulsed by what he'd seen. Repulsed? That thought made her stiffen angrily, and she jerked her arm away. "Since my mother died, not that it's any of your affair. Nor does his malady make him any less a man deserving of respect! My father is much beloved by the people of this parish, tinner, fisherman, and shipbuilder alike, and I'll not have you—"

"Cease your bloody tirade, woman. I merely asked a simple question," Donovan said through his teeth, tempted to grab her by the shoulders and shake her. Hell and damnation, he had only to open his mouth and she thought the very worst of him! "You're right, it's none of my business— as long as he's capable of saying the proper words when it comes time for the wedding."

"Oh, he'll say them, though I'll be choking on every one."

"You'd best choke on the rest of your venom too," Donovan advised dryly, glancing beyond Corisande as Frances came charging through the kitchen door, the stout housekeeper's face red as a beet, her rolling pin held high. "And smile prettily, my love. It seems the reinforcements have arrived."

"You stand away from her there, do 'ee hear me, stranger?" Frances blustered as Corisande groaned. "Never you fear, Corie, they're coming soon to help us, Dr. Philcup an' the constable! I didn't know who to fetch first so I sent up a cry for 'em both an' came back as quick as I could—"

"It's all right, Frances. Papa's fine. I'm fine. Everything's fine." Corisande tensed as she felt Donovan draw her possessively into the crook of his arm, but somehow she managed a lighthearted tone. "And put down that rolling pin, will you? I can't have you cracking the man I'm going to marry over the head—"

"Marry?"

The rolling pin hit the ground with a thud, Frances looking as if she were about to totter, her slack mouth forming words that gave no sound. At once Corisande rushed to her side, but Donovan got there first, lifting the stricken, heavy-set woman in his arms with nary a grunt.

"Have you any brandy?"

Corisande nodded. With a last glance at her father, who seemed oblivious to the commotion as he tended his geraniums, she led the way back inside, skirting the puddle of spilt goat's milk and smashed crockery by the door just as Linette, Marguerite, and Estelle, Luther yapping at her heels, came shoving and pushing into the kitchen.

"What's wrong with Frances?" blurted out Estelle.

"Oh, Corie, is that him? The man you were kissing?" came Marguerite's excited query, her eyes agog.

"I wasn't kissing—" Corisande's sharp retort died at the warning look Donovan threw her; instead, she focused upon helping him seat Frances in the high-backed settle near the open hearth. "Linette, fetch Papa's brandy from the cupboard, but watch out for that mess. Quickly now!"

The twelve-year-old did as she was bade, her eyes very wide as she brought forth the dusky brown bottle, her gaze more upon Donovan than Frances. "You do look like a Gypsy, just as Johnnie Morton said."

"So I've been told." Donovan accepted the bottle from the young girl and poured a generous amount in the glass Corisande held out to him, watching silently as she urged the housekeeper to drink. Frances coughed a few times as she swallowed, her pale eyelids fluttering, but within a moment she'd downed the entire amount, her color much improving.

For good measure, Donovan poured her a second glass, then helped himself to a healthy swallow, the rich, amber liquid providing molten warmth all the way to his stomach. He needed fortification, too, surrounded as he was by a near fainted housekeeper, a bride-to-be with the temper of a shrew, a trio of girls who could but stare at him, and a scruffy-looking dog, more rat than canine, that persisted in sniffing ominously at his boots.

Oh, yes, let him not forget that poor wretch, the Reverend Easton, puttering near dotty as a hatter in the garden, and his new temporary family was complete. It was enough to make a man drink, and he did, taking another good swallow, grateful at least that the brandy was far better than passable.

"Your father has a commendable taste in spirits," he said to Corisande, not missing the slight flaring of her eyes. "French, best quality. Haven't tasted the like since my regiment captured an enemy general outside Madrid. The fellow was fleeing with his beloved supply on a packhorse. Hated parting with it."

"It was a gift from a parishioner." Surprised to hear that Donovan had been an officer in Spain and yet eager to change the subject, Corisande turned her attention back to Frances, who'd downed the second glass without any assistance at all and was now fairly glowering at her. "Are you feeling better?"

"Ais, so I am, Corie Easton, even if 'ee gave me one of the biggest shocks of my life. Marrying, are 'ee? An' I've never before even seen the man!" Frances glanced at Donovan, saying in apology, "Pardon me, sir, 'ee were kind to help me, an' I'm sorry to have come at 'ee with my rolling pin. But Corie's like one of me own brood, she is, though she's always been one to do exactly as she pleases. An' now jes proves it." The housekeeper looked back at Corisande, her voice heavy with disapproval. "An' what poor manners 'ee have too! You haven't even told me your man's name—"

"Lord Donovan Trent, Frances, if you'd only let me speak," interrupted Corisande, exasperated. "His brother is the Duke of Arundale. I know it's terribly sudden—quite unexpected, but—"

"You're going to marry him, Corie?" Estelle had scooped up Luther, hugging her little dog close as she gazed uncertainly at Corisande. Before she could answer, Donovan sank to his haunches in front of the child, his expression, to Corisande's amazement, grown almost tender.

"Yes, we're to be married—very soon, I'm pleased to say. But you needn't worry about your sister. I'll take good care of her. Now tell me, is your name as pretty as Linette's?"

"Estelle Marie?" The little girl looked thoughtful for a moment, then shrugged. "I s'pose, but I think Marguerite's is the prettiest of all. 'Course, she's not always as nice as her name. Just the other day she tromped on poor Luther's tail—"

"Estelle Easton!"

"It's true, Marguerite, and you know it! You pulled my hair too!" Linette chimed in, Corisande certain she'd never seen Marguerite more chagrined. But in the next instant the pretty fifteen-year-old blushed bright pink to her roots when

Donovan smiled at her, though Corisande could see it didn't reach his eyes, his massive shoulders rigid as he rose.

"Sometimes I don't get along very well with my brother either."

He didn't say any more, but even if he had it would have probably been drowned out by the sudden fierce pounding at the front door, a booming male voice demanding entrance.

"Oh, Lord, Constable Curtis!" Frances heaved rather tipsily to her feet and rushed from the kitchen, Linette, Estelle, and Luther scurrying after her while Marguerite remained planted to the floor. That is, until she realized that she was the only one left in the kitchen besides Donovan and Corisande. Her blush deepening, she looked about her distractedly as if she weren't sure which way to turn.

"Papa's in the garden, Marguerite. By the geraniums. Why don't you see how he's doing?"

"Oh—oh yes, Corie. Of course I will." Smiling gratefully, Marguerite skipped over the spilt milk and fled outside, her rich auburn curls flying.

That left Corisande alone, at least for the moment, with a man whom she was growing to despise more and more. She grabbed a broom and a dustpan and set to work cleaning up the mess on the floor, her back turned purposely to Donovan.

"Would you like some help?"

"Oh, my, no, I think you've helped enough already. Charmed them all quite handily, I'd say. Rose Polkinghorne, Frances, my very impressionable sister Marguerite—"

"Jealous?"

She whirled, stunned. But one look at his sarcastic expression and she turned right back to her task, deeming his ridiculous comment not even worthy of a reply. Her heart was racing, though, which only made her madder as she emptied the dustpan into a bucket. She was almost finished when he spoke again.

"You missed a shard . . . over there by the cupboard."

"I *see* it, thank you." Corisande scooped up the last bit of broken crockery, then straightened to glare at him, no longer able to contain herself. "Forgive me if I sound overly rude, but don't you have somewhere else you can go? You've obviously accomplished your aims—met my family, spread the word about our impending wedding, even ordered me a gown—"

"Which leaves the license and a ring."

"A ring too?" Corisande's tone was mocking as she plunked the broom and dustpan beside the bucket. "Goodness, my lord, you're going to a lot of trouble for a vicar's daughter. You should be glad you didn't meet my friend Lindsay instead, and convinced her to play your wife. You might have felt the need to spend even more coin for your sham wedding."

"Lindsay?"

"Yes, Lindsay Somerset, gone to London for the Season only three days ago. Her father is Sir Randolph, a baronet—"

"I wouldn't have wasted my time with her. No marriageable young woman of the gentry would agree to such a plan, not if she wanted her reputation left intact for a true marriage."

Donovan knew at once he'd gone too far at the stricken look on Corisande's face, but the thing had been said. He couldn't take it back. Nor did he have a chance to soften the blow as Frances bustled into the kitchen, a plump arm hugging Estelle on one side and Linette on the other while Luther barked and spun in circles around their feet.

"Ais, what a day this has been! I told the constable an' the good doctor that all was well, Corie, but they're waiten at the front door, hoping for a word with Lord Donovan. They want to wish him well, an' you too. 'Tesn't every day that a duke's son comes to Porthleven an' picks a bride from one of our very own."

Donovan looked to Corisande, but she still stood staring at him as if she couldn't believe what he had said. He could swear he saw pain in her gaze, too, but it was gone so quickly when he went and took her by the hand, her lovely brown eyes now sparking with fury, that he was certain he must have imagined it. Yet she came with him willingly— although she was ominously silent—as he led her from the kitchen and down the hall, the hubbub outside the parsonage growing louder as they passed through the parlor.

"Saints in heaven, have 'ee ever heard such a stir, Corie?" Frances said excitedly from behind them. "It sounds as if the entire village is here!"

It looked like it, too, Corisande seethed to herself as they stepped into the sunshine, a sea of faces there to greet them. People she'd known since she'd taken her first steps and babbled her first words come to see the man she'd be marrying within the week, the man who'd blatantly stated just a few moments ago that he cared nothing for her reputation.

Such outrage filled her that she was tempted to expose the ruse right then and there—they should know Lord Donovan Trent for the horrible, self-centered man he was!—but she remained silent as a stone, her thoughts upon the sweat-soaked tinners toiling fathoms underground, who by now must surely know of their change in fortune. She kept silent and smiled like a besotted idiot as good wishes were thrown her way, while Donovan was deferred to and bowed to and fawned over until at last she felt as if she might retch if she witnessed another moment of such spectacle.

Donovan must have sensed her mounting revulsion, for he led her abruptly to his horse and drew her into his arms for all to see. She stiffened, but at the dark warning in his eyes, she forced herself to relax as he brushed his lips upon her forehead.

"Don't forget, Mrs. Polkinghorne awaits you, my love. Tell her I want the dress finished by Monday morning for our wedding at eleven. I'm off to Helston to see the bishop about a license, but rest assured I'll see you at Sunday service tomorrow. In fact, I'll be counting the hours."

That said, he bent his head to kiss her cheek, and Corisande seized her chance, flinging her arms around his neck and drawing him down so she could hiss into his ear, "Bastard! You think you're so very, very convincing, don't you—"

She didn't get to say more as Donovan's lips covered hers so suddenly that she gasped aloud, but the warm pressure of his mouth stifled that sound too. It couldn't stifle the astonishment rippling through the crowd, however. Corisande's ears burned as she heard embarrassed coughs and children giggling.

Yet still Donovan kissed her, his mouth moving over hers as with a strange hunger until she felt light-headed, her face on fire, her body going almost limp against him. Only then did he raise his head, Corisande fluttering open her eyes to find that lazy, charming smile upon his lips and wry amusement—amusement!—in his devil's eyes.

"I'll miss you too."

He released her before she could respond and mounted Samson while Marguerite came rushing over to her side, her sister fairly breathless.

"Oh, Corie, you're so lucky! He's so dashing, so handsome . . ."

And so mistaken if he thought she was some naïve country miss he could toy with, Corisande fumed as Donovan rode away, Marguerite half swooning beside her.

Oh, yes, bloody mistaken, and she couldn't wait to set him straight. In fact, she was counting the hours.

∾ Eight ∾

·

It was late by the time Donovan arrived home, so late that when he let himself in the massive oaken front doors, neither of the two housemaids were there to receive him.

He wasn't surprised. Imagining the shiftless pair had long since retired to their rooms in the attic, he was grateful at least that they had left a lamp burning in the immense entry hall, the dim, flickering light shrouding in shadow a dilapidated interior that must have at one time been quite grand.

Henry Gilbert had told him that the estate had changed hands many times in the past century before being bought by Donovan's father, the last owner an elderly viscountess who had wanted a more modest country house closer to London. She'd cared little about the ancient abandoned mine at the northeast corner of her property, not seeing its potential as had the Duke of Arundale. After he ordered the sinking of deeper and deeper shafts, a rich lode of tin ore was struck, making Arundale's Kitchen one of the most profitable in west Cornwall.

Not that his father had spared many shillings on the up-keep of the house and grounds, Donovan thought disgustedly to himself. Nor to pay a fair wage to the miners—no, tinners, as Corisande had so graciously corrected him. As graciously as a spitting cat. But at least he had found the perfect way to silence her in a pinch, his bride-to-be quite kissable for a shrew.

Quite bloody kissable.

Frowning, Donovan shook off the memory of Corisande's soft parted lips and moved to the sweeping staircase. But he switched his course at the last moment and headed for the library instead, wondering if Gilbert had purchased the few items he had requested that morning on the way to the mine. Soap, shaving paste, and a razor to start. The house was bare of such simple necessities, and he hadn't enjoyed a good shave since his short overnight stay at Arundale Hall.

He had asked for paper as well, pens, ink, and more candles and lamps to light the place, especially the library. And good brandy, of course, if Gilbert could find it. Obviously not too difficult a task, considering the superb quality of the spirits Donovan had tasted at the parsonage.

He was no fool. Smuggling had to be rampant along this godforsaken coast, given the high taxes levied upon so many goods to help pay for the war. A sizable portion of the Reverend Easton's parishioners were no doubt chin-deep in the running of contraband from France to Cornwall. How else could such fine brandy have found its way to a vicar's cupboard?

Donovan wished he had a strong dose of that brandy now as he opened the door to the library, anything to help him stomach writing a letter to Nigel about his impending marriage. He might have found a way out of his miserable predicament, but what he had to do to gain his inheritance still chafed like hell. No, he wouldn't allow himself to sleep until that letter was done. He'd be damned if he would allow a new day to start on such a galling note—

"What the devil?" Donovan came to a halt at the sight of Henry Gilbert fast asleep in a tattered wing chair drawn close to the fireplace. A fireplace that, amazingly enough, wasn't cold, black, and empty but filled with fat logs that burned brightly, the lively hiss and crackle of the flames a welcoming sound in this drafty place. Gilbert's discordant snoring, however, was anything but pleasant, the agent's mouth hanging open and his bony elbows dangling over the arms of the chair.

"Nothing like an honest day's work to tire a man," Donovan muttered dryly, wondering how a fellow so slight could make such a racket. He moved to wake him, but a full decanter of brandy flanked by a pair of cut-crystal glasses set to one side of the marble mantelpiece caught his attention. Reminded with a grim jolt of the letter he must write, he decided rousing Gilbert could wait. A moment later, the brandy was poured and snaking a warm path down his throat, a vintage almost as fine as the Reverend Easton's.

"Good man, Gilbert. Good man."

Donovan's loud-spoken compliment had the desired effect, Henry's snores coming to an abrupt halt as he blinked open his eyes. Upon seeing Donovan, the agent lurched at once to his feet, nearly upsetting the chair.

"Oh—oh, my lord! I had no idea—"

"Sit down, Gilbert, and get your bearings. I don't want you tumbling into the fire." As Henry obliged him, plopping bleary-eyed and silent into his chair, Donovan sat himself on the edge of the worn desk and took another deep drink. "I take it you were waiting for me to return?"

"Why, yes, my lord. I thought you might like to know that all was done to your satisfaction. I hired a new man to captain the mine, Jonathan Knill's the name—"

"The tinners will work for him?"

"Gladly, my lord. Knill's well liked, his family long known in the parish."

"Excellent. And the tinners' pay?"

"Doubled it just as you asked, which drew quite a cheer from the men. And when they heard a share of wheat would be doled out to each family on Monday morning, enough good couldn't be said—"

"About Miss Easton, I hope," Donovan cut in as he rose

to refill his glass. He poured a brandy for Gilbert, too, the agent accepting it with a look of some surprise. Donovan doubted that his father had ever shared a drink with the man, or any employee for that matter. "She made quite an impression on me this morning, enough for me to ask her to be my wife. But I suppose you've already heard that we're to be married."

Before he answered, Henry took a good swallow of brandy, his hand slightly shaking as he lowered the glass. "Yes, my lord, the talk in Porthleven was of little else but you and Corisande Easton. But of course, I knew from His Grace's letter that you might be seeking a bride—"

"My brother wrote you a bloody letter?" Donovan knew he had roared like a tyrant, but he couldn't contain himself at this news. "About my personal affairs? By God, when?"

"I . . . I just received it a week past, no more." Henry Gilbert's prominent Adam's apple bobbed nervously, but he managed to rush on. "His Grace asked that I assist you in any way I could—in making introductions to some of the local gentry, of course, if needed. The letter stated that the Arundale family is in desperate need of an heir, thus your haste today in choosing a bride is quite understandable."

"Quite," Donovan echoed tightly, reining his anger as best he could. It was damned difficult—how thoroughly Nigel had seen to every detail, and before Donovan had even agreed to come to Cornwall!—but he now had the perfect explanation for his odd behavior in the stable that morning. "So it must be equally understandable to you, then, why I want Miss Easton to reap full credit for my decisions made earlier in the day. It made her happy, you see, to think that it was her own doing, and thus endeared her all the more to my proposal of marriage. She doesn't know, of course, that an Arundale heir is of the utmost importance—as you say, a matter of haste. Any young woman would find the matter most indelicate, perhaps even unpleasant—"

"Of course, of course, my lord, have no fear that I'll not honor your confidence. It is the very least that I can do."

Donovan had to summon all his will not to scowl as Gilbert gave him a conspiratorial wink. Instead he raised his glass, and the agent quickly followed suit.

"A toast, then, to my coming marriage."

They drank, downing the brandy in one swallow—well, Donovan did. Henry Gilbert began to cough and wheeze, his thin shoulders hunched and his eyes watering as Donovan pounded him several times on the back.

"Are you all right, man?"

"Yes, my lord, thank . . . thank you. I was fine until I thought of how close I came to being skewered this morning. Forgive me for saying so, Lord Donovan, but I don't envy your choice of a bride. Perhaps you should reconsider. Take a few more days. There must be other young ladies who would gladly—"

"No, Gilbert, my proposal's been accepted. It would be dishonorable not to proceed."

"But her temper, my lord—"

"A passionate spirit, nothing more. Stands up for what she believes in, an admirable trait, really. Very impressive."

"But she wanted to kill me! She would have, too, if you hadn't been there. You saved my life!"

Donovan sighed, growing weary of defending a young woman whom he imagined wouldn't think twice about taking a pitchfork to him either. "Enough, Gilbert. I'm sure now that Miss Easton's cause has been championed, she'll be as docile as a spring lamb. In fact, I guarantee it. She would tell you herself that she couldn't be more pleased about our marriage. You've nothing to fear from my bride. Nothing at all."

Donovan hoped he didn't sound as doubtful as Henry

Gilbert looked at that moment. Corisande, as docile as a lamb? That thought was so preposterous that he considered another glass of brandy, but he'd had plenty enough already to see him through the vexing task that lay ahead. Without saying more, he sat down at the desk and drew pen and paper toward him while Gilbert, recognizing Donovan's cue that he wanted to be left alone, headed for the door.

"Oh, yes, my lord, I've placed the other things you wanted in the master suite. If there's nothing else—"

"Jack Pascoe." Donovan looked up, his expression grim as he met Gilbert's eyes. "Was he gone from the mine as I'd ordered?"

Henry Gilbert nodded, swallowing hard.

"No trouble?"

"None, my lord. I imagine he's already left to find work in another parish. He's no family here."

"Good. Take yourself home, then. I'm meeting Miss Easton tomorrow morning at church, so you'll have to post this letter for me. You've done well today, Gilbert. See that it continues."

Another mute swallow and the man was gone, leaving Donovan to stare at the blank page before him. Resentment, ah, it was thick and deep enough to choke him, but he had only to think of Paloma—was she safe? Was she well? God help him, it had been months since he'd seen her. Would she even remember him?—and he began to write, furiously.

To find his little daughter he would write a hundred such letters. A thousand! Anything!

Soon, if the fates were willing, soon he'd have his money and be heading back to Lisbon, his father, Nigel, and their bloody plans for him be damned.

∾ Nine ∾

"Maybe he's not coming, Corie. Maybe Lord Donovan's changed his mind—"

"Shh, Marguerite, for the last time. I'm sure he'll be here any moment. Now please keep your voice down! The service is about to start. And tell Linette and Estelle to stop squirming!"

Corisande frowned down the mahogany pew at her two youngest sisters, both girls twisting in their seats to peer behind them—at least until Marguerite hissed for them to face front and sit still. They obeyed but only for an instant, first Linette and then Estelle glancing over their shoulders as if they couldn't help themselves. When Marguerite joined them, Corisande sighed with exasperation and gave up, keeping her eyes trained forward even if they could not.

She'd be damned if she was going to watch for Lord Donovan Trent to make his grand entrance into the church like the conquering hero. In fact, she hoped he wouldn't come at all. Already she felt as if every eye in the packed sanctuary was trained upon her, a low flurried buzz of conversation and speculation taking place behind white-gloved hands and fluttering fans.

She'd never seen the church so crowded, no, not even on Easter Sunday. There had been no need to erect the cardboard figures her father insisted upon using to fill the normally empty back pews, a curious practice begun not long after her mother had died and her father's unsettling eccentricities had frightened away—at least temporarily—many of his flock. It seemed every parishioner from Porthleven to Arundale's Kitchen, including much of the local gentry, had made the trek to service—no doubt having heard the big news and come to gape at her and marvel at her astounding good fortune.

Oh, she'd overheard some choice comments already, begun the moment Donovan had ridden away yesterday afternoon.

"A duke's son, truly? And Corie Easton? Don't mistake me, she's a good, hardworking girl, we all know it to be true. Helped us all, she has, time and again. But that temper! Lord help him, the poor man will need the patience of ten saints!"

"Such a handsome young gentleman too. Not that Corie isn't pretty in her own right. But, oh, my dear, that scar on her face. What a pity. Doesn't seem to bother the man, though."

That thoughtless remark had sent Corisande hurrying into the parsonage with her three sisters and Frances in tow, all of them peppering her with questions that required ridiculous answers in keeping with a young woman who'd just been swept off her feet by most likely one of the most eligible gentlemen in Britain.

"Aren't you excited, Corie? It's so romantic!"

That from Marguerite, of course, who seemed satisfied when Corisande gave as giddy a smile as she could muster.

"Where will you live, Corie?"

At Lord Donovan's house—the crumbling eyesore, she'd added mutinously to herself. Linette's second question quickly followed: "Can we come and live there too?"

"Of course not, 'ee silly girl," Frances had said with a fond laugh. " 'Ee have a good home here with your papa. An' I'll be stayen to watch over 'ee, so never you fear."

And lastly, just before Corisande managed to escape upstairs to her room, came another breathless query from Marguerite that Corisande had hoped to avoid.

"Oh, Corie, it must feel so wonderful to be in love. Really, truly in love. Tell me what it's like, will you?"

"It—it's all so new," she'd fumbled, hating the deception, hating to lie to her family. "I haven't even had a moment to think, Marguerite. We'll talk later, I promise."

She had fled then, sinking against her door with enormous relief. But indignation had gripped her, too, and she had gone straight to her small writing desk set before the lace-curtained window and penned Lindsay a long letter telling her everything.

Someone had to know the bloody truth! Corisande wouldn't be able to bear it otherwise. And she could trust Lindsay to hold her tongue. She could trust her dearest friend with her life.

And she most certainly didn't want Lindsay to hear from someone else that she was getting married—and for her to think that Corisande had found the man of her dreams virtually overnight—oh, no! She had made it quite clear in the letter that Donovan was self-centered to his core and cared about nothing but himself, hardly the upstanding, principled man she envisioned marrying one day. She'd mentioned, too, what Donovan had said about her reputation, his words still smarting like a slap—

"Oh, Corie, he's here! He's here!"

Corisande stiffened at Marguerite's announcement, allowing herself only the merest glance over her shoulder as her three sisters wriggled excitedly like fresh-caught pilchards beside her. What she saw made her breath stop, and no doubt every other woman's in the congregation, as the most handsome man she'd ever seen strode down the center aisle toward them.

If Donovan had been dressed casually yesterday, this

morning he looked every inch the gentleman, from his clean-shaven face and startlingly white cravat to the tailored lines of his dark blue coat, fawn-colored breeches, and black riding boots polished to a bright sheen. Suddenly she felt quite shabby in comparison, her dove-gray cloth dress a poor cousin to the colorful concoctions Rose Polkinghorne was making for her. But none had been ready, and so she had worn her very best, which obviously wasn't good enough —oh, for heaven's sake, what did she care anyway? That cad! That bounder! It wasn't as if she gave a halfpenny for what Lord Donovan Trent thought of her!

Her face burning, Corisande slid over reluctantly just as Donovan reached the pew, her sisters bumping into each other as they slid down too. In the next instant, Donovan was seated beside her, his hard thigh pressing against her leg, which made her cheeks feel hotter still.

"Forgive my tardiness, my love," came his low aside as the congregation erupted into a full-throated hymn. "The servants my brother hired for me arrived early this morning. The whole place was in an uproar."

"You mean your brother's 'eyes and ears'?" Corisande whispered back, certain that her sarcasm would be masked by the resounding singing. "How bloody lovely."

"My thought exactly." Indeed, waking up to a houseful of Nigel's spies hadn't been Donovan's idea of a rousing good morning. He had not only found Ogden moving silent as a ghost about his bedchamber, the somber middle-aged butler laying out finely tailored clothes that Nigel had ordered made for him—another detail seen to weeks before Donovan had returned to England!—but in virtually every other room was a servant either dusting, scrubbing floors, or cleaning windows. Even the two sullen housemaids had been enlisted, the pair working harder than Donovan had thought possible.

Not surprisingly, Ogden had already been informed of

Donovan's imminent wedding by Henry Gilbert, who had stopped by the house shortly after the servants' arrival to fetch the sealed letter bound for Arundale Hall. Thus Ogden's sharing of the news created the unholy commotion of Donovan being accosted by the frantic housekeeper, Ellen Biddle, and Grace Twickenham, the red-faced cook, the moment he went downstairs, both women clamoring to know what special preparations should be made to welcome his new bride.

A bride who looked about as happy to see him as a condemned criminal bound for Tyburn, Donovan thought dryly, sending a smile beyond Corisande to his three young soon-to-be sisters-in-law. Estelle and Marguerite smiled back readily, but Linette stared at him with some wariness, this serious-faced middle child reminding him most of Corisande.

"If you please, my lord, you're only encouraging my sisters to fidget. They should be paying attention to the service!"

Donovan met Corisande's flashing brown eyes, glad that the hymn had covered her irritated whisper. It seemed the hours they had spent apart had made her even less inclined to honor the role they must play, and he was determined to remind her. "Of course, my sweet darling, forgive me. We'll let them pay attention to the service while I pay attention to you. Fair enough?"

Corisande gasped as Donovan tunneled his arm through hers and pulled her none too gently against him. "What—?"

"Shh, my love. That's better. Let's give your father's flock what they came to see, shall we?"

Corisande's face had never felt hotter; she was mortally aware that everyone in the congregation must surely be staring at them. She tried to slide her arm back through Donovan's, but to no avail. She was no match for his strength. The overbearing lout held her as if in a vise, and she couldn't budge.

"Easy now, dear heart, or you'll confuse your sisters," he whispered firmly as the hymn swelled to a close. "I wouldn't be averse to kissing you right here in front of the pulpit if it will ease your mood. That certainly seemed to work well enough yesterday. What's it going to be?"

What's it going to be? Corisande screamed incredulously to herself, wondering if Donovan would really make good on his threat. Seething, weighing the odds, she had only to glance at the steely look on his handsome face to know he would probably relish such a display. Resignedly she forced herself to relax against him. There was nothing else she could do.

But she didn't look at him again for the remainder of the service, not even when he laced his strong fingers through hers and began to rub her palm lightly with his thumb, a curiously soothing sensation. No, not even when he leaned over to whisper in her ear after her father's sermon was done that he'd heard few vicars preach with such conviction.

Only when the last hymn was being sung did she glance at him again, and, as if he had been waiting for that moment, he lowered his head to murmur a husky warning for her ears alone, "When you feel a flash of temper coming on, think of the tinners, my love. Henry Gilbert tells me they're singing your praises. Let's keep things that way, shall we?"

She was caught and she knew it, at least while they were in public. But there would come a time when they would be alone, oh, yes, and she could hardly wait.

Corisande's arm was cramped when Donovan finally released her, wooden pews creaking all around them as parishioners rose to their feet. And just as she had known it would, the ingratiating nightmare of yesterday afternoon was repeated as people swarmed forward to offer good

wishes, the local gentry falling all over themselves to welcome Donovan into their midst.

To her relief she saw Frances rush forward from the back
where she'd been sitting with friends and shepherd her sisters away, while in front of Corisande Druella's parents, a
very rotund Baron and Lady Simmons, came barreling
along. But the hapless couple was cut off as a path suddenly
opened among the parishioners to make way for an impos-
ing figure of a woman, her familiar stentorian voice greeting
those on the left and right as if she were the bloody queen.

"Oh, Lord."

"Someone you know?"

Corisande nodded mutely at Donovan as the woman
drew closer, her massive corseted breasts reminding one of
the wide prow of a warship, her lavender silk dress rustling
and her double chin jiggling. Upon her powdered face was
an imperious look to which Corisande had long ago grown
accustomed, the woman's narrow, high-bridged nose giving
her the ability to look snootily down upon all she surveyed.

Just the way she was now staring at Corisande, though
her shrewd blue eyes quickly shifted to Donovan as she
extended a plump gloved hand.

"Olympia Somerset, my lord," she announced before
Corisande could introduce her. "What a distinct pleasure to
welcome you to Porthleven, although"—she glanced dispar-
agingly at Corisande—"a few days' notice of your imminent
arrival might have allowed my stepdaughter, Lindsay, to be
here to greet you as well. Yes, such a pity."

Corisande held her breath while Donovan said nothing
for what seemed the longest moment, nor did he make a
move to offer Lady Somerset the least courtesy. Only when
the woman arched a thin painted brow, looking at Donovan
somewhat uncertainly, did he take her hand and bow ever
so slightly, an audible murmur of relief rippling through the
church.

Wondering at his behavior, Corisande glanced at him to find he had stepped closer to her, a faint scowl on his face, his arm around her back in almost a protective fashion. Unsettled by a sudden rush of warmth, she immediately dismissed the ridiculous thought. Lord Donovan Trent was merely playing his part, convincingly as usual.

"Allow me to introduce my husband, Lord Donovan," Olympia added in a tone that gave no hint of her earlier discomposure, stepping aside to reveal a slight graying man who had silently trailed in her wake like a shadow. "Sir Randolph Somerset. We would be so honored if you'd dine with us at Somerset Place, perhaps tonight—"

"Tonight won't be possible," Donovan interrupted smoothly, feeling no small amount of disgust at the woman's insulting behavior toward Corisande as well as pity for the poor miserable-looking wretch who'd been fool enough to take her to wife. "But perhaps sometime in the near future . . . after our wedding."

"Oh, yes, that would be lovely. Of course, you must know by now that Lindsay and Corisande are the dearest of friends. Close as sisters, I'd dare say. We'll almost be like family."

Stunned to her toes, Corisande gaped as Olympia gave a regal nod of her head and then swept away, another wide swath opening for the woman like the parting of the Red Sea. But Corisande had no time to dwell upon the first public acknowledgement she'd ever heard from Lady Somerset's lips that she and Lindsay were friends as more parishioners crowded forward to introduce themselves to the son of a duke.

She was certain nearly an hour had passed by the time the church was emptied, leaving her and Donovan, finally, incredibly alone.

"Pleasant people. Well, most of them," he said as Corisande brushed past him and moved down the center aisle, inspecting the pews both right and left. "Did you lose something?"

"Not at all. I'm checking to see that no one left anything behind. It's one of my duties."

"Duties?"

"Of course. I always close the church after Sunday service, then I count and record the tithes in the parish accounts, look over the register—"

"But what of the churchwardens?"

Corisande shrugged. "None have been elected for three years. I manage well enough, and the parish trusts me. Things run quite smoothly here."

"But your father? Does he help—"

"My father is already at home in his study, where he's most comfortable," Corisande broke in stiffly over her shoulder. "Sunday mornings tire him dreadfully. He puts everything he has left into his sermons. You said yourself that you'd seen few vicars preach as well as my father."

"So you heard me. I wasn't sure—"

"Yes, I heard you and your ridiculous warning as well." Corisande swept up an abandoned white ladies' glove and spun to face him, struck anew by how magnificently handsome he looked in the sunlight streaming through the arched windows and wishing she wasn't so inclined to notice. "And I don't need *you* to tell me to think of the tinners! If not for them, for their families, I wouldn't be suffering your—your loathsome attentions—"

"Loathsome? I don't recall any woman ever complaining before that she found me loathsome."

"Oh, I'm sure you haven't, being the charming Don Juan you are," Corisande bit off sarcastically. "No wonder you don't want to be married. Why ruin such a blissful existence? Lord knows how many innocent women you've despoiled along the way!" Furious now, she wadded the glove in her hand, wishing it was something harder that she could throw at him. "We may have a part to play, my lord, be it a few days or a few weeks until this miserable charade is done, but I'll not have you thinking I'm some naïve country twit eager to be seduced by the likes of you! You may not care in the least about my reputation, but I do!"

There. It had been said, however indelicately. In her father's church on Sunday morning no less! But Corisande felt much better—no matter that her face was on fire—and stared indignantly at Donovan even as he stared straight back at her. For a long moment, he said nothing, then a wry half smile touched his lips.

"Clearly my attentions yesterday offended you."

She reddened further, dropping her gaze to the crumpled glove in her hand. "That, and what you said about why you wouldn't have wasted your time with Lindsay."

Again Donovan grew silent, so silent that Corisande couldn't help looking up to find that his smile had disappeared, his dark eyes burning into hers.

"My words were thoughtless, I admit. But I have every confidence that your strength of spirit will carry you through any trial our temporary union might cost you."

"How kind of you to say—" Corisande began tightly, thinking the man could be very glib as well as charming, only to have him wave her to silence.

"I'm not finished. As for the other, I cannot promise that I won't kiss you again, given that we're soon to be 'happily' wed and must appear as such to the good people of Porthleven. But those occasions might be less frequent if you would keep your hot temper in check—"

"That's very difficult for me."

"So I've seen."

"Considering who you are, of course," Corisande added bluntly. "If it wasn't for the tinners—"

"I know, I know. You wouldn't be suffering my loathsome attentions." Donovan sighed heavily, rubbing his hand across his forehead. "It seems we're talking in circles here, except for me to say that I have no plans to seduce you."

"*That* I'm very glad to hear," Corisande spouted, although for the life of her, she couldn't understand why her face was feeling so bloody warm again. But it truly felt like fire when Donovan continued, his voice growing brusque as his gaze swept her.

"I meant that as no insult, of course. You're quite an attractive young woman—that pale gray color suits you very nicely, by the way. But we've a business arrangement, Corie, nothing else."

"I—I'd appreciate it if you wouldn't call me Corie," she stammered, wondering where her composure had suddenly flown, wondering if she'd ever felt her heart beat any faster. "Only my family and friends—"

"I *will* call you Corie," he interrupted firmly, "since it would be strange for me not to. Everyone else does. Besides, the nickname suits you. Corisande is lovely, but—it's French, isn't it? Your sisters' names too."

"Our mother was French, but as I told you yesterday, that's none—"

"I know. None of my bloody affair. Good God, woman, do you know you're one of the most exasperating . . . !" Donovan didn't finish, shaking his head as he looked away.

Which was fine with Corisande. She desperately wanted this uncomfortable line of conversation to end, desperately wanted her face to stop burning and her heart to stop racing, and definitely wanted this perplexing man out of her life.

"I've work to do," she said stiffly, turning back to her task of inspecting the pews. "You needn't wait for me. Frances makes a lovely Sunday dinner, unless, of course, you've other plans. Which I'm sure you do. There must be a hundred things that need to be done, considering we're to be married tomorrow, and I imagine sons of dukes are very busy people—"

"Not at all," he broke in gruffly, making her start. "My plan is to spend the whole blessed day with my lovely bride-to-be, just as any eager bridegroom would do. I've spies at the house, remember? Why would I want to go there?" He leaned against a pew, the whole massive length of him, and crossed his arms over his chest. "Do what you must, then we'll go over to the parsonage together."

"Oh, no, I'm not going home for dinner. I spend Sunday afternoons at the poorhouse, then I make calls for my father well into the night, so if you're hungry, you might as well join Frances and my sis—"

"I'll wait for you, woman! What more do I have to say?"

"Well, you don't have to shout." Her spine as rigid and straight as a poker, she huffed away, grumbling, "Swept off my feet? Ha! More like lost my mind—"

"I heard that."

She frowned and clamped her mouth shut, determined not to say another word.

⚮ Ten ⚮

Which was impossible, really.

Donovan was such an infuriating man, much of what he said provoking her, that she soon gave up any notion of holding her tongue.

"You may keep the parish accounts now, Corie, but I imagine there are already those among the congregation wondering who will tend to such things once we're married."

"Thankfully you and I won't be married very long," Corisande retorted, as Donovan followed her outside into a balmy spring day after she'd completed her duties. "I'll explain to any who ask, of course, that careful thought must first be given to electing a competent churchwarden and that I don't mind at all filling in while they deliberate, and by that time, sir, *we* will be happily annulled. Things will go on just as if you'd never been here."

A pleasant notion indeed, Corisande thought as she hurried down the stone church steps, not waiting for Donovan.

Of course, she'd never considered that her marrying one day might affect things, because her husband would fully share in her work, not want her to stop. He wouldn't be a privileged aristocrat like Lord Donovan Trent who thought only of himself and his own amusements, oh, no—

Corisande gasped as Donovan suddenly caught her hand

and pulled her up short, his strong fingers enmeshing with hers.

"I said I would wait for you, woman, not run after you like a pup. Now, shall we slow our pace to a promenade and proceed together to the poorhouse?"

She wanted to rant at him, half for startling her and the other half for pure spite, but passersby in the street made her force a smile instead and say through gritted teeth, "As you wish, my love."

He smiled back, all white teeth and masculine charm, and settled her hand comfortably in the crook of his arm, which only angered her further. But she took some comfort in gloating over how totally out of his element Donovan would be at the poorhouse, like a pilchard out of water as he was surrounded by orphaned children, the aged, and the infirm. He would probably flee for the nearest door, sickened by the smell of filled diapers and the sight of drool . . .

"Here we are," Corisande announced almost gaily in front of a neat two-story brick building, eager to see his handsome face turn green. She even took his big hand and led the way up the few stairs, her move clearly surprising him as he raised a thick black brow. As soon as she opened the front door, she felt almost giddy as the smell of curdled milk porridge and mackerel and potato pie greeted them, hardly palatable fare for a highborn gentleman such as he.

"Ah, Corie, I wasn't sure you were coming today."

Corisande smiled at the thin, kind-faced woman who rushed forward to greet them, then turned to Donovan. "Mrs. Eliza Treweake, the good governess here. Eliza, Lord Donovan—"

"Oh, yes, I've heard all about him," Eliza gushed before Corisande could finish, the woman's bright blue eyes crinkling at the corners as she smiled warmly at Donovan. "Such an honor for you to come and visit us, my lord. I'm so happy for you both too. A wedding tomorrow? How wonderful!"

"Yes, it is wonderful," Donovan agreed pleasantly, giving Corisande's hand a firm squeeze. "And such a pleasure to meet you, dear lady."

"Yes, well, I'm sorry we're late, Eliza." Pointedly tugging her fingers free from Donovan's, Corisande stepped further into the entrance hall as the sounds of children laughing and spoons clattering against china carried from behind the closed doors to the dining room. "There was so much to do at the church today. We had such a crowd."

"Ah, no trouble, no trouble. I hope you don't mind, but we already began our meal. The children were so hungry we couldn't wait."

Corisande nodded in understanding and followed Mrs. Treweake through the broad double doors, knowing Donovan was right behind her. Although she was fuming again at the insufferable man who took every opportunity to torment her, she was able to feel a bit smug again, too, at the lively commotion that greeted them.

At one end of the long oaken table sat the older folk, most contentedly focused upon their generous helpings of Cornish pie and mashed turnips while a dozen boisterous children of varying ages squirmed upon wooden benches set along the sides. At the far end, an attendant bustled around three gurgling babies in high seats, and it was between these littlest ones and the wriggling children that chairs were brought for Corisande and Donovan. Plates heaped high and steaming cups of watery tea soon followed, as Mrs. Treweake took her place at the quieter end of the table between poor Alice Ripper, who was blind and quite feeble, and a crippled old tinner by the name of John Thomas.

"Enjoy your Sunday dinner, my lord." Corisande knew she was grinning like a fool into her food as Donovan picked up his fork, but her smile soon became a look of pure amazement when he began to eat with gusto, clearly enjoying his meal.

"Wonderful fish pie, Mrs. Treweake," Donovan offered a few moments later when his plate was almost empty. He glanced over at Corisande, who was staring at him incredulously, and, imagining her thoughts, couldn't resist adding in a low sarcastic aside, "Surprised, my dear? You shouldn't be. We Don Juans must keep up our strength no matter what's put before us. One never knows when an innocent maiden ripe for despoiling might come along. No, one never knows."

"Cad!"

Her emphatic whisper was drowned out as a baby nearby began to wail, the exasperated attendant throwing up her hands as she spun to face Mrs. Treweake.

"Little Mary won't eat 'er porridge, ma'am. I've done everything—"

"Here, I'll help." Corisande had begun to rise, but Donovan caught a handful of skirt and pulled her back into her chair.

"No, no, you finish your meal. I'll give the girl a hand." Donovan was on his feet before Corisande could utter a word, her eyes so filled with surprise that he bent down and whispered in her ear, "Your food's growing cold, my love. Better eat."

He almost laughed when she glanced down at her plate then back at him, furious sparks in her gaze. But his attention flew to the baby, a chubby little thing with flyaway wisps of dark hair and big brown eyes, when she began to wail afresh. At once he went and scooped the child from her chair, a painful well of emotion gripping him as he held her close.

"Ah, Mary, the milk porridge isn't agreeing with you today?"

He'd spoken in low, soothing tones that, if not completely

quieting the child, at least eased her distress to whimpers and slowed her flood of fat tears. Jouncing her gently, he strolled to the nearest window where he shifted her to one arm and pointed at some birds fluttering from shrub to shrub in the small neatly tended garden outside.

"Those little wrens seem to like the lemon verbena, don't they? Do you see them, Mary? And such a nice song they make too. Ah, look, there they go!"

Donovan smiled to himself, taking almost as much delight in watching the child as Mary—grown quiet and wide-eyed, her pudgy little finger pointing too—seemed fascinated by the birds. But his enjoyment brought him fresh pain as well, and he stared out the window, thinking of another child with beautiful brown eyes, his child, who would be nearly three years old now, that is, if she was still alive . . .

"I think Mary might eat now, milord. Would 'ee like for me to take her?"

Donovan turned from the window, nodded, and handed the child to the attendant as his eyes met Corisande's across the room. She was studying him, a tiny frown between her brows, but when he came around the table toward her, she immediately left her chair and went to assist Mrs. Treweake, who was helping one of her elderly charges rise to his feet.

Which left Donovan to retake his seat heavily, the mounting confusion at the table as the children finished their meals and clamored to be excused so they could go play outside making his head pound. And with Corisande purposely ignoring him—though, hell, why should that bother him?—and all three babies beginning to wail in unison, startled by the noise, and restless children beginning to run like wild heathens around the dining room, he could take it no longer.

Corisande was startled, too, when Donovan came up behind her and caught her by the elbow, his low growl grating in her ear as he steered her toward Mrs. Treweake.

"We're leaving. Now. Thank the governess for the meal and say what else you must—that we've many things to do before the wedding, *whatever*—but do it quickly, Corie."

She bristled, wanting to resist, but his harsh grip on her arm brooked no argument. Somehow she found it within herself to smile as she made a hasty excuse to Mrs. Treweake, the poor besieged woman surrounded by so many squealing children hopping up and down like rabbits and weary older folk anxious to return to their places before the sitting room fire that she looked almost relieved to see them go.

Corisande was relieved, too, when at last she and Donovan had stepped outside, her cheeks so flame-hot with anger that only fresh air could cool them. Fresh air and an explanation, but that, she saw from the numbers of people strolling in the street and enjoying the sunshine, would have to wait until they were alone once again.

To that end, she summoned the last ounce of her composure and said pleasantly, "Perhaps you might help me once we're back at the parsonage, my lord. As I told you earlier, I've calls to make for my father, and everything's ready in the stable. I've only to hitch the cart to Biscuit—"

"Yes, let's head to the stable. I left my horse there."

With that brusque reply, they walked silently the rest of the way, only speaking to greet passersby. When they were almost to the stable, no one else between them and the door, Donovan let down his guard completely, as deep and forbidding a scowl on his face as ever she'd seen. He was tense, too, his hand at the small of her back propelling her forward as if he thought her long legs weren't carrying her fast enough. She was breathless when they entered the small building, Biscuit nickering to them from his stall.

But Corisande paid no heed to Biscuit as she whirled

around, her jaw dropping in surprise to find that Donovan was already hauling a very fine leather saddle onto Samson's broad back.

"You're leaving?"

"Marvelous deduction. Yes, I'm leaving."

Affronted by his sarcasm, she felt the heat explode in her cheeks along with her temper. "Well, at the very least you could explain why you hustled me from the poorhouse as if I'd done something wrong. Unless, of course, the place unnerved you just as I imagined it would. Babies, old people, cripples. Not your sort of company, I'm sure. And I don't know what point you were trying to make with little Mary—going out of your way to charm everyone as usual. Oh, you looked very convincing, as if you've held babies before, and I thought for a moment you might even go so far as to try to feed her and then clean a dirty bottom or two for good measure—"

"Hell and damnation, woman, does your shrew's tongue never stop?"

Stunned, Corisande gaped at Donovan, not so much because he had just insulted her but because he looked almost tortured, his eyes strangely desperate. Yet he turned away so quickly to lead his horse from the stall that she wondered if it might have been a trick of light. The stable was always filled with shadows no matter how sunny the day . . .

"I thought we were to spend the whole day together," she said as she followed after him, feeling more than a bit of the sting now that he had called her a shrew. "The whole *blessed* day, as I recall. What of your brother's spies—"

"Spend the rest of the day with you?" Donovan had spun, gripping the reins in his fist as he scowled back at her. "I'd rather be flogged with a horsewhip than endure that pleasure. Not until we're married, woman, shall I force myself to spend another hour in your presence."

He turned and was gone, striding out into the sunshine as if he couldn't leave the stable fast enough.

Which left Corisande alone, well, except for Biscuit.

"So much for our charade," she muttered as the piebald pony snorted and shook his shaggy white mane. "The man can't stomach being around me. Thinks I'm a shrew." She glanced over at the cart, filled with blankets and medicine and tins of smuggled tea, all the things she needed to make calls on some of her father's more needy parishioners, and suddenly realized she didn't quite feel like going anymore.

At least not by herself. Oh, Lord, she hadn't actually been looking forward to . . .

"Not bloody likely," Corisande huffed under her breath as the sound of Donovan riding away carried to her from outside. If anything, she'd merely wanted to see him squirm when faced with more unfortunate souls; yes, of course, that was it. Squaring her shoulders, she went to lead Biscuit from his stall. "The surly bounder. I doubt now he'll even show up for the wedding. Probably decided to find himself another temporary bride."

Which she hoped for the tinners' sake, Corisande had to admit grudgingly to herself, wouldn't be true.

"Will there be anything else, my lord? Another brandy?"

Donovan shook his head, waving Ogden away without a word as he stared into the fire. But on second thought, he decided to speak up just before the butler closed the library door.

"All is in readiness, Ogden? I want everything to be as near perfection tomorrow as possible."

"It will be as you desire, my lord. Grace has yet to leave the kitchen for the night—the wedding breakfast has her most preoccupied—and Ellen Biddle is seeing to last details as well. I can vouch for her highly, Lord Donovan. She is an excellent housekeeper."

"I have no doubt of it." Indeed, the industrious woman had worked wonders with the place in the span of one day—Donovan had scarcely recognized the entry hall when he had returned to the house late that afternoon. Sparkling marble floors, no dust to be seen anywhere, furniture he'd thought no better than kindling polished and looking like new. Even the grounds and stable had been spruced up and repairs made, Henry Gilbert overseeing a good-natured crew of tinners who'd been more than happy to work on their Sunday off, anything for Corie Easton, they'd said to a man.

Yes, the transformation was bloody amazing. But what would be more amazing was if he'd have a bride to bring home tomorrow. Now *that* would be a true miracle.

"If there's nothing else, my lord . . ."

Donovan looked up, his thoughts in such an unpleasant furor he wasn't surprised he'd forgotten the somber-faced butler was still hovering at the door, and the man probably ready to drop on his feet at this late hour. "Get yourself some sleep, Ogden. Well done."

"Thank you, my lord. Good night."

Ogden was gone as silently as he had come, a good quality in a spy, Donovan mused dryly. Not furtive, just unassuming. The kind of servant one could easily forget was near until it was too late, the damage done. But then again, if there was no more role to play . . .

Cursing to himself, Donovan lunged to his feet and went to the window where he stared out at the darkness.

If Corisande failed to meet him at the church, he'd only brought her mutiny on himself. Good God, he had caused his own damned torment by holding that child! He'd never felt more wretchedly impotent, overwhelmed by frustration and rage that he was sitting in a poorhouse in Porthleven, Cornwall, instead of back in Spain looking for Paloma along with the men he'd hired to help in the search.

Yet he hadn't needed hours of riding across the heath to tell him that his fury had been misplaced, Corisande unjustly bearing the brunt of his pain. She'd had every right to be angry at him. He'd acted abominably, his temper getting the best of him, and then to call her a shrew . . .

"She *is* a bloody shrew," he muttered wryly, wondering how long it had taken her to finish her calls and if she was home safe and sound.

Add to that exasperating, quick to anger, stubborn . . . impassioned, intelligent, determined—Corisande Easton was made of far sterner stuff than he deserved, no matter she was only a temporary bride, if she showed up at the altar tomorrow morning and agreed to be his wife.

❧ *Eleven* ❧

"It's quarter past eleven, my lord—"

"I know that, Gilbert!" Donovan snapped, ready to wrap Henry's gold pocket watch around the man's scrawny neck.

Growing more uncomfortable by the moment, Donovan shot a glance at the church entrance, then back at the animated group sitting in the front pew in their finest clothes and bonnets—Estelle and Marguerite, who were alternating between grinning at him and blushing, Linette, who couldn't seem to sit still, the girl forever twisting around to see if Corisande was coming, and Frances, who was plucking at her sleeve, the bellflower-blue kerseymere apparently not lying straight enough to suit her.

Meanwhile, the Reverend Easton was puttering between the altar and the sacristy, apparently unconcerned that his daughter was fifteen minutes late for her own wedding . . . if, indeed, the poor fellow even remembered whose wedding he'd come to perform. But right now, that was the least of Donovan's concerns.

Frances had told him at five to eleven that Corisande's calls had run quite late the night before, which had made her sleep longer than usual. Thus she'd missed entirely her early morning appointment with Rose Polkinghorne for the final fitting of her wedding dress, the poor seamstress frantic when Corisande finally appeared that she wouldn't have the work done in time.

It hadn't helped that the fine pearl buttons ordered from Penzance had yet to arrive and— Bloody hell! Why was Donovan recounting this entire mess in his mind? The fact remained that Corisande was not here and probably had no intention of arriving for the wedding, or else she planned to show up in one of her drab pea-green dresses with her bun askew and tell him he could jump off a cliff for all she cared, his inheritance be damn—

"My lord, my lord! Look!"

Donovan did look, the fierce throbbing in his temple all but forgotten as Corisande entered the church, tense relief pouring through him that she was, indeed, dressed from head to toe in white. She paused, their eyes meeting across the pews, and it seemed to him that she looked suddenly relieved as well. Then she was hurrying down the aisle toward him, but instead of going to meet her, Donovan could but stare, stunned.

He had known beautiful women, but in that moment Corisande rivaled them all, no untidy ragamuffin now as the bright sunlight pouring through the windows made her a shimmering vision in silver and white. A vision made all the more startling in the soft clinging drape of her dress, the satin so thin and delicate as to reveal a most tempting female shape, long, long legs, wondrously curved hips, a narrow waist, that Donovan's pulse began to pound.

Good God, this was hardly the time to be wracked by lust, in a church no less, her father the vicar only feet away, and for a woman he had no bloody intention of touching!

But matters were only made worse as Corisande drew closer, Donovan's eyes drawn to the seductive swelling of her breasts against her low décolletage—he hadn't forgotten the feel of those pert breasts pressing against his arm— and the beauty of her bare throat brushed by tendrils that shone a rich burnished auburn next to her white skin. He would never have guessed her hair was so long, falling almost to her waist beneath a sheer lace veil that covered her head and framed her face, her cheeks glowing pink with color, her eyes—

"Oh, Lord."

"My lord?"

"Nothing, Gilbert, nothing," Donovan muttered, leaving his agent's side to greet the woman whose lovely eyes were filled with outrage as if she'd just read his lustful thoughts. He held out his hand to her, wondering almost resignedly if she might still renounce him, especially now, but Corisande took his hand with a stiff smile and allowed herself to be led to the altar.

"No need to be nervous, my love." Donovan clasped her hand tightly, as much to warm her icy palm as to remind her to try to relax in front of her family. "You look beautiful. Those extra fifteen minutes were more than worth the wait."

An extra interminable fifteen minutes that had been hell for her, Corisande fumed, all of them spent wondering while Rose Polkinghorne hastily sewed and pinned her into this ridiculous dress, if Donovan would even be at the church. She'd been told a pair of fancy carriages had rumbled past Rose's house, but she refused to believe Donovan had driven the smaller one until she saw him in the flesh. Ha! She needn't have worried. He might have lost his temper yesterday but he showed no ill effect today, looking more the handsome Don Juan than any man should in his fine claret-colored wedding coat and leering at her to boot!

Uncomfortably reminded of the lecherous squire Druella Simmons had married last week—was it only a week ago?—Corisande was glad Lindsay wasn't here to witness this wedding, even if it was a ruse. And as for not feeling nervous, was he mad? Heaven help her, she'd have to be on her guard now, Donovan proving with those treacherous dark eyes that he was hardly a man of his word.

"Here, Corie. I brought you some flowers from the garden. I hope you like them."

Corisande turned to accept the bouquet of fragrant purple veronica from Marguerite, who gave her a quick kiss on the cheek and then returned to Frances's side at the front pew. All of her sisters were beaming at her, yes, even matter-of-fact Linette was smiling, too, which caused a painful tug at Corisande's heart.

She hated terribly to deceive them, but it was for a very good cause. So many families would be helped by this sham marriage. It was time to look forward and, instead of grumbling over the injustice of it all, simply bear the next few weeks of Donovan's company with as much grace as possible.

She had been a bit strident these past days, a bit shrewish, yes, she could admit it after thinking long and hard yesterday about her behavior, and God knows she didn't want to jeopardize an agreement that would make life better for so many throughout the parish. Lord Donovan Trent might be a Don Juan, but she would show him that *she* honored her word even if he could not. Play the rapturous bride? With pleasure!

"I believe your father's ready, darling."

Corisande glanced up from her sweet-smelling bouquet to see, indeed, that her father was drawing near with his opened prayer book in hand. Doing her best to ignore the stab of guilt that she was deceiving the man she held so dear, she turned to Donovan as her father reached them and bestowed upon him a gloriously blissful smile that would have done Lindsay's flair for the dramatic proud. "Oh, my lord, I'm so happy this moment has come at last! So truly, truly happy."

At once, Donovan looked so startled that Corisande wanted to laugh, but the wedding ceremony had begun, their small number of witnesses rising to their feet.

Corisande had heard the service performed so often since childhood that she listened with half an ear, not wanting to focus upon sacred words that to her, right now, meant nothing.

She answered where she must, taking care to look adoringly at Donovan as they repeated their vows, then blessedly the short ceremony was over, the marriage register signed, the delicate gold band like a cold weight around her finger. But what wasn't cold were Donovan's lips when he drew her into his arms and kissed her, his mouth, so warm and insistent, moving intimately over hers.

At first she thought to pull away, but that wouldn't do, no, not with everyone watching. Instead she melted against him just as any happy bride would do, her arms winding around his neck as she began to kiss him back.

She really wasn't sure if she was doing it right, having no prior experience except for the other day, but she decided she must be close when she felt him tense as if in surprise— although she wasn't tense, not at all. She felt quite wonderful, dizzy almost, this kissing business more than pleasant and something over which she'd be damned if he had all the control. Two could play—

"All right, woman, enough. There's no need to overdo it."

Corisande snapped open her eyes, Donovan's terse whisper hardly what she would have expected from the happy groom. Nor would she have expected his look of irritation as she slid her arms from his neck, but it was gone in the next instant as Frances rushed forward, the housekeeper dabbing at her eyes with a white silk handkerchief while Linette, Estelle, and Marguerite all clamored round to give Corisande a hug.

"Oh, Corie darlin', Lord Donovan. I'm so thrilled for 'ee both! What a lovely wedden—"

"But you're crying, Frances!" piped up Estelle, looking momentarily concerned.

"Ais, child, don't mind me. I always cry like a new babe at weddens, I do. Means nothing more than I'm happy too."

"Yes, my lord, Lady Donovan, allow me to offer my sincerest congratulations!" enthused Henry Gilbert, although the agent's eyes grew alarmed when Corisande frowned at him, as much for him cutting into their little group before she could speak to Frances or her sisters as that she despised the man. She couldn't help it. The skinny little weasel had caused so much hardship these past three years . . .

"It appears, Gilbert, that my new bride has been rendered speechless with happiness." Donovan suddenly spoke up with a firm squeeze to Corisande's elbow. "But perhaps if she knew how hard you worked earlier this morning, handing out bags of grain to the tinners until your fingers were raw, she might find it in her heart—"

"Yes, thank you, Henry, truly," Corisande cut in sweetly —oh, no, even Donovan's infuriating little warnings weren't going to rile her!—as she glanced from him to the agent, who despite her soft words took a few cautious steps backward.

"I—I'll wait outside with the carriages, my lord."

"That will be fine, Gilbert. We won't be long."

Confused, Corisande looked back to Donovan as the agent hurried down the aisle, his long blue coattails flopping against his skinny legs. "Surely we're not leaving already. Frances has made a lovely meal, rabbit pie and plum pudding—"

"I'm afraid Grace Twickenham, my new cook, has prepared a special wedding breakfast for us as well. I'm sorry that I neglected to tell you sooner but—"

"Ais, Corie, we've no problem here," Frances interjected with a wide grin. " 'Tes a fine idea to go to your new husband's house an' a fitting one too. An' I know the girls wouldn't mind at all seeing such a grand place, would 'ee?"

"Oh, Corie, can we?" Marguerite's eyes shone with excitement while Estelle hopped up and down.

"I want to go to Donovan's house! I want to go to Donovan's house!"

"You shouldn't call him Donovan," chided Linette in a half whisper, looking askance at her younger sister. "At least not until he says it's all right—"

"He's your brother-in-law now, Linette. Of course you must call him by his Christian name." Corisande threw another radiant smile at Donovan. "Isn't that right, my love?"

Donovan nodded, silenced as much by the stunning beauty of Corisande's smile as his vexation that he could be so strongly affected by it.

What the hell was she up to? One moment she'd looked angry enough to spit, then the next she was playing the eager bride to the hilt, no, overacting was a more apt description. Overacting as shamelessly as a second-rate vaudevillian, and he wished she would stop. He had gotten quite used to her frowns, her angry glances, her name-calling, and constant indignation, albeit she'd usually behaved well enough when others were around, but these damned smiles were another matter altogether, heating his blood and making his pulse pound, and when she'd kissed him . . .

"Well, I suppose we should be on our way if everyone is agreed." Somewhat unnerved by the way Donovan was staring at her, his dark eyes the veriest black, Corisande added, "If that's all right with you, darling. I wouldn't want to disappoint your new cook."

"Ais, now, we don't want to do that!" Frances blurted out to Corisande's relief, the housekeeper breaking the unsettling current between her and Donovan. "Come on with 'ee, girls. We'll quick put away the meal and then settle ourselves in one of those fine carriages, shall we?"

"No, no, I want to ride with Corie and Donovan!" Estelle protested as Frances took her small hand. "Please, Corie . . ."

Corisande opened her mouth to say yes, deciding suddenly that she didn't relish the thought of being alone with Donovan all that way, only to have Frances firmly reply before she could utter a word.

"Silly lamb! There'll be times aplenty to ride with your sister an' her husband, never 'ee fear. But not on their wedden day." With that, Frances and her crestfallen charge headed down the aisle accompanied by Marguerite and Linette while Corisande, sighing to herself, turned back to Donovan.

"I . . . I should see about my father. Sometimes it takes him a while . . ." She didn't wait for a response—the man was still staring at her!—but half fled to the sacristy. "Papa? Did you hear? We're all going to Donovan's—"

She didn't finish, her father to her surprise having already changed from his vestments and meeting her at the door with a gentle yet somehow sad smile on his face, his eyes slightly wet.

"Papa, are you all right?"

"You look . . . you look like your mother today, Corisande. All in white . . . so beautiful."

She swallowed hard, unable to say anything for the longest moment. But then suddenly Donovan was beside them, his voice sounding as deep and strong as her father's had been broken and shallow.

"I'd be honored, Reverend Easton, if you would accompany us to my home." Donovan glanced at Corisande. "Our home."

She stiffened—the lies, oh, the lies!—but at once reminded herself of her new resolve. "Yes, Papa, please come with us."

To her surprise again, he nodded; she'd fully expected

him to refuse their invitation, preferring the solitude of his study. She had hardly seen him these past few days, well, except for Sunday service and then again late last night when she'd returned to the parsonage to find him outside in the garden, sitting upon the bench with his head in his hands. But she hadn't disturbed him; she had seen him like that many times before.

Strangely enough now, though, he seemed almost eager as the three of them walked together down the aisle, and Corisande took note that her father's step seemed less slow and labored. Perhaps the wedding had heartened him, which made her feel guilty all over again, but she quickly shoved away the thought.

Once outside, she watched him crinkle his eyes at the bright midday sun, this lovely third day of April the warmest the season had yet offered—Joseph Easton even smiling when Marguerite waved gaily to them from the second and much larger carriage.

"Frances said I could wait here, Corie. Isn't it grand?"

Corisande didn't have a chance to answer as Donovan's voice sounded beside her.

"Gilbert! Help me with the good reverend."

At his command Henry came running, Corisande ignoring the sensation of interested stares upon them from dozens of onlookers on the street and at their windows as she watched the two men lead her father to the carriage. It was then that she noticed Estelle running from the parsonage as fast as her short legs could carry her, her sister grinning from ear to ear and clutching Luther to her breast.

"Frances?" Corisande called to the housekeeper, who appeared in the doorway with Linette in tow. "Did you . . . ?"

"Ah, Corie, the poor child looked so glum when we came out of the church. She asked if she might bring the dog, an' I didn't have the heart to say no. Would 'ee?"

In truth, Corisande didn't mind at all, but she couldn't help wondering what Donovan might say. He hadn't seemed very fond of Luther the other day when the tiny mutt had been circling round his boots . . . yet did she care? Smiling, she lifted the skirt of her wedding dress and went to meet Estelle, hearing Frances's terrified cry for her to get out of the way almost at the same moment her little sister suddenly stopped and stood openmouthed, Luther yapping in her arms.

"What . . . ?" Corisande heard the ominous rumbling and whirled in place, her eyes widening in horror as two huge pilchard barrels rolled toward her, the salted fish flying out all over the street. But she didn't think of herself. She ran instead toward Estelle, snatching up the stricken child and dodging out of harm's way with no more than an instant to spare, her heart slamming in her ears as the heavy barrels thundered past her and crashed into the parsonage wall.

∞ Twelve ∞

"Corie!"

The cry hadn't come from Frances but Donovan. Corisande spun to find him running hard toward her, on his heels Henry Gilbert and lastly, half stumbling, her father. Yet her eyes weren't drawn to them but to Donovan, his face taut, his pallor ashen as he reached her and pulled her, Estelle, and a yowling Luther into his arms.

"Good God, woman, are you all right?"

"I'm fine, yes. We're fine," Corisande croaked as Estelle began to wriggle between them.

"I can't breathe, Corie, and . . . . and you're both going to squish Luther!"

Laughing nervously to herself, giddily in fact, the full force of what had narrowly been avoided hitting her, Corisande met Donovan's eyes as he seemed to laugh, too, and released them. But he wasn't smiling, no, not at all, as he glanced grimly at the smashed and splintered staves while Corisande was suddenly surrounded by her family, Henry Gilbert, and wide-eyed onlookers who had witnessed the near disaster.

"Lord help us, did 'ee see those hogsheads come a-tumbling?" cried an old Cornish shipwright to no one in particular, everyone clamoring and talking at once.

"I think they were ones set against John Killigrew's house 'cross from the church," shouted another man, naming a respected Porthleven fisherman. "Stacked an' waiten to go to market, they were, but no export market to be found for 'em same as the rest of us, thanks to that bugger Napoleon and his damned blockade!"

Corisande sighed heavily as the noisy crowd around her grew larger and understandably belligerent, their comments now more centered upon the village's plight of being unable to sell last year's bumper catch of pilchards than on the accident that could have taken her life, Estelle's, and poor Luther's. Donovan must have read her mind, his tone as tense and irritated as his expression as he addressed the villagers.

"Did anyone see what happened? Anyone at all?"

A mute chorus of shaking heads and apologetic stares greeted his query, one woman piping up, "We were watching the hubbub in front of the church, milord, if 'ee don't mind me saying so, and with Corie looking so lovely today . . ."

A sudden flurry of concurring compliments flew around the gathering, so many that Corisande felt her face redden. "The barrels must have tipped," she concluded with a shrug, eager to be done with the whole unpleasant matter. "Stacked too high, I suppose, perhaps a bit carelessly, an easy enough thing to do." She looked down at Estelle, who had just planted a kiss on top of Luther's bedraggled head. "How about a nice carriage ride, sweet? Would you like that?"

"Oh, yes, but only if I can bring Luther. He's never ridden in a carriage, and I think he'd like it. May I, Donovan?"

Somewhat disgruntled by how her little sister had warmed so quickly to Donovan, Corisande was nonetheless grateful when he nodded, which drew from Estelle a high-pitched squeal of delight. Hugging Luther, she slipped through the dense crowd as easily as a minnow and ran toward the shiny black coach as she had only moments before, clearly none the worse for all the excitement.

Corisande couldn't say the same for Frances, however, the poor woman still pale and uncommonly silent. "Everything's all right, Frances, really. You see?" Corisande did a slow twirl for the housekeeper's benefit. "Even my dress came out without a tear or scratch. Now, is the meal put away?"

Frances nodded shakily.

"Good. Take Marguerite and Linette with you to the carriage, and we'll be on our way, sure to have a lovely time." Corisande looked round the circle of faces. "Papa?"

She had seen him among the villagers, keeping to the back, which for him wasn't at all strange. He'd been pale as a ghost, too, which had made her heart go out to him, but now he was nowhere to be seen.

"Papa?"

"I believe I saw the Reverend Easton enter the parsonage, Lady Donovan."

That from Henry Gilbert, whose large Adam's apple bobbed as he swallowed as if he'd summoned all of his courage just to speak to her. Meanwhile, she had to summon all her will not to frown.

Lady Donovan. No, she didn't like the sound of that lofty title at all, but let her not forget her resolve . . .

"Thank you, Henry." Then she opened her mouth to tell Donovan that she'd fetch her father if he wanted to wait for her by the church, but he took her hand firmly before she could speak and began to lead her through the crowd to the parsonage, Corisande gaping at him in some surprise. "I . . . I could have gotten Papa by myself—"

"If it's all the same to you, my love, I'd prefer to see you safely there and then back to the carriage."

Astonished at the sudden warmth flooding her face, Corisande just as quickly reminded herself that her temporary husband was anything but altruistic. Oh, he'd done a magnificent job already of looking concerned and outraged as any proper groom would do, surprising her with the intensity he had displayed. But now was not the time to commend him, although she certainly planned to do so when they were alone . . .

"It doesn't look as if the wall is damaged." Donovan had paused near the front door, his gaze raking the site where the barrels had crashed against the sturdy gray stone of the parsonage, now splattered with bits of salted fish. "I'll send Henry Gilbert back later to clean up the mess."

Oh, he'll love that, Corisande thought to herself as Donovan proceeded into the house, still gripping her hand tightly and leading the way. But they had no sooner entered the front passage than he suddenly stopped and pushed her none too gently against the wall, holding her by the shoulders, the fierceness of his action making her breath catch. And her heart, she'd never felt it pounding so hard when he leaned toward her, the buttons on his coat grazing her breasts, his eyes searching hers.

"You are sure you're all right, Corie?"

She'd never heard such a deep huskiness in his voice, and for a moment she could only stare up at him, wondering at this man whose moods could change so drastically from one day to the next. Yesterday he'd wanted nothing to do with her, calling her a shrew, and now she could almost swear he was truly concerned.

But, of course, that couldn't be. He must be toying with her again, even when he'd said yesterday he wouldn't, the lout! He'd said as much in a holy church, too, which proved he was as trustworthy as a snake and, oh, she was feeling infuriated again and quite, quite shrewish and to hell with playing the rapturous bride!

"Of course I'm bloody well fine," she said, keeping her voice very low so her father wouldn't hear. "And just because we're married now, my lord husband, don't you dare think for a moment that anything has changed between us. No, not even in your dreams!"

Stunned, Donovan wasn't sure for an instant whether to smile or frown. He was stunned at himself, too, not wholly certain why he'd pinned her against the wall. Something had come over him—good God, just thinking about those huge barrels crashing toward her . . .

"You . . . you insufferable oaf! Are you going to release me so I can find my father, or not?"

Now Donovan smiled, much to Corisande's indignation as her face grew a rosy pink, but he couldn't help himself. It appeared to his relief that the woman he knew was back, and with a vengeance, but what was this latest accusation—

"So I was right, you bloody lecher! You are thinking—"

"Thinking what, woman?"

"Shh, my father might hear you! Must you shout?"

"Must you call me preposterous names?" Donovan countered, any humor he'd found in the situation gone altogether as vexation gripped him. "Hell and damnation, woman, I am not a lecher."

"Oh, no? What was all that in the church, then?"

"All what?"

His question was rewarded with a sigh of pure exasperation, Corisande staring at him as if he were a complete idiot.

"If you've something to say . . ." he prompted, knowing full well what she'd meant, but nonetheless finding a bit of perverse pleasure in baiting her. The woman had called him a lecher—she deserved it! "All what, Lady Donovan?"

"Your . . . your looking at me and leering, what else could I possibly be talking about?" she finally spouted in an outraged whisper, her cheeks reddening even more as she struggled to free herself. But Donovan held her tight, determined that they would have this matter out.

"Not leering, Corie, 'admiring' is more the word. Perhaps more intently than I should have, given the situation—"

"That's an understatement!"

True, Donovan thought to himself, "admiration" was hardly the word to describe what he'd felt in the church. Now wasn't, either, for that matter, which didn't please him. Doing his best to ignore the indignant rise and fall of her breasts as she began to struggle again, he continued gruffly, "You look very lovely today, Corie, and I am a man inclined to notice beautiful things."

Corisande froze, more aware in that moment of Donovan's overwhelming masculinity than she wanted to be. He was simply standing too close and holding her too tightly, the strength in his hands alone proving altogether disconcerting, his clean, virile scent invading her senses, Donovan so tall, his body so massive, that she felt nearly smothered against the wall. Not an unpleasant sensation at all, but something wholly exciting—oh, Lord, whatever was coming over her?

"Please, we should talk of this later," she said, feeling no small amount of desperation. "I want to find my father, and —and I'm not bloody beautiful! Lindsay is beautiful, and Marguerite is very nearly so, and . . . and why is it that a wedding dress and veil make people say the most ridiculous things when they know—"

"Corie."

She started, meeting his eyes. Dark midnight eyes held an understanding of her now that she didn't want to see. Furious with herself, she dropped her gaze to stare blindly at her feet.

"Once again, you haven't allowed me to finish. Nothing is any different than what we discussed yesterday. But as you said, we can talk later if you wish—"

"I do wish! I wish for you to kindly release me so I can look for my father—oh!" Corisande nearly toppled forward when Donovan abruptly let go of her shoulders, but of course he was right there to catch her, which only made her more angry. With an agile twist she was free of him, half storming through the parlor and down the hall to her father's study.

"Papa?"

Grateful at least that they had been so far to the front of the house that he couldn't possibly have heard them, Corisande was even more relieved when she found that his door was closed. But he wasn't inside his study, she soon discovered, which made her gaze jump at once to the windows. They were securely shut, not like a few days ago when she'd spied him out in the garden. Of course, the garden.

Corisande hurried from the darkened room, her eyes widening as she entered the kitchen, which still smelled fragrantly of Frances's cooking. Donovan stood next to the high-backed settle where her father was sitting as eerily silent as a stone, Joseph Easton giving neither of them any notice as he stared with unblinking eyes at the glowing red embers Frances had carefully banked in the center of the hearth.

"Reverend Easton—"

"Please, Donovan, let me talk to him." Ignoring his raised brow, which no doubt indicated he was more surprised she'd called him by his Christian name than that she'd interrupted him, Corisande sat down next to her father and placed her hand gently on his arm. "Papa, please, you musn't be distressed about those silly barrels. It could have happened to anyone—"

"No!"

Corisande sat back stunned, her father's vehement outburst the last thing she would have expected from him. The tears now streaking his drawn, ashen face were another matter. Corisande felt her own eyes grow wet at the shock he must have suffered when he thought she and Estelle were in danger. But they were both fine, her father had surely seen that . . .

"What am I to do? What am I to do?"

The despair in her father's voice was heartrending, and Corisande looked at him in confusion. "Do about what, Papa? Has something else happened? If so, you must tell me—Papa?"

She'd felt him stiffen an instant before he lurched to his feet and headed for the door, but he turned abruptly, his eyes moving from her face to Donovan's. Desperate eyes that held a fervent pleading while he stood there for the longest moment, looking as if he wanted to speak but saying nothing. Then he was through the door and gone, walking stiffly into the garden.

At once Corisande flew to follow him, but she didn't get far as Donovan caught her arm. She turned upon him, incensed.

"Let me go, damn you! I've never seen him like this—"

"Leave him, Corie. It's clear that he wants to be alone. Give him some time."

"Time? How could you possibly know what my father needs? You don't even know him!"

"No, but I saw his face. I've seen that look a thousand times on the battlefield when the cannon smoke has cleared and the ground is slippery with blood. When an infantryman wipes the burning sweat from his eyes to find his comrades lying wounded and dead around him—"

"Oh, forgive me, I almost forgot that you're a veteran of the war in Spain," Corisande broke in sarcastically, Donovan's face hardening at her biting tone.

"Not a veteran. I'll be going back as soon as my business here is done."

Corisande felt a stab; he had said the word "business" so coldly, and of course he'd meant their temporary marriage and—and bloody hell, what did she care if he planned to return to Spain? Thinking mutinously that she, too, couldn't wait until their arrangement was done, she tried to yank her arm free.

"Infantrymen, battlefields, I don't see what any of this has to do with my father!"

"He's been badly shaken, Corie. You saw him. He's probably never come so close to losing you, or even thinking that he might have lost one of his daughters."

"Or else he overheard everything from the front entryway, and for that I blame you! If you hadn't grabbed me—"

"Corie! Lord Donovan?"

Corisande gave a small gasp as Frances came bustling down the hall toward the kitchen, while Donovan at once released Corisande's arm and swept her into an embrace— an embrace! She felt like wrenching away, but she forced herself to nestle her head against his chest and throw her arms around his waist instead, making it look, quite convincingly, as if she were hugging him back.

"Oh! Oh, my, 'ee two! Here I thought there might be some trouble with the good passon an' I came to see if I could lend a hand but—where is the Reverend Easton?"

"He's gone out to the garden, Frances." Donovan felt Corisande tense in his arms, but he held her firmly, smoothing the delicate veil that covered her hair. "I'm afraid my new bride is quite distressed about her father. He's upset, too—those damned barrels . . ."

"Ais, so I was right. Nearly scared the life from me, the accursed things!" Frances went to the kitchen window, clucking her tongue in dismay. "I'll stay here with the passon, Lord Donovan. You an' Corie go on your way—ah, such a thing to spoil a lovely wedden an' the girls being so excited too."

"No, no, Frances, I'm sure Papa will be fine." Corisande

lifted her head, doing her best to gather together the shreds of her resolve and trying not to glare at Donovan. "My husband believes Papa just needs some time to collect himself, and I can't but agree, so there's no need for you to stay. And you're just as excited to see the house as my sisters. It wouldn't be fair if you didn't come with us too."

That said, Corisande pulled herself free of Donovan's arms and with a last look at her father, who was sitting on the bench staring out across the vast sunlit heath, she led a still reluctant Frances from the kitchen.

"Ah, me, look at your poor flowers," the housekeeper bemoaned a few moments later as they walked past the spot where Corisande's bouquet of purple veronica lay crushed into a paste upon the street. "Lord help us, I don't even want to think—"

"So we won't, Frances." Corisande's voice was firm. "It's a lovely warm spring day, and we've a fine carriage ride ahead of us. *That's* what we'll think about, nothing more."

Which was much easier said than done, Corisande thought to herself, glancing over her shoulder at Donovan, who was following close behind them, his dark eyes meeting hers as he looked up from what was left of her bouquet. At once she turned back around, her face heating most uncomfortably at the memory of how he'd grabbed her in the entryway and told her nothing had changed between them.

Somehow she felt as if something had changed and she didn't like it, no, not at all.

Donovan didn't like it either. Dammit, he didn't like the way those crushed flowers made him feel and certainly not the memory of Joseph Easton's pleading eyes, as if the man had been trying to tell him something.

Those barrels, an accident? Somehow Donovan doubted it. But he couldn't attend to the troubling matter now. He had a bride to take home, a spitting, irritating, altogether perplexing termagant of a temporary bride who no doubt intended to make his life most interesting for the next few weeks.

God help him. He'd gotten his wish.

∞ Thirteen ∞

"More tea, my lady?"

Corisande stared into the fire, impatiently twirling the tiny silver spoon around and around between her fingertips.

"Would you like more tea, my lady?"

"What . . . ?" Corisande looked up in surprise at Ogden hovering just behind her chair, the spoon clattering onto the bone china saucer. For heaven's sake, she hadn't even heard the butler come into the room! Did all of these bloody servants walk about the place on tiptoe?

"Forgive me, my lady. I startled you—"

"No, no, Ogden—well, actually you did startle me a little but . . ." Corisande didn't finish, the man's expression as placid as a basset hound's while her heart was pounding. In fact, Ogden resembled a basset hound although his eyes weren't dopey at all, but quite keen. Reminded again of what Donovan had said about spies, she forced a bright smile. "More tea would be fine, Ogden. Thank you."

As the butler silently obliged, Corisande let her gaze roam for the hundredth time around the immense drawing room where Donovan had left her almost a half hour ago. In fact, everything about this house was immense, at least compared to the parsonage, from the high-ceilinged rooms to the solid English furnishings.

She'd felt quite ridiculous that afternoon in the dining room, sitting at one end of a monstrous oaken table while

Donovan sat at the other, her three sisters, Frances, and
Henry Gilbert placed at evenly spaced intervals along the
sides. Not that she wanted to be closer to Donovan. She'd
had enough closeness for one day, thank you very much,
although the carriage ride hadn't been too terrible since
Estelle—and Luther—had been allowed to join them after
all. But at that dining table she'd practically had to shout to
reply to anything Donovan said, making the wedding breakfast with its many courses more of a trial than she could
have anticipated.

She'd never seen such an embarrassment of food, including a saddle of roasted mutton and a baked ham that could
have fed the poorhouse for a week, nor tasted the like of
mulligatawny soup, pungent with Indian curry, and potted
pheasant. Frances, after being assured by Corisande again
and again that her father would be fine, was finally able to
relax and proceeded to enjoy herself immensely, delighting
in each new dish and then spending the remainder of the
day exchanging recipes in the kitchen with a very flattered
Grace Twickenham.

Meanwhile Estelle and Linette had nearly eaten themselves sick, while Marguerite had barely touched her food,
so overawed was she with her surroundings. After the
double-iced bride's cake was served, all three girls, Luther
skittering among them, had spent the day eagerly exploring
much of the house and grounds with Donovan as their
guide, and he'd insisted that Corisande come too. Which
was fine because she hadn't wanted to be left alone with
Henry, although he disappeared soon after the meal to return to Porthleven to clean up the mess at the parsonage.

And to fetch her one valise, forgotten earlier in the day
and which Corisande had packed very lightly. Why bring
more? Poor Rose Polkinghorne was furiously stitching new
dresses for her, although Corisande hoped Donovan's inheritance would come soon and she wouldn't have to wear

them. Each was as impractical and revealing as her wedding dress, and after Donovan leered at her so in the church, no, no, *admired* her as he had so smoothly insisted—

"Will there be anything else, my lady?"

Corisande started again, realizing that Ogden had poured her tea, added a fresh log and stoked the fire, and then walked to the door without her giving him any notice at all, her thoughts running rampant. Lord, she was tired . . .

"No, Ogden, but—do you know if my husband is still meeting with Mr. Gilbert?"

"Yes, my lady, I believe so. Would you like for me to carry some message to His Lordship? Or perhaps, since it grows late, I could have Miss Biddle show you to your room—"

"No, no, I'll wait here. I'm sure he won't be much longer . . ."

Not that she cared, Corisande thought as Ogden nodded and left the room, well, other than that she longed terribly to feel a soft pillow under her head. But she had to make some attempt to play the wistful bride, abandoned as it were, if only for a short time, by her newly wedded husband.

Yet it was rather strange, really. She and Donovan had no sooner bid good night to her family—Linette and Marguerite waving drowsily from the carriage while Estelle, an exhausted Luther snuggled and snoring in her lap, already lay fast asleep against Frances's deep bosom—than he had led her to this room and excused himself, saying he had summoned Henry Gilbert to the library and that he would return shortly. But that had been a while ago now, while here she sat drinking tea . . .

"And more tea," Corisande muttered, her gaze flying from her brimming cup to an elaborately carved sideboard where a decanter of golden sherry gleamed among cut-crystal glasses. Except for some wine with her meal, she'd drunk her fill of tea all day. A long grueling day, and who knew how much longer Donovan would keep her waiting?

Corisande couldn't resist. She wasn't normally one to drink spirits, well, except on those nights after working hard to land a cargo of smuggled goods when she'd shared a nip of brandy with the men who risked their lives to cross the Channel for the good of the parish—and admittedly, to line his own pockets as well, Oliver Trelawny, the grizzled captain of the cutter *Fair Betty* would often laugh.

But tonight was different. Soon she and Donovan would be alone for the first time since the parsonage . . .

Corisande half flew from her chair to the sideboard and poured herself a generous amount, the sweet fortified wine infusing her with warmth as she nearly emptied the glass.

It was silly, really. She shouldn't be so nervous. She had nothing to fear. Donovan might have been leer—admiring her, but he knew better than to risk even the thought of touching her. Of course he must know, too, that she would scream to high heaven if he did so much as touch her and bring this whole houseful of spying servants down upon them, and then what would he say? No, he'd be a fool to threaten his inheritance now when it was so near to his grasp. A damned bloody fool.

Feeling better and certainly more confident, Corisande took another long swallow, then refilled her glass and walked back to the fire.

For heaven's sake, it was just as ridiculous that she was spending so much time worrying about Donovan when she had so much else to think about. Like her visit to see Oliver Trelawny last night, for one. She had imagined he would be concerned about her impending marriage, so after she had finished her calls she'd gone to see him at the comfortable quayside inn he ran with his wife, Rebecca, when he wasn't out fair trading, and discovered she had been right.

"Lord, Corie, how do 'ee expect to go on helping with the landings when you'll be marrying on the morrow? Do 'ee think your husband will be pleased to find 'ee gone from his bed late in the night when I've need of you?"

Her face burning, Corisande had wanted terribly to tell him the truth about her marriage, although at that point she hadn't been sure a wedding was even going to take place. She trusted the gruff, white-bearded captain with her life. But Oliver had been known a time or two to boast in his cups, and she couldn't risk that he might somehow let the truth slip.

"Lord Donovan knows how much helping the tinners means to me," she had hastily explained. "Helping the fishermen and their families in Porthleven too. It's been such a terrible time all around, and . . . and I wouldn't have considered marrying him otherwise! If I say I'm needed at a sickbed or some such thing, I'm sure he won't question me."

Oliver had pondered for a long moment, tugging at his thick beard, then he slowly nodded.

"Very well, Corie, we'll give it a try. Lord knows, you're a wonder at hiding goods an' sending them on their way, so I don't want to think of going forth without 'ee." His raspy laughter had filled the back room. "An' since 'ee assured me three years past there'd be a spot reserved in heaven if I split my trading profits with you so's 'ee could help the poor, I don't want to gamble with meeting the Old One instead, no, indeed. He'll have to save his red-hot fork for another damned soul!"

Yet Oliver had sobered an instant later, his weathered face grown very serious as he leaned toward her across the scarred table. "I hope this fine gentleman treats 'ee well, Corie. 'Ee know I think of you like me own daughter, an' after 'ee did so much to help my poor Sophie . . ." His voice catching, the burly sea captain had paused to shake his head, his eyes wet when he looked up again. "Well, Lord Donovan'll answer to me, is all I'm saying. You know good an' why."

Yes, she knew good and why, Corisande thought as she lifted the glass to her lips and downed the rest of the sherry, her hand slightly shaking. Lord help her, even now the memories . . . the blood, the screaming, the knife blade gleaming bright . . .

A sudden chiming made Corisande jump; her gaze flew to the ornate ormolu clock on the mantelpiece. Ten o'clock. And still no sign of Donovan.

"So much for playing the attentive bridegroom," Corisande said under her breath, which was fine with her. But what wasn't fine was waiting any longer. She was bloody tired! Discussing their next smuggling run had kept her at Oliver's until way past midnight, then she'd had to tend to Biscuit, poor pony, the long day exhausting him entirely, then try to sleep while wondering if Donovan would appear at the church or not—oh, enough!

She didn't need him or Miss Biddle to show her to her room. After all, Donovan had conducted the grand tour earlier that day, so Corisande knew the master suite was on the next floor. There was her bedchamber, then a cozy sitting room, and his much larger bedchamber. Nothing to be nervous about at all. Separate rooms, separate beds, and a door between that could be locked. Perfect.

So why did she suddenly feel the need for yet another glass of sherry? Resisting the impulse, Corisande set down her glass and left the drawing room, heading at once for the staircase.

The door to Donovan's library was still shut. No matter. At the top of the stairs, she turned into the right wing of the house, remembering what Donovan had said about how filthy and rundown everything had looked upon his arrival last Friday.

She would never have imagined such disorder, so clean and well maintained did the house look now, thanks to Miss Ellen Biddle, he had said. A pity these corridors and rooms would be empty and dark in only a few weeks' time, for despite what she'd thought in the past, she had to admit that the house was quite impressive, even lovely. But again, what did she care?

Corisande was almost to her chamber when she heard laughter and young women's voices. She stopped, the door slightly ajar, and peered into the room.

Two housemaids were turning down the bedclothes; Corisande recognized one of them as the sullen, unkempt girl who had told her last week that Henry Gilbert wasn't at home, failing to add that the Arundale agent had moved to a smaller residence on the estate. But she wasn't unkempt now, both housemaids' appearance neat as a pin, their aprons starched and white. More wonders accomplished by the amazing Miss Biddle, that much was clear.

"I don't see why we're turnin' down the sheets. It's not as if she'll be sleepin' 'ere tonight."

Her breath catching in her throat, Corisande leaned closer.

"No, but what old Miss Biddle says goes, 'aven't you learned that by now, Bess? You're going to find yourself discharged, you will, quick as a blink if you're not careful to mind."

"Well, it makes no sense to me," came the petulant reply, but soon husky giggles erupted. "Bloody 'ell, she'll be one sore chit tomorrow, wouldn't you say, Meg? As Fanny tells it—just this morning she did, too, whilst she was polishin' the silver and I was settin' up the table, well, she said His Lordship won't be wastin' any time in getting 'imself an heir this night. Seems Lord Donovan didn't want to marry, oh, no, but then he'll never see his inheritance. Bloody sad problems these nobs 'ave, eh? Seems His Grace of Arundale's wife is barren, well, only because His Grace won't sleep with her, so the chore's left to Lord Donovan and his common little bride."

"Bess!"

"It's true! She's barely better than us, a dotty vicar's daughter, that one. Fanny said His Lordship had to find 'imself a country girl, a good breeder, to be exact. And so he did, quick as a jackrabbit, but I wish to 'eaven he'd looked no farther than my hips here. Wide and deep, they are, good for plowin' both day and night! And wouldn't I like to be the one sharin' Lord Donovan's bed. God help me, I feel all wet sometimes just lookin' at 'im!"

"Bess, enough now! Fanny's probably just running her big mouth. She's only a scullery maid. How could she possibly—"

"By sleepin' with His Grace's solicitor, you pudding head! Aye, just before Fanny left to come here. Wilkins, she said his name was—though she says he wanted her to call him 'lambkins,' the strange little fart. Seems they shared a bit of wine and one thing led to the other—aw, come on, Meg, a rousing good tumble's always the thing to loosen a man's tongue."

"Aye, I suppose you're right."

"So I am! Look at the rubbish that knobby-kneed scarecrow Henry Gilbert used to tell me! How he wanted to marry me and take good care of me, whilst 'ere I am, plumpin' the pillows for some common Cornish chit with an ugly scar on her face and no breasts to speak of. Ah, but I'll just bide my time till Lord Donovan's done his duty and filled her belly, then when he casts 'is eye about, I'll . . ."

Corisande couldn't hear more; the two housemaids must have gone into the other room. But she didn't need to. Her blood thundering in her ears, she rested her forehead on the doorjamb, incredulous.

Donovan needed an heir? That . . . that . . . God help her, there were no words to describe what she thought of him now. If he had tricked her, and it bloody well sounded as if he had, she wouldn't waste time with a pitchfork, oh, no. As an army officer, he was bound to have a pistol in the house. Yes, perhaps in his room, and she had only to find it. Then she would confront him and demand to know the truth!

"Corie?"

She spun, her heart slamming, as Donovan strode toward her; it was too late now, she knew, to look for any pistol. But she had her shrew's tongue—wasn't that what Donovan had called it?—and, thank God, that had never failed her.

"Fiend," she spat, not surprised when he stopped in his tracks, those midnight eyes growing hard as he glanced behind him to see if any servants were near. "You bloody, bloody fiend! Oh, yes, I know all about you now. You need an heir, do you? An heir because your brother the Duke of Arundale won't lie with his own wife—"

"Who told you this?" Donovan cut her off, never having seen her look so furious. He moved toward her, but she dashed farther down the hall, keeping a good distance between them. Good God, if he didn't catch her and silence her soon . . . "Corie, answer me. Where did you hear—?"

Donovan didn't finish, spying movement out of the corner of his eye as he passed Corisande's bedchamber. He stiffened as he recognized the two housemaids who had been hired long ago by Henry Gilbert, the young women laughing at something and talking between themselves while they closed the heavy velvet draperies. Hell and damnation, he would kill Henry if that fool had said a word to these women!

"Leave my wife's room. Now."

Both housemaids whirled to stare at him wide-eyed; he had clearly startled them. And his tone had clearly frightened them, for both women looked pale of a sudden and only too eager to oblige him. They dashed past him without a word and were gone, not even looking over their shoulders, which led him to believe that somehow they must surely have played a part in upsetting Corisande.

Corisande.

Donovan looked down the corridor toward his room, but she was gone, his door wide open. But he wasn't fool enough to rush in after her. Oh, no, his short three day acquaintance with this hot-tempered, unpredictable woman was enough to tell him that caution should be his guide. Instead, he stole into her bedchamber and then through the sitting room, pausing for an instant to glance inside his own room.

She was there, standing behind the door leading out to the corridor, waiting for him, a fireplace shovel raised high as if she fully intended to bash him over the head as soon as he walked into the room. She looked so intent, so vengeful, and yet so ridiculous standing there in her white wedding gown with black soot spotting her veil, that he thought he might laugh. He knew he was smiling, and when she suddenly turned, spying him, he simply gave up the chase and went to the fireplace where he sank into a deep wing chair, shaking his head.

"You . . . you think this is funny?"

She sounded so outraged and yet almost disappointed as she lowered her weapon uncertainly.

"Funny? Not at all, but what would you have me do, woman? Take up the poker and challenge you to a duel?"

∽ Fourteen ∽

A duel? Was the man mad? Corisande glared at Donovan, so angry that her face felt ablaze, yet she couldn't be sure if it might not be due to the sherry. She felt a bit dizzy, too, but oh, no, she wasn't going to drop the shovel—or her guard—for a moment. Lifting her weapon once more, she took a step from the door.

"You must feel very clever, don't you?" she demanded through her teeth. "You knew damned well I'd never agree to marry you if you'd said anything about a bloody heir, so like the detestable, deceitful, self-interested—"

"Loathsome?"

"Yes, loathsome!" Corisande blurted out, enraged even more that he would make jokes and toy with her at such a moment. "Like the loathsome, despicable miscreant you are, you decided to wait and surprise—"

"There's no surprise, Corie, because there's no heir. At least I've no need of one. Put down that shovel and close the door so we can talk."

Now she gaped at him, wondering incredulously how he could sit there like some pompous monarch issuing commands while she fully intended to do him bodily harm . . . but—but wait. Hadn't he just said he needed no heir? Corisande blinked, suddenly wishing she hadn't downed those two brimming glasses of sherry so quickly.

"Very well, *I'll* close the damned door. No bloody sense in the servants overhearing more than they know already."

Donovan thrust himself from his chair so suddenly that Corisande gasped and stepped backward, her heel entangling in the hem of her dress. But he was there to catch her almost before she felt herself falling, looking at her quizzically as he firmly took the shovel from her hand.

"You're jumpy tonight, wife."

Corisande tensed, the infuriating wryness in his voice enough to vanquish the fuzzy cloud settling over her brain. "If I'm jumpy, it's only because you've made me so! Now let go of me!"

"As you wish."

He did, too, and before Corisande had a chance to regain her balance she fell backward, landing with a startled cry on her bottom. That drew no response from Donovan as he returned the shovel to its hook by the fireplace, then went to shut not only the door to his bedchamber, but her door as well.

Within a moment he was back, looking mildly surprised that she was still sitting quite ungracefully on the floor, her dress twisted about her knees. But when his gaze fell to her white-stockinged calves, lingering there, too, Corisande scrambled to her feet and stood somewhat dizzily, glowering at him. Damn that sherry and damn him too!

"There. Now at least we have some privacy. Perhaps now, too, you're in more of a frame of mind to talk."

Oh, she was in a fine frame of mind, all right, but before she could utter a single word, Donovan put up his hand.

"Allow me, Corie. I don't know what you overheard from those two maids—it was the maids, yes?"

She nodded through clenched teeth.

"As I thought. By God, I'm going to strangle that Gilbert!"

"Gilbert? What are you talking about?" Corisande demanded as Donovan began to pace in front of her, his strides reminding her of a restless beast prowling a cage.

"The only way those chits could have known anything was if Gilbert told them. He knew I was coming to Cornwall to find a bride, thanks to a recent letter from my brother, who also informed him that the Trents of Dorset were in dire need of an heir."

"So you did trick me!"

"No, I didn't trick you! Nigel could have all the heirs he wanted if he'd only sleep with his wife, but I can hardly blame the man. Charlotte is a fright."

"That's unkind."

"But true. Nigel didn't choose her, my bloody father did . . ." Sighing with exasperation, Donovan ceased his pacing and shoved his fingers through his hair. "That's not the point anyway. Simply put, Corie, I didn't marry you to father an heir. I told you I needed the money. My inheritance. That's all I want out of this mess, nothing more. As far as I'm concerned, Nigel and his grand scheme for an heir can go to hell!"

Stunned by the raw vehemence in his voice, Corisande watched as Donovan began to pace again, even more restlessly than before.

"So now you know what you overheard tonight isn't true, and by God, as soon as I see Gilbert I'm going to—"

"Why are you still blaming Henry? It wasn't he who told Bess about this heir business but Fanny, the scullery maid. And Fanny was told by some fellow named Wilkins."

Donovan stopped to stare at her incredulously. "Wilkins?"

"Yes, your brother's solicitor." Corisande felt her cheeks growing very warm as she debated what else was seemly for her to reveal, and how to politely say it. She cleared her throat. "It seems that Fanny and Wilkins shared a glass or two of wine and then . . ."

"Oh, good God!" Donovan circled in front of the fire-place and then brought his hands down hard against the mantel, bracing himself there as he scowled into the fire. "That little bespectacled . . ."

He didn't finish, but Corisande could imagine what he must be thinking. Which wasn't exactly what she was thinking. Suddenly a giggle burst from her throat, then another, which made her clamp her hand over her mouth when Donovan turned to look at her, a black brow raised.

"I said something funny?"

Corisande lowered her hand, grinning like an idiot, she knew, and which she blamed wholeheartedly on the sherry. "No, but Meg did. It seems Fanny told her this Wilkins likes being called, well . . . lambkins."

"Lambkins?"

Hearing Donovan say it only made Corisande giggle again, and this time she simply couldn't stop. It was so ridiculous! Grown people wanting to be called such silly names? And she wasn't laughing by herself, either, as a slow grin spread over Donovan's face, nothing like that devilishly charming smile at all, but something more boyish and, oddly, much more appealing.

He began to chuckle, shaking his head as he looked at the fire and then back to her, while she had to hold herself around the middle, she was giggling so hard. Her ribs hurt!

"Oh, Lord." Her words had come out with a gasp, and finally she bent over slightly at the waist to catch her breath. But when she threw back her head, still laughing to herself, she saw that Donovan wasn't chuckling anymore, just staring at her with a strange look on his face. Suddenly self-conscious, she dropped her arms slowly to her sides, the room grown silent but for the soft crackling of the flames.

"You should do that more often, Corie. Laugh. Smile. It becomes you."

She didn't know what to say. There really didn't seem to

be anything she could say. Rubbing her lips together nervously, she glanced beyond him to the door leading to the sitting room. It had been closed, too, which made her grow even more flustered, a sudden gush of words jumping to her lips.

"I should go . . . to my room, I mean. It's late and—and I'm very tired. Good night, Donovan."

Hugging her arms tightly around her middle, Corisande went to walk past him, nearly jumping out of her skin when he reached out and blocked her way.

"You can't go, Corie. You have to sleep in here tonight, with me."

If he had said she must walk on water, she couldn't have been more surprised. Or more alarmed than she'd ever felt in her life, and she tried to bolt past him toward the door. But his arms were around her before she could blink, strong massive arms that held her still against his body though she struggled mightily, a big hand clamping over her mouth when she inhaled to scream.

"Easy, Corie, you haven't let me finish! We have to share the same bed. It's our wedding night. But I'm not going to touch you, woman! How many times must I assure you of that? You'll have your side, and I'll stay on mine—and for God's sake, that bloody mattress is wide enough so we won't even be lying close to each other! But we have to make things look convincing to the household, remember?"

She'd already ceased struggling well before he had finished, embarrassment flooding her as he slowly drew his hand away from her mouth. "Of—of course, I knew that," she stammered, trying to cover for behaving so ridiculously and yet trying not to look in the direction of that huge canopied bed. "Our wed-wedding night."

"Exactly. Now, your valise is over there behind the screen if you'd like to change."

"Change?" she parroted, once again feeling quite stupid when Donovan smiled wryly and released her.

"Unless you want to sleep in your wedding dress. But I doubt that would be very comfortable."

"No, no, probably not," she said half to herself, only too grateful to be free of Donovan's unsettling embrace. Without meeting his eyes, she rushed to take refuge behind the screen like a terrified mouse looking for its hole, which only made her feel more chagrined. Staring blindly at her valise set upon an embroidered stool, she fought to regain her composure.

Whatever was the matter with her? For heaven's sake, she'd faced tougher trials! This situation wasn't dangerous or life-threatening, no, not like coming face to face with armed Customs men in the dark of night, or braving boiling surf to help drag to shore a near-drowned fisherman. It was the sherry, and it was her own blessed fault for drinking so much of the stuff, making her act like a ninny, a dimwit, a flustered goose!

"Would you like some champagne, Corie? It might make you feel better."

"Oh, Lord." Now what was she to do? Tell him no, thank you, she'd already downed half a bottle of spirits in the drawing room? Then he'd think she was a drunkard and—oh, she didn't care what he thought! Champagne might actually make her feel better, she decided, her fingers still trembling as she began to pull clothing out of her valise and scatter it about her. "Yes, yes, all right. That would be nice."

"Have you ever tasted champagne before?"

She was tempted to say no, not wishing to reveal any more about herself than was absolutely necessary—theirs was a business arrangement, after all—but then she shrugged. "Once. At Lindsay's twentieth birthday this last February." Corisande smiled to herself as the cork popped, the sound bringing back uproarious memories. Lord, how

Lindsay had made her laugh! "We borrowed one of Lady Somerset's precious bottles for the occasion and had ourselves quite a giggle."

"So Lindsay is younger than you, then."

"No—" Corisande froze, wanting to kick herself. "I mean, yes, she's—"

"Here's your champagne."

Corisande took the long-stemmed crystal goblet Donovan held out to her above the screen, hoping he hadn't heard what she'd said. She didn't want him to know that she was younger, well, she supposed it didn't really matter now that they were married. Oh, why couldn't her thoughts stop tumbling over themselves? And where was her nightgown? How could she possibly find anything while holding this silly glass? It was so full, she would surely spill champagne over everything . . .

Wholly exasperated, Corisande drained the goblet in two long swallows and set it upon the floor behind her, then began to dig once more through her valise. She came up triumphant this time, grateful at least that Rose Polkinghorne hadn't yet stitched her a new nightgown. Hers was sturdy white flannel with a plain collar that came up to the chin. She wouldn't have to worry at all about anyone ogling her tonight.

Corisande pulled the pins from her hair and whipped off her sooty veil, wondering what Donovan was doing as she draped it over the top of the screen. He had gotten so quiet of a sudden. Ah, no matter. She began to work at the back of her dress, her fingers searching for the pearl buttons, until she remembered with a start that there were no bloody pearl buttons. That's why Rose Polkinghorne had had to sew her into this dress. No time to do anything else . . .

"Oh, no."

"Problems?"

Corisande frowned. Was the man forever listening for her

every word? She rested her head against the screen, her heart starting to pound. Now what was she going to do?

"I think I can help."

She looked up and almost wished she hadn't as she gulped, swallowing air.

Donovan was standing stripped to the waist just beyond the screen, his powerful-looking shoulders more broad than she could have imagined, his chest matted with black hair that narrowed to a thick trail down the center of his taut, muscled abdomen and then disappeared into his breeches. Thank heaven, he still wore his breeches! Oh, Lord, oh, Lord—

"I noticed you had no buttons at the church. Frances had said they failed to arrive from Penzance so . . ." He shrugged. "There's really only one thing we can do."

"Do?" she echoed, staring stupidly as he held out his hand to her. Before she even realized what she'd done, she placed her palm in his warm one and felt him drawing her from behind the screen, drawing her closer and closer, until suddenly he spun her around so she was facing the other way.

"It will look better anyway . . . to the servants."

Corisande felt his hands gripping the satin fabric at her shoulders and her underlying shift, then she heard a rending sound that seemed to echo around the room. A rending that went all the way down to her hips, and she cried out as cool air touched her skin. Clutching what was left of her dress to her breasts, she fled back to the screen, not daring to look behind her.

Which was probably a good thing. She wouldn't have liked the look in Donovan's eyes, and he certainly didn't like what seeing her bare flesh had just done to him.

With a low curse, he walked back to the bed and continued to strip from his clothes, hoping Corisande would have the sense not to peek at him behind the screen. If so, she might faint dead away; he doubted she'd ever seen a man afflicted with his current plight. He was so hard it hurt, his turgid member standing at full attention as he cursed again his brilliant idea to rip her out of her dress.

When he'd seen the lovely curve of her back and the dimpled flesh above her buttocks . . . sweet rounded buttocks—ah, God, why was he torturing himself? And there had been no stays, no stays at all, which meant those saucy breasts were nature's own tantalizing design. With a pained grunt, he climbed into bed and yanked the covers to his waist, then reached for his glass on the side table and downed the champagne in one gulp. Oh, yes, he'd gotten his wish, and it was fast becoming a bloody nightmare!

First she'd had to start laughing on him, her eyes alight and sparkling as he'd never seen them, her gleeful grin causing the strangest tug at his heart, and then he'd even encouraged her to smile more often! And now this . . . this madness seizing him, his lower body full and heavy and throbbing and no promise of release in sight. If she came from behind that screen in some clingy, semitransparent muslin nightgown with her pink nipples showing through, he couldn't say what he might—

"Donovan?"

He groaned inwardly, cursing for a third time the painful bulge between his legs.

"Donovan, I'm ready to come out now. Have . . . well, have you finished changing?"

Changing? He almost laughed, but it would have held little humor. He braced himself, saying as normally as he could, "I'm in bed, Corie. There's nothing to fear. Bring your glass, and we'll have another sip of champagne, then we'll go to sleep. Does that suit you?"

He heard no response, but imagined she must have found his reply agreeable for he saw a flash of virginal white from behind the screen. He squeezed shut his eyes. Oh, God, give him strength. No nipples, please. It had been too damned long . . .

"Here's my glass, Donovan. Should I turn out that lamp by the door?"

❧ *Fifteen* ❧

Donovan opened his eyes, sheer relief flooding through him and no small amount of incredulity, too, as his gaze swept over Corisande.

Flannel? Good God, he'd seen such stuff on small children but never a grown woman. Enveloped from her toes to her chin, her slim arms swathed in long cuffed sleeves, her auburn hair flowing down her back, Corisande looked more a hesitant, wide-eyed young innocent than the half-naked temptress who had fled only moments ago behind the screen, a very good thing. So what was this disappointment filling him? Hell and damnation, he wanted nothing to do with the chit!

"Yes, turn out the lamp."

Corisande flinched, Donovan's voice a surly growl that took her by surprise. He hadn't sounded so gruff when she had asked if he'd finished changing and . . . oh, dear. Her eyes dropped again to his bare chest when he leaned forward to take her glass, her heart already beating hard as a drum as she tried to reassure herself anew that he *must* have changed into some sort of sleeping wear. She didn't know what men wore to bed, but surely he wasn't—

Not even wanting to consider the matter further, Corisande hastily lifted her gaze, but Donovan was already occupied with pouring more champagne. Oh, Lord, she already felt as bloated as a fish. She couldn't possibly drink any more until she had . . . oh, this night was becoming increasingly more unbearable and more embarrassing than she could have ever imagined!

"Is . . . well, could you tell me where the water closet—"

"Over there through that door. By the wardrobe."

Still pouring champagne, he hadn't bothered to look at her, and for that Corisande was grateful as she hurried on bare feet across the room. His voice was as gruff, too, but right now she didn't care. She felt ready to burst, her head in a fog, her legs feeling wobbly beneath her, and probably the last thing she needed was more champagne.

While Donovan wished he had another bottle as Corisande half stumbled into the water closet and shut the door behind her. Two bottles! If nothing else, that would have numbed him. But he had only the one, and it was empty now, the two goblets filled to the brim. He didn't bother to wait for her, his champagne gone when she reappeared a few moments later.

"Don't forget the lamp."

She glanced at him, but said nothing, which was somewhat of a surprise. Surely his churlish tone must be irritating her, and he certainly wished it would.

A rousing show of temper would probably do them both some good. Help them to get some sleep, too, each hugging their own side of the bed with their backs turned belligerently to the other like two encamped enemies exhausted from battle. Watching her douse the lamp, the room falling into darkness but for the dying orange flames in the fireplace, Donovan wondered what he could say to make her flare up at him. Or maybe all he had to do was make some move toward her . . .

"Oh . . . oh, no!"

Donovan heard a dull thud followed by a heavy thunk as

if something had fallen, making him throw back the covers. "Corie?"

A low groan greeted him, and Donovan lunged from the bed. His heart pounding, for a moment he couldn't see her, for that corner of the room was so dark. But then he spied a still white form on the floor near the wardrobe. He rushed to Corisande's side and dropped to his haunches.

"Corie? What happened?" He got no answer though she moved clumsily this time, her hand flying to her forehead. He did the same, pushing away her trembling fingers to place his palm gently over her brow, a telltale lump already forming above her right temple.

"I—I tripped," came a weak faltering voice that didn't sound anything like Corisande at all. "I hit . . . I hit the wardrobe and—"

"I know, Corie. Shh, don't talk for a moment." Donovan scooped her up in his arms, trying to assure himself that there was little cause for alarm as he carried her to the bed. It was only a small bump, and after a full night's rest she'd be as good as new and eager to spar with him again, he had no doubt.

Yet she felt so limp in his arms, so helpless, and he didn't like it at all. Strangely, it made him feel helpless, too, which was even more bloody unnerving, just like earlier in the day when those pilchard barrels had been crashing toward her and he'd been too far away to do anything but cry out her name.

"Easy, Corie, lie still now," he commanded softly, placing a down pillow beneath her head and then pulling the covers to her chin. "I'll get a wet cloth for that bump and some water for you to drink."

"Yes, water. Please, water," she agreed in a raspy voice that had grown somewhat stronger. "No more champagne. No more sherry."

"Sherry?"

She didn't answer, moaning softly to herself as she rolled her head from side to side until suddenly she froze, her fingers digging into the covers. "The bed! Oh, God, what's happening to the bed? It's spinning—"

"It's not spinning, woman, you're spinning," Donovan cut her off dryly, realizing now exactly what she'd been talking about.

It must have been a damned good amount of sherry too. One glass of champagne wouldn't have made her feel so ill, or caused her to trip over her own feet, though it had probably made things worse. No wonder his surliness hadn't riled her. The chit was as pickled as a mackerel! And, just as he'd feared, in the next instant he was racing to bring the washbasin to the bed before she was sick all over herself. Donovan held her head and swept her long hair out of her face as she leaned over the edge of the mattress and retched and moaned, and retched some more.

Finally, when she was done, he was able to leave her to get rid of the basin and fetch wet cloths and a gobletful of water; Corisande drank so thirstily that he thought she might become ill again, so he took the glass away. After wiping her face and mouth, he pressed a fresh cloth to her forehead, the bump as big as a robin's egg now and quite tender. She sucked in air through her teeth and cried out, trying to push his hands away.

"Dammit, woman, you need this for the swelling! Lie still or you'll only start spinning again."

That dire warning seemed to work as she sank back onto her pillow and grew quiet, so quiet that several moments later he thought she'd fallen asleep. Sighing heavily, Donovan left her side and climbed back into bed, but he didn't lie down, propping some pillows behind him to sit staring at what was left of the fire.

So much for his wedding night. He might have a temporary marriage, but he couldn't say the evening hadn't been memorable. In fact, he doubted he'd ever forget it.

First she'd wanted to whack him over the head with a shovel.

Then she'd nearly driven him to distraction with a body any man might kill for.

And lastly, she'd walked smack into a wardrobe and nearly scared him half to death, only to come very close to being sick all over him.

Bloody hell, he deserved a drink. And fortunately there was one more glass of champagne.

"So mean. So mean . . ."

Donovan turned to find Corisande had rolled over onto her side and was clutching her pillow, her body curled into a ball.

"Corie?"

"So mean! Bess . . ."

He couldn't tell if she was awake or dreaming, her words coming in half-whispers that sounded hoarse, distressed. Sliding closer, he laid his head down close to hers and prodded gently, "The housemaid, Corie? Bess, the housemaid?"

In answer, she clutched her pillow more tightly, a broken sigh slipping from her lips. It sounded so sad, Donovan couldn't help but move closer, drawing her into his arms. He held his breath, but she didn't resist, instead pressing her cheek against his shoulder.

"What did she say, Corie?" he whispered, freeing one hand so he could stroke her silky hair. A second ragged sigh broke from her throat, this one even more heartwrenching than the last.

"Ugly . . ."

He tensed, anger filling him. "Bess said you're ugly?"

"Scar . . ."

Her voice had sunk to a whisper and, as she pressed even

closer, Donovan could feel a warm wetness where her face was buried against his shoulder.

". . . ugly. So cruel. They don't know . . . don't know . . ."

He said nothing as her voice trailed away, her breathing so deep and regular he knew she was fast asleep. While he lay there, his throat so tight that he could barely breathe. But he didn't want to move, not right now. He didn't want to wake her.

Instead he gathered her close and rocked her gently, as a father might cradle a hurting child.

Corisande half opened her eyes, a blurred shadow passing in front of her. Groaning at the dull throbbing in her head, she was barely aware that the indistinct shape had stopped and now hovered over her.

"Oh, you poor, poor dear. To be sick on your wedding night? Such a shame. Nerves will sometimes do that to a bride. But I've tea for you, and a nice hot bath is ready, my lady. Shall I help you to sit up?"

Corisande recognized the brisk, capable tones of Ellen Biddle even before she could focus clearly upon the housekeeper's kindly face. What was that the woman had said about nerves? About her being sick? She tried to speak, but nothing came out except a hoarse croak, her tongue as dry as wool and practically useless.

"Oh, my, yes indeed, you need tea, my lady. Here, if you'll raise yourself just a bit—that's right, now I'll plump these pillows for you. There."

Corisande was amazed; one moment she'd been lying flat on her back feeling wretchedly helpless and disoriented, and now she was comfortably reclining while Ellen poured her a steaming cup of tea from a white china pot decorated with tiny blue flowers. Comfortable at least, but for the painful ache above her right temple, Corisande flushed with chagrin as fuzzy memories came rushing back at her.

Oh, dear, had she really tripped and fallen headlong into that wardrobe? And now that she thought about it, she vaguely remembered becoming ill but little else after . . .

"Sugar? Cream?"

Corisande shook her head, to which the housekeeper gave a concurring smile.

"Plain is how I like my tea too. Well steeped, hot, just the thing to start the day. Here you go, my lady."

Corisande no sooner accepted the teacup and took her first sip than the housekeeper was bustling across the room, her plain black dress and starched apron rustling efficiently. A spare middle-aged woman with premature gray hair beneath her neat white ruffled cap, Ellen Biddle had to be one of the most energetic souls Corisande had ever seen.

"A pity, but it seems the sunshine has left us today." With firm no-nonsense tugs, Ellen drew aside the forest-green velvet curtains at the windows flanking the balcony doors and tied them back with thick gold-braid ropes. "The fog broke a short while ago, but I fear not the clouds. It looks certain to rain, maybe even storm. Wretched weather for traveling, but there it is. At least you had a fine day for your wedding, my lady."

"Traveling?" Relieved that she had regained the use of her voice, Corisande stared in confusion as Ellen came back around the bed. "I don't recall anyone saying—"

"Oh, my, no, I didn't mean you, my lady, or His Lordship." The housekeeper's face drew into a sudden frown. "Good riddance, is what I say. Those two girls were a handful of trouble. Well, not so much Meg, although she followed along after Bess like a silly milk cow. A pity too. She was a good worker. But His Lordship said that she and Bess must go this very morning, and Fanny too. I warned the girl her loose tongue would bring her trouble, but—"

"Lord Donovan . . . I—I mean, my husband sent them away?" Incredulous, Corisande had to believe it must be so when Ellen firmly nodded.

"Oh, yes, indeed. His Lordship came to see me before the sun was up, quite angry he looked too. Said he'd have no servants in this house speaking ill of you, my lady. Said those three must be gone before you opened your eyes this morning, and so they were, sent to catch the mail-coach in Helston just after dawn. Meg and Bess bound for Weymouth and Fanny back to Arundale Hall where she'll have to explain herself to His Grace, no doubt. I believe Lord Donovan sent along a sealed letter."

Corisande leaned her head back against the pillow as Ellen paused to refill her teacup; memories swam before her now, fresh and vivid. The unsettling conversation she'd overheard between the housemaids, Bess discussing her so callously, and how furious Donovan had been, threatening Henry Gilbert with injury to life and limb until Corisande had told him that Fanny—

"I must apologize for those girls, my lady."

Corisande looked at Ellen, but the woman seemed reluctant to meet her eyes as she set the china pot back upon the tray.

"I don't know what all was said between the three of them, but . . . well, it troubles me to no end to think your upset last night might have been caused . . ."

Ellen didn't finish, instead glancing down uncomfortably at her hands, which led Corisande to guess that the housekeeper had probably heard—Ogden and the other remaining servants as well, for that matter—much of Fanny's gossip on their way to Cornwall. But something told her that she would never have heard a word of such talk from this woman's mouth. Ellen Biddle had a strong air of decency about her that made Corisande doubt, too, that she could possibly have agreed to be a spy. But Corisande supposed she could never be sure.

"It was a simple case of nerves, Ellen, nothing more," she said, deciding it was a good time to show that if she'd overheard anything, she'd granted it little credence. "Certainly no reason to trouble yourself. All the excitement, the long day. I'm sure you understand."

"Oh, yes, of course, my lady."

"So it's not worth discussing any further. Have you seen my husband?"

Ellen at once looked relieved that their conversation had taken a swift turn although her clear gray eyes held a touch of what Corisande could swear, to her dismay, was pity.

"In the library, my lady. But I believe he plans to leave shortly with Mr. Gilbert. His Lordship said he wouldn't be home for luncheon—he mentioned something about business at the mine, but surely by supper—"

"Oh, dear, I have to wait to see him until supper?" Corisande broke in with mock alarm, hoping to show the housekeeper, too, that her wifely devotion to Donovan had not been shaken. "You must go to him, Ellen, right this minute, and tell him I'll be downstairs as soon as I can to say good-bye." She set her teacup with a clatter onto the tray. "Did you say I've a bath ready?"

"Yes, my lady, in your bedchamber. I've also hung up your clothes in the wardrobe, but your wedding dress . . ." The housekeeper cleared her throat delicately. "I fear your wedding dress is beyond repair."

Her face suddenly burning, Corisande chose to skip over that subject altogether. She threw aside the covers and rose somewhat shakily, not surprised when Ellen caught her arm to steady her. But she didn't want the woman's help, however well-meaning, this business of having servants constantly hovering around her quite unsettling. And now she had to contend with them feeling sorry for her too; Lady

Donovan, the poor little country simpleton, so naïve, so trusting, so blind. Oh, she couldn't wait to have her normal life back again!

"I'll be fine, Ellen. Really. You don't have to stay to wait upon me. And I'd be so disappointed if I miss my husband . . ."

"Oh, yes, of course. I'll see to it right away." Having swallowed the cue, Ellen hustled away only to pause at the door. "If you need anything, my lady, there's a bell pull in your chamber. Someone will come straightaway, well, at least we'll do our best. We're rather shorthanded now. If you know any local girls who might wish for employment here at the house, I'd welcome your recommendation."

Corisande sighed to herself as the housekeeper disappeared, thinking that there were many women in the parish who would leap for joy to have steady work to help their families. But to give someone a job that would last only a few weeks? Maybe days, if she got her wish and that inheritance came soon from Dorset. It would be cruel to build such hopes. Ah, but she couldn't think of it now. She had to hurry if she was going to catch Donovan. She had a few things to say to him, and they *didn't* include a pleasant good-bye.

Corisande felt her cheeks growing hot again as she hastened from his bedchamber and into her own without a backward glance, grateful to be gone from the place. Grateful, too, in a way that she had become ill. Oh, she hoped she'd retched and retched. That must have repulsed him and kept him far, far away from her! Maybe she should drink a good strong dose of sherry every night.

A sharp queasiness in her stomach made Corisande quickly abandon the idea, the high-backed metal tub placed before a freshly stoked fire looking quite inviting as her knees suddenly felt a bit wobbly too. Within a moment, she had stripped out of her nightgown and settled with a long sigh into the steaming bathwater that smelled heavily of lavender oil.

Which she supposed made sense, considering that the fragrant herb was well-known as a restorative for hysterical women. Ellen Biddle must have poured a whole bottleful into this tub, probably believing that Corisande hadn't been stricken with nerves as much as a frenzied fit after discovering she'd become an overnight bride simply to serve as brood mare for the heir to the dukedom of Arundale.

Nerves! Had Donovan told the woman that? It was a perfect excuse to explain why she'd been ill, though. Lord, if the housekeeper, and Donovan for that matter, only knew the truth—

"Miss Biddle said you wanted to see me, wife?"

∽ *Sixteen* ∽

Corisande shrieked and covered her breasts with her hands, water splashing onto the floor as she sank as low as she could into the tub. It was only then that she realized Donovan had spoken from behind her, and she craned her neck to glare at him.

"How—how dare you! Get out! Get out, I tell you—"

"Enough, Corie." He gave her no indication that he intended to go anywhere as he continued to lean against the doorjamb to the sitting room, his arms crossed casually over his chest although he looked taut with tension. "There may be fewer servants in the house now, but that doesn't mean you can raise the rooftop with your infernal shouting."

"Then don't creep up like . . . like a bloody snake behind me!" she sputtered, incensed. "Having to sleep together in the same bed to make things look cozy and proper between us is quite another thing than you standing there watching me bathe. Now please leave!"

With that she faced front and sank down further to her chin, which, to her chagrin, only made her knees rise higher, the tub too small to accommodate her long legs. But bare white knees were better than her breasts bobbing in plain view, no matter that Donovan was standing well behind her. She closed her eyes and counted to twenty, then hazarded a glance over her shoulder to discover he had gone.

Oh, Lord, that made her wonder if he had stormed from their suite altogether, and here she wanted to talk to him!

Corisande grabbed one of the thick cotton towels hanging over a wooden rack and wound it around herself as she climbed from the tub, water splattering the rug as she raced to the wardrobe. It was such a relief to see some of her own familiar clothes again. She didn't bother to dry herself fully but shrugged into a thin linen shift first, then one of her wool dresses, followed by plain white stockings and her sturdy walking shoes.

Her first thought as she hastily gathered her hair into a loose bun was to run downstairs to catch him, but she supposed she should check the other rooms first. He might not have left. She flew into the sitting room, stopping short as Donovan turned dark brooding eyes upon her from where he stood by a tall window.

He didn't look happy at all, and she imagined that was due to her shrewish outburst. Even if he had interrupted her at her bath, she shouldn't have shouted at him like a fishwife and called him a snake. That hadn't been wise, no, not with servants lurking around. In fact, she felt a bit guilty about it, but he had startled her so badly—

"I see you're feeling none the worse for last night."

He didn't sound very happy either, no, not at all, Corisande thought with some apprehension, swiping a damp tendril from her face. "Actually my stomach feels a little odd. I'd never have imagined one could become so ill after bumping one's head."

"Helped along by a glass of champagne, of course."

Corisande looked at him uncertainly, his tone having grown even more brusque. "Well, yes, I suppose I shouldn't have drunk it so quickly—"

"Or half emptied the decanter of sherry in the drawing room. I suggest if you've a mind to drink spirits in the future, you keep it to a minimum, Corie. Nerves will suffice as an excuse for our wedding night, but not again if we're to make things look as if you've been properly bedded. Are we understood?"

She gaped at him, bristling and feeling quite embarrassed by turns. Properly bedded? Lord, she wasn't going to touch that one at all, but the other . . .

"I'm not a drunkard, if that's what you're thinking and—and, well, I don't care what you think! Anyone in my place would have done the same thing. You were meeting with Gilbert, and I was left waiting and waiting—and I don't see why I'm explaining myself to you anyway! If you just came up here to rant at me—" Corisande didn't finish, suddenly eyeing Donovan warily. "How did you know about the sherry? One of the servants could have drunk—"

"You told me yourself. Just before you got sick."

She frowned. "That's not possible. I'd have remembered. I remember tripping and bumping my head."

"And becoming ill?"

"Yes, of course! I told you my stomach still hurts."

"But you don't remember telling me about the sherry."

"No."

"Or anything else, for that matter, after you were sick."

He was looking at her so oddly that Corisande began to feel quite nervous. "Why did you say that? Is there something I should have remembered?"

When he gave no answer, merely staring at her, his handsome face set and unreadable, she felt a flush race from her scalp to her toes, her sense of unease growing. "You didn't . . . I mean, we didn't . . . oh, Lord, surely not—"

"No, we *didn't*, but your not knowing is another damned good reason to stay away from the sherry, wouldn't you say?" Donovan interrupted gruffly, ending her torment. Time to end his too—damn if he couldn't drive the image of her sitting naked in a tub out of his mind!—and get on with why he'd come to her room in the first place. "I was already on my way to see you when I met Miss Biddle in the hall. She mentioned she'd asked for your help in replacing some of the household help, so you must know—"

"Yes, I know," came the snappish reply, Corisande's deep brown eyes full of angry fire. "How gallant of you to come to my rescue, kind sir! It must have been a fine show, indeed. I wish I'd seen it! Ah, yes, the vengeful husband protecting his bride! But I fear you're too late, the damage already done."

"What damage?" Donovan demanded, not liking it at all that her sarcastic words had stung. "Those girls are gone, enough said."

"Ha! You think by dismissing them the gossip has stopped? A story like that has wings, my lord. It's already flown through the servants. By the end of the day, everyone in the parish will have heard every detail and think I'm a fool. A silly romantic fool for believing that a fine aristocratic gentleman like yourself could come and sweep me away, a vicar's daughter, while all you actually wanted was a good breeder to help you win your inheritance."

"Bess said that too? A good breeder?"

"She said a lot of things."

Corisande's voice had grown so quiet that Donovan felt his throat tighten, much as it had last night. And good God, it was bloody ridiculous! He didn't want to feel sympathy, he didn't want to feel anger for the hurt she'd suffered, he didn't want to feel anything when it came to this long-legged waif of a woman.

Why, just look at her, dressed once more in her dowdy ragamuffin clothes and probably quite happily too. She wasn't anything at all like the sophisticated women he'd known, women whose perfume alone could fill a man with lust. This chit smelled medicinal, reeking of lavender. Nothing sensual there. Damned unpleasant too!

The only good thing he could say about her, Corisande

wasn't like those grasping title-hungry virgins who'd been thrust at him every Season until he'd gone to war. She wouldn't have looked at him twice if not for the business arrangement she'd accepted, not to benefit herself, but the people she cared about. In fact, she despised him! Despised him, and she didn't know a damned thing about him. So why should he care if her feelings had been hurt—oh, hell, enough!

Donovan glanced out the window to see that Henry already waited for him below, their horses saddled and snorting in the heavy drizzle. The man had worked fast. God, how Gilbert had tripped all over himself to swear he hadn't betrayed Donovan's confidence. It had been almost laughable. But the last thing he felt like doing right now was laughing as he grimly turned from the window to find Corisande scowling at him.

"Obviously, my lord husband, you've nothing further to say, which doesn't surprise me in the least. After all, it was never a question of *your* reputation—"

"Or yours, woman, if you'd pause to consider things a moment before spouting at me. Is that bloody possible?"

Stunned that he had raised his voice at her, and so harshly, too, Corisande clamped her lips together, which apparently was just what Donovan wanted.

"Excellent. Now, as for your reputation, it doesn't matter what the servants think, or the parish, or the blessed whole of Britain. Good marriage, unhappy marriage, indifferent marriage, it doesn't make a damned bit of difference. And believe me"—Donovan's voice grew even harsher—"unhappy marriages are far more common among those of my station than the blissful roles we've been playing—which is exactly my point. You don't have to pretend that you're happy anymore."

"I—I don't?"

"No. In fact, it would probably be better if you acted as if you hate me, at least for a time, considering the terrible surprise you've just suffered. That shouldn't be too difficult for you."

His sarcasm was so biting that Corisande could only stare at him, never having seen this darker side of Donovan before . . . well, except a few days ago in the stable, and even that hadn't been as bad.

"Nothing to say? You surprise me, Corie. I'd have thought you'd be ecstatic to know you're free to act however you please—ah, no matter. Do what you will. Just remember, people can think whatever they want about us as long as they don't suspect our marriage is a purely temporary arrangement. That's the *only* thing you and I need be concerned about."

"Why did you dismiss Fanny and the others, then, and not simply reprimand them?" Corisande asked, confused. "That would have made the most sense instead of leaving poor Ellen Biddle short of help and with three times as much work to do— Donovan?"

He had strode past her so abruptly that she stood stunned, but before she thought to go after him he had spun back to face her, his eyes an angry black.

"Stick to your affairs, Corie, and I'll stick to mine. Is that understood? Those young women overstepped their bounds, upsetting the peace of this household. They should have known to keep their gossip well to themselves." With that he strode into his bedchamber but stopped again, his swarthy face grown as dark and hard as she'd ever seen it.

"Oh, yes, something else that might please you. I plan to spend much of my time at the mine, at least during the day. So you won't be plagued with my presence. I've also informed Miss Biddle and Ogden that you will be continuing with your charity work throughout the parish and with helping your father, and that I wholeheartedly approve. So you see, your life hasn't changed so drastically. You'll be busy,

I'll be busy. The time will fly, and soon we'll be free of each other's company forever. I've sent a letter to my brother to let him know that yesterday we became husband and wife, as well as a formal announcement to the London papers. That should make things move swiftly. Now, was there something you wanted to speak to me about?"

Corisande shook her head, speechless.

"Good. I'll see you at supper. By the way, you might wash that lavender smell from yourself before you go out. It's damned overpowering. Not pleasant at all."

Gasping softly, Corisande felt her cheeks growing hot as Donovan moved to the door.

"Have the coachman take you wherever you need to go. No matter the state of our marriage, you're Lady Donovan Trent now. There are certain proprieties to be observed. I don't want you going out alone."

"But—but that's ridiculous! I've always gone everywhere by—" Corisande jumped, the door slamming behind Donovan before she'd even had a chance to finish. Outraged, she almost went after him but instead ran into his bedchamber and threw open the balcony doors, cool rain pelting her face as she went to grip the iron railing. She was determined to tell him exactly what she thought of his preposterous command as soon as he emerged from the house, and she didn't care if the whole estate heard her. She wasn't one of his regiment to be ordered about!

"Why—why, Lady Donovan. Should you be standing there? It's begun to rain, you'll take a chill."

Corisande looked at Henry Gilbert's upturned face, tempted to snap at the man—of course she knew it was bloody raining!—but something Donovan had said made her hold her tongue.

Do what you will.

Oh, yes, he had said those words as plain as the rain dripping off her nose. So why bother screeching and hollering? He was going his own way, she would go hers. What could be better? He probably couldn't care less what she did anyway.

That thought stuck with her as Donovan strode outside, Henry gesturing to him that she stood on the balcony. But Donovan barely gave her a glance as he donned his hat and mounted Samson, then spun his stallion around and urged him into a gallop. Within moments, he and Henry had ridden from view while Corisande stood shivering on the balcony, feeling strangely hollow inside and quite, quite alone.

It was clear that he'd dismissed her from his mind as easily as flicking lint from his greatcoat. She was money in his pocket, nothing more. Why, he'd scarcely given her a look while she was . . .

"Standing here like a bloody fool getting soaked and chilled to the bone, is what you're doing, Corie Véronique," she muttered to herself, running back inside the room. Lord, what was the matter with her? So she was alone. Wonderful! She wanted to be free of his company, yes, forever. She could hardly wait!

She shut the balcony doors against the rain and then ran her hands over her face, which made her stop and stare at her palms, her skin fairly reeking with a distinctive smell.

She smiled.

So Donovan didn't like lavender, hmm?

❦ *Seventeen* ❧

"Are you sure this is the place, Gilbert?" Donovan studied doubtfully the crumbling white cottage with its small shuttered windows, no smoke pillaring from the stone chimney. "Looks quiet as a tomb."

"He's probably still sleeping, my lord. Jonathan Knill said he'd heard Pascoe was working the last core at Great Work mine, so he wouldn't have come home until after dawn."

"I'm surprised the bastard was able to find work at all," Donovan said tightly as he dismounted and left Samson to nibble at the sparse grass alongside the muddy road. And as a bloody mine captain no less. Gilbert had brought the astonishing news this morning, though Great Work in neighboring Breage parish was so huge that there were a dozen such men overseeing hundreds of tinners. Jack Pascoe ranked the lowest of them all.

To Donovan the man was just that, the lowest of filth. If he discovered Jack Pascoe had had anything to do with those pilchard barrels yesterday, bearing some murderous grudge against Corisande . . .

"All right, Gilbert, let's get on with it," Donovan said in a terse whisper as Henry crept along in his wake, the agent's eyes round and apprehensive. Henry's eyes grew even rounder when Donovan pulled a pistol from inside his greatcoat. "Stay behind me if you want to and remember, if there's trouble, duck the hell out of the way."

"Y-yes, my lord. Duck, oh, yes. That I'll certainly do."

Thinking dryly that he would have probably done just as well to leave Gilbert back at the estate, Donovan signaled for Henry to get out of line with the door and to stand flush against the cottage wall, the agent nearly tripping over his scrawny legs in his haste to oblige. "Easy, man. Easy."

"Yes, yes, forgive me, my lord," Gilbert whispered back, his large Adam's apple pumping.

Donovan inhaled very slowly, waiting, listening, then took a step backward and violently kicked in the door, the weather-worn wood giving way with a splintering crash. As he rushed inside he heard a raspy intake of surprise and a woman's scream, high-pitched and terrified, Donovan making out a pair of humped shapes atop a mattress in one dark corner.

"Get up! Both of you!"

The dark-haired woman obeyed him at once, whimpering in fear as she half stumbled to her feet and came forward into the light from the doorway, a soiled blanket clutched to her fleshy, sagging breasts. "Lord have mercy, sir, what have we done? I—I don't even live 'ere—"

"Wait outside, woman."

She fled, skittering out the door like a plump terrified rabbit while Donovan pointed his pistol at the corner.

"I said get up, Pascoe—"

"Ais, so I am, so I am! Must 'ee bluster an' shout?" came a decidedly surly voice, Jack Pascoe not even bothering to cover his wiry-limbed nakedness as he rose from the mattress on the floor. "What do 'ee want here, my lord? God in heaven, an' look what 'ee did to my door! Smashed it t' bits —eh, there! Is that Henry Gilbert standen outside? I see you, 'ee bloody scarecrow, an' 'ee better keep yer bugger's eyes off my woman or I'll—"

"You'll what, Pascoe?" Donovan demanded. "Push a few hogsheads down a hill and hope you'll crush the man? Just like you did yesterday in Porthleven? But then it wasn't Gilbert you were after, was it?"

A long silence fell over the cottage; Donovan felt a vein pounding in his temple now that the man hadn't immediately proclaimed his innocence. Just when he thought he'd have to grab the fool and throttle an answer out of him, a low, hoarse chuckling broke the stillness. Jack Pascoe scratched his crotch as he shuffled forward into the light, the red hair on his head dirty and matted and sticking up like a rooster's comb.

"Ais, I should have known you'd come looking for me. But I didn't do it—though I've no liken for that bitch 'ee took for your bride."

"So you know what happened," Donovan said through his teeth, suddenly tempted to shoot the man right then and there.

" 'Course I do! One of the mine cap'ens from Great Work saw the whole thing—visiting his dear old mother in Porthleven, he was. Said those barrels caused quite a stir. Wish I'd seen it. But I was already at the mine, an' 'ee can ride right out there an' check for yerself too. Spent the whole day there an' into the night, then, for my first core, just to get used to the place. 'Tes huge, 'ee know, five times bigger than yer little place and richer to boot. And fancy them hiring me so fast after leaving your mine only this past Saturday—"

"Fancy them firing you, too, if I hear the slightest word that you're making the tinners suffer as you did at Arundale's Kitchen," Donovan cut him off, sickened by the man's smug smile that he was very pleased to see had suddenly faded. "The same thing, too, if you're seen anywhere near my wife or her family. Are we understood, man?"

Jack Pascoe didn't readily answer, but his pocked face had turned a mottled red that nearly matched his hair. Yet finally he spat, "Stuck on that meddling wench, are 'ee?

Well, more's the worse for 'ee, then. I hope she yells yer ears off like she used to holler down into the shaft whenever she came looken for me, calling me names that would make the saints blush. I think she might have followed me, too, if it wasn't that the men'll have no women down in the mines. Bad luck, 'tes, and I wish you plenty of it with that one!"

Donovan smiled grimly, thinking that he could tell this man a thing or two about having his ears yelled off. But now that he knew Pascoe hadn't been involved in yesterday's incident, he wanted out of a cottage that stunk of urine, sweaty unwashed bodies, and sex. He lowered his pistol and left the place without another word, Jack Pascoe shouting after him.

"Eh! What of my door here? I hope 'ee plan to pay for it, my lord. A good door costs dear these days, it does!"

"Give him five shillings," Donovan ordered Henry, who was hard-pressed to keep his eyes off the woman's fat, jiggling bottom as she ducked back into the cottage. "Gilbert?"

"Oh, yes, yes, my lord. At once!"

Donovan didn't wait for the transaction to be completed but strode away, inhaling deep breaths of fresh drizzly air as if he could cleanse himself of the unnecessary filth he'd just encountered. The man was disgusting, living like a rat in a hole—

"All done, my lord. Where to now? Arundale's Kitchen?"

Donovan nodded at Gilbert, his jaw clenched as he glanced back at the cottage. "Why does Pascoe live like that? He must have some coin to his name. God knows you paid him like a king when he was under our employ, and I've no doubt that he stole his share from the tinners."

"Gambling, my lord. Terrible voice. And women." Henry gave a nervous shrug, clearly having nothing more to say and probably afraid to.

But it was enough for Donovan. His insides churning to

think that their family agent could have given so much power to a man who was no more than scum, he didn't trust himself to speak as he caught the reins and mounted Samson while Henry clambered atop his horse.

But finally, after they'd ridden some distance from Pascoe's cottage, he had calmed himself enough to ask, "Did my wife really do that? Yell down into the shafts?"

Gilbert bobbed his head, looking somewhat apprehensive after Donovan's long silence and more than anxious to please. "Oh, yes indeed, she did. You could hear her across the heath sometimes if the wind was right, all the way to the house. I'm ashamed to admit it, but that was always a good sign it was time for me to hide."

Donovan couldn't help smiling. It was all so ridiculous, really. Jack Pascoe heading deep into the earth, Henry Gilbert no doubt diving under a bed, and all because one angry-eyed, sharp-tongued woman had the conviction to stand up to injustices she was determined to change. Good God, she was admirable!

His smile faded just as quickly as it had come, Jack Pascoe's words ringing in his mind.

"Stuck on that meddling wench, are 'ee?"

Bloody hell, was that how he appeared? Surely not. He'd gone to see the man because he had his business arrangement to protect, nothing more. He'd be damned if he was going to start over with some other country chit, oh, no. One wife was enough for any lifetime, even if she was only temporary . . .

"It must have been an accident, my lord. I don't see any other way around it."

Donovan looked over at Henry Gilbert, who blinked at him in the thickening rain.

"Those barrels, I mean. If it wasn't Jack Pascoe—"

"We'll be keeping our eye on him all the same, no matter what that bastard said." His tone must have been dire, for

Henry gulped, the man keeping any further thoughts to himself as they galloped in a spray of mud toward Arundale's Kitchen.

"Are 'ee sure that I can't send one of the men along with 'ee? It'll be dark before you're halfway home—"

"So then I'll be riding in the dark," Corisande said firmly as she shrugged into her cloak, although she eyed Oliver Trelawny with fond suspicion. "If you're acting like this because I'm a married woman now, well, it's silly! It's not as if I haven't ridden across the heath at night a thousand times before. And on Biscuit, too, while this evening I've a young strong gelding to carry me."

"Maybe so, but it should have been a carriage, especially in this foul weather. But you've always been a stubborn one, an' I'm sure that new husband of yours can vouch for that. I still can't believe Lord Donovan didn't insist 'ee let his coachman take 'ee about—"

"The coachman was more than glad for the day off," Corisande lied guiltily, but she turned before Oliver could read anything in her eyes, and headed for the heavy oak door leading out of the inn's back room. They always met here to discuss their business, a quiet private place well away from the tobacco-smoking, ale-drinking, story-telling customers. But at the door she turned, her expression grown serious. "Godspeed, Oliver, and fair winds. The weather seems to have turned against our favor but—"

"Ais, Corie, when has a gale kept me from Brittany? I love it all the better, an' it keeps the king's excisemen at home in front of their fires where they can cause no trouble! We'll see you in a few days' time with a shipload of niceties for the good gentry, yes?"

She nodded silently, smiling, then lifted her hood over her hair and stepped outside. At once the door was almost flung from her hand by a strong, salty gust of wind, which only made Oliver curse behind her.

"See? A carriage would have kept 'ee nice an' dry an' well out of this mess!"

She waved and left him standing shaking his head after her, his burly bulk filling the doorway and limned in lamp-light, while she went to retrieve her mount from the small stable next door. But Oliver was gone back inside when she rode out a few moments later, ducking her head against the stiff wind whipping off the harbor.

Lord, she supposed a carriage would have been nice but she shoved away the thought as she nudged the big brown gelding into a trot. In no time she'd left behind the snug, well-lit houses lining the quay and moved farther into the village, and soon even those familiar houses—including the parsonage, which made her wish she was going there instead—receded into the distance and swiftly gathering darkness as she rode out across the heath at a full gallop.

She would probably be late for supper, but there was no help for it. She'd had so much to do. Taking time out for the wedding yesterday had put her so far behind.

First she'd stopped at the parsonage to check on her father, Corisande finding him in his study poring over his books. He'd said virtually nothing to her, no, not even wishing her Godspeed when she left his room, which she'd found strange. But Frances assured her that everything seemed back to normal although Linette, who already missed Lindsay so much, had apparently cried herself to sleep.

So Corisande had gone straightaway to the church schoolhouse to see her sisters, excusing them for a few moments from their studies to give hugs all around. Her heart ached at how usually matter-of-fact Linette clung to her after Marguerite and Estelle left to return to their desks, her sister's pretty brown eyes swimming with tears.

"Oh, Corie, can't you come back to be with us? I miss you so much. It isn't the same! Nothing's the same!"

Her throat tight, Corisande had wanted so badly to assure her that, yes, she would be home very soon to stay. She had long sensed that perhaps Linette had suffered the most when their mother had died, being only four and too young to understand that Adele Easton would never return. And now with Lindsay having left and Corisande, too, Linette looking so miserable . . . ah, but she couldn't tell her the truth. At least not yet.

"Linette, I'm married now, sweet. I have to stay with my husband. That's the way of things, and someday you'll have your own home and family. But I'll still be here if you need me. I'm not very far away, after all."

Thankfully Linette had seemed to understand, smudging away her tears with the palms of her hands although her small chin had still trembled. Corisande had almost been relieved to leave her, and with a host of other things to do—visiting the poorhouse to see that Eliza Treweake had everything she needed for her charges, tending for a few hours to the church accounts, and then meeting with Oliver to make some last arrangements for their next shipment of contraband—she'd had very little time to worry further—

"What . . . oh, Lord! Easy, boy!"

A gust of such violent force had suddenly hit them broadside that the gelding had ground to a halt and tried to rear, Corisande gripping the reins with all her might and fighting to maintain control of the frightened animal and keep her seat.

"Easy! Easy now, boy!"

They wheeled in place, the horse snorting and blowing and tossing its head, but finally the poor creature grew calmer as Corisande continued cajoling and soothing him.

"It's all right, boy. Just a sou'westerly, and a healthy one too. Didn't that Henry Gilbert ever take you out on a ride before in such lively weather? If he had, you wouldn't have been so surprised."

The gelding nickered, shaking his thick mane, which made Corisande feel as if they could start out again. She rubbed his neck first a few times and then veered him around, catching her bearings and . . . and . . . who in blazes was that?

Corisande squinted against the cold drizzle hitting her face and peered through the near pitch-black darkness at the undeniable shape of a horse and rider some distance away. They weren't moving either, just standing there beside a stunted tree, which was odd. The weather really was quite miserable. Who would be outside if he didn't have to be?

"Hello!"

The whistling wind sucked up her cry, but surely the rider must have heard her. Yet he still wasn't moving—oh, Lord. It couldn't be. Had Donovan ridden out to meet her?

Here she'd hoped he might even still be at the mine, and then he wouldn't have known at all that she had chosen to ignore his ridiculous command. Now he probably planned to play the outraged husband and lecture her all the way to the house about the correct behavior for the wife of a lord, but oh, no, she was going to have none of it!

"On with you, boy! Go!" Corisande kicked the gelding into a gallop, but the big horse surprised her, probably so eager to be home and well out of the approaching storm that he lengthened his strides to a breakneck run.

Which was perfectly fine with her. Donovan would have no hope of catching them now, no, not even riding his fine steel-gray stallion. They'd had too great of a head start, and just to make sure, she glanced over her shoulder and saw that, indeed, they were being followed; but Donovan was still so far back that he almost blended into the darkness.

Facing front, Corisande smiled giddily as she hunched

down over the gelding's lunging neck and held on tightly, her hood flying off her hair, her cloak billowing and snapping in the wind. She may have decided that she was going to behave as if she and Donovan had the happiest marriage in Britain no matter what had happened—although she'd been encouraged that no hint of Fanny's gossip had yet reached Porthleven—but right now, it was just she and Donovan out here in the windswept dark where no one could see them.

Why not frustrate him entirely by refusing to wait up for him? Why not show him that she needed no silly carriage to take her here and there, her riding skills quite capable, thank you very much! She began to laugh with sheer exhilaration, the lighted windows of the house appearing through the thickening trees as they thundered into the wide valley that nature had cut through the heath.

Just she and Donovan, and she was still well ahead of him, a quick glance telling her that he had nonetheless gained some ground no matter that she could barely see him. But she could hear him, his stallion's hooves pounding the ground while her heart began to beat faster and faster. With a whoop of triumph she burst through a line of elms and onto the drive and pulled up tight on the reins, mud and stones spraying behind them as she brought the heaving gelding to a halt.

Right in front of the entrance door.

Donovan stood waiting for her in the lamplight, his swarthy face truly ominous to behold.

Wholly stunned, Corisande glanced behind her but there was no rider in sight. None.

She gulped.

Oh, Lord.

❦ Eighteen ❦

"Looking for someone?"

Breathless, Corisande spun to face Donovan, not really sure what to say. "Yes . . . well, I mean, no, no, I'm not. Of course not. There's no one there." She glanced behind her again, staring into the darkness, hearing nothing, no pounding hooves—for heaven's sake, she hadn't imagined it!—and looked back at Donovan. He couldn't have beat her to the house, that was bloody impossible, so who . . . ? "Is . . . is Henry Gilbert here?"

"He went home five minutes ago." Donovan nodded brusquely in the opposite direction. "He lives *that* way."

"Yes, yes, of course. I knew that." So much for Henry following her, she thought, growing more confused than ever and a mite alarmed. Should she tell Donovan what had happened? He didn't look very happy; in fact, she hadn't seen him look or sound anything but surly since last night when she'd come out from behind that screen. She doubted he was in any mood at all to hear her incredible story—

"Are you planning to just sit atop that horse or come in for supper?"

"Of course I don't intend to sit out here all night!" she snapped, only to catch herself when she spied Ogden walking stiffly to the door. The happiest marriage in Britain, remember?

It was more for her family than anything else. If Linette

was so distressed just to have her gone from the parsonage, she could imagine how her sister might feel if she believed Corisande was unhappy. Marguerite too. It would crush her. She truly thought Corisande was in love. So for now she would play the part, however difficult—and the way this night was going, she was clearly in for a chore.

"Oh, hello, Ogden," she began breezily, very much aware that Donovan had stiffened. "My husband says that supper is ready."

"Yes, my lady, so it is. I've come to tell you that Grace is ready for me to serve."

"How wonderful! I'm simply famished." She glanced back at Donovan to find him scowling at her but, unperturbed, she gifted him with the most contrite smile she could muster. "I'll be in shortly, my love, as soon as I return my horse to the stable. I know you can't be happy that I didn't use the carriage today, but I so enjoy riding. And this gelding is so much faster than Biscuit. Surely you can forgive me."

He said nothing, which didn't surprise her. The visible tension in his body was enough to tell her that he wasn't amused at all by her remorseful performance, although she didn't care what the man thought! Actually she was quite beginning to enjoy herself. Suddenly the tables had been turned, and now *she* had become the bold charmer. But it was no more than he deserved for all the false smiles he'd given her and, to that end, she gave him another grin of her own.

"You're much too serious, Donovan," she playfully chided him. "It's really no large matter. I know you'll be a dear and understand. I'll be right back—"

"I'll take the horse."

Donovan had come down the steps and reached up to lift her from her mount almost before she could blink, but Corisande wasn't going to let this golden opportunity escape as her feet touched the ground. She flung her arms around his neck before he could blink, saying innocently, "There, you see? I knew you'd forgive me. Oh, Donovan, I've missed you so much! Did you and Henry have a good day at the mine?"

Donovan was so startled, he found himself leaning toward her, his eyes upon her smiling lips, his arms going around her, but he stopped himself just in time. The wily chit! What new game was she playing now?

"We had a fine day," he muttered, disengaging himself but not too abruptly. Ogden was standing there watching them like a somber-eyed hound, after all. Even if the servants thought he'd married for monetary reasons, he couldn't just shove her away like an indifferent cad. Good God, he wasn't his bloody father! "You'd best go inside," he added gruffly, not liking at all the tempting pressure of Corisande's hands upon his chest. "It's starting to rain."

"Ah, so it is. You're such a dear to think of me. Don't be gone too long, darling."

Gone too long, *darling*? Clenching his teeth as Corisande ran up the steps and hurried inside, Donovan vowed in that moment to hire extra help before tomorrow was done. If there were only footmen around the place, he could follow her right now and take her aside and demand what she was up to, but first he had to go to the damned stable. That is, unless . . .

"Ogden, you take the horse to the stable."

The butler's eyes nearly bugged from his head, and he backed up inside the door. "Me—me, my lord? But I don't know anything at all about horse—"

"It's simple, man! You hold these reins and lead the way. He'll follow you, nothing more to it than that. And when you get to the stable, just call for Will the coachman. He'll handle things from there."

"Oh, oh, but I—"

"Go to it, man." Donovan cut him off, having sprinted up the steps. "Don't worry about supper being served late. We'll await you in the dining room."

At least that's where he believed he might find Corisande, Donovan thought darkly to himself, leaving Ogden shaking his head as the man disappeared outside. Donovan strode across the entry hall past the drawing room, but he stopped suddenly and retraced his steps, intuition striking him. Good God, if Corisande was emptying the sherry decanter again . . .

Donovan was nearly tempted to kick in the door to catch her red-handed, but somehow he restrained himself and entered the room quietly, deciding that might be just as effective as he soundlessly closed the door behind him. Yes, Corisande was there, standing with her back to him in front of the fire, and she looked as if she were lifting something to her mouth, her head tilting as she made to drink—

"Dammit, woman, stop right there!"

Corisande spun, so startled she nearly dropped the small bottle of perfume she had just pulled from her cloak pocket. Her heart hammering, she stared at Donovan, who was staring right back at her, although he looked somewhat confused as he glanced from her to the sideboard and then back again.

"What . . . what is that you're holding?"

Corisande felt a wave of irritation as she realized what he must have been thinking, but she made herself answer sweetly as she held up the bottle in one hand and the cork stopper in the other. "This?"

"Of course, *that*. What else could I have meant?"

"Oh, a glass of sherry, perhaps? Maybe the whole decanter?"

He stiffened, scowling, while Corisande merely smiled, her aggravation all but forgotten as she felt immense enjoyment in teasing him. "It's perfume, my love. Something I found today in Porthleven. I've never really worn any before, but now that I'm Lady Donovan, well, it seemed the thing to do." She took a quick moment to dab some at her throat, which was exactly what she'd been about to do before Donovan had startled her, then held out the bottle. "Would you like to smell for yourself . . . ?"

When Donovan shook his head, obstinately holding his ground, Corisande shrugged. "As you wish. It's a lovely scent, I assure you, though probably not as fine as perfume you'd find in London. But it was the best I could afford." She closed the bottle and slipped it into her pocket, then turned back to the fire and swept off her cloak, shaking it free of moisture before folding the garment over a chair. "It didn't take you very long at the stable. I thought I'd wait for you in here. The fire looked so inviting, and that dining room is so huge and drafty—"

"I didn't go to the stable, Corie."

Corisande whirled around, Donovan having come up so close behind her that she nearly fell into him, his big hands locking around her upper arms to catch her. But he didn't let her go, instead jerking her against him.

"I had Ogden take your horse to the stable so I could come and find you. What game are you playing now, woman? I thought we'd dispensed with the happy bride."

Donovan's harsh grip was hurting her, but she refused to show her pain. She also refused to give in to the anger threatening to overflow, instead remembering her sisters as she said evenly, "You may be done with your charade, my lord—and it seems from your recent churlish behavior that you are, but I'm not comfortable playing the martyr. I don't want to appear the wronged bride, the miserable bride, the spiteful bride. Besides, I heard no whiff of any gossip about us today in Porthleven, so there's simply no sense in acting as if something is wrong. I'd prefer to go on just as we were before, if you don't mind—"

"Dammit, woman, I do mind!"

His outburst was so vehement that Corisande could only stare, but in the next instant Donovan looked almost angry with himself as he abruptly released her and went to sink into a wing chair.

"Ah, do what you will."

"That's what you told me earlier, and I fully intend to."

"Like wearing that damned lavender perfume?"

Corisande almost smiled, for he sounded so much like a sulky young boy. But he didn't look like a boy, oh, no, her spending a full day away from him making her all the more aware of just how acutely masculine he was, the room fairly crackling with his presence. Shoving away the disquieting thought, she murmured, "I didn't think you'd noticed."

"Noticed? Ha! You can smell the stuff halfway across the room."

"Yes, I thought you'd like it."

That comment brought another scowl, Donovan's tone accusing as he glared at her. "You're enjoying yourself, aren't you?"

"Actually, I am," she admitted, probably the first time she had said anything to him with such honesty. "I don't know why it should make you so furious, either, but I suppose since you've gotten what you wanted—at least as far as finding someone to marry you—there's no more reason for you to act anything but a callous, ill-tempered boor—"

"Is that what you truly think of me—no, woman, don't even answer that," Donovan just as quickly amended, shoving his fingers through his jet-black hair. "Hell and damnation, I already know."

He sounded so disgruntled, Corisande didn't know what to make of it, but she had no chance to say anything as a loud knock sounded in the room. Immediately Donovan lunged from his chair and went to throw open the door, revealing a rather mussed Ogden, his white gloves muddied and his clothes somewhat askew, yet his dignity still quite intact.

"The horse is in the stable, my lord, and supper is served."

As Ogden turned stiffly to lead the way, Corisande thought Donovan might go ahead without her. But to her surprise, he held out his arm to escort her, clearly resigned to the role she wanted to play although he still didn't look very happy about it. In fact, she doubted that for the brief duration of their marriage, she would ever see him smile again, which made her feel oddly wistful. He had the most handsome smile, and that boyish grin last night . . .

"We're not going to the guillotine, Corie. Just to supper. Unless of course, Grace's roast beef and Yorkshire pudding is overcooked now thanks to you coming home so late. Upon a horse, no less, not inside the carriage that I requested."

"Ah, yes, but you've already forgiven me for that, remember?" she said lightly as they proceeded arm in arm to the dining room, although her mood suddenly didn't feel so light.

She wasn't sure why, either, which was just as strange. Perhaps Donovan's surliness was simply wearing her down. With her luck, she'd probably prattle by herself at one end of that absurdly long table while Donovan swirled his wine at his end and said little . . . which was exactly what happened.

Lord, Ogden must think she was a ridiculous chatterbox to have carried on and on about her day—well, as much of it as she could safely discuss, leaving out her meeting with Captain Oliver Trelawny altogether and the unsettling incident on the heath—but she'd had to do something to fill the silence. Thankfully a glass of red burgundy had helped, but she'd pointedly been given only one while Donovan's glass was refilled twice though he had barely touched the last.

Then he'd been given a snifter of brandy after their dessert of buttermilk cake—a familiar Cornish recipe of Frances's that had given her some comfort, Grace Twickenham thoughtfully doing her best to help Corisande feel at home —while she was served a bracing hot cup of green tea. But she didn't want bracing, she wanted to go to bed. Tomorrow would be as full a day as the one she'd so exhaustively described. Oh, Lord, and she had only to think of that huge mattress she must share with Donovan to start feeling nervous all over again.

She wanted to get to their room first. Oh, yes, she wanted to be safely under the covers with her eyes closed and her back turned before Donovan even came up the stairs. So she began to yawn well before he'd finished his brandy, great, long, exaggerated yawns she did little to hide.

And she ceased talking too. Why continue when she was speaking largely to herself? The only time Donovan had showed any interest was when she'd mentioned Linette crying herself to sleep, and he'd said at once that her sisters were welcome to visit the house as often as they wished. She'd been surprised, warmed by his response actually, and had thanked him, but as for the rest, she might as well have been conversing with a brick wall, Donovan was so brooding and unsociable. At last she could stand the weighty silence no longer, and she rose from her chair.

"Go on up if you'd like," Donovan said gruffly before she could utter a word. "I'll be there shortly."

So at last the man speaks! she fumed, using every bit of her restraint not to lash out at him and thank him for the enlivening pleasure of his company. Instead she said, primarily for Ogden's benefit—the butler had been standing stiff as a statue beyond Donovan's chair and listening to them all night, after all—and quite meaningfully enough to raise a stoic brow, "Don't be too long, Donovan, my darling.

I'd be so disappointed to fall asleep before you kiss me good night."

Oh, Lord, had she really purred that ridiculous nonsense? Was she mad? Seeing that Donovan had stopped swirling his brandy, his midnight eyes full upon her as she hastened from the room, Corisande wanted to kick herself, but instead she fled up the stairs.

It was the nervousness taking over, she was certain of it. Making her tongue rash. Making her foolish. Last night at least she'd had sherry and champagne to dull her senses, but tonight she had nothing to calm her racing heart. Yet she remembered her heart pounding last night too—oh, bloody hell, she didn't want to think about it!

Corisande saw that her bed was turned down again the moment she entered her chamber, and wishing in vain that she might sleep there alone by herself, she quickly shed her clothes and groped inside the wardrobe for her flannel nightgown . . . but it wasn't there. Groaning to herself, she found instead a gossamer bit of muslin trimmed with delicate pink lace, and she knew at once that Rose Polkinghorne must have come to call.

There were two new dresses, too, but she didn't waste time looking at them. She slipped the muslin nightgown over her head—for heaven's sake, there was nothing to it!—and felt her face grow red with embarrassment. The fabric was nearly transparent, and it wasn't voluminous either, like her flannel, but hugged the curves of her body like nothing she had ever worn before.

Corisande groaned aloud this time, wishing she had thought to bring her cloak with her. She would have liked nothing more in that moment than to douse herself from head to toe with lavender perfume. But the damned cloak was in the drawing room while she was here, and with Donovan no doubt on his way upstairs . . .

She didn't tarry any longer, pulling the pins from her hair

and dropping them onto the floor as she raced through the sitting room. Thank God she didn't need the water closet tonight. She could just dive into bed and bloody hide, that thought making her bolt into Donovan's room all the faster—

"Good God, woman, are you trying to run me down?"

∽ Nineteen ∽

Corisande gasped and veered to avoid careening into Donovan as he sidestepped to avoid her too. Spinning around, she gaped at him, loose strands of hair half covering her face, but she wasn't so blinded as not to see that his shirt was hanging open—oh, dear Lord, he was already undressing!

At least, he had been undressing. Now he was simply staring at her, his gaze sweeping over her from head to foot. With a shriek she crossed her arms over her breasts, demanding in a hoarse croak, "Turn around this very instant! Damn you, Donovan Trent, turn around!"

But Donovan didn't want to turn around. God help him, he wanted to stare and stare, the hissing fire burning brightly enough that he could see nearly every tantalizing inch of Corisande just as God had made her. And her nipples weren't pink as he'd thought they might be last night, but a dusky brown he could plainly see through her nightgown even as she desperately tried to cover herself. A dusky brown like the muslin-veiled triangle at the heart of her thighs.

"What are you doing here? I—I only left the dining room a few moments ago. What are you doing here?"

She sounded nearly beside herself, her voice having become a high-pitched squeak. It was enough to make Donovan cease his staring, barely, and look at her stricken face.

"What do you think I'm doing here, woman? You told me not to be too long, and I do sleep here."

She opened her mouth to speak, but this time no words came at all. Instead she turned and fled toward the bed and tore back the covers, leaping beneath them and pulling them up to the bridge of her nose.

In fact, she looked like a tousle-haired mouse peeping out at him, and thank God, too, that Corisande had covered herself, giving him much-needed respite to calm his thundering senses. He'd almost gone after her, the sight of her trim, heart-shaped bottom all the temptation any man should be made to stand in one lifetime. Ten lifetimes! He doubted he'd ever seen any woman fashioned more seductively, lithe and long-limbed and yet curved and round—

Groaning to himself, Donovan went to the washbasin and filled it with water, then bent over and splashed himself full in the face. He did so, not once but several times, wishing that it wasn't tepid but ice-cold. Ice-cold to stop this infernal burning inside him, this madness he seemed scarcely able to control.

By the time he stopped splashing himself he was drenched, his chest matted and soaking, his shirt dripping wet, as well as his breeches and boots. And yet he felt like hanging his head in the water, doubting the dunking had done him any good.

Dammit, why *had* he raced up here? Corisande hadn't meant those bloody words, he knew that, which was nothing new to him.

He'd been called darling countless times before, my love, my heart—by elegant, beautiful women who uttered such endearments as easily as they changed lovers. Even Nina hadn't meant them, lovely ebony-haired Nina with her sultry dark eyes and scarlet lips, his mistress for a time and the mother of his child. And it had suited him fine, always had. He'd never been bothered at all, no, never given it a second thought or yearned for even a moment that those words might be heartfelt.

Until now.

Something was gnawing at him, eating at him, and he didn't like it. He didn't want it! He'd never before considered the possibility . . . God, it was ridiculous! This . . . this whole insane attraction for a woman he bloody well intended to leave, to annul, to forget! With a low growl, he splashed his face again, but there was more water on himself and the floor than in the basin.

"Do . . . do you always make such a mess when you bathe?"

Donovan fell still, snorting wryly to himself as he held his face in his hands although he felt not a whit of humor.

Bathing? Was that what the chit thought he was doing? Hell and damnation, Corisande was more a raw innocent than he had ever imagined. That realization couldn't have proved more grounding either; at least she had no idea what havoc she'd just caused inside him. Thinking it was time he got hold of himself and saw to what else needed to be done, Donovan straightened and grabbed for a towel.

"I . . . well, surely you know that I didn't mean what I said in the dining room. It was only for Ogden—to make things look convincing. I really didn't mean it at all."

Donovan glanced over at the bed, Corisande apparently having calmed herself enough to drop the covers to her chin. "No?"

His tone was so heavy with sarcasm that Corisande bristled, but she made herself relax, imagining he was simply offended that she'd commented about him making a mess.

And he had made a mess! She had never seen anything like it, water splashing all around him, hitting the wall, cascading onto the floor and soaking the carpet. She hated to think what he would do with a whole tubful of water . . . but, of course, she had no intention of ever seeing him sitting in a tub or watching Donovan dry himself for that matter. She averted her eyes as he stripped off his sodden shirt and began to towel his chest and under his arms, Corisande even going so far as to roll over so she was facing the other way.

"That's probably a good idea. I wouldn't want to offend you while I undress."

Stiffening again at his sarcasm, Corisande rolled back over, a retort ready to fly—and then wished she'd stayed put facing the opposite wall. Donovan was standing with his back to her, a back so broad and powerful and incredibly contoured with sinewy muscles that she couldn't help looking at him, although she told herself that she should turn away at once.

She stared almost transfixed as he bent over to tug off his riding boots, his muscles flexing, his arms looking strong and powerful, too, and she certainly knew that to be true. She'd felt them around her more than once; why, even tonight when he'd pulled her against him in the drawing room, Donovan's body lean and so hard—

"Perhaps I should stand behind the screen if you're going to ogle me."

She gasped to find Donovan studying her, his expression as dry as his tone although his eyes held a disturbing hint of what she had seen in them before when he'd been staring at her. "I—I wasn't ogling you. I was looking at the mess you made, is all. I can just imagine what Ellen Biddle is going to think tomorrow morning—"

"That's not the only mess she'll find." He cut her off cryptically, his hands moving to his breeches. "I sleep naked, in case you'd like to know. So you might want to—"

"Naked?" Corisande half screeched, forgetting her resolve to play the happy bride altogether as she clutched the covers against her breasts. "You mean . . . last night, you . . . no sleeping wear at all?"

"None. Never worn the stuff. Too confining."

"Too confining?" Her voice had again become a high-pitched squeak, but that was the last of Corisande's worries as she rolled over so fast that she nearly tumbled from the bed. Clutching the edge of the mattress, she tugged the bedclothes well over her ears, but that didn't prevent her from hearing Donovan's every slightest movement, an intense flush of heat racing from her scalp to her toes as he pulled off his breeches and tossed them to the floor.

She squeezed her eyes shut as he walked about the room, first dousing lamps and then stoking the fire, her heart beginning to pound.

And when he came toward the bed, his side of the bed, and yanked back the covers, she thought she might choke, her breath strangled so in her throat. Oh, Lord, what she would give for a glass of sherry now—no, the whole decanter! She remembered nothing of this last night; she doubted she would have even considered coming out from behind that screen if she'd known he had stripped down to his skin.

She waited and waited, feeling as if she were turning blue while Donovan had yet to climb into bed. Then she heard a sharp intake of breath and a low curse, and her eyes flared wide. What in heaven's name . . . ?

She rolled over onto her back despite the sudden compression of the mattress, crying out and sitting bolt upright as a knife blade flashed in the firelight. "Donovan! Dear God, what—"

"Shh, woman, I'm not trying to murder you, if that's what you're thinking . . . just making things look as if you've been properly bedded—damn! I cut too deep."

Corisande heard another sharp intake of pain, understanding flooding her as Donovan leaned on one knee over the center of the bed, the room not so dark that she couldn't see blood dripping onto the clean white sheet from where he'd slit the inside of his forearm. Oh God, she'd seen such a pool before when she'd gone with Oliver's wife, Rebecca, to help tend to their daughter Sophie after her wedding night. But then there had been so much more blood and ugly purple bruises and tears, so many tears—

"Get me a towel, Corie, before I make this look more a pig slaughter than a deflowering—dammit, quick! I'm bleeding all over the place."

Corisande was already scrambling from the bed, nearly tripping in her haste to reach the washbasin.

"Careful, woman! I don't want you bumping your head again. Then we'll really have a mess on our hands."

She grabbed a sodden towel since she couldn't find a dry one, and rushed back to the bed, Donovan sitting at the edge with his hand clamped over the wound. "Here, let me," she commanded urgently, sitting down beside him and pressing the towel to his flesh when he removed his fingers. "Turn your arm upright—that's it. That should help the bleeding to stop."

She sat there for long moments as neither one of them spoke, Donovan wincing as she gradually released the pressure. At last she decided she could lift the towel, the wound still oozing but not bleeding as profusely as before. She pressed gingerly around the area with her fingertips, marveling at the muscular strength she felt in the slightest flex of his arm.

"I doubt you'll need a bandage. Does it hurt very much?" She glanced up when Donovan didn't answer to find him staring at her, their faces only inches apart. She gulped, suddenly feeling quite woozy inside, her gaze falling from his eyes to his lips, sensual, masculine lips so close to hers she could feel the heat of his breath upon her. "I . . . I said does it hurt—"

"Not anymore. You've a very gentle touch, Lady Donovan. Where did you learn to nurse so capably?"

His low, husky voice brought chills to her spine, strange, wonderful chills that made her shiver and yet feel quite warm all at the same time. "F-Frances, I suppose. She's seen to all our scrapes and bumps, and I've helped at birthings too. We've only one doctor in the parish, and the tinners could rarely pay . . ." She gave a tiny shrug, inhaling softly when her shoulder rubbed against Donovan's. "It's common sense, really."

"Not at all. Birthings, helping your father, helping out at the church, the poorhouse, the schoolhouse, watching after your sisters, hollering down mine shafts—"

"Mine shafts? Who told—?"

"Henry Gilbert, for one." Donovan's voice grew even huskier as he brought his face closer, causing Corisande's breath to snag in her throat. "You're quite amazing, Corie. Bloody amazing. Is there anything you can't do?"

Corisande had no voice to answer, Donovan's mouth so near to touching hers that she found herself closing her eyes and tilting her head, every part of her suddenly aching to believe that she had truly heard sincerity in his voice. But she no sooner felt the stirring pressure of his lips upon hers than she started as if stung— Dear Lord, what was she doing? What was she thinking? With Donovan's gift for sarcasm? He was mocking her, not praising her. Mocking her! Oh, she could already hear his taunting voice . . . *"You said you wanted a good-night kiss, didn't you?"*

"No, don't you dare kiss me!" Her hoarse cry sounded like a thunderclap in the room as she pushed away from him, Corisande just as horrified that she could have been sitting there nearly atop Donovan's lap, and he was naked— wholly naked—while she was practically naked too!

"Corie?"

"No, I don't want to hear any more! You're mean and cruel and—and I hate you!" Feeling stupid and so ridiculously naïve, she lurched to her feet only to jump in surprise when something hard clattered to the floor, barely missing her toes. She looked down but then backed away, saying brokenly through the tears swimming in her eyes, "I—I don't like knives. You'll have to pick up the damned thing yourself!" Then she spun and ran around to the other side of the bed, never more grateful that it was so huge. She climbed in and pulled the covers tightly over her head, biting her clenched hand and feeling a total fool that she could be crying.

Donovan sat at the edge of the bed for a long, long time, shaking his head and wondering what the hell had just happened. He could hear muted sniffles under the bedclothes, but eventually they quieted, Corisande, he imagined, having fallen asleep.

Eventually he lay down, too, after returning the knife to the bottom wardrobe drawer where he kept his pistol. But he couldn't sleep, instead listening to the mounting wind whistle and howl outside and glancing from time to time at the still, shrouded figure on the opposite side of the bed. She looked more like an Egyptian mummy underneath all those bedclothes than his temporary wife.

Hell and damnation.

Women.

⊂⊃ Twenty ⊂⊃

Men!

If it wasn't enough that Donovan continually occupied Corisande's mind, this past interminable week had proved a trial like nothing else she'd known, now that Oliver Trelawny's whereabouts plagued her, too, and she was growing more worried by the hour.

Staring out the window into the pitch-dark night, Corisande hugged her arms to her breasts as she looked for the signal that she'd been awaiting for three days now. It wasn't ten o'clock yet, though she still couldn't help looking.

Corisande sighed and glanced over her shoulder at the small gilt clock above the mantel. No, only quarter to ten. Fifteen minutes yet to wonder and worry if Oliver and the twenty-man crew of the *Fair Betty* were back safe and sound from France. Lord, what could have kept them?

Oliver hadn't sailed out early last Wednesday morning as he'd planned, the gale he'd so welcomed becoming a fierce spring storm that had churned up the sea and slashed the Cornish coast with torrential rain, delaying his departure until Friday before dawn. Those two days for Corisande had been the worst, when she'd been cooped up in the house with Donovan because the weather was simply too foul to venture out.

Oh, he'd left her alone. He'd left her alone all week, in fact, those first several rainy days by staying in his library much of the time and saying he had work to do. So she'd played the agreeable wife and left him alone, too, spending her time reading dusty old novels and exploring the house with Ellen Biddle.

It hadn't been her idea, but the housekeeper had seemed eager to get started on what yet needed to be done around the place, and she wanted Corisande's opinions. Of course, Corisande knew nothing about the latest styles in drapery and upholstery fabric and the best ways of arranging furniture, but she tried to show suitable interest. Yet all the while she couldn't help thinking again of how within weeks every room would be shuttered and closed, the house settling once more into dust and disuse.

Oddly enough, the thought had bothered her. *Everything* seemed to be bothering her, so she tried to keep such troublesome musings out of her head.

Like the fact that Donovan rarely spoke to her. No, not even in front of the servants, which had made her task of appearing content all the more difficult. He was especially silent at night when that dreaded time came for them to adjourn to bed, but thankfully much of the awkwardness had been eased straightaway when he'd gruffly said it made no difference in whose room she was found sleeping in the morning now that she had been "properly bedded." Since then, he had made no other reference to that disconcerting night, clearly not wishing to discuss it further, and neither had she.

That bothered her too. Not that he wouldn't discuss what had happened but that it had happened at all.

Oh, Lord, she still couldn't believe she'd come so close to allowing Donovan to kiss her. He might have done so before, but this time had been different, disturbingly different. She didn't like to admit it, but she'd wanted him to kiss her. At least for a split second before she'd come to her senses.

It was all so ridiculous. What a stupid fool! To think she

had believed for even an instant that Donovan might have spoken sincerely—that sarcastic, self-centered cad! Then her getting so upset, crying even. Bloody ridiculous!

Her face blazing at the memory, Corisande looked outside again, but she saw nothing, only inky blackness. Sighing more heavily this time, she began to pace although she didn't stray very far from the windows.

When the storm had finally passed and she'd been able to go about her business, she had felt as if she'd been released from prison. But not before Donovan had insisted on Friday morning that she first see the document he had drafted saying the tinners would continue to be paid fairly no matter the state of his personal affairs or his whereabouts, which had bothered her too.

And it bothered her that she should be bothered! So Donovan could think of nothing but annulling their marriage and returning to Spain. Good riddance! And where was Oliver, that grizzled rogue? The *Fair Betty* should have been sighted late Saturday, and here it was Tuesday night . . .

Corisande swatted at the blue velvet draperies when another glance outside proved fruitless; with another ten minutes to kill, she needed something to clear her mind.

One bright spot in the week had been a letter from Lindsay, posted the very day Corisande had written to her about Donovan, so Lindsay had known nothing yet about her temporary marriage. Held over in Helston because of the storm and delivered to the parsonage on Friday, the letter had been raced over to her at the church, where she was working on the accounts, by a breathless and giggling Estelle, an indignant Linette, and Marguerite hard on her heels.

"A letter, Corie! From Lindsay!"

"I had it first, too, but Estelle took it from me," Linette had groused, scowling at her younger sister only to glance back pleadingly at Corisande. "Remember, Corie? You said we would read it together—"

"And me!" Estelle had chimed.

"Me too!" Appearing as eager as the others, Marguerite had looked expectantly at the letter, her lovely brown eyes alight. "I want to hear about London, Corie. Go on, open it!"

So Corisande had done so, perusing the letter very quickly to make sure there was no reference to Donovan and their sham marriage before she'd read it aloud, delighting in every word. She went to the writing desk now and retrieved that same letter, smiling to herself as she plopped onto the bed.

Suddenly it felt as if Lindsay were there in the room with her, breathlessly recounting everything she'd seen since she'd gone to London, her somewhat reckless handwriting spilling forth in an animated tumble as lively as her speech . . .

Oh, Corie, I can hardly believe I'm here! So many things to tell you—where to begin? London is so very, very grand, and so much bigger than I'd expected! I've never seen so many people—ah, but more of that later!

Aunt Winifred is a dear, though terribly cowed by Olympia, poor thing. It seems she received reams of instructions on where I'm to go, how I'm to deport myself, how I'm to dress, the people I must meet—what silly rubbish! You know I hope to strike out on my own, but Aunt Winnie is quite excitable, even more than I remember—Lord, her lady's maid, Matilda, doesn't dare leave the house without smelling salts in hand! So I must take care—oh, Corie, you won't believe what I've to tell you!

Some things here are so strange. I've seen gentlemen in corsets! Yes, corsets, their waists cinched so tight they look like plump-breasted pigeons, and their collars so starched

*they can no easier look to the left and right than if their
necks were encased in plaster . . .*

Corisande let the letter drop to her lap, imagining what it
must be like to see such startling things.

Of course, she didn't regret that she hadn't gone to London; she would never have met Donovan and . . . and for
heaven's sake, that wasn't the point either! She wouldn't
have been able to help the tinners on such a vast scale if not
for Donovan, and that was virtually the only thing for which
she had to be thankful about meeting him!

Corisande focused once more on Lindsay's letter, but she
felt all bothered again and hardly in the mood to read. And
she still had five minutes to go, she saw irritably as she
glanced at the clock. Lord, if that signal didn't come tonight—

"Corie, may I come in?"

She froze, her gaze flying to the sitting room door, a door
she'd left pointedly closed all week as a clear sign that Donovan was not welcome. He hadn't made any move to disturb
her until now—bloody hell, why tonight of all nights? It was
almost ten o'clock and, oh dear, she'd retired early, claiming
a headache, and here she was dressed in her sturdiest
clothes and ready to go out at the first sign . . .

Corisande had only a moment to leap into bed, still holding Lindsay's letter, fully clothed, shoes and all, and yank
the covers under her chin before she heard Donovan enter
the room. Her eyes were squeezed shut, and her heart
raced. She made no move at all as he crossed to the bed, but
she knew at once he didn't believe she was sleeping when
she heard him sigh heavily.

"You haven't bothered to douse the lamps, Corie, and I
heard you pacing just a few moments ago. You can't have
fallen asleep that fast."

She didn't readily open her eyes, moaning instead. "Of
. . . of course I was pacing. My head hurts so . . ."

"Then I should have Ellen Biddle bring you a pinch of
laudanum in some tea—"

"No, no, I don't want any laudanum!" Realizing that
she'd half shouted, Corisande tried to control her annoyance as she stared up at Donovan. "I mean, my headache
isn't all that terrible, but it does hurt. I—I'm sure I'll be fine
if you'd allow me to sleep. Would you please turn out the
lamps for me, Donovan?"

He seemed taken aback by her docile request although
quite reluctant, too, to leave her side, the tension in his
body plain to see. "Actually, Corie, I thought we should
talk—"

"Please, Donovan, not tonight." Her gaze skipped to the
clock—oh, Lord, it was almost ten!—and then back again to
his face. His expression had hardened. "It's so late, and I'm
so tired. Tomorrow would be better."

"Very well, very well, tomorrow."

He didn't sound at all as if he wanted to leave, sighing
with exasperation, but finally he went to douse the lamps,
plunging the room into darkness but for the low red glow of
the fire. She could sense his barely restrained agitation as he
came back around to stand beside the bed, but she gave as
audible and as wide a yawn as she could summon, rolling
over onto her side and snuggling her head into the pillow.

"Thank you, Donovan. Good night."

No answer came but for the sitting room door closing
behind him a long moment later, even the dull thud sounding disgruntled.

Somehow Corisande managed to wait another moment,
just to make certain he didn't come back in again, then she
could stand it no longer as the clock began to chime ten.
She was on her feet and over to the windows in a flash,
taking care to move silently, her breath stopping as she

spied a lantern's yellow glow far off in the distance, the light swinging back and forth in an arc.

Thank God. Thank God.

She was cloaked and heading to the door in the next moment, her every thought concentrated upon getting to the stable as quickly as possible.

The men who had signaled her wouldn't be waiting for her, but on their way already to crisscross the parish and alert the others that the *Fair Betty* was anchored near to shore and waiting to be unloaded. Trusted tinners, farmers, fishermen in Porthleven, and even a few gentry would be converging at the prearranged cove by midnight with scores of hardy ponies, small boats, and willing hands ready to assist in an endeavor that had lined some pockets with coin, true, but brought hope to many lives too.

And thank God Ellen Biddle and she had gone exploring about the house, Corisande thought as she moved stealthily into the hall and closed the door silently behind her. She had only to creep a few feet to find the panel on the opposite wall that wasn't solid at all but a concealed doorway opening into a servants' staircase that led to the basement.

With a low exhalation of relief she hurried down the narrow wooden steps, hoping, though, that she wouldn't run into anyone. The huge spotless kitchen was silent and empty, Grace Twickenham having retired to her room.

Cautiously Corisande stepped past the cook's door, light streaming beneath it, only to freeze against the wall when Grace called out, "Is that you out there, Ogden? Well, if you're planning to make yourself some tea, I'll not have you leaving a mess. Mind now, I worked my knuckles raw to polish that kitchen. I want it to stay that way!"

Corisande didn't wait to see if the woman popped her head out the door, but fled to the servants' exit leading out the back of the house. With a prayer of thanks she plunged outside into the balmy night air, smiling to herself, too, at the thought of somber-faced Ogden being ruled by a house-ful of women servants. Well, there were the two young foot-men who'd joined the household last week, the main reason why Corisande had opted not to use the front door.

She couldn't relax, either, for there was still the obstacle of the stable. But fortunately Will Brighton, the stocky, ami-able coachman, was nowhere in sight, making it easy for her to saddle the big brown gelding whose name she'd learned from Henry Gilbert was Pete. A plain, unassuming name for a wonderful animal, but she'd scarcely had much chance to ride him, having deferred to Donovan's request that she take the carriage.

But that had been not so much to oblige him as that she was still puzzled by what had happened last week; she had no idea who could have raced across the heath like a swoop-ing bat to catch her.

She shivered at the unsettling memory; well, she might have an idea, but that made her shiver too. She didn't want to think about it and right now she didn't have the time. No, not even to wonder why Donovan, oddly enough, had wanted to talk to her after a week of brooding silence. Quickly she led Pete from the stable and mounted.

"Shh now, Pete, not a sound." Corisande drew up the reins and squeezed her knees together to get the gelding moving, but only at a walk at first. "Easy now, until we're far enough away from the house . . ."

The horse tossed his head and chewed at the bit, clearly eager to stretch his legs, and made Corisande wince when he gave a full-throated whinny just before they cut through the tall copse of elms lining the drive. But there was no help for it, and she urged the animal into a gallop, hoping that no one would think anything was amiss.

At least they wouldn't be seen, the night so pitch-black that if she hadn't known the rough surrounding countryside since childhood, she might have been reluctant to venture forth. She veered the gelding to the southwest and rode hard, astonished to see the familiar lantern light some way off in the distance.

Had the men decided to wait for her after all? They weren't standing where they'd been before but were heading toward the coast, which made sense. She cut to the left a little and rode straight for the light, Pete's hooves thundering so hard that she didn't hear her name being roared from the house.

∾ Twenty-one ∾

"Corie!"

Good God, it was useless! Cursing to himself, Donovan ran for the stable, his lungs already afire from sprinting so hard to get outside.

Hell and damnation, where was she going? He'd just stepped out onto the balcony when that whinny had cut through the night, and he'd watched in disbelief as a cloaked rider was swallowed up by the dark. He hadn't needed to check Corisande's room to know it was her—the wily chit! She must have been fully clothed under those covers, pleading a headache and then meekly as a dove asking him to douse the lamps, when all the while she'd simply been waiting for him to leave so she could . . .

"Go where?" Donovan growled under his breath as he dashed inside the stable and made for Samson's stall, his horse throwing back his head and snorting a greeting.

The last time Corisande had ridden anywhere by herself had been a full week ago; Donovan had never before seen her so flushed and exhilarated as when she'd galloped in from the dark. She'd glanced behind her as if looking for someone—bloody hell, he hadn't really considered it before now. Might she have gone to meet a lov—

Donovan didn't finish the thought, telling himself fiercely as he saddled Samson and vaulted onto the animal's back that it mattered nothing to him where she was going, just that she had ridden out alone.

He hadn't been concerned as long as she seemed willing to use the carriage, but now—dammit, he didn't trust Jack Pascoe to stay away from Corisande no matter the dire threats he'd made the man. He hadn't wanted to alarm her but he could see now that he should have given her some warning about the potential danger. He should have known she'd eventually do something like this.

"My—my lord? Is there some trouble?"

"Out of my way, man!"

A sleepy-eyed Will Brighton nearly toppled backward in his long white sleeping gown in his haste to stand clear of the stable doors as Donovan rode past him out into the night. But he had barely left the lights of the house behind him when he heard a high-pitched whinny from somewhere out on the heath that froze his blood.

A terrified horse. How many times had he heard that sound on the battlefield? Heard it from his own mounts as musket and cannon fire hit and thundered all around him, some of the poor animals even cut down beneath him?

Oh, God. Corisande.

"No, no, leave him alone! Who are you? Who are you?"

Corisande's piercing shrieks rent the air as her hooded attacker swung the lantern a second time at her horse's head, the stricken animal rearing out of the way and pawing the air in fright. She clutched at the reins, fighting for control, but when the lantern made a third blinding arc, the gelding reared so high that Corisande went tumbling from his back and hit the ground with a painful thud, knocking the breath from her body.

She was so stunned that she could only lie there on her stomach, the taste of dirt in her mouth, while poor Pete, whinnying shrilly, galloped away. The world around her had suddenly been plunged into darkness.

Dear God, what was happening? She'd ridden toward the light, catching up with the solitary man swinging the lantern, only to have him turn upon her, and then . . . and then—

Corisande screamed as she was suddenly hauled to her feet by someone with such immense physical strength that she felt nearly weightless. She began to fight, flailing her limbs, but she might have been a child's doll for how easily her attacker spun her around. The next thing she knew, an arm went round her neck to half strangle her while a harsh voice whispered in her ear, "You will hear me, woman. You will hear me . . ."

Corisande scarcely could hear, the sharp ringing had grown so deafening in her ears as she fought to breathe, the man's arm pressing like a cruel vise against her throat. She began to claw at him, wildly, desperately, when suddenly she was shoved to the ground, and receding footfalls plunged through the thick gorse as hooves came thundering toward her.

Dragging in huge gulps of air that stung her lungs, an instant later she felt someone drop to his knees beside her, turn her over gently, and lift her into a pair of strong arms.

"Corie . . . dear God, woman, are you all right? I saw a man running away, but he disappeared into the dark. Did you see his face? Did you recognize him?"

She flickered open her eyes, astonished as much to find Donovan holding her close as that she could see him, the lantern uprighted and spilling light upon them from only a few feet away. So it hadn't gone out. Her attacker must have dropped the lantern in the grass just before he dragged her to her feet. Her attacker . . .

"You! You arranged this, didn't you?" Corisande croaked, irrational fury filling her as she tried to twist free

of Donovan's arms. "You've hired someone to frighten me
. . . to kill me!"

Donovan could only stare, wondering incredulously as
she squirmed and wriggled if she might have hit her head
again for the utter nonsense she'd just spewed.

"So you don't deny it! You think it's going to be too much
trouble to annul me so you're going to see me done away
with instead! Let me go! Get away from—"

"Of course I didn't hire someone— Good God, woman,
will you never cease to think the worst of me?"

That seemed to quiet her, but she was still looking at him
with such mistrust that Donovan sighed heavily and released her. Corisande scrambled to her feet and spun to
face him.

"Those barrels," she accused, swiping hair out of her
eyes. "I—I never thought of it until now, but you had someone push them over so they might hit me, didn't you? On
our wedding day!"

Deeply stung that she was persisting in her preposterous
tirade, Donovan rose to stand in front of her. "Do you truly
think me so diabolical, Corie? I had nothing to do with
those bloody barrels, but I suspected that Jack Pascoe might
so I went to see him last week. He denied any involvement,
but I'm certain, especially now, that it was no accident."

She didn't say anything for a moment, her dark eyes having grown wide as saucers. It was very clear she'd been
frightened terribly by the attack; he almost couldn't blame
her for lashing out at him. But it still hurt . . .

"You saw Jack Pascoe?"

He nodded, and Corisande looked at him uncertainly
now. "Saw him, threatened him, told him to stay damned
well away from you and your family. But it looks as if he's
due another visit—the bastard. I'm going to break—"

"It wasn't Jack."

"Who? The man tonight?"

Corisande bobbed her head, trembling so visibly that Donovan was tempted to pull her into his arms. But he held his ground; she was talking to him now at least, more rationally, as calmly as could be expected. He didn't want to upset her again so he prodded gently. "Who was it, then, Corie? Did you see his face?"

"No, no, he wore a hood. But he was much bigger than Jack, taller. Then the lantern fell, and I couldn't see anything when he grabbed me around the neck—"

"He grabbed you around the neck?"

"Y-yes, and tried to choke me. He was strong, so strong."

When she winced, her hand moving to her throat, Donovan felt such rage that he could have killed at the moment, if he'd only found the man. He looked around them but he knew he'd never find the culprit in this inky blackness. Yet if he did . . .

"I—I was followed too. Last week when I rode home through the storm—"

"You were followed?" Donovan shouted, and Corisande took a nervous step backward. He couldn't believe she hadn't said anything to him until now. "Good God, Corie, why didn't you tell me?"

"Y-you looked so angry with me—for taking the horse, being late for supper, being your wife, I don't know! I didn't think you'd want to hear . . ."

Donovan cursed to himself as Corisande lapsed into indignant silence, knowing he shouldn't be surprised she hadn't confided in him. It was bloody true. He'd hardly made things easy for her this past week, which was why he had finally abandoned his resolve to have little to do with her and gone to her room, his infernal attraction for the woman be damned!

He'd wanted to apologize for his surly behavior, for trying to kiss her and upsetting her—hell, not that he'd meant to upset her. But now that she'd tricked him, he didn't exactly feel like apologizing although he was glad, he couldn't deny it, that that night she hadn't been looking behind her for a lover. Yet where then, tonight . . . ?

Later, man, later, Donovan told himself as Corisande sighed brokenly, rubbing her temples. Again resisting the overwhelming urge to take her in his arms, he asked quietly, "Do you feel well enough to ride? If you'd like, we can walk a short way first—"

"No, no, I'm fine." Actually Corisande felt as if she were coming out of some overwrought haze.

Oh, Lord, had she really accused Donovan of hiring someone to kill her? She felt chagrined suddenly, but tried to justify herself too. He'd been so hostile since the wedding, and then there was that night with the knife when he'd said something about murdering her, which had probably given her the idea in the first place. How was she to know? Someone who'd clearly meant her harm had been swinging that lantern, luring her like a ship onto the rocks when she had thought it was Oliver's signal—oh, God. Oliver.

"I have to go," she said shakily, realizing now that she had no idea if the *Fair Betty* had arrived safely or not.

"Go?"

Corisande heard Donovan's astonishment, but ignored him as she peered into the dark, looking for Pete. "Yes, I have to go—"

"I hope you mean back to the house."

Now what was she going to say? she thought crazily, wondering how she could possibly convince him to let her continue on her way, and alone.

"No, no, not the house. One, uh, one of the tinners' wives is expecting her third babe tonight. Peggy Robberts—she lives not more than a quarter mile away," Corisande explained hastily, concocting a fanciful story that would have done Lindsay's wild imagination proud as she named a woman whom she knew to be only a week or so away from giving birth. "She asked me to help and sent her husband, Morton, to throw stones at my window—"

"Stones at your window."

Trying not to be daunted by the skepticism in Donovan's voice, Corisande rushed on. "Yes, to let me know when it was time, we'd arranged it just that way. But he went on ahead so poor Peggy wouldn't be alone and—and I was just about to leave when you knocked on the door. I didn't know what you'd say so—oh, Lord, I can't fail her, Donovan! Peggy needs me."

"So we'll ride there together. You've no horse after all."

"Yes I do! Look!" Corisande couldn't believe her good fortune as Pete suddenly wandered into the wide arc of light cast by the lantern, the gelding looking none the worse for the night's events. "There's Pete now, Donovan, so everything's fine. You don't have to trouble yourself—"

"Are you mad, woman?"

He yelled so loud that she jumped.

Donovan stood glaring at her. "You were just attacked by some bloody stranger wearing a hood, no idea who the wretch might be—nearly throttled, mind you,—and I'm to let you travel on by yourself as if nothing happened?"

She gulped, venturing the smallest nod, which was greeted by a scowl so deep that her heart sank.

"I haven't gone through this much trouble, Lady Donovan, to lose you now. Oh, no, one temporary bride is quite enough, thank you. I'll not be taking another, and that I bloody well swear."

His vehement words had stabbed her more painfully than she could have imagined. Corisande lifted her chin, knowing full well what he was going to say next. So well, in fact, that she beat him by saying, "You're coming with me, then."

"Exactly. I'm going to follow you like a shadow, woman, closer than a shadow, until this whole inheritance business is done. Crashing pilchard barrels, someone following you

home, someone attacking you out here on the heath and
nearly strangling the life from you—oh, yes. I'm not going
to let you out of my sight."

But what would he do after he'd gotten his inheritance?
Corisande was tempted to ask him. What would happen to
her then when he wasn't around to accompany her? But she
held her tongue, knowing he probably wouldn't think twice
about her welfare once he was on his way back to Spain,
which hurt even more. So much so that she refused to think
about it further, wondering instead how she was going to get
rid of him.

She knew he'd meant his words; she'd heard that impos-
ing tone before. But she wasn't giving up, not yet. Resigned
at least for the moment, she nodded, saying softly, "Actually
I'd be grateful for your company. But you don't have to stay
the whole night. It might not be pleasant—to hear the child-
birth, I mean, the screams, the pain. Peggy has never had a
very easy time of it—"

"*That* I'll decide."

As he went to fetch her horse, Corisande realized she'd
more than meant she was glad she wouldn't be alone, the
darkness all around them suddenly become a threat. Yet
what was she going to do? If Oliver was back from France,
he was the one who needed her help tonight, not Peggy
Robberts. Silently she accepted Donovan's assistance as he
gave her a leg up onto Pete's back, the horse pawing at the
ground.

"Here, Corie, take the lantern."

Corisande reached out to oblige him, but the gelding
pranced sideways, whinnying shrilly.

"I think you'd better hold it," she said as she drew hard
on the reins and sought to soothe the horse. "Poor Pete was
nearly struck three times by that lantern, at least until I fell
off . . ." She didn't go on as Donovan's handsome face was
once more transformed by a deep scowl. Instead she

changed the subject altogether as he hung the lantern on his saddle and mounted, asking lightly, "What had you wanted to speak to me about tonight, Donovan? I'm sorry that I had to deceive—"

"You didn't *have* to deceive me, woman." His voice was harsh, although he seemed to make an effort to relax his tone as he brought Samson alongside her and Pete. "You could have told me the truth, Corie, and spared yourself, spared me—" He abruptly went silent only to meet her eyes, his expression grown serious. "I came to ask you for a truce. It's been a difficult week—"

"Only because you made it so difficult," she interrupted, eager for Oliver's sake to be on their way, yet wanting to hear what Donovan had to say, his sudden candor astonishing her. "You haven't been the most agreeable company, churlish, ill-mannered, I could go on and on."

"I know, and it's been wrong of me. I owe you a very great debt after all. I'm sorry if I've made you miserable."

"You haven't made me miserable," she lied, realizing that that was exactly how she'd felt and for reasons she had no wish to contemplate. "Just made me look a complete fool in front of the servants, is all, chattering to myself at supper each night like a dotty parrot while you've merely sat there—"

"Yes, you have been talking quite a bit lately."

Astonished even more to see a hint of a smile on his lips, Corisande flushed with warmth. "I don't see anything amusing here. And as for you owing me a debt, I imagine that's exactly what got you into so much trouble in the first place and why you're apologizing to me, too, implying you intend to act more the civil gentleman. My goodness, the lengths to which you're having to go to save your bloody neck!"

"What are you talking about? What trouble?"

"Your gambling debts, of course! That's all you've talked about since I've known you—how much you need the money. Well, unless it's a very grand lifestyle you crave back in Spain, my lord husband, I'd say you've probably wagered yourself into quite a deep hole with your fellow officers—"

"Good God, woman, is that what you think has brought me to Cornwall? Gambling debts?"

Corisande gaped at him. His voice had almost gone hoarse with incredulity. But before she had a chance to reply, he looked away from her, shaking his head and muttering to himself.

"Of course that's bloody well what you think. Why would it be otherwise? You don't know a thing about me."

"What was that, Donovan?"

"I said you don't know a damned thing about me!"

"N-no. No, I don't," she stammered, struck by the wildness in his eyes as he'd turned back to face her. "Not much anyway. But it's not as if it really matters—given the circumstances, I mean. You said it yourself, Donovan, well, that soon this will all be over, and then we'll be free of each other's company forever. Remember?"

He was silent for so long that she began to think he had no intention of replying, but finally he murmured half under his breath and with a wryness that surprised her, "So now I'm a Don Juan with gambling debts. Amazing. Bloody amazing."

She didn't know quite what to make of it, either, when he began to chuckle, and she shifted uncomfortably on her horse.

"Donovan, I think we should go. Peggy—"

"By all means, wife, lead the way! The poor woman needs your help! Lead on, lead on!"

Corisande did lead the way, setting off at a gallop almost gratefully as Donovan's chuckling became rich, full-throated laughter that incredibly enough made her feel like chuckling too. But she didn't know why she should be laughing.

He *was* a Don Juan with gambling debts, or at least he hadn't denied that's why he needed the money.

So why was *he* laughing?

☙ Twenty-two ❧

Donovan was still chuckling when they arrived at the tiny cottage a few moments later, the ride requiring even less time than Corisande had expected. But she wasn't smiling, her heart battering at her breast as she quickly dismounted and ran to the front of the cottage, turning back with a small gasp to call to Donovan, "Give me one moment, will you? I don't want to startle poor Peggy with both of us beating down her door."

She spun as he gallantly bowed his head to her, thanking the heavens for whatever strange mood had come over him to make him so biddable. She knocked twice but didn't wait for a reply as she heard someone shuffling to the door, instead rushing inside the darkened two-room cottage so suddenly that she nearly knocked over poor Morton Robberts. His mouth hanging open, the russet-haired, freckle-faced tinner stared blearily at her as if he'd just stumbled into some bizarre dream.

"Don't look so startled, Morton, it's only me, Corie East—Corie Trent. And don't ask me any questions, I've no time! I need an enormous favor from you, from both you and Peggy—"

"Who is it, Morton?" called a sleepy voice from the pitch-dark adjoining room. At once Corisande grabbed a candle stub from the rough-hewn table and lit it upon the open hearth, then cupped the flame and hurried into the back where a very pregnant young woman no older than herself was already struggling to sit up in bed.

"It's Corie, Peggy, but I can't tell you much more right now than that I need a favor from you and quickly!"

"Corie?"

"Yes, yes—here, let me plump that pillow for you." Corisande fixed the candle to the windowsill, her voice softly pleading as she did her best to make the woman comfortable. "Don't excite yourself, Peggy, there's nothing wrong. Only my husband's waiting outside—"

"Lord Donovan's outside?"

"Yes, because I told him you were having your babe tonight, and that I had to come and help."

"But I'm not—"

"I know, Peggy, I know, but I can't explain everything now. I need you to moan, good and loud, too, just how you might if the babe were coming. Could you do that for me? I'll tell you more when I can"—she spun to face Morton, who was looking at her now as if she were half-mad—"and, Morton, you must say yes to anything Lord Donovan asks of you, could you please, please do that for me? Oh, dear, I know this is terribly strange, but if I told you Oliver Trelawny's behind my coming here, would it help?"

At once Corisande saw understanding flood the young man's eyes. It was common yet closely guarded knowledge among the tinners that the burly sea captain was a friend and benefactor to them all. Greatly encouraged, she rushed on.

"Suppose my husband asks if you came and threw stones at my window tonight to let me know that the babe was on its way—"

"I'll say, ais, milord, so I did, a good handful too."

"And suppose he asks if the babe's coming tonight?"

"I'll say, ais, milord, far's I can tell 'tes true, but my dear Peggy's the fairer judge than me."

"Thank you, Morton. That's perfect. Perfect!"

Relief and gratitude spilling through her, Corisande took a moment to squeeze Peggy's hand, and then she raced for the door.

She wasn't surprised to find Donovan leaning just outside against the whitewashed wall. Hoping desperately that he hadn't overheard her speaking with the Robbertses, she beckoned for him to enter just as a terrible moan split the air, followed in quick succession by another. Donovan at once stopped in his tracks and looked at her doubtfully, glancing just as doubtfully inside the cottage as a third moan, this one even more pain-wracked than the last two, came spilling forth from the inner room.

"It's all right, Donovan, you can come in," she encouraged him, astonished that his swarthy face had seemed to pale. "Peggy and Morton were honored to hear you'd accompanied me—"

"No, no, I think I'll wait out here," he said, backing away as another moan shattered the stillness. "Go on, Corie. Do what you must."

"But it's going to be a long night, Donovan. Peggy's pains are just getting started." Corisande gestured to an uncomfortable-looking stool by the hearth. "You could sit there, or, well, are you sure you wouldn't rather come back for me in the morning? I fear it's bound to get worse, much worse. Peggy's always been a screamer, poor thing—"

"Oh God, enough."

He'd waved her to silence, but that didn't quiet the hoarse moan crescendoing into a keening wail that seemed to burst from the back room, punctuated now by the cries of two young children awakened in the loft. Corisande had no sooner glanced over her shoulder as Morton rushed up the narrow wooden ladder to comfort them than she looked back to find Donovan had disappeared.

"Donovan?"

She raced outside, trying not to show how relieved she felt that he was already mounting Samson, clearly anxious to be gone.

"I'll be back for you in the morning, Corie."

She nodded, struck again by how unsettled he looked when another of Peggy's convincing moans carried out into the night. Men. It was a good thing they weren't the ones made to bear children. They'd never withstand it.

"Don't dare cross the heath without me. Do you understand? Wait until I can come for you. And if you must step outside for any reason, make sure Morton Robberts is with you."

She nodded again, rushing forward when Donovan held out the lantern.

"Here. You might need the extra light."

"Oh, yes, I'm sure we will. Birthing can sometimes be quite a mess."

He swallowed hard at that comment and was gone, disappearing into the dark as Corisande rushed back inside the tiny cottage.

But she wasn't there long. She waited five minutes, no more, encouraging Peggy to give a last few groans and moans for good measure, then Corisande, too, was galloping out into the black night, doing her best to force back her fear that someone who meant her grave harm might yet be lurking as she turned her thoughts to Oliver Trelawny and the *Fair Betty*.

"Ais now, Corie, you've lectured me enough for one night. I know 'ee were worried, but I'm safe an' sound, 'ee can plainly see, an' I've the finest cargo of French brandy moving ashore that Cornwall has ever known! You'll soon see, too, that it was well worth it for me to wait those few days in Roscoff until I had the stuff aboard when the gold guineas start filling our pockets!"

"*And* the coffers for the poor, Captain Trelawny," Corisande reminded him with mock sternness, taking care to keep her voice down so it wouldn't carry across the deep cove to shore, although Oliver didn't seem concerned at all that he wasn't whispering. It was because the night was so dark, she knew, doubting herself that any king's excisemen would be straying about on such a bleak evening as Oliver threw a beefy arm around her shoulder.

"Ha! Those coffers will be filled to such overflowing 'ee won't know what to do with it all!" Laughing heartily, Oliver steered her to the cutter's starboard railing where his crew was hoisting eight-gallon kegs over the side into waiting rowboats. "Go on with 'ee now an' mind the landing, Corie, me brave girl! I want to be finished here in no more than an hour's time so I can sail home to my Rebecca."

Corisande hesitated at the rope ladder, wondering if she should mention to Oliver that someone had mimicked their signal to lure her into danger earlier that night, but he seemed so eager to be on his way to Porthleven harbor that she decided to wait. Instead she hauled her cloak and skirt between her legs and clambered expertly over the side and down the ladder, easing herself into a rowboat that she could see from the pyramid of kegs was quite full.

"No more, no more, we don't want to capsize," she warned the two dark-clad men who settled down at once to their oars. She signaled, and they pushed away from the sixteen-gun cutter, their small craft quickly replaced by others waiting to be loaded and then rowed to shore.

As the boat lumbered through the calm waves, Corisande peered at the black forbidding cliffs where she knew tinners armed with stout cudgels and muskets stood watch to give warning if strangers should approach by land or sea. In fact, everyone had been assembled and waiting at their places when she'd arrived at the secluded cove and saw that the *Fair Betty* had, indeed, made it back safely from Brittany.

Which had convinced her at once that the first lantern signal at ten o'clock had come from their own loyal men. But the second? Somehow her attacker had known she would leave the house upon seeing the signal, which meant, too, that he must know of her involvement in fair trading. So either there was an informer among them, God help any fool who betrayed their sacred trust, or somehow she and Oliver had been overheard at the inn . . .

Corisande's dark thoughts scattered as the rowboat came to a scraping halt upon the beach. She jumped out over the prow to keep her shoes well out of the water, having no wish to explain any suspicious salt stains to Donovan. Immediately a host of waiting hands unloaded the rowboat while Corisande hurried farther up the beach to where a line of thirty pack ponies waited patiently, two kegs apiece already strapped to their backs.

"Are you ready to go, John?" she whispered to the tall, lanky farmer standing near the lead pony.

She got a nod, no more, the man as reticent as a clam, which was a virtue in a smuggler.

"Head to Helston, then. Stanley Hawkins is waiting at the Golden Lion to take every last keg off your hands. We want top price for this load, though. Don't accept anything less, or we'll hear of it from Captain Trelawny. Godspeed."

And so it went, Corisande rushing about the beach as more heavily laden rowboats were hauled onto land, the precious kegs first counted and then either strapped onto ponies or carried up and out of the cove along winding stone-strewn paths to where carts and wagons waited to convey the contraband throughout the Cornish countryside. At least half of tonight's shipment would be sold outright to innkeepers like Stanley Hawkins or local gentry friendly to the trade, while the rest of the kegs would be hidden in caves, down deep wells, or stowed away in cellars and then dispatched later as time and opportunity allowed.

"Godspeed, Tobias. Take care with that load, now. Captain Trelawny says it's the finest brandy he's ever brought home from Roscoff. Top price, don't forget."

Then to another, "We'll be expecting to see you back from Falmouth by Thursday, Michael. Godspeed."

And still another: "Godspeed, Thomas. First, Squire Bellamy in Marazion, then on to Penzance and the White Horse Inn with the rest. Godspeed!"

Corisande was nearly exhausted by the time the last of the kegs had faded with their silent bearers into the night, her legs cramped from running back and forth across the sand and up and down the narrow cliff paths so many times that she'd lost count. But she hadn't lost count of the kegs, oh, no.

There were six hundred forty-two, and she never lost track of the thirty different directions in which she'd sent them and how many kegs with whom. Add to that two hundred pounds of Dutch East Indies tea and six bales of Brussels lace, and her head felt crammed with places, names, and numbers.

Usually now she would make her way to the church and then neatly record everything in a ledger she kept under one of the altar flagstones, partly so she wouldn't forget and partly to relieve her mind and enable her to sleep. Oliver had long since turned the *Fair Betty* for Porthleven, the cutter never lingering after the hold had been emptied, but heading back to the safety of the harbor. In fact, he'd left a few hours ago; it always took three times longer to dispatch goods than to unload the ship.

But tonight Corisande had no wish to head for Porthleven even though she could have asked some of the tinners just now drifting home from their lookouts to accompany her. Yet then they'd all have to walk—most of the tinners had come on foot to the cove—and the sky was already beginning to lighten to the east. By the time she finished with the account book it would be light, and she couldn't risk Donovan arriving at the Robbertses' to find her gone.

She would just have to risk riding back to the cottage alone, although the prospect was daunting as Corisande untethered Pete from a stunted tree and mounted. She took a cautious look around her, but it was still so dark she doubted she would see any hint of danger until it was too late. That thought made her kick Pete at once into a gallop, her thighs so sore that it was difficult to grip his sides. Yet she urged him to run even faster. Surely if she rode hard enough, no one would dare try to stand in her way to stop her—

"Oh, Lord."

Corisande's hands froze at the reins as she heard a second loud snort behind her, the sound only another horse would make. And she'd been the only one with a horse left at the cove, all the pack ponies and carts and wagons long gone. Oh, Lord. Oh, Lord.

She didn't glance behind her. She didn't breathe. Instead she kicked Pete into a full run and rode as hard and as fast as she ever had in her life, the gelding lunging powerfully beneath her.

Within moments, she'd made it to the Robbertses' tiny cottage, thinking it the most beautiful place imaginable as she slid from Pete's back and raced to the door. It was only then that she dared to glance behind her, her heart stopping at the distant dark shape on horseback cutting to the southwest and heading back as if to Porthleven.

God help her, why was she being followed? Who could wish her harm? If not Jack Pascoe as Donovan had said— and that snake of a mine captain made the most bloody sense of all!—then who?

Shaking with fear, Corisande ducked inside the cottage; she gasped to find the two small rooms lit brightly, a cheery fire crackling in the hearth, and candles glowing at windows shuttered against the night. And, as if he'd been waiting for her, Morton Robberts, with a shy grin on his face, sat at the table.

"The babe's come, Corie."

"The babe?" Incredulous, Corisande glanced from him to the adjoining bedroom where Peggy lay cradling a tiny swaddled bundle in the crook of her arm. "Oh, Morton, the babe?"

"Ais, indeed, our first little girl. I think my Peggy wants to name her Corie Olivia, too, after all the excitement 'ee an' your going to help Oliver Trelawny brought to our house. What do you think?"

Corisande was speechless, both elated and chagrined. She threw off her cloak and ran into the bedroom, her terrifying ride all but forgotten as she dropped to her knees beside the bed. "Ah, Peggy, is she all right? She's come too soon, hasn't she? Oh, Lord, I'm so sorry—"

"Hush now, Corie, everything's fine. She's only a few days early, and my Morton knew just what to do, no trouble at all, thanks to him watchen 'ee the last time with our Jimmie. Isn't that right, Morton?"

Corisande glanced over her shoulder, the young tinner's face split from ear to ear in a proud grin that nonetheless held a good bit of amazement at himself too.

"Ais, so I did, so I did. An' now you've something to show Lord Donovan when he comes to take you home, eh, Corie?"

Corisande could but shake her head, grinning from ear to ear, too, as Peggy invited her to sit upon the bed so she could welcome the newest Robberts.

❧ Twenty-three ❧

Corisande fluttered open her eyes as the thin wail of a babe started her awake.

For a confused moment, she stared at the rough hand-hewn timbers some four feet above her head, unsure of her whereabouts until another wail carried to her from below, the fretful cry of a newborn. At once the previous night's events came flooding back to her, but she didn't move. She was too sore. Instead she turned her head and smiled softly at the two young boys still sound asleep in the crude crib next to her mattress, Jimmie Robberts, all of one, his tiny thumb resting near his puckered mouth, and his three-year-old brother, Morton, who shared his father's name, freckles, and bright russet hair.

Such beautiful children, and now they had a new little sister too. Corie Olivia. Corisande still couldn't believe it. She never would have forgiven herself if anything terrible had happened, but fortunately all was well.

Except that her body felt stiff as a board, she groaned to herself, especially her legs. She wondered how she was ever going to get down out of the loft. She barely remembered climbing up here, she'd been so exhausted, and that couldn't have been more than a few hours ago. She'd fallen asleep almost at the moment her head had touched the straw-filled mattress, slumbering as soundly as if she'd been lying on the softest goose down. She could have slept longer too. Ah, well. Maybe if she closed her eyes . . .

"Ais, 'tes a fine, fine thing 'ee did for us, milord. I've been meaning to say something to you—I've seen 'ee nearly every day at the mine but I s'pose this is as good a time as any. I was one of the tinners 'ee spoke to that first morning 'ee came to Arundale's Kitchen with Mr. Gilbert. It was just after dawn, an' I'd hiked in t' work my core. Might you remember me?"

"Yes, I do. It was very brave of you to come forward when most of the other men held back. Very brave."

Corisande stiffened, her eyes flaring wide.

Donovan was here already? Then again, she had no idea what time it was—it could be almost noon for all she knew. And what was Morton saying to him about Arundale's Kitchen? She raised herself on her elbows to peep into the room below but she saw no one, realizing that the voices were carrying to her from a small chink in the wall just above her head.

"It wasn't bravery, milord, but fear for my dear Peggy and my children that made me speak out. We hardly had bread on the table as it was, an' then for Cap'en Pascoe to cut our wages, I didn't know what to do. I gave my food to Peggy for the babe—she was so sickly there for a time, I thought I might lose them both. 'Course Corie—forgive me, milord, Lady Donovan—tried to ease our way, bringing what she could to help us, God bless her, but it wasn't just us suffering but all the tinners and their families. Until 'ee came that morning, milord. I could tell just from talking with 'ee that things were going to get better."

"You've my wife to thank for that, Morton."

"Ais, milord, I know, but I was watching 'ee with Cap'en Pascoe. I saw 'ee talken to him alone before I went down the shaft an' I saw his face when he stormed away. He said nothing to any of us, but we knew, milord, we knew something grand had happened. He just disappeared with no word at all, an' we had no mine cap'en until Mr. Gilbert came back later and hired Jonathan Knill to the job. An' then when we heard our wages were doubled an' grain coming on Monday—"

"I said you've Lady Donovan to thank, man."

"Ais, maybe so, but I've you to thank, too, milord. You're a good, honorable man, Lord Donovan, I'll tell it to anyone who asks me, I will! An' when we heard 'ee were marrying our Corie Easton, all of us tinners couldn't have been more pleased that she'd found a man with compassion and charity enough to match her."

Compassion and charity enough to match her? Incredulous, Corisande was even more astonished as Morton's voice suddenly became choked with tears.

"I don't know how to thank 'ee, milord. I've a sweet new babe inside the house, a little girl, an' my Peggy—God help me, for a time I feared she wouldn't have the strength to push the child from her body or live herself to see that day . . ."

Corisande wiped at her eyes as Morton grew silent, knowing well the terrible anguish he must have suffered. She'd seen it throughout the entire parish, seen it on so many faces, seen the desperation in so many eyes, heard it in so many voices—until Lord Donovan Trent had come to Cornwall, yes, that couldn't be denied. That is, until she'd made her devil's agreement with him; it was pitiful to hear how poor Morton had been fooled. If the tinner only knew . . .

"Let's go see your new daughter, man, not stand out here." Donovan's deep voice carried into the loft, filled with emotion Corisande had never heard before. Except, wait . . . she had heard it before—in the stable after they had left the poorhouse that Sunday and Donovan had called her a shrew. She'd been railing at him about holding little Mary—

Corisande gasped as the cottage door swung open, and she fell back onto the mattress, pulling the woolen blanket up over her nose to lie there still as a stone. But a soft chortle made her look at the crib, little Morton Robberts plopping onto his back, too, and pulling his blanket over his head while Jimmie stared at her with a bemused smile and sucked his thumb. Noisily.

Oh, Lord.

She knew she was lost when young Morton began to laugh, sweet, husky laughter that made her smile in spite of herself, the little boy taking great delight in raising himself up only to fall back again, tugging the blanket over his head as he played his newfound game. Corisande couldn't help it. She sat up and then dropped back to the mattress, disappearing underneath the blanket for only an instant before she yanked the cover from her head and blurted out, "Boo!"

Little Morton shrieked, Jimmie giggled, and she laughed, too, leaving the mattress on all fours, albeit stiffly, to crawl to the crib. She couldn't stand up anyway—the thatched roof was too low—so she went right up to the wooden rungs, stalking the boys like a tiger while Jimmie's blue eyes grew round, and little Morton scrambled, squealing, to the far side of the crib.

"Having fun?"

Corisande froze, unable to see Donovan for the hair covering her flushed face. "Yes, actually, I am," she said with less embarrassment than she might have imagined, although she did feel a mite ridiculous being caught crawling about on her hands and knees. She tossed back her head to get the hair out of her eyes, her gaze meeting Donovan's.

He was smiling at her from the ladder, a warm, easy smile that made her heart jump. She hadn't seen him smile in so long—which immediately made her suspicious. But then again, it made sense, considering last night he had said he wanted a truce, even apologizing to her, and of course she knew why he'd done that. God forbid that he threaten his inheritance . . .

"I was just coming in to see the Robbertses' new babe. A girl, Morton told me."

"Yes, she's beautiful." Corisande held on to the crib as she rose into a hunched position, careful lest she knock her head on the low timber beams. At once little Morton held out his arms to her, demanding, "Out! Out!"

"Here, give him to me."

Corisande obliged, wincing at the soreness of her body as she picked up the little boy and handed him to Donovan, who then disappeared down the ladder. She followed suit with Jimmie, glad that Donovan reappeared to take this child too. Then it was her turn, her legs so wooden that she feared she might fall as she swung out onto the ladder until she felt Donovan's strong hands encircle her waist to lift her down. Her face burning, she said nothing, relieved when her feet touched the packed dirt floor and he released her.

"Th-thank you. I'm rather stiff this morning—"

"I'm not surprised," he broke in, the smile still upon his face although now it didn't quite reach his dark eyes. "After your being thrown from a horse, of course. And helping a babe into the world can be no easy thing."

Corisande didn't reply, suddenly feeling quite uncomfortable as her gaze shifted to where Morton already sat beside his wife, their two young sons clamoring to see their new sister. Morton and Peggy looked uncomfortable, too, the deception behind last night obviously at that moment lying heavily upon them—which made Corisande decide that she and Donovan would not be staying long. Leading the way into the little bedroom, she quickly stepped aside so Donovan could approach the bed.

"She is beautiful," he murmured when Peggy held the

mewling child out to him and he settled the babe into the crook of his arm.

Again Corisande was struck as she had been days ago at the poorhouse by the incongruous sight: as big and powerful-looking a man as Donovan Trent holding a tiny infant who had begun to cry piteously from almost the moment she left her mother's arms. But instead of becoming nonplussed, he began to jounce the baby gently, a tender smile appearing on his handsome face that tugged like a pain at Corisande's heart, making her wonder how things might be if Donovan were more like the man he appeared, right now, to be . . .

"Have you named her yet?"

"Corie Olivia, milord." Morton coughed to clear his throat. "After Lady Donovan, of course, for coming to help us an' . . . an' after my wife's mother."

Donovan nodded and handed the baby back to Peggy without saying more.

Corisande grew nervous at the awkward silence that had suddenly settled over the room but for the two little boys playing on the floor. "I—I think we should go. But if you need anything, Peggy, anything at all, you've only to send Morton to let me know."

"That I will, Corie, an' thank 'ee again."

Corisande scarcely heard her; she'd already left the bedroom and gone to grab her cloak from a peg near the hearth. But she didn't bother to put it on as the bright sunlight streaming inside the front door told her the day was warm. She ducked outside gratefully—for heaven's sake, what had come over her in there?—Donovan following hard on her heels.

"Funny, you don't seem very stiff anymore, wife. Helping with Corie Olivia must not have been so difficult for you after all."

Donovan wasn't surprised that Corisande had spun to

gape at him, his sarcastic tone hardly what he had intended. But he was angry, dammit, furious. He had told himself a hundred times while coming to fetch her that he would be able to contend with the ruse, the lies. That what Corisande had done last night was her own business! But now he felt like grabbing her and shaking her hard.

He'd already come close when he'd seen the trouble she was having on the ladder. Good God, he'd be sore, too, if he'd done half of what he had seen her accomplish on that beach. Corisande had probably given no heed to the danger she faced if any customs officers had been on the prowl. Probably given little thought, either, to the brutal attack only an hour before, when she should have been indoors and safe. And that was the whole bloody problem! When was the damned woman going to think of herself before putting everyone else first?

"I'll get the horses."

He brushed past her, knowing she was staring after him and no doubt wondering what had brought on his latest foul mood. But let her think what she would. Hell and damnation, what could be worse than what she thought of him already? A heartless cad, a despoiler of innocent women, a gambler, a murderer? Which made it all the more ridiculous that he should be so concerned about her, but he was, God help him, he was. More than he could have ever thought possible.

"Bloody fool," Donovan muttered to himself as he untethered Samson and then went to Pete, who nudged him with a velvety nose. He'd found the animal still saddled and grazing free some hundred yards away; Corisande obviously had been so frightened after she'd been followed back to the cottage that she hadn't thought to see to the horse.

But Donovan had wanted to frighten her, so badly that she wouldn't dare set foot outside again until he came for her. He'd almost believed her clever story about the Robbertses, probably would have, too, if he hadn't overheard everything from outside the door. Chasing her from that cove was the least she deserved for lying to him, although the babe coming after all had been a surprise. But when he'd set out after Corisande last night, no idea where she was bound, only to discover incredibly that she was involved in smuggling—

"I can manage from here, thank you very much!"

As she snatched Pete's reins from his hand, Donovan watched grimly as Corisande hoisted herself onto the big gelding, grimacing in discomfort.

"I could have helped you, Corie."

"I don't need your help," she snapped as she veered the horse around, "and as for your sarcasm, my lord, though I've no idea what you were implying, it's clear that the truce you spoke of last night was very short-lived. I'll see you back at the house."

She kicked Pete into a gallop and was gone, leaving Donovan to mount Samson with a low curse and ride after her. But he didn't have to push his stallion very hard; Corisande had slowed Pete to a walk within moments, which didn't surprise him, given how she'd winced in pain just in mounting. He caught up with her easily, but she didn't look at him, lifting her chin and keeping her face forward as if he weren't even there.

"I wasn't implying anything, Corie. I'm sorry," he said, having no intention of revealing that he knew about her smuggling. Why upset her further? He would only be a part of her life for a very short time longer, and he'd do bloody well to remember that fact. "And the truce—"

"The devil take your truce, Donovan! Act however you wish, pleasant, unpleasant, it makes no difference to me. If you're worried about your money, don't be. I'm not going to threaten our agreement just because you're absolutely the most insufferable man I've ever known."

"Ah, I'm insufferable now? Well, at least you didn't say loathsome. I never liked being called loathsome."

✑ Twenty-four ✑

Corisande glanced at Donovan, astonished at the wry smile on his face. Lord, she would never understand the man! One moment sarcastic, the next apologizing, the next making jokes and smiling. But she didn't want to understand him. She wished she wasn't riding with him either. If she wasn't so bloody sore, she could have made it to the house without having to say another word . . .

"Corie Olivia Robberts. You must be honored."

"I am," she said stiffly, facing front again.

"At least it's something interesting to write about—to your friend Lindsay, I mean. A letter came from her just as I was about to leave this morning—"

"A letter from Lindsay?" Corisande had drawn up sharply on the reins, coming to a halt as Donovan reined in Samson too. He reached into his dark blue riding coat and drew out the letter, a black brow raised as he handed it to her.

"Addressed to Lady Donovan Trent, no less. News travels fast."

"She . . . she must have seen the wedding announcement in the papers." Not liking that she was feeling quite uncomfortable again, Corisande clutched the thick packet in her hand. "And I'm sure Lady Somerset wasted little time in writing to her. The woman has a nose for what's happening in the parish nearly as keen as Rose Polkinghorne's."

"Yes, a letter came from Lady Somerset too. An invitation to dinner, actually, which I accepted. I'm surprised she gave us this long—unless, of course, you've other plans for tonight? Someone else with a pregnant wife coming to throw stones at your window?"

"No, no other plans," Corisande murmured, not liking the way Donovan was looking at her. Grateful that the Robbertses' baby had come—it would have been impossible to try to explain a false alarm to him—she glanced down at the letter, her fingers itching to break the rose-red seal. But she nudged Pete back into a walk instead, deciding it would be better to wait until she was alone. God knows what Lindsay had to say, considering she knew everything—

"Aren't you going to read it?"

Corisande started, flushing to the roots of her hair as Donovan caught up with her, Samson matching Pete's slow stride. "No, I think I'll wait—"

"Not on my account, I hope. I won't look, if that's what concerns you, Corie. There isn't anything new about London that Lindsay could tell me anyway. Go on, enjoy your letter."

She gulped, but her curiosity was overwhelming. Perhaps Lindsay had some more funny stories for her. She could use some levity right now. Anything to take her mind off the man who was dogging her like a shadow just as he'd promised last night.

If not for that reason, she might have suggested he ride on ahead, but that was as likely to happen as Napoleon to surrender. So she broke the seal and opened the letter, the sunshine so bright that she tilted the cream-colored paper to one side, away from Donovan, and began to read.

Oh, Corie, where to start? I received your incredible letter, and I could hardly believe it! To think you're married! And to a Trent of Arundale! Of course, I know you said it's only temporary, but I must tell you of the most startling things—

"How is she?"

Corisande started, looking up to find Donovan staring at her. "Who?"

"Lindsay, of course. She's well?"

"Yes, yes, but I haven't read very far," Corisande said with exasperation, clearly enough that Donovan waved her back to her letter, which irked her. She didn't need his permission! Taking care to grip the reins tightly enough so Pete wouldn't begin to wander aimlessly, she settled back with an irritated exhalation to her letter.

. . . but I must tell you of the most startling things. I had already written you a letter in answer to the one with your astounding news, but I was so busy—Aunt Winnie hasn't given me a moment's peace, she's so determined to follow Olympia's every last instruction to the letter, dragging me to dressmakers and out shopping and then in the evenings— oh, dear, Corie, I'm losing my train of thought. Anyway, I had no chance to mail my first letter, which was a very good thing. All I knew of Lord Donovan Trent was what you told me in your letter, and of course, since it was a secret, I couldn't ask anyone about the dratted man. At least I thought him dratted at the time. But back to the topic. The moment your wedding announcement appeared in the papers—truly, I've never heard such a stir! Everyone was talking about it, well, about your husband anyway. I went to a ball that very night, and the entire place was abuzz—

"Is Lindsay having a good time?"

Corisande must have jumped, for Pete suddenly pranced

to the side, nearly making her lose her seat. This time it was Donovan who caught the reins, and Corisande glared at him as he brought the gelding under control.

"I thought you wanted me to enjoy my letter!"

"I do—"

"Then please don't interrupt me, Donovan."

Especially not now, Corisande thought somewhat nervously as he shrugged his massive shoulders and looked away. Good Lord, if he knew the letter was about him . . . and where was her place anyway? Oh, yes.

. . . went to a ball that very night, and the entire place was abuzz. All the eligible young ladies and their mamas were terribly disappointed to hear that Lord Donovan had wed, and everyone, of course, was wondering about you, Corie, but that wasn't the most extraordinary thing. Somehow I came upon a conversation between some young gentlemen who knew Lord Donovan well and spoke of him quite fondly. They couldn't believe he'd wed either, because Lord Donovan had sworn years ago that he would never marry. It seems his parents had a terrible marriage, a dreadful arranged affair—Lord, they painted his father the Duke of Arundale as an absolute monster, and of course we already know that to be true from Arundale's Kitchen. His poor mother ran off with an Italian count, Corie, can you believe that?

Anyway, according to these gentlemen, it seems Lord Donovan had defied his father for years in so many ways, disgusted by the man—hating him even—and determined to be anything but like him. He was forever giving away his money to beggars, prostitutes, and countless charities though he would tell his father he'd lost it all to gambling just to get some more he could give away. That made the gentlemen laugh and laugh, Corie, because Lord Donovan had never once been known to gamble since his father had loved it so.

Corisande lifted her eyes from the letter, suddenly feeling quite unsettled as she glanced at Donovan. But he wasn't looking at her, the man leaving her alone just as she'd sharply bid him. Her heart beginning to pound, she focused once more on the page, feeling almost as if she didn't want to continue, but unable not to.

They went on and on, Corie, recalling how Lord Donovan's father had tried to force him into a marriage four years ago, but he'd left Britain to fight under Wellington. One of the men, Freddy, they called him, said Lord Donovan had tried to talk him out of marrying for money just before he left and how Freddy wished he'd listened, his life a bloody mess. They laughed, but it wasn't funny, Corie, all of them wondering what could have made Donovan finally take a bride. Another gentleman guessed it might have something to do with his inheritance, but they couldn't see Lord Donovan caring a whit about money—he never had before—which made them say then that maybe he had simply fallen in love.

"She's written quite a letter, hasn't she?"

"What?" Startled, Corisande met Donovan's eyes, her heart fairly thundering.

"The letter. It's long, several pages."

"Y-yes, it is long. It's Lindsay's first Season—it's all so new to her. Balls, shopping—"

"Hunting for the wealthiest gentleman she can find to marry. The loftiest title."

Corisande heard the sudden bitterness, something she might have missed before. But now . . . "No, you're wrong, Lindsay's not like that at all," she said vehemently. "Lindsay's different. She doesn't care about those things. That's why I admire her so much."

"I'm not surprised. Considering she's your dearest friend,

I mean. I doubt you'd have wasted your time with her if she was anything less than someone you could respect."

She heard a tinge of bitterness there, too, but Donovan had turned away again, and she quickly returned to Lindsay's letter. Yet it took her a moment to be able to focus on the page, her thoughts racing. Dear God, could she have been so wrong about him? Like a phantom voice, Donovan's words last night suddenly came back to ring loud and clear in her mind . . . *"You don't know a damned thing about me!"*

"Oh, Lord," she murmured under her breath, finding her place to reread Lindsay's hastily scrawled lines.

> *. . . but they couldn't see Lord Donovan caring a whit about money—he never had before—which made them say then that maybe he had simply fallen in love. Which is why I had to write a new letter to you, Corie! Lord Donovan doesn't sound anything like the horrible man you described in your letter, no, not at all! Self-centered? Caring about nothing but himself? It's as if we're talking about two different people. To me, Lord Donovan sounds more like the man you said you wanted to marry, remember? When we made our secret pact the day before I left for London? Someone who cares about helping people and righting wrongs? And you have married him! Oh, Corie, I've heard he's terribly handsome and brave and highly respected by his fellow officers, and his friends here wish him the best and you, too, even though they don't know you. But I know you better than you think I do, and I can just imagine the trouble you've been giving him with that temper of yours and all the while thinking the worst of him—*

"We're nearly home, Corie. Maybe you might want to finish reading later."

Corisande glanced up to see that, indeed, the huge Tudor

house was appearing through the trees. She had only another few paragraphs of Lindsay's letter to go, but maybe she had had enough for now. Her head was spinning, her thoughts in a whirl, and now something was plaguing her terribly, something she'd heard about only a short while ago . . .

"Donovan."

She had his attention, his eyes upon her, but suddenly she felt as if she had a huge lump in her throat. For heaven's sake, did she want to know or not? If she'd been struck by a blinding lightning bolt, she couldn't have been more stunned by everything Lindsay had told her. Did she really want to suffer another shock when deep down she already sensed his answer?

"I . . . well, I was wondering—"

"Careful, Corie, tighten up on the reins! Do you want your horse to walk headfirst into a tree?"

She gasped, so lost in her private quandary that she hadn't even noticed she'd let the reins slip in her hands and Pete was veering ominously close to the stately line of elms flanking the drive. Quickly regaining control, she pulled the gelding back closer to Samson, but she knew the moment was lost.

Suddenly she didn't want to hear Donovan tell her that, yes, he had gone very early to Arundale's Kitchen on the same morning they had made their agreement, where he'd spoken to young Morton Robberts among others and learned firsthand of the tinners' wretched plight.

She didn't want to hear that he had spoken to Jack Pascoe either, sensing Donovan had fired that bastard from the mine hours before he'd even met her and learned she would do almost anything to help the tinners and their families.

Anything. Even marry a man she despised.

Which led her to realize she hadn't needed to marry Lord

Donovan Trent to see life improved for the tinners, although he'd made her believe that that was so. But why?

He certainly hadn't married her for love—leave it to Lindsay to hear something like that and latch onto it, hoping for Corisande's sake that it might be true. She could just imagine that was what the rest of Lindsay's letter had to say. So she should write right back and tell her romantic friend that Donovan couldn't bloody wait to annul her and return to Spain! In fact, their sham marriage would probably be over in days, even hours. Surely a letter with that wonderful news would be coming anytime soon from His Grace, Nigel Trent, the Duke of Arundale.

"Corie?"

She turned her head as if snapping free of some dream, her eyes meeting Donovan's as he reached up to help her down from her horse. She hadn't even realized they had come to a stop in front of the house, and a liveried footman already hovered to take Pete and Samson back to the stable. But she barely saw the servant, her pulse pounding as she felt Donovan's hands slide around her waist; she felt his strength as he lifted her easily and drew her toward him to set her upon the ground, his expression intent as he searched her face.

"Was there something you wanted to ask me? I'm sorry if I startled you back by the trees, but I didn't want to add bruises to the stiffness you're feeling already."

Another apology. This one uttered so sincerely, she could almost feel herself believing that he might truly care about her welfare. Almost.

"It was nothing. I'm tired, Donovan. It was a long night, and I got little sleep. I'll hardly prove enlivening company at the Somersets' if I don't get some rest."

"Go ahead, then. We're not expected there until six—"

Corisande was gone before he'd finished, leaving him to stare after her as she went inside. And the first thing she did when she got to her room moments later was to crumple Lindsay's letter and throw it into the fire.

∽ Twenty-five ∽

"I can't believe I agreed to come here."

Corisande's hiss had been meant for Donovan's ears alone, but the stiffly dressed footman taking her cloak raised a brow. She shot a glare at him, and he turned away, leading the way to the Somersets' drawing room although she was loath to follow. Only Donovan's firm hand at her elbow made her move forward reluctantly.

"You see? Even the servants are haughty in this wretched place. I don't know how Lindsay withstood it. I never liked coming here."

"You sound as if you rarely visited."

"Ha! Lady Somerset never wanted me to. The last time was for Lindsay's twentieth birthday party, and oh my, Lady Somerset wasn't very happy to see me appear at her door. But we got her back, Lindsay and I."

"With the champagne?"

Corie nodded as she glanced at Donovan, warmed more than she wanted to be by his amused smile. Warmed to her toes, and it was so ridiculous too!

So she'd been wrong about why he didn't want to be married—and the man wasn't a Don Juan. So he wasn't a gambler, either, or anything at all like his late father. He'd still married her because he needed money—tricked her into becoming his temporary bride, no less!—and what about how surly he'd been to her?

She wished he would go back to being surly, too, instead of holding to his bloody truce. His amiability was just making everything worse. And she wished she'd never read that letter; the thoughts roiling through her mind had prevented her from getting any rest this afternoon.

"Ah, Lord Donovan, come in, come in!"

Corisande felt his hand tighten at her elbow as they entered the drawing room; she sensed he didn't like Olympia Somerset any more than she did, and yet he had accepted the invitation, she supposed because it was necessary that they appear socially as husband and wife. And to turn down the premier hostess of the parish? Heaven forbid.

She'd told Donovan in the carriage that Lady Somerset had only asked them to dinner because of who he was. It didn't have anything to do with her. And here was perfect proof. Corisande might have been invisible for all the notice Olympia gave her, the woman one huge rustling mountain of green silk as she rushed forward, her eyes wholly on Donovan.

"I'm so honored, Lord Donovan—Oh, Randolph dear! Bring our guest a brandy, will you?"

Corisande winced for Lindsay's father as he turned away from coming to greet them with a near-inaudible sigh; if there was ever a man who should annul his wife straightaway, it was Sir Randolph Somerset. But she doubted after eight years with such a hideously domineering woman he had the will to speak up, let alone to be rid of her.

"Excuse me, Donovan, will you? Lady Somerset."

Corisande was spared hardly a glance from her hostess as she crossed the room to Sir Randolph. At once a kindly smile split the man's face when he saw her coming, making him look much less browbeaten and weary, his grayish-blue eyes filled with warmth.

"Ah, Corie, you're lovely as a picture in that yellow dress.

I've been wondering how you were doing. With Lindsay gone these past two weeks, I feel as if I've lost you as well."

"I'm fine, Sir Randolph, truly," she murmured, noting how the crystal decanter was shaking as he tried to pour brandy into a glass. "If you'd like, I could help . . ."

"No, no, I have it. Drank too much of the stuff today, I fear, but"—he glanced toward his wife, lowering his voice— "not a word to Olympia now, Corie, are we agreed? A man has to have some pleasure—"

"Randolph!"

Corisande winced again as the decanter hit the glass with a ring and Sir Randolph cursed under his breath.

"Good heavens, man, what could be taking you so long? I said a brandy for our guest—oh, dear, you must forgive him, Lord Donovan. Welles, our butler, is seeing to the dinner—"

"It's no matter," Donovan said tersely, doing his utmost to remain civil. But it was becoming quite difficult, especially when Lady Somerset leaned toward him conspiratorially, the woman's massive breasts brushing against his coat as she clucked her tongue in sympathy.

"Such a trying week you must have had since your wedding, my lord. A new bride, and one so . . . well, how shall I put it? One so *unaccustomed* to the way of things. That's why I withheld my invitation until now. So Corisande might adjust, of course."

"Adjust, madam?" Having a good idea as to exactly what the woman was implying, Donovan took a step backward only to have Lady Somerset draw closer, her voice dropped almost to a whisper.

"Oh, yes, indeed. She must have had a terrible shock, poor dear, but surely by now she's cast aside any romantic illusions and come to understand that many members of our class must marry to secure their family's lineage or fortune. I truly feel for you, my lord. To be hastened into a marriage

—having to choose a bride so quickly. It's a pity, truly, that my husband's daughter, Lindsay, wasn't here. She's quite aware of her responsibilities, oh, yes, indeed, I saw to her education on that score myself. I'm sure you would have had a much easier time—"

"I already have a wife, Lady Somerset, and so far I'm quite content, thank you," Donovan cut in, thinking with regret that Corisande had been right about gossip flying through the parish. He wanted to say more—hell and damnation, having her discussed so callously by this woman was infuriating!—but here Sir Randolph came with his brandy . . .

"Sorry about that, old man. Damned glass cracked, had to fill another."

Donovan gave an unconcerned shrug, tempted to tell the poor bastard that he would have cracked a glass, too, if he had someone of Olympia Somerset's ilk bellowing at him across a room. He took a drink, his gaze meeting Corisande's. She looked entirely reluctant to join them, miserable even as she stood all alone near the fireplace, and he didn't blame her. Dammit, he should never have brought her here, with Lady Somerset rudely snubbing her from the moment they'd walked in the door. There had to be something he could do to make her feel better.

"I hope the brandy is to your liking, my lord. Oh, splendid, here's Welles now. Shall we adjourn to dinner?"

"Actually, madam, the brandy tastes a bit off to me."

Donovan heard a horrified gasp, which was exactly what he had hoped. Lady Somerset looked quite stricken as she glanced at his glass. "*Off*, my lord?"

"Yes, not quite what I'm accustomed to." He set the glass down with a decided thunk of distaste, pleased to see, too, the astonished look on Corisande's face. "It's dreadful, really, but don't trouble yourself. The barrel could have been bad."

"Bad—oh, my, no, surely not. Welles? Didn't you procure the brandy just this morning? You told me the fellow said it was the very best!"

"Yes, my lady, so he did, so he did," the red-faced butler, as round and squat as a barrel himself, hastened to assure her while Corisande chewed her lower lip, wondering if the brandy might have been from Oliver Trelawny's shipment last night. Oh, Lord, she hoped not . . .

"I thought it tasted fine," Sir Randolph said to no one in particular. Lady Somerset turned round to glare at him.

"Then it couldn't have been fine because you're certainly no connoisseur!"

"I said it was no matter." Donovan's bored voice rose above the storm while Corisande looked at him in amazement, never having heard him use such a snooty, aristocratic tone. "Didn't you say something about dinner, madam?"

Lady Somerset spun to face him, her double chin bouncing. "Why, yes, yes, I believe everything is ready. Welles?"

"Ready, my lady, yes, everything's ready," the butler assured her, rushing forward to lead the way.

"Splendid, then, I'm famished," Donovan announced. "If I may escort you, madam, to the dining room? Sir Randolph, I'll entrust my wife to you."

Corisande had never seen Lady Somerset so flustered as the woman took Donovan's arm and left the room with him, never seen Lady Somerset nonplussed ever before for that matter, and she was immensely enjoying the spectacle. It seemed Sir Randolph was enjoying himself, too, a bemused grin on his face as he offered Corisande his arm. But she waved for him to wait a moment while she went to the small table where Donovan had left his brandy, glancing over her shoulder to make sure he and Olympia weren't waiting for them in the entry hall before she lifted the glass and took a healthy sip.

"Well? Is it off?"

Relief poured through Corisande as the brandy snaked a warm, silken path down her throat, but to Sir Randolph she gave a noncommittal shrug. In truth, she was no connoisseur either, yet it certainly tasted better than any spirits she'd tried before.

"I suppose my husband would know," she said lamely, hoping Sir Randolph wouldn't feel too offended. But he didn't look offended; instead, he seemed quite eager to make their way to the dining room as he again offered his arm. Corisande was eager, too, giddy excitement rushing through her as she wondered what Donovan could possibly be up to. Dear Lord, it was almost as if he were baiting Lady Somerset on purpose.

"Yes, a quaint little place you have, Lady Somerset, indeed. Cornwall never ceases to astonish me."

A quaint little place? Corisande would never have called the Somerset residence quaint. Why, it was nearly as large as Donovan's home, and certainly more ancient. Surely he could see that, too, she thought as she accompanied Sir Randolph into the dining room to find Donovan studying the paintings adorning the walls as if he were in some museum, while Lady Somerset seemed to be hanging in agitation upon his every word.

"Hmmm."

Hmmm? Was that all the man planned to say? About a large painting by an Italian master of fat cherubs making music, Lady Somerset's pride and joy? It appeared so as Donovan took his seat at the silver-laden table. Lady Somerset's face was beet-red as she swatted away the assistance of a footman and signaled for Welles to begin the meal.

Donovan at once sent back his turtle soup, saying it wasn't quite hot enough.

Then, to Corisande's complete astonishment, he sent it back again, saying it had scalded his tongue.

She began to giggle into her linen napkin; she couldn't

help it, but Donovan's raised eyebrow finally made her stop. But he hadn't looked stern, no, not at all. She would swear he was smiling behind his napkin, too, and so was Sir Randolph. At least until he tried to send away his soup, saying he'd never liked turtle, and Lady Somerset in an exasperated huff sent all the bowls away, demanding that the first course should start at once.

Donovan made no complaints about the wide array of dishes appearing at the table—Lady Somerset clearly had gone out of her way to impress him—no, not complaining through the first course or the second. They chatted pleasantly about the weather and the fine choice of wines, nothing controversial at all. But as the third course began, he waved his hand and pushed away from the table.

Lady Somerset's jaw dropped in dismay.

"But—but, my lord, there is the best yet to come. Almond custard and potted pheasant with imported figs and apple tart, my cook's specialties—"

"I am one man, madam, not twenty. Perhaps if you've so much food yet remaining, you might send it to the parish poorhouse. I'm sure Mrs. Eliza Treweake would be very happy, indeed, to offer such delicious fare to her charges."

"Yes, Olympia, I think that's a damned marvelous idea," Sir Randolph spoke up, clearly emboldened by Donovan's example. "You really had the cook make too—"

"Oh, be still, Randolph!" So irritated now that she didn't seem to care how she might appear to Donovan, Lady Somerset turned upon Corisande. "Obviously you've been filling your new husband's head with the same ridiculous notions you foisted upon our Lindsay! Well, I'll have none of it, my girl, not in this house."

"Are you asking us, then, madam, to take leave of your kind hospitality?"

Corisande's gaze jumped to Donovan, whose voice was so forbidding that she began to feel nervous. Suddenly the situation wasn't so humorous anymore, although Lady Somerset at once appeared to back down.

"Of—of course not, Lord Donovan, pray forgive me. Perhaps I did have my cook prepare a bit too much food—yes, I can see that now."

Lady Somerset *didn't* say, however, as she signaled for the footmen to clear the table, that she planned to send the remainder to the poorhouse, which didn't surprise Corisande. Nor was she surprised that Donovan had suggested such a thing, although even that morning she would have been dumbstruck.

But that he would treat Lady Somerset in so arrogant a manner, yes, that had surprised her. Delighted her, too, and she smiled at him across the white-clothed table. It had been so wonderful to see Olympia Somerset undone. Lindsay would never believe it . . .

"Welles, serve port to the gentlemen while Lady Donovan and I retire to the drawing room."

"I think not, madam," Donovan said firmly, as warmed from the smile Corisande had just gifted him as the wine served at dinner. He rose from his chair, having no intention of letting her go anywhere alone with their hostess, not when he'd done his utmost to cheer her. "No insult to you, of course, Sir Randolph, but it grows late. I think Corie and I must bid you good night."

"No insult taken, old man."

Hearing the telling slur in Sir Randolph's voice, whose eyes had grown puffy and bleary from too much drinking, Donovan felt great pity for his host. He had taken a liking to Sir Randolph from the moment he'd seen how warmly the man had welcomed Corisande; now, as Lady Somerset threw her husband a withering glance, Donovan couldn't help wondering what had ever made him marry such a witch.

"Are you sure we can't persuade you to stay longer, my

lord? We could all retire to the drawing room, if you prefer—"

"Let them be, Olympia, for God's sake," Sir Randolph
broke in to everyone's surprise and, apparently, his own. He
cast a halfway apologetic look at his outraged wife and then
got up shakily, a footman rushing forward to steady him as
he waved a hand to the door. "Come, I'll walk with you."

Corisande didn't wait for Donovan but left the table and
hurried to offer her arm to Sir Randolph, who leaned upon
her heavily as they left the dining room. Donovan was right
behind them. Lady Somerset made no effort to follow, obviously too incensed to move.

Which was perfectly fine with Corisande. If she never saw
the woman again in her lifetime, it would be too soon, but
she didn't feel the same at all about Lindsay's father. Especially when he turned to her as the footman shadowing
them went round to open the front door.

"Have you heard from my daughter, Corie?"

"Yes, yes, I have," she murmured, struck by the sadness
in Sir Randolph's eyes. "Lindsay's fine, having a lovely time.
I'm sure you'll get a letter, too, very soon. I know she must
miss you terribly."

"Ah, if she doesn't write, it would be no unexpected
thing. The life she had here was not a happy one . . . well,
after her mother died. I don't think she's ever forgiven me
for bringing Olympia into this house." Then abruptly he
shrugged and smiled wanly. "Don't mind me. Go on, go on.
A good night to you both. You certainly made it one for
me."

Corisande gave him a kiss on the cheek. The man reeked
so miserably of wine and spirits that she was grateful when
Donovan whisked her cloak around her shoulders and led
her outside. But she didn't readily accept his hand up into
the waiting carriage, looking back as the front door closed
behind them.

"I can't believe he said that about Lindsay—that she's never forgiven him. Lindsay loves him dearly. She endured Lady Somerset all these years because of him! I've never heard her say one ill word about her father."

"That doesn't mean such a hurt isn't there. Even close friends can't know everything about each other, Corie. Do you think Lindsay knows everything about you?"

She didn't answer; she couldn't, her throat suddenly grown so tight as she stared at Donovan that she was unable to breathe. That he could have voiced, however indirectly, the very thing . . .

"Hell and damnation, woman, it was only a simple question! Don't look so glum. I would have thought you'd be smiling with delight as we drove away. Ah, well, all that wonderful arrogance for nothing."

∞ *Twenty-six* ∞

Corisande gaped at him, stunned. "So it *was* on purpose —oh!"

Donovan had scooped her up and deposited her inside the carriage so abruptly that she had to fight to catch her breath, her stomach flipflopping in her throat.

"Shh, Corie, do you want the old termagant to hear us?" he demanded as he climbed in beside her and rapped on the roof. The carriage at once rolled into motion as Will Brighton snapped his whip over the two matched bays' heads. "At least now she isn't quite sure *what* happened. Let her wonder."

"But why . . . ?" Corisande didn't finish the question as suddenly she and Donovan were cast into heavy shadow when the lights of Somerset Place faded away, the carriage lanterns providing only a dim glow. She felt him shrug, the two of them sitting so close together that his arm rubbed against hers.

"The woman was irritating. And rude. Treating her husband like a lapdog. Intolerable to watch."

"Oh."

Corisande didn't know why she felt so disappointed as a weighty silence fell between them—for heaven's sake, what had she expected? That Donovan would say he'd done it all for her? He might be more of a gentleman than she'd ever imagined, but she didn't need him to stand up for her, no, not at all, nor did she want his protection—

"Of course, she wasn't very kind to you either. That was damned intolerable too."

Her stomach suddenly turning upside down, Corisande glanced at Donovan to see that he was staring at her in the dark, and she quickly looked away. "I—I grew used to Lady Somerset's rudeness a long time ago—"

"Well, there's no excuse for it. We were invited guests in her home, but she ignored you from the very start."

"That shouldn't have surprised you. I told you her invitation had absolutely nothing to do with me. But you're the son of a duke—"

"Yes, dammit to hell, so I am, and most of the time it's brought me nothing but trouble." He gave a dry laugh that to Corisande held bitterness too. "Except tonight, of course. Rank does sometimes have its benefits. Did you see her face when I sent away the turtle soup?"

Corisande began to chuckle, shaking her head. "Oh, she was aghast, she really was. And her beloved painting, Donovan. I'm sure she expected glowing compliments, but you sat down at the table with hardly a grunt."

"A grunt? I don't grunt, wife. I said 'hmmm.' "

"Well, it might as well have been a grunt. I've never seen anyone's face so red. That was Sir Randolph's wedding gift to her, you know. She wanted that painting desperately, so Lindsay told me, and Sir Randolph bought it for her at an auction."

"He should have sold Lady Somerset at that auction instead," Donovan said bluntly, chuckling now too. "For a shilling."

"No, I think a pence. Definitely a pence." Corisande laughed at the thought, imagining Olympia Somerset surrounded by a roomful of silent, horrified bidders. But she really began to laugh when, to her surprise, Donovan suddenly raised his voice to a high-pitched falsetto, intoning, "Oh, Randolph dear!"

It was so ridiculous, hearing him mimic Lady Somerset, and she didn't think she'd ever giggled so hard. When she was able to calm herself she had to try it, too, but this time she added with a haughty ring, "Bring our guest a brandy, will you?"

"Oh, yes, that was much better than mine."

"No, no, yours was better."

"Really? Good God, that woman had a vicious flair for ordering her husband about, didn't she?" Donovan's laughter had abruptly died down, and so did Corisande's as he added almost under his breath, "Poor fool. Another marriage made in hell."

As silence reigned once more except for the carriage's rumbling and creaking, Corisande turned her head to find Donovan wasn't looking at her any longer but staring out the window into the black night, his body gone tense beside her. So tense that she couldn't help but think of Lindsay's letter and of last week, too, when Donovan had said unhappy marriages were far more common among those of his station. Something inside her suddenly wanted to know more, much more.

"You . . . well, you make it sound as if all marriages are miserable."

"From what I've seen, most of them are. Bloody miserable."

"My parents' marriage wasn't miserable. They loved each other dearly."

"Then they were lucky. My parents hated each other. Of course, my father deserved to be hated. You were more right about him than you could ever know. He was a bastard through and through. Everything to him was money. He married for money, made my brother, Nigel, marry for

money, ruined people's lives for money—just look at
Arundale's Kitchen. And he played with money."

"Gambling?"

She knew Donovan's eyes were full upon her now, and
she swallowed hard.

"Yes, gambling. But never enough to threaten his
dukedom. That's why he squeezed every last shilling out of
his business ventures. My mother couldn't stand it, the dev-
astation the man wrought for years without blinking an eye.
She finally left him when a woman who worked at one of my
father's cotton mills came to Arundale Hall to tell him that
her three children had all starved to death that past winter
for want of food. Do you know what my father did, Corie?"

She shook her head, dread filling her.

"He hit her across the face when she refused to be silent,
knocking the poor woman down the steps. She struck her
head at the bottom and died. My mother never spoke a
word to him again."

Corisande didn't know what to say, the bitterness so thick
in the air she could almost taste it. And she supposed some
of it was aimed straight at her. Yet if Donovan was no
gambler, why hadn't he just said so? He'd never denied
anything of which she had accused him—but then again,
why should he? He probably didn't care at all what she
thought of him—which hurt . . . more than she could have
ever imagined.

"So your parents were happy?"

Astonished at how quiet Donovan's voice had become
after the horror of what he'd just told her, Corisande nodded. "Yes, they were. Very much."

"What happened? To your mother, I mean."

"A fever struck the parish, and many died. My mother,
Lindsay's mother—"

"Lindsay's mother too?"

"Yes. We'd known each other before, but I think that's

what drew us close. Her losing her mother, me losing mine. It was a terrible time."

"And your father?"

Corisande sighed, drawing her cloak more tightly around her shoulders, the thin muslin dress Rose Polkinghorne had made her offering little warmth against the night's cool air.

"He's been as you've seen him since the day my mother died, although he was worse at first. We had to beg him to leave her grave—he loved her so much. They'd never been apart for even a day since he'd saved her from a shipwreck. She'd just escaped from France, the Revolution, only sixteen years old. But that's all I ever knew. My mother never talked about her life there. She always said her life had begun the moment she met Papa."

Falling silent, Corisande couldn't believe she'd shared so much with Donovan; it had come out of her like a flood. He must have been amazed, too, for he said nothing for long moments until he exhaled heavily.

"I envy the man."

Corisande looked at Donovan in disbelief, his face hidden in shadow. "My father?"

"Yes, to have known so rare a thing as what he shared with your mother. Not based upon money, or arranged, or forced upon him, but found only by the purest chance."

"And look what it did to him."

Corisande had spoken so softly that she doubted Donovan had heard her, his words unsettling her entirely. All she could think of was how her father had wept and wept as if he couldn't stop, wept for days while she huddled with her sisters, closing her eyes and ears to pain more wretched than she ever wanted to hear again. She had seen then how much it hurt to be in love, and had vowed she wanted no part of it. No, never. Never—

"Corie."

Donovan's voice was so husky that she felt shivers spiral

down her spine; suddenly she wished that the carriage wasn't so dark so she could see his face, not just hear him.

"I just wanted you to know that you looked very beautiful tonight at the Somersets'. I didn't say anything earlier, but I should have. You were stunning."

Wholly astounded, Corisande bit her lip, tears springing to her eyes. Beautiful? Stunning? Damn him, now he was taking his bloody truce too far!

"I don't care if you thought I was no more decorative than a turnip!" she blurted out, bunching her cloak and shifting away from him. "I've no more need of your ridiculous compliments, my lord, than you defending my honor to Lady Somerset—oh! What are you— Let me go!"

Donovan had grabbed her forearm, drawing her back toward him though she tried to brace her feet upon the carriage floor, but it was no use. The damned leather seat was too slippery. With an outraged gasp she was brought up hard against him, his arms locking around her to prevent her from escaping even as she braced her hands upon his chest.

"How . . . how dare—"

"Easy, woman, easy! I only want to know why it upsets you so terribly to hear such praise. Is it that bloody scar on your face?"

Corisande was so astonished, she felt her jaw drop, her body going limp in his arms as if the wind had been knocked from her.

"So that's it, then, isn't it? Good God, Corie, is this how you want to go through life? Denying to yourself that you're a damned lovely woman and thinking when anyone says so they're mocking you? So you have a scar. It's never once bothered me—in fact, from the first moment I saw you it only made me wonder what happened to you. What did happen?"

"I—I was cut," she said hoarsely, feeling ridiculous as

tears began to spill down her cheeks, but she couldn't stop them. "Three years ago. A girl from Porthleven, Sophie Trelawny, married a terrible man, a monster. He fooled us all, me, her parents, even poor Sophie—he'd always seemed so nice. But he nearly beat her to death on their wedding night—oh, God, there was so much blood."

She bent her head, sobbing silently now as Donovan's arms tightened around her.

"Shh, Corie, shh, you don't have to tell me any more if you don't want—"

"We . . . we all took turns sitting with her," she went on, scarcely hearing Donovan as the horrifying memories assailed her. "Her parents, myself, Frances, sitting at her bedside and caring for her while a search went on for the man. But a few days went by, then a week, and they never found him. Everyone thought he'd fled from Cornwall, but he came back. He came back the night I was sitting alone with Sophie."

"Corie, it's all right—"

"He'd been drinking for days, the bastard, and he kicked in the window. He had a knife and he went for the bed while Sophie could only scream, too weak to move. I tried to stop him, but he knocked me to the floor, and when I came back at him again, he turned and cut me. I fell—I thought he was going to kill me, he was standing over me and I saw the knife and Sophie was screaming and screaming . . ."

Corisande clutched Donovan's coat even as he coaxed her to stop, jerking at the deafening memory of a pistol shot exploding in the room.

"Oliver Trelawny killed him—he'd heard Sophie screaming, poor, poor Sophie. She never recovered, died only a few days later. She'd lost too much blood . . ."

"Ah, Corie . . . Corie . . ."

Corisande gave no heed to Donovan's soothing whispers as she buried her face against his shoulder and squeezed her burning eyes shut, a great shuddering sigh escaping from her. But a long moment later, she felt him ease her backward, suddenly very much aware of what he was doing as he cupped her face in his hand, his thumb slowly tracing over her cheek . . . her scar . . .

"You must wear this as a badge of honor, Corie. Don't ever allow anyone to make you think that it's ugly. It's a thing of beauty, of courage. God help me, I've never known a more amazing woman than you. Never."

His vehemently whispered words plummeting to the very heart of her, Corisande had never felt her pulse pounding so hard as he tilted her chin, his finger tracing over her lips for the barest moment before his mouth captured hers.

She started, pulling back, but he only brought her that much more fiercely against him, his kiss as fierce, as wild. She felt suddenly as if she were drowning, Donovan drawing the very breath from her body, and she thought to fight him, if only to breathe, to live. At least until her arms found their way around his neck and she clung to him as fiercely, drawing from him, too, what he seemed to crave so desperately from her.

"Donovan . . ."

She'd said his name with a voice that sounded not her own, hoarse, shaking, and she trembled from head to toe as his tongue swept deep into her mouth. Her fingers entwining in his hair, she pulled him closer, gasping when she felt his hand slip inside her cloak and cover her breast, her nipple taut and swollen beneath his palm. A palm that began to slowly circle, the thrilling pressure of his hand filling her with a yearning so powerful she felt she might explode from its sheer intensity.

So, too, came a fierce awareness as she was suddenly pulled onto Donovan's lap that she not only yearned but wanted to give, *ached* to give this man a part of herself that she'd given to no one ever before. And it was the most frightening realization of her life, the swaying, rumbling carriage, the all-encompassing dark, their panting breaths, Donovan kissing her throat, her ear, her face as his hands moved over her body and tugged her dress up over her bare thighs like a dizzying dream from which she now desperately wanted to wake.

God help her, no, she wasn't falling in love with him, she wasn't! It was impossible, it was—

"Sorry, my lord, we'll 'ave to drive round to the stable, we will. There's 'alf a dozen carriages in front of the house and no room for us—Lord, wot a commotion!"

∞ Twenty-seven ∞

Donovan cursed under his breath, more because Corisande had suddenly flown from his lap to the opposite seat than at anything the coachman Will Brighton had just shouted out to him. But he cursed aloud when the carriage came to a jolting halt, and Will added incredulously, "It's His Grace of Arundale come to call, my lord! All the way from Dorset!"

Corisande's amazement must have matched Donovan's, for she quickly dabbed at her eyes with her sleeve and then readjusted her dress while he nearly kicked open the carriage door. Dammit, no word from Nigel first? No bloody warning? Donovan waited for Corisande to follow after him, not surprised when she refused to accept his assistance as she descended from the carriage.

"Corie, I had no knowledge of this—" he began, only to fall silent as she turned blazing eyes upon him.

"It appears our wait is over, my lord, your brother come personally to grant you the wonderful news of your inheritance! As you hoped, things have moved quite swiftly after all. Shall we go and welcome them?"

She held out her hand to him, and Donovan had no time to dwell upon the catch in her voice or that her fingers were trembling as they proceeded together to the house. The entrance was ablaze with light as footmen—most of them obviously Nigel's from their splendid royal blue and silver livery—hurried up and down the front steps carrying in baggage and huge traveling trunks. Standing at the door was Ellen Biddle, her face a bit pale, no doubt at the unexpectedness of her guests, but directing the flow of traffic quite capably all the same.

"Up the central staircase and to the left, all of you. His Grace of Arundale's chamber will be the first door on the right, Her Grace's the second."

"That hasn't bloody changed," Donovan muttered to himself as the housekeeper suddenly spied them and came flying down the steps.

"Oh, my lord, Lady Donovan! Their Graces only just arrived—five minutes past, no more. I sent them to the drawing room for refreshment, and Ogden is seeing to their needs, but of course they've brought a host of servants with them and even a trio of musicians! His Grace informed me they intend to stay only a day or so, and then they're bound for London—oh, my goodness, so much to do. I've already asked Grace to prepare a light supper, the guest bedrooms are being readied, and fires lit. Is there anything in particular you think Their Graces might require?"

Perhaps another two floors to separate them? Donovan thought dryly, although to the housekeeper he shook his head. "It seems you've things well in hand, Miss Biddle. We'll await your notice of supper in the drawing room."

"Oh, yes, my lord, of course. And how fortunate for you and Lady Donovan to arrive at such an opportune time."

Donovan felt Corisande tug her hand free at that remark and proceed up the steps ahead of him, her cheeks ablaze when he caught up with her inside the entry hall. But she refused to meet his eyes, appearing quite nervous as she glanced toward the drawing room. Meanwhile, Donovan was suddenly hard-pressed to think of anything else but what had happened in the carriage, the memory of Corisande's silky thighs making him clench his teeth. God help him, one moment longer, and she would have been his bride in every sense of the word—

"Donovan, old man!"

"Oh, Lord . . ." Corisande had whispered to herself, but Donovan must have heard her; suddenly she felt him take her arm and propel her forward as a grinning gentleman who looked a shorter, rounder, and much less handsome version of Donovan came striding across the immense hall to meet them. In fact, she couldn't help thinking that based upon appearance alone, Donovan would have made a far more impressive duke than this slightly dissipated-looking man whose dark eyes swept over her with some surprise.

"Why, you've done quite well for yourself, Donovan— she's lovely. Corisande's the name, am I not right, dear lady?"

She nodded, but before she had a chance to utter a word, Donovan propelled her onward toward the drawing room, saying over his shoulder to his brother, "I'd like to speak with you in the library, Nigel. Wait for me there, if you will." Then to Corisande, he added very low, "I won't be gone long, Corie. My brother's wife, Charlotte, whines incessantly about everything, but do your best to entertain her. If all else fails, ask her if the musicians might play for you. I believe Nigel keeps them close at hand just to drown out her complaints."

With that, Donovan left her standing alone just outside the drawing room while he turned and strode after Nigel, who had obligingly disappeared into the library.

Bloody bastard! Of course Donovan couldn't wait to talk to his brother, so eager to hear about his inheritance that he hadn't waited even two minutes before ridding himself of her. Just as she imagined he could hardly wait now to annul her and be on his way back to Spain—oh, God.

Corisande closed her eyes, feeling suddenly almost dizzy, the pain of that reality cutting her so deeply. But in the next instant she lifted her chin, intoning vehemently to herself, "It doesn't matter. It doesn't matter!" as she moved to the drawing room door.

So Donovan would soon be leaving Cornwall. Good riddance! She wanted him to go! So far, far away that there would never be any chance of her seeing him again. And she wanted whatever had awakened inside her to go away too. *Please,* please, *make it go away* . . ."

"Lady Donovan, are you all right?"

Corisande started, spinning to find Ellen Biddle looking at her with concern.

"Yes—no, no, I'm not," she murmured, Nigel's disagreeable wife the last person she felt like meeting right now. "I'm sorry, Ellen. Could you please give my regrets to the duchess? Something must have disagreed with me at dinner tonight—I'm sorry."

Corisande fled, avoiding even looking at the library door as she dodged two footmen carrying a trunk and raced up the stairs.

"Good God, couldn't you have at least written and given us some notice that you intended to visit?"

Donovan wasn't surprised that Nigel's grin had faded, yet his brother still seemed unconcerned, giving him a shrug.

"Sorry, old man, there really wasn't time, and Arundale Hall was in an uproar for days. Charlotte always goes mad each year with packing before we leave for the Season, so I stayed well out of her way and took myself elsewhere—"

"I can bloody imagine." Donovan cut him off, surmising his brother had kept himself well amused by his mistresses.

"Actually, Donovan, it's not at all what you think. I say, you're just as ill-tempered as ever. I had hoped that marriage might have mellowed you a bit—oh, hell, look what it's done for me."

Nigel sounded so disgruntled that Donovan almost

laughed; instead he went to pour them both a good, stiff brandy.

"Damned good idea, brother." Nigel grunted as he dropped into a deep wing chair. "I feel as if I've been traveling for days now and, by Jove, I have been! To London, then back again to Christchurch to fetch Charlotte, and then here—"

"You've been to London?" Donovan set down the decanter, growing tense as Nigel gave him a nod and an enigmatic smile.

"So I have, so I have. But hand me that brandy first, then I'll give you the news I came so far to deliver to you myself."

Donovan obliged him, Corisande's words after she stepped from the carriage suddenly ringing in his mind: *"It appears our wait is over, my lord, your brother come personally to grant you the wonderful news of your inheritance!"* She had sounded upset, yes, and sarcastic, but something else, too, her voice strangely breaking . . .

"Are you just going to stand there, Donovan? Share a toast with me, old man! The necessary papers have been signed, the money transferred to your bank, the controlling share of the mine in your name. The inheritance is yours, and I'd say you earned it in record time. Father would have been pleased—no, elated—and so am I!"

Donovan stared at his brother almost stupidly, the moment he had so anticipated not anything at all as he would have imagined. He should have been glad—hell, he had all the money now he could possibly need to search for Paloma and he was vastly relieved, there was no denying it. He should have been damned eager, too, to head out at once for London so he could arrange an immediate annulment and then catch the first naval ship bound for Lisbon. But he wasn't.

Hell and damnation, he wasn't.

Donovan drank, half draining his glass while Nigel looked on with approval.

"Good show! Marrying wasn't so difficult after all, was it? It's only the trials that come later—but no, no bloody bemoaning tonight. And you certainly can't complain. I'll admit I was a mite concerned when you wrote to say you'd decided upon a local vicar's daughter, and then when Fanny came back wailing at how unkindly you'd treated her and saying your bride had a scarred face—"

"Fanny said . . . By God, I should have flogged those women from my house instead of just throwing them out!" Donovan roared, incensed. "Corie got that scar trying to save someone's life—"

"Easy, man, I said that as no insult," Nigel broke in, his gaze suddenly speculative as he studied Donovan. "Your wife's a beauty, scar or no, which I was very glad to see. I imagine it's been no trouble at all bedding her, not like the times some of us have had with our wives . . ."

He didn't continue, a look of such distaste on his face as he rose to pour himself another drink that Donovan knew Nigel was thinking of Charlotte. Just as he was thinking once more of Corisande and how she'd wound her arms around his neck and kissed him so passionately, moaning his name—

"Another for you, brother?"

Donovan shook his head, his blood already heated enough, and it wasn't because of the brandy. Instead he waited until Nigel had retaken his seat before asking, "Why did you go to London? Couldn't you have sent Wilkins to handle everything for you?"

"Oh, yes, but I had something else to accomplish." Nigel paused for a drink, the same enigmatic smile on his face as he lowered his glass. "It's all been taken care of, Donovan. You need have no fear of getting yourself blown to bits any longer—or I should say, *I've* no fear—"

"What are you talking about?"

"Your service under Lord Wellington is done, man. Finished. An official dispatch releasing you from further duty has been sent to his headquarters, so you need harbor no notion that you must return to Spain. I need you here, Donovan, and now your marriage has given me the means I needed to ensure you may stay in Britain. Besides, you've already given four distinguished years to the defense of the Commonwealth, longer than most men of your station. It's time you think of yourself, of your bride, of having children and prospering here in Cornwall."

Donovan kept silent, struck by the thought that even a week ago this news would have sent him into a rage. To have Nigel so ordering his life? But that his service in the army was over did not so much concern him.

He still must return to Spain for Paloma's sake, but not yet. He couldn't leave yet. He would send money at once to the trusted men he'd hired to continue the search for his daughter while he was away in England, but Corisande needed him, too, although she'd never admit it. She was in danger, and not until whoever had attacked her was found and punished . . .

"No argument, Donovan? No scowls? No curses? I say, old man, you surprise me. You're acting much different than you did at Arundale Hall. Maybe marriage has mellowed you after all."

"And I'm bloody surprised you didn't wait to hear some word from Ogden before you set off for London."

"No, no, I decided all must be well after hearing what you did to Fanny and her cohorts—" Nigel abruptly went still, looking at Donovan with some chagrin, although an instant later, he shrugged. "There's much at stake here. The Arundale dukedom, man, what did you expect? But Ogden has already assured me that everything is as it should be—unless you've something to tell me?"

"No more than that I don't want my wife troubled with news of my inheritance. Or anything else we've discussed. It was hard enough for Corie when those housemaids—damn them, all that business about my marrying her for an heir. I don't want to see her hurt again."

"Yes, yes, I imagine you don't."

Nigel was staring at Donovan so intently that he began to feel uncomfortable, going to refill his glass after all.

"Well, well, brother, so it's finally happened."

Donovan tensed, but he didn't turn around. "What's happened?"

"Oh, I think you know. I envy you too."

Donovan didn't reply, downing his brandy and heading for the door while Nigel rose from his chair and followed him.

"Don't worry, old man, as far as I'm concerned, we came here simply to meet your bride. I only hope Charlotte hasn't made her regret marrying into our family."

Donovan half spun, and Nigel started back a step. "Dammit, I didn't consider Charlotte. Does she know why—"

"Ha! The less that woman knows of anything, the better. I told her the same thing I just said to you, that it was fitting we meet your new wife. But do you think that made her whine any less? Good God, she drove me half-mad—complaining about the length of the trip, how she'd rather be in London already, until I couldn't stand it anymore and rode in another carriage. But I still had to listen to her moan at every stop, how she was being jostled to pieces, how—"

Donovan didn't want to hear anymore either, and he ducked outside the library, nearly colliding with Ellen Biddle, who was waiting for him outside the door.

"Oh! Forgive me, my lord! I didn't know if I should interrupt you so I waited—"

"What is it, woman?" He cut her off a bit too sharply, so

intent was he on rescuing Corisande from his sister-in-law. "I'm sorry. Is supper ready?"

"No, not yet, but—well, Lady Donovan has retired, my lord. She asked me to give her regrets to Her Grace, which I did, but your wife looked so pale, I was worried for her and thought you should know—"

"Best go to her, old boy," Nigel interjected, tipping his glass in a wry salute. "Damn, if you don't have all the luck. Think there's any way we can get Charlotte to retire for the night?"

Donovan didn't answer, feeling truly sorry for his brother at that moment as he left them and raced up the stairs. But he forgot Nigel, forgot Charlotte, forgot everything as a moment later he knocked on Corisande's door.

Then he cursed to himself. Why was he knocking? She was his wife! He pushed open the door just in time to see Corisande fly across the softly firelit room and dive into bed, throwing the covers over her head.

It made him chuckle, relief filling him, too, but he sobered when he heard a small plaintive voice call to him brokenly from under the bedclothes. "Go away!"

Good God, it almost sounded to him as if she'd been crying. He drew closer, hearing muffled sniffles, and grew concerned all over again.

"Corie?"

"Go away!"

"No, I'm not going away until you tell me what's wrong—"

"Nothing's wrong! I'm just glad this whole bloody thing is finally over!"

Her outburst striking him like a fierce punch in the gut, Donovan couldn't help saying as vehemently, "Well, it's not over, woman, I'm sorry to disappoint you. If you must know, my brother and his wife merely came to Cornwall to welcome you into our family. It might be a couple more weeks before the whole matter of my inheritance is settled, so it appears we're still stuck with each other whether you like it or not!"

Corisande couldn't believe it, her heart hammering in her throat. A couple more weeks? Nor could she believe the wild elation surging through her, but she only had an instant to dwell upon the sheer ridiculousness of her feeling so happy before the covers were suddenly wrenched away from her head, and Donovan stood above her, a dark, looming silhouette beside the bed.

"Are you going to lie there, or will you accompany me back downstairs to greet my brother and sister-in-law properly? They came all this way—"

"I don't care if they just arrived from America!" she spouted, indignant and shivering in her thin nightgown, too, as she tried to tug the bedclothes away from him. "I already made my excuses, so go away—oh!"

Donovan had lifted her bodily and set her with a jarring thump on the floor; the next thing Corisande felt was a stinging slap to her bottom as she shrieked in surprise.

"You've got two minutes to dress, Corie, or you'll get another and harder too. Now move."

She did, so stunned that he had spanked her like a child that she ran to the wardrobe and clutched about for her clothes in a panic.

But it was even more unsettling that they were alone and in the dark, just as they had been in the carriage. When he'd told her her scar was a thing of beauty and he'd kissed her and touched her breast and run his hands over her thighs and . . . and she wanted no part of it! She wanted no part of him! God help her, a couple more weeks?

That thought made her dress faster than she ever had in her life, more than eager to get back downstairs as she flew out of her room and down the corridor, not waiting for Donovan.

∽ Twenty-eight ∽

"Oh, dear, do you have to go in there? It's so dreadfully stuffy in this carriage, and we've already been riding about for hours now and—"

"Then get out, Charlotte, and take a nice walk along the quay," Corisande suggested through clenched teeth as an Arundale footman opened the carriage door and helped her to step down. "I won't be but a moment, I promise."

"But it's growing so cloudy and windy, surely you can see that. I just know the moment I step outside it would start to rain, and then my hair would be ruined and my dress and my lovely new parasol, and, oh, dear, should you go into that inn? It looks quite common and—and it might be dangerous."

"It's not dangerous, Charlotte. I told you I've good friends who live here." Doing her best to bridle her temper, Corisande forced a smile at the sallow-faced, pinch-nosed young woman who stared at her doubtfully from the dim interior of the carriage. "Truly, a walk would be lovely. You could get some fresh air—"

"Oh, my, no, and smell all that horrible fish?"

That did it, Corisande had had enough. Without another word, she spun and crossed the cobbled road, kicking herself that she had been the one to suggest she and her sister-in-law take an afternoon drive instead of waiting around the house for Donovan and Nigel to return from Arundale's Kitchen.

She'd had her own motives, too, visiting Oliver certainly one of them, but now she wished she'd risked going alone instead of having to endure Charlotte's constant whining. She should have known, starting with last night, that the woman had little good to say about anything—complaining ceaselessly about being abandoned in the drawing room, the rigors of the journey, the lateness of the supper. Then breakfast this morning had been served much too early, and her bed had been lumpy, the fireplace smoky, on and on and on . . .

Sighing, Corisande had to agree with Donovan as she stepped inside the Trelawnys' inn. Charlotte, Duchess of Arundale, was a fright, her fretful chatter about as pleasant as fingernails scraping across a chalkboard and her breath almost unbearable although the woman couldn't entirely help her bad teeth—

"Corie, dear, I was just thinking of 'ee! Come in, come in!"

Corisande smiled at Rebecca Trelawny as the plump older woman wound her way past trestle tables where a few patrons sat smoking pipes and drinking home-brewed ale. But upon reaching her, Rebecca gave a nod to the back room.

"I've something to tell 'ee, Corie, but not here, eh?"

Corisande nodded and followed, wondering where Oliver might be. The sea captain usually held forth in the inn, telling tall tales to his customers. "Actually I can't stay long, Rebecca," she began as the woman quietly closed the door to the back room. "I came to see Oliver—"

"He's not here, Corie, that's what I wanted to tell 'ee. He asked me to have one of the men bring 'ee a note, but the day's slipped away from me. He sailed out to Brittany again at mid-morning, he did, so pleased with the coin already coming in from that fine brandy that he went to try and fetch some more. Said he knew there was a chance for another shipment into Roscoff but he wouldn't know for sure until he got there. Aw, that man of mine. Gone for days an' now gone again!''

Corisande was somewhat stunned; Oliver hadn't said a word the other night about the chance of bringing back more of that brandy. She was suddenly worried too.

She had wanted to tell him about the attack and how the man had known their signal, but it wouldn't do any good to say anything now. She didn't want to worry Rebecca; the poor woman already had been asking her husband for months if he might cease his fair trading and enjoy sitting at home with her in front of the fire.

"Well, I hope it doesn't take him as long to return this time," Corisande murmured, and Rebecca nodded in agreement.

"Ais, I told him if that shipment wasn't there to come back straightaway, an' he promised me, Corie. No ifs or an's about it! An' my Oliver holds to his word. So 'ee can look for the signal tomorrow night, an' if it doesn't come, you'll know there was none of that good brandy to be found." Rebecca's hand moved to the door. "Now, can I give 'ee a nice hot drink before 'ee must be on your way? A piece of buttermilk cake?"

Corisande shook her head as she stepped outside the room, though buttermilk cake, especially Rebecca's, which she always served with a dollop of sweet cream, did sound inviting. But by now Charlotte was probably quite overcome by dreaded fish odors, so she'd best hurry. She gave Rebecca a hug and then drew her cloak more snugly around her.

"Ais, a good idea, wrap yourself tight. A gale's brewing, I fear, a nor'westerly, so my Oliver should be well clear of it, but I'll be praying hard tonight, all the same."

"I'll say a prayer too."

" 'Ee do that, Corie dear. A vicar's daughter's prayer is surely worth two of mine!"

Corisande smiled, turning to the door only to be bumped suddenly out of the way as three men who'd just gotten up from their chairs shouldered past her without even an apology.

"Ais, those dockhands!" Rebecca snorted with exasperation as the door slammed behind them. "Rude as can be and not getting any better! Been here almost two weeks now an' haven't left an extra pence for me cleaning their rooms an' cooking them meals, an' nary a thank you either. Pah! Foreigners! Oh, dear, no slight upon your dear mother, though. But these fellows—come here to find work when there's barely enough for our own? Pah!"

Corisande shrugged. "Everyone has a right to earn bread, Rebecca. It's no matter."

She gave the still-grumbling woman another hug and then stepped outside. The whistling wind had picked up tremendously in the few moments since she'd entered the inn, so strong now that her skirt whipped around her legs. And obviously Charlotte had noticed, too, the duchess waving to her frantically to hurry.

"Oh, dear, oh, dear, we're going to be blown into the sea! We'll never make it back to the house, I know it! We'll tip over, the horses will stumble in the mud, we'll drown!"

"Drown in what? The heath?" Corisande muttered to herself as she ducked her head to the wind and went to the carriage, a footman waiting to assist her. But she waved him away, saying to an incredulous Charlotte, "I was hoping we might stop first to meet my family but—"

"Oh, no, oh, no, we must get back to the house!" the frenzied duchess interrupted before Corisande could finish. "Climb into the carriage before you're blown away!"

"I'm not going to be blown away and I'm not getting into

the carriage," she shouted, beyond all patience now. "You go ahead, I'll get home somehow later. Either that, or have Donovan come for me. I'll be at my father's house—I haven't seen him and my three sisters for several days. Are you sure you wouldn't like to come with me and—"

Again Corisande didn't get to finish as a powerful gust of wind suddenly tore the carriage door away from the footman and slammed it shut with a bang, while Charlotte shrieked in terror for the coachman to drive on at once. Corisande barely had time to step out of the way as the black ducal coach jerked into motion, and the hapless footman had to run after to swing himself up onto the back platform.

"Yes, hurry, you don't want to be blown into the sea," Corisande said with a wryness that would have matched Donovan's if he'd just seen this ridiculous little episode.

Oh, Lord, Donovan.

She began to walk quickly toward the parsonage, trying not to think of how angry he might be once he discovered she'd stayed behind in Porthleven. Of course, she had no intention at all of journeying across the heath alone; if the storm proved too bad and Donovan couldn't come for her, she would just spend the night in her own bed, her narrow single bed, not anything like the huge bed she'd shared those two nights with Donovan . . .

Corisande shivered, not wanting to think of that either. Nor how he'd stared at her so strangely all through supper last night, looking at her almost as if he'd never really seen her before. Of course, it could have been because her hair was mussed and her dress askew; she'd pulled on her clothing in the dark after all. And certainly she didn't want to think about how vastly disappointed he must be to have to wait longer for his inheritance—Oh, for heaven's sake! Why think of Donovan at all?

So she tried not to, wondering instead when she was going to be able to write down all the figures of Tuesday's landing in the ledger she kept hidden in the church. She supposed after she visited her family she might have some time, that is, if the gale grew worse and there was no chance of Donovan coming to fetch her—

"Donovan again, always Donovan," she said aloud, resignedly, grateful that the parsonage was only another few houses away. A blast of wind, laced now with cold rain, hit her with tremendous force and so suddenly that she half spun, looking back down the darkening street as she braced herself against a cottage wall.

Villagers were rushing outside to close banging shutters and shoo their children indoors while dogs barked at the low, heavy clouds scudding across the sky. And the harbor was alive with activity as boats were lashed to the docks, a few larger vessels anchored farther out bobbing upon the angry, steely-looking waves, their masts dipping and swaying. Other than that, the streets were nearly empty where she stood, well, except for those three men huddled as if talking among themselves down the hill.

Corisande turned and kept walking, then slowed down.

Three men? Strange. She glanced over her shoulder to see that they were no longer huddled but coming up the street at her pace, their capped heads lowered against the wind and shoulders hunched. She'd scarcely thought twice about it at the inn, but could they be the same ones who'd bumped into . . . ?

Corisande began to walk faster, glancing behind her to see that the men were now walking faster, too, which made her heart jump. Then she immediately told herself she was being silly. It was growing dark, but there was still enough light to see quite well, and she was in the very center of the village. Surely she had nothing to fear. So why, then, was she suddenly so nervous?

She didn't want to, but she hazarded a quick glance behind her to find to her immense relief that the three men were gone. Where, she could not say, but she didn't waste time wondering. She half flew into the parsonage, where the comforting warmth of the place and the smell of Frances's leek and potato pie greeted her like an old friend.

"Hello? Anyone here?"

At once a clatter arose from the kitchen as wooden chairs scraped against the floor and Luther began to yip, and her sisters came spilling down the narrow hallway at a run.

"Oh, Corie, is she here? Is she here?" That from Marguerite, who embraced Corisande excitedly while glancing past her into the parlor.

"The duchess, Corie! Where's the duchess?" piped Estelle as Luther spun and pranced and yapped at her feet.

"Oh, so you heard Donovan and I have important visitors?" Not surprised that the news must have flown like tonight's gale through Porthleven, Corisande bent down to give her youngest sister a hug and then moved on to Linette, who flung her slender arms around her neck.

"I don't care about any silly duchess, Corie. I'm glad just to see you."

"And I'm very glad to see you too," Corisande murmured, giving Linette a good squeeze before releasing her. "But I'm sorry to say the duchess decided to go home. Charlotte doesn't much like storms. Doesn't like much of anything, for that matter."

"Did she take her shiny black coach with her?" Her voice very small, Estelle looked crestfallen. "Johnnie Morton saw you riding in a huge, shiny black coach—with men in fancy clothes sitting on a funny little seat. He came hollering back into the school to tell us."

"Yes, it was quite big with a crest and silver mountings and footmen in fancy clothes, and I'm afraid they all went home with the duchess. But I'm here, and something smells very good in the kitchen. Do you think Frances made enough for me too? Where is Frances?"

Suddenly there was an uncomfortable silence as all three girls looked at each other, none of them looking at her.

"She's not in the kitchen? Marguerite?"

"She's out trying to get Papa to come in for supper, Corie. She told us to stay inside—the storm coming and all —and she knew, too, that you might be stopping by—"

"What do you mean, trying to get Papa to come in?"

Again the silence, Estelle looking up with very big eyes at Marguerite while Linette chewed her lower lip.

"Well, is somebody going to answer me?"

"He doesn't want to come inside, we don't know why," Marguerite said in an uncertain voice. "He's too busy digging holes."

"Holes?"

A chorus of nods greeted her incredulous query; Corisande stared at them in confusion. "Where? Why?"

"I told you we don't know." Tears filled Marguerite's eyes. "He's been outside in the garden—"

"Well, of course, that explains it, then," Corisande broke in as she moved down the hall. "You know how he loves to spend time out there tending the flowers."

"But all day long, Corie, and into the night?" Marguerite called after her while Linette and Estelle followed closely at Corisande's heels, and Luther skittered ahead into the kitchen. "I don't think he's slept at all for two days."

Growing concerned now, Corisande said as reassuringly as she could, "Go on, all of you, sit back down and eat your supper. It smells wonderful. I'll go see if I can help Frances, all right?"

But they didn't sit down, instead following Corisande to the kitchen door until she spun and said in her sternest voice, "I said to go finish your supper. Everything will be fine, you'll see."

They silently obliged with long faces, their chairs scraping dully, not at all the boisterous girls who had greeted her only moments ago. It was as if seeing her had given vent to unspoken fears, but Corisande couldn't worry about them now as she went outside into the garden, astonished at how dark it had grown. A thick rain was falling, too, scratches of lightning cutting across the pitch-black sky. And the wind, the wind had become a wild thing that tore at her clothes, her hair, whistling shrilly as it whipped across the heath.

"Frances! Papa!"

She ran deeper into the garden, but she didn't see them anywhere, a great sense of unease swamping her.

"Frances?"

"Here, Corie! Here!"

She whirled, relief overwhelming her as she spied Frances and her father just outside the garden wall. She ran and pushed open the metal gate, barely dodging a yawning hole some two feet across illumined by a great flash of lightning.

"Be careful, they're all around!" Frances warned, waving her back inside the garden. "The good passon's fine, Corie, never 'ee fear! Go back now! I'll have him into the house quick as a wink!"

Corisande doubted it would be quick as a wink since her father walked more slowly and more stooped than she'd ever seen him, his snow-white hair plastered to his head, his clothes drenched. She made a move to come and help, nearly slipping into another hole just inside the wall. Good Lord, how many holes—

"Oh, God!"

Corisande's hand flew to her throat as two cannon explosions in close succession rocked the earth, rumbling over the village as loud as any thunder. As lightning flashed brilliantly around them, she could see Frances's stricken face that must have surely matched her own.

"Lord help us, Corie, that alarm hasn't sounded in over a year! 'Tes a ship! They've sighted a ship in trouble!"

∽ Twenty-nine ∽

Corisande gasped as a third cannon blast shattered the night—which meant only one thing: the ship must have already struck the shore, with who knew how many lives at stake.

"Get Papa inside—see to him, Frances!"

Corisande ducked her head against the slashing rain and ran back through the garden to the house, taking care to watch for any treacherous holes. Her three sisters scattered away from the door as she burst inside the kitchen, their faces pale and their eyes wide.

"Papa's fine. Frances is bringing him back to the house," she explained hastily, wiping the moisture from her eyes. "See that he eats, and drinks some hot tea. A ship's in trouble, and they may need him to . . ."

Corisande didn't finish but raced down the hall, her sisters well understanding that their father might be needed to perform a burial service if anyone drowned—though she prayed that help would arrive in time for those poor desperate souls. To her relief, she saw as she stepped outside that the village was alive with commotion, men and their wives, too, tugging on cloaks and caps and coats as they rushed from their houses and jumped onto pony-drawn wagons already rumbling down to the harbor.

She ran to a passing cart; villagers outstretched their arms to give her a lift up, and she clambered aboard, breathlessly murmuring her thanks as she joined the flight to help strangers in trouble. It seemed in only moments they'd reached the water and there everyone set off on foot, running north along the beach. Some men had huge twists of rope thrown over their shoulders while still others half dragged, half carried rowboats across the sand. A tar barrel stood lit and burning brightly atop a nearby cliff to show them the way.

It only took a brilliant flash of lightning to spot the distressed ship fifty yards from shore being buffeted by a tremendous sea, her eerily white sails split and tattered. It looked to be a fishing vessel, and Corisande's heart pounded hard for a moment when she thought it might have been the *Fair Betty* returned home because of the fierce gale. At once a hue and cry went up to man the boats, while a host of villagers suddenly dashed into the boiling surf to drag a limp survivor to shore.

Corisande was stunned to see another exhausted swimmer struggling through the breakers to reach the safety of the beach, and she rushed with four others to help. The water was bitterly cold and dragged heavily at her skirt, while the sand shifted dangerously beneath her feet with the powerful undertow. But she managed to grab onto the man's collar while the others grabbed his arms and legs and hauled him to dry land.

"There's seven hands . . . seven hands still aboard without Hodge an' me," the man gasped, coughing up water as he looked to where the other sailor was surrounded by villagers farther up the beach. "An' Captain Briggs an' his young son . . . we were bound with a load of mackerel for Falmouth . . . tried to run the storm . . . we're the only ones who know how to swim . . ."

As the man fell into a fit of violent hacking, Corisande did her best to lift his shoulders so he wouldn't choke.

"I'll stay with him. Tell the others there are still nine

people on board!" she shouted above the roaring wind to the villagers who had helped her drag the sailor to shore, waving them away to alert the men climbing into the row-boats. But already several boats had headed into the crashing waves, only to be tossed about like bits of cork and overturned, spilling their occupants into the sea.

At once people forged into the heavy surf to save their own. Corisande's heart sank as another streak of lightning lit the sky and she saw that the ship now listed ominously. God help those poor people, there wasn't much more time—

"Hell and damnation, woman, must you forever place yourself in harm's way?"

Corisande gasped as she was hauled to her feet, barely able to see Donovan's expression in the darkness although she could hear the scowl in his voice. She could tell, too, from how tightly his hands were gripping her shoulders that he must be furious she'd not returned in the carriage with Charlotte, but there was no time to think of that now.

"Donovan, this man swam from the ship, but there are still nine on board including a little boy! They've already tried to launch some boats . . ."

Corisande's words were drowned out as a great anguished cry went up along the beach when another rowboat was cast back onto shore by the churning sea. She saw then that several men with ropes tied around their waists were plunging into the water in a valiant attempt to reach the ship before it foundered. Donovan must have seen them, too, for he turned back to her and shook her hard, his voice brooking no argument.

"Stay here, Corie, where I'll know to find you. Don't move an inch!"

She didn't have a chance to reply as he left her and ran to the water's edge, where a cluster of villagers gathered round him to tie a lifeline about his waist as well. Then Donovan was gone, disappearing into the waves while Corisande's heart flew to her throat.

That's what she had meant to ask him—if there might be some way he could help—but now that he was swimming out to the ship as the storm was shrieking and thundering and blowing all around them, she had never felt more frightened. The water was so cold, the waves like mountains. Oh, Lord, oh, Lord . . .

Corisande dropped to her haunches as another fierce fit of coughing seized the sailor, but to her surprise he waved her away as if sensing her unease.

"I'm all right . . . go on if 'ee want to join the others."

Corisande shook her head, but when three women came rushing over with blankets, one of them saying that he should come with them to the overhang of a cliff where a bonfire had been lit, she was only too relieved to see the man helped to his feet and led away.

She knew Donovan had told her to stay put, but she hurried down the beach anyway. She wanted to make sure that the villagers holding his lifeline were ready to haul him in as soon as they saw him swimming back to shore—and not to pull too hard either. Last year a rescuer had been swallowed up by the sea when his rope had snapped . . .

"No, Donovan will be fine. He's going to be fine," she intoned to herself, dodging two men who had suddenly gotten in her way. But she was no sooner past them than she felt a jarring tug that nearly felled her, her sodden cloak yanked from behind as someone else grabbed her around the neck and clamped a rough callused hand over her mouth before she had a chance to scream.

And she tried to scream, struggling in mute terror as she was half dragged along the beach, realizing with a horribly sick feeling when no help came that everyone was too intent upon watching the desperate rescue to see her plight. It was so pitch-dark at this far end of the beach, too, so dark and the wind howling so bitterly that she could hear nothing but the blood thundering in her ears.

Two men now held her, one with his arm curled around the back of her neck and his hand still clamped firmly over her mouth while the other gripped her right arm cruelly, twisting it as if daring her to try to escape. Then to her horror, a third man suddenly appeared almost out of nowhere and strode toward them, and Corisande was sickeningly certain that these were the very same men who must have been following her to the parsonage, who had bumped into her so rudely at the inn—

"Let her go! No one can hear her scream now."

Corisande recognized that harsh voice at the same moment she was knocked forward onto the sand, an ice-cold wave hitting her full in the face. She'd had no idea they were so close to the water. Her eyes burning from the salt, she tried to rise but instead found herself hauled to her feet and then thrown forward again, and this time the water was much deeper, another frigid wave breaking over her head.

"No . . . please, no!" she sputtered tearfully, scrambling through the churning surf on hands and knees as she tried frantically to get away. She shrieked when a third time she was dragged to her feet and again she was pitched forward, her body tossed and rolled like flotsam as a violent wave crashed over her, then another and another.

Her fingers clawing at the sand, she feared in that moment that she was going to drown. And when she felt a heavy foot settle atop her back to hold her face down in the icy water, she was certain of it.

She wildly flailed her limbs, her lungs ready to burst, the pounding so fierce in her temples she felt her head was going to explode. Until something suddenly gave way deep inside her, her struggles growing sluggish, her clothes become so heavy, dragging her down, down to drift around her like a watery shroud . . .

"*Non, non, madame,* I did not bring you here to kill you."

Corisande cried out as she was slapped hard across the face, scarcely aware that she'd been dragged from the water until she felt another brutal slap that made her see blinding white light in front of her eyes. The next thing she knew, she was staring up at the sky, rain stinging her face as she gasped and coughed and sputtered for air.

"Now you know when you hear from me again, madame, you will not doubt that my words are true. You will not doubt me!"

Corisande heard gruff laughter and low voices conferring and then nothing more, the wind sucking up all sound but the waves crashing upon the beach. It wasn't until long, heart-pounding moments later that she dared to believe she was alone. Curling onto her side, she lay there numbly, her limbs and her wet clothes so heavy that she wondered if she could move. It was only when she heard a faint cheer coming from the opposite side of the beach that she remembered . . .

Donovan.

Somehow she rose to her hands and knees, crawling across wet gritty sand until she felt she could rise. She stumbled, fell, and rose again as another cheer split the night, much louder this time, the distant orange light of a bonfire drawing her like a moth to a flickering flame.

Somehow she made herself walk faster when she heard another cheer, finally managing to run as lightning flashed overhead, a thunderclap booming seconds later. She might have thought she was coming upon a joyous celebration if not for the tension suddenly cutting the air: at least a hundred villagers were gathered in a tight crowd at the shoreline and staring out at the sea.

"What's happening?" she rasped, nearly falling into two men who turned to look at her, clearly stunned that she was soaked from head to toe, her clothes caked with sand. "Tell me! What's happening?"

"Why, haven't 'ee seen, Corie? The ship's splitting apart, but all the crew are saved except for two."

"Two?" she echoed hoarsely, peering through the crowd to see the hunched blanketed figures being led across the beach to the bonfire. But she didn't see Donovan anywhere and she began to push her way through to the water, mounting fear clawing at her throat, until finally she came upon two sets of grim-faced men who were pulling hand over hand at thick ropes stretched taut.

"Is he still out there? My husband? Lord Donovan?"

"Ais, Corie," one man spoke up, though none of them turned for even a moment from their crucial labor to glance at her. "Lord Donovan and John Killigrew, bringing in the last of 'em, the captain and his boy— There, lads! There! I can see 'em now, pull easy, pull easy!"

Corisande felt scalding tears jump to her eyes as she saw four distinct shapes emerging from the surging darkness that was the sea, the fisherman John Killigrew with a small boy clutching to his neck and Donovan only a few feet behind holding fast to a heavyset man who appeared to be unconscious. As cheers went up along the shore, Corisande held her breath.

They were still some twenty yards out, but already villagers were wading into the breakers as far as they dared, and she waded out, too, a sudden violent gust of wind nearly knocking her off her feet. She heard a loud cry and glanced behind her to see one of the groups of men who'd been pulling suddenly rushing into the waves. It was then that she saw a rope had snapped, and she cried out, too, spinning back to see with horror that Donovan and the captain had disappeared under the waves.

"No! Donovan! Donovan . . . !"

Desperately she lunged for deeper water, the sand slipping beneath her feet, only to feel someone grab her from behind.

"Corie, Corie, 'ee can't help him! The waves will take 'ee out too!"

"No, let me go! Let me go!"

She fought and flailed her arms, but her captor refused to release her, dragging her back even as villagers rushed to help John Killigrew and the boy as they were hauled exhausted onto shore. Nearly choked by rasping sobs, Corisande stared in shock at the black churning sea, full of debris from the shattered ship . . . white bits of sail, planks of wood—

"Over there! Help him, men! We can grab him now—the water's not too deep!"

Corisande found herself suddenly free as people began to run farther down the beach. Her heart began clamoring in her breast as Donovan emerged from the waves hauling the limp captain in his arms. Both men were at once surrounded and helped to shore by a cheering, jubilant crowd. But she couldn't reach him, her legs suddenly giving out beneath her, and she went down in the sand, unable to see for the tears blinding her eyes.

Unable to see anything until what seemed no more than an instant later, when someone fell to his knees in front of her and pulled her into his arms.

"Corie . . ."

She held on to him for dear life, not caring that Donovan seemed a block of ice, his skin and his clothing as wet and cold as her own. But suddenly they were borne to their feet by a host of villagers and swept along to the bonfire where all the other rescuers and survivors sat huddled, both she and Donovan soon enveloped in blankets, mugs of hot tea laced with brandy thrust into their hands.

But she couldn't drink, merely staring at him as he stared back at her, his breathing still labored, his eyes the color of midnight as, incredibly, a wry smile came to his blue-tinged lips.

"You look as much a mess as I feel, woman. Sand in your hair, on your clothes. What happened?"

⚭ Thirty ⚭

Corisande didn't know what to say; there were so many people gathered beneath the rocky overhang. Thankfully Donovan was distracted as the captain of the fishing vessel was suddenly brought round by a shot of brandy poured down his throat, the man breaking down and weeping openly as he embraced his son.

As more cheers went up, and many villagers crowded forward to commend not only Donovan, but also all the other rescuers for their bravery, Corisande drank her tea, grateful for its warmth. But nothing could thaw the chill that was descending over her, and she stared silently into the sputtering bonfire, her attacker's cryptic words echoing in her mind . . . *"Now you know when you hear from me again, madame, you will not doubt that my words are true. You will not doubt me!"*

She sat there and stared even as people began to leave for their homes, and one by one the survivors were helped to their feet and taken off to eat a warm, hearty meal and spend the night in beds generously offered by strangers. She was scarcely aware of anything until she felt Donovan touch her arm and she jumped, dropping her mug into the sand.

"Corie, I said it's time we leave. Didn't you hear me?"

Donovan got no reply, only a mute shake of her head; Corisande's face was so pale, her teeth still slightly chattering, that he couldn't wait to get her home.

Good God, she had probably helped to drag the survivors to shore—no wonder she was soaked to the skin. She must have been knocked from her feet a time or two and won a good dunking for her efforts to have so much sand clinging to her, too, her hair matted to her head. She didn't protest when he helped her to her feet and wrapped the blanket more snugly around her shoulders, but her legs seemed so wobbly that he lifted her into his arms and carried her out from underneath the overhang. The wind was not so strong now, the gale having lost some of its wild fury.

He was amazed he didn't feel worse after battling the waves. When that rope had snapped and he'd gone under, nearly losing his grip on the captain, he'd known apprehension, yes, but he hadn't allowed himself to doubt for an instant that he would make it back to shore. He'd had only to think of Corisande, dammit, how she had defied him again, putting herself at grave risk, and how he planned to let her know just how furious he'd been when he had met the ducal carriage rumbling at a breakneck pace toward home and discovered she was not inside with Charlotte.

But not tonight, Donovan thought to himself, wondering at how strangely still Corisande was as he strode to a narrow outcropping where he'd left Samson. His horse was soaked, too, snorting almost in indignation at him, but at least the animal had had protection against the wind.

He hoisted Corisande into the saddle and then mounted behind her, thinking she must be exhausted, indeed, when she leaned back against him, again making no protest when he wound his arms tightly around her and kicked Samson into a gallop. This wasn't at all the Corisande he'd left earlier in the day, when she had hardly spoken to him and more often than not refused to meet his eyes. That woman was nothing like the one who had hugged him so fiercely back there on the beach as if . . . as if . . .

Sighing heavily, Donovan told himself to be content that

she was safe and sound in his arms. Yet he wasn't content, God help him, he wasn't.

"Here's some nice hot tea, my lady, I'll put it right here next to the bed. I don't like to see you still shivering so. The bath should have helped. If you'd like I could fetch another blanket for you—though we're a bit short right now with Their Graces being here and all their servants—"

"I'm fine, Ellen, really," Corisande murmured, plucking absently at the sleeve of her flannel nightgown. "I think maybe if I just get some sleep . . ."

"Oh, my, yes, of course, sleep is probably the best thing for you, my lady. To think of you outside in all that wind and rain and sloshing about in the sea. I'll be grateful that you don't come down with a bad cold or worse!"

Corisande closed her eyes as the housekeeper tucked in the covers one last time, then turned down the lamp by the bed. "If you could give the duke and duchess my regrets—"

"Ah, no trouble there, Her Grace has already retired for the night, but I'll say as much to His Grace. He's waiting downstairs in the library for Lord Donovan to finish his bath and join him, though I heard him ask Ogden to let His Lordship know he wouldn't mind at all if Lord Donovan decided to retire, too, after the night he's had. Actually, His Grace was humming. Seemed quite content to be alone. I can't say that I blame him—oh, dear, I'm rattling on, and you need your sleep. Good night, my lady."

Corisande had already rolled onto her side, listening with half an ear as Ellen stoked the fire one last time and then left the room. Fleetingly she wondered if Donovan was making as much of a mess at his bath as he had at the washbasin that one night, water splashing everywhere, but she immediately pushed away the image, not wanting to think about water at all.

It had been terribly difficult even getting into that tub,

and when Ellen had poured a pitcher of water over her head to rinse the sand from her hair, her heart had begun to race so fast that she at once had wanted out. She imagined her pillow would be covered with the gritty stuff come morning, but she didn't care. She just wanted to sleep, please, please, to sleep so she wouldn't think anymore—

"Non, non, madame, *I did not bring you here to kill you.*"

Corisande gasped and pitched onto her back, the harsh voice so loud in her head it was as if she had heard it all over again.

". . . *kill you . . . kill you . . .*"

Dear God, the man almost *had* killed her, nearly drowning her! What was happening? Why was she living this nightmare? What had he meant about not doubting him?

Corisande threw back the covers and half stumbled from bed, trembling to her toes. She tried to take a sip of tea, but the cup was shaking so fiercely in her hand that she at once set it down again, fearing she might drop and break it. Instead she walked unsteadily to the curtains and peered through the rain-spattered windows, wondering if her attackers were out there, watching the house, watching her.

Three men, but only one had spoken to her, a Frenchman, she was certain of it, and they were at war with France! Rebecca had denounced the men staying at the inn as foreigners. Hadn't she guessed their origin? What of Oliver? A Frenchman who had said Corisande would be hearing from him again. Dear God, did he plan, then, to kill her?

"Corie?"

She shrieked and spun, embarrassment flooding her as Donovan came toward her, the soft lamplight streaming through the sitting room from his bedchamber limning his powerful silhouette. "I—I'm sorry. I didn't hear you knock—"

"I didn't knock, woman. Are you all right?"

She gave a small laugh, a shaky, empty laugh, and spun back to the curtains. "I'm fine, of course, I'm fine—"

"Screeching when someone says your name is fine?"

"I didn't screech."

"Yes, you screeched. Which was actually a good thing to hear, considering you haven't said two words to me since I found you on the beach. I came to see how you're doing and I'm not leaving until you tell me. How does that suit you?"

Corisande rested her forehead upon the velvet curtain, her shoulders slumping.

"Corie, you're not yourself. I know tonight was a trial for both of us, but you're made of sterner stuff—"

"No, I'm not." Exhaling brokenly, Corisande didn't recognize the tremulous voice that had escaped her and neither apparently did Donovan. She felt tears sting her eyes as his hand touched her shoulder.

"Woman, that didn't even sound like you. What do you mean, you're not—"

"Not for something like this . . . it was so horrible—"

She gasped, folded so suddenly into Donovan's arms that she scarcely realized he'd reached out for her. Nor had she realized he was wearing no more than breeches as her cheek pressed against the crisp thick hair that matted his chest. Unbidden, tears began to spill down her face, not because he held her so closely, but because it felt so comforting to be held.

"I know the shipwreck was horrible," he murmured, slowly stroking her hair. "But it turned out well—no one drowned. It was damned astonishing, really, given the seas . . . Corie?"

She had begun to sob, great wrenching sobs that came from the very depths of her as she turned her face to his chest and wept unabashedly.

And Donovan began to hope, to hope desperately, that she might be weeping for him.

"I've always been a good swimmer, woman. Maybe I should have told you that before I ran off—"

"He tried to drown me, Donovan. I thought I was going to die."

He froze, intuition kicking at his gut as he held her away from him only to have her nearly collapse, she was sobbing so wretchedly. With a low curse he swept her into his arms and carried her into his room, into the light where he could see her face. A face that was flushed red from crying, her eyes filled with such despair that his heart seemed to twist inside him as he went and sat down with her on the bed.

"Who tried to drown you, Corie? For God's sake, what happened tonight?"

"Th-the same man from the heath . . . when you went into the water. I . . . I know you told me to stay put, but I came down the beach so I could be closer and—and they grabbed me."

"In front of everyone? How could that—"

"No one was watching me, Donovan. They were watching you and—and the other men and the ship! I tried to fight but—oh, God, they took me to the other side of the beach, and a man came out of the dark and threw me into the water again and again and again . . ."

Donovan pulled her fiercely against him as a terrified cry burst from her, and her arms flew around his neck as if by holding on to him she could will the horrible memories away. But he didn't want her to stop—he wanted to know everything that had happened. He clenched his teeth as she began to cry again, wishing desperately that he had been there, wishing that he could have helped her . . .

"You said he tried to drown you, Corie?"

"Yes, he—he held me down with his foot. The water was so cold, so deep, and my chest hurt so terribly . . . and then I couldn't struggle anymore—"

"God help me, woman, no more, no more." Donovan

hugged her more fiercely, incredulous that he could have been out saving strangers' lives while the woman he loved . . . the woman he loved . . . !

"He said . . . he said he hadn't brought me there to kill me, Donovan, and then—"

"Tomorrow, Corie, we'll speak of this tomorrow," he whispered, cradling her against him like a child. This time she fell quiet, her sobs becoming a great shuddering sigh that tore at him as deeply as anything she'd said. So deep that he felt a sudden wetness in his own eyes as he held her head against his heart, his cheek resting against her hair.

No wonder she had been soaked to the skin and covered with sand. He should have known she might be in danger, even with so many people around . . . damn him for not recognizing the peril. He couldn't think of it anymore! He didn't want to think about it, not now, not now. He only wanted to hold her, to feel the warmth of her, to have her close. Gently he lifted her chin; her beautiful brown eyes, still brimming with tears, met his as he traced the fullness of her lips with his thumb.

"Corie, I want you to stay with me tonight. I want you near me, to know you're safe. Please, woman, tell me you'll stay."

∞ Thirty-one ∞

Corisande went utterly still, no more able to breathe at that moment than when she'd fought so futilely beneath the waves.

She stared up at Donovan, at his lips, so very near now to her own, certain that her heart was pounding as fiercely as his, his rampant heartbeat pulsing in her ear. And when his mouth touched hers, so tenderly, so gently, more a whisper than a kiss, she knew she wanted to stay. To be near him, to know that he, too, was safe, to feel the wonder of his arms around her long, long into the night—

"No!"

She twisted free of Donovan's embrace so violently that she fell to the floor, the cry that had ripped from her throat as ragged and desperate as her sudden overwhelming thought that she must get away. Dear God, no, she didn't want these feelings! She didn't want them!

Fresh tears blinding her, she scrambled to her feet even as she heard Donovan coming after her, felt him catch her arm, but she wrenched herself away, rushing headlong for the drawing room door. But he was there blocking her way, and she dashed the other way, not heading for the door leading out into the corridor for fear he would block her there, too, but grasping her way frantically along the windows, among the curtains, until she found two smooth handles and yanked open the balcony doors.

In seconds, she was gripping the iron railing, thick rain pelting her face as she looked down wildly at the drive below.

It wasn't too far. She could jump and then run and run and run and never stop—

"Corie! Good God, woman, what are you doing?"

One leg already over the railing, Corisande fought with all her might as Donovan caught her round the waist and hauled her back onto the balcony, spinning her to face him. He shook her hard, not once but twice, such pain in his voice that she went still while he shook her a third time.

"Why are you so afraid of me? Why? I would never hurt you!"

"I—I'm not afraid of you!"

"Then why are you running from me?"

She didn't answer, couldn't answer, glancing behind her and thinking crazily that the railing was still close enough for her to reach if only . . .

Corisande cried out as Donovan pulled her against him, his fingers tunneling through her rain-soaked hair, his husky voice almost pleading.

"Corie, don't fight me. Don't run from me. Let me show you that I would never hurt you. That you can trust me! Let me show you . . ."

His mouth found hers before she could speak, his kiss filled with such unbridled passion that she knew at once she was lost, those same feelings coming back with a vehemence that she now felt wholly powerless to fight. Suddenly she couldn't be closer to him, nearer to him, her hands moving up his wet, matted chest to the massive breadth of his shoulders as his arms tightened around her.

The rain was cold, but everything else was so warm, his lips moving so hungrily over hers, his tongue as it thrust deep into her mouth, his skin that seemed to be on fire. She felt on fire, too, despite her soaked nightgown, the sturdy flannel clinging heavily to her body. So heavily that Donovan soon groaned in frustration against her mouth, his hands moving over her wildly as if searching for some way to reach her skin.

"Come. This damned stuff must go."

His lips never leaving hers, she was swept so unexpectedly off her feet that she felt her heart leap to her throat and she threw her arms around his neck, the balcony doors kicked shut behind them as he carried her back inside. But she scarcely noticed the sound for her blood pounding fiercely in her ears, or that suddenly she wasn't being carried anymore but lying upon the bed.

Only when she felt a small nip at her breast did she flare open her eyes to find Donovan kneeling astride her, looking more swarthily handsome than she could ever remember him, his eyes become as jet-black as his hair.

"Useless things, nightgowns. Shall we be rid of this one?"

He had whispered so huskily that she shivered, staring up at him as if cast in some seductive spell. Staring up at him as he bent his head to kiss her, his tongue first sweeping languorously across her lips before he pressed his mouth possessively to hers. But he didn't kiss her long, kneeling over her again as he gathered two fistfuls of flannel and slowly, his eyes full upon her, rent the soaked fabric from collar to hem, while Corisande gasped as her body was bared to his gaze.

Donovan drew in his breath, too, unable to tear his eyes from her . . . from the translucent whiteness of her skin and her dusky brown nipples to the auburn curls between her thighs, sweet dark curls he longed to touch, longed to feel wet and closing around his sex but not yet, not yet. She lay like a gift before him, a rare, exquisite gift, and he would not rush, no matter that he was already so hard and aroused he thought he might explode. No, no, he would not rush.

He could see that she trembled; he was shaking, too, her

sudden, wondrous acquiescence giving him more than hope
—that she would entrust him with her body, this woman
whom he thought of no longer as a temporary bride. God
help him, if he made her his wife tonight in every sense of
the word, maybe she would one day entrust him with her
heart . . .

"Are you chilled, Corie?" he asked softly, his gaze moving once more to her breasts, small beautiful saucy breasts
with droplets of moisture upon them that must have trickled
from his shoulders.

As she shook her head, he bent over her and flicked away
a tiny crystalline drop with his tongue, feeling her start beneath him, her eyes half closing at the sensation. He found
another droplet and flicked it away, continuing slowly, teas-
ingly, above her taut lovely nipples, below them and all
around them but not touching her there yet, not yet. Only
when he came to the last tiny bead of moisture did he gently
swirl his tongue around a nipple. Corisande arched her back
and moaned deep in her throat while he marveled at the
rose-scented sweetness of her skin.

"No lavender?" he couldn't resist teasing her in a
whisper, not surprised when her eyes flared wide.

"N-no, I don't like it either."

He chuckled deeply but grew sober when he leaned down
to kiss her parted lips, then the rapid pulsebeat at her
throat, her breasts. "Ah, but you will like this, Corie, I
promise."

He gently began to run his fingers over her body, barely
touching her, his hands gliding over her ribs and her belly,
then up her breastbone to her throat and shoulders, lightly,
softly, taking a moment to free her arms from her sodden
sleeves and cast the torn nightgown from the bed before he
ran his fingertips all the way down her beautiful torso to the
silken insides of her thighs. He was rewarded when

Corisande began to tremble all the more, her breathing coming faster, much as his own.

"Ah, Corie, do you like this too?"

He ran his hands back up to her breasts, touching her, oh, so gently, the pads of his fingers drawing close to her nipples and then circling away in a seductive game of cat and mouse until she tried to push away his hands and writhed beneath him. But she jumped, crying out when he finally grazed her nipples with his fingernails, and he gave in, too, to the urge nearly driving him mad and bent his head to suckle hungrily as Corisande wound her fingers in his hair and brokenly voiced his name.

He groaned in answer long delicious moments later when, her nipples wet and flushed a deeper brown from his touch, he finally left the bed to pull off his breeches, his swollen sex springing free. He saw her eyes widen, but to his relief she didn't faint dead away. He knew he was a big man, even when not fully aroused, yet he had no intention of rushing her, of taking the slightest chance of hurting her except to make her sweetly, sweetly suffer. Quickly he returned to the bed and enfolded her in his arms.

"Shh, Corie, we have all night. Let me show you that you can trust me. Let me . . ."

Corisande caught her breath as, once more, Donovan found her lips and kissed her deeply; she was already so lost to the wonder of everything he had been doing to her that she gave no thought of protest. She felt so strange, like nothing she'd ever known before, languid, and yet her skin tingling with his every teasing touch. Just as he was teasing her now, lifting his mouth from hers to roll her gently onto her side, and then shifting his body until he was almost flush against her.

Again his hands began to move over her, caressing the small of her back and her bottom with so feather-light a touch that she felt goose bumps sweep across her skin. But she inhaled sharply when one of his hands slipped between her legs from behind, his fingers gently brushing against her sensitive flesh, his breath upon her neck incredibly warm as he whispered in her ear.

"Shh, woman, I think you'll like this too."

She did, she couldn't deny it as Donovan touched her softly, making her squirm against him, a strange heat inside her growing ever hotter. He slid his fingers back, splaying his hand on her bottom and then slipping them to the front once more until she wasn't only squirming but trembling uncontrollably at the sensations plummeting through her. Over and over he teased her, until she could barely open her eyes when Donovan finally eased her onto her back; she felt drugged from the pleasure.

But she almost screamed when she felt something very hard nudge her at the center of her thighs, nudge her at the swollen, tingling place where his fingers had been only an instant before; she was stunned to find Donovan supporting his massive body on one arm as he half lay on top of her, her legs spread wide. And he was holding himself, his eyes burning into hers as he slowly, gently, rubbed that soft aching point with his flesh.

It was her last conscious thought as she cried out, her fingers digging into the mattress . . . and nearly Donovan's last conscious thought as well. To have Corisande lying beneath him, trembling, moaning, her beautiful body spread to him, her woman's flesh so wet and hot and quivering to accept him was the sweetest torture he'd ever been made to bear.

But he made himself move very gently though he was dying to thrust himself deep, deep inside her, entering her only the slightest bit before he pulled himself out, making her suffer, too, as sweetly as he had known she would. He teased her again and again until she was panting his name and clutching wildly at his shoulders, begging him to release her from something he knew she had never experienced before.

Begging him desperately while her body had begun to shake as he was shaking. His sex was throbbing so mercilessly that it was the most difficult thing he had ever done not to bury himself inside her warmth, her tight softness, and grant himself the release he so craved.

Only her mounting whimpers made him hold fast, her flesh beginning to pulse and quiver and contract around him until Corisande threw back her head and suddenly arched her hips to meet his. Donovan was unable to contain himself any longer as she screamed incoherently at the height of her surrender. With a ragged gasp he thrust through her maidenhead, his body gone rigid as he was rocked by the deepest, fullest release he had ever known.

"Ah, God, Corie! Corie . . . !"

Corisande heard Donovan's hoarse cries only dimly through the ecstasy that consumed her, expanding out from an incredible fullness deep inside her that she scarcely realized was his body until she opened her eyes long moments later, feeling entirely sated. Donovan was resting upon his elbows, the weight of him pressing her down into the mattress, a tender smile upon his lips though his eyes held concern.

"Did I hurt you, Corie?"

She shook her head, remembering a twinge of pain, but it had been nothing to the pleasure. At once she felt him relax upon her, and she relaxed, too, unable to keep from closing her eyes.

"Ah, no, woman, ah, no. No sleep yet."

She felt him lift his hips from her slowly, flickering her eyes open in surprise when he sank just as slowly back inside her, but not all the way, his body rubbing against her, teas-

ing once more that soft sensitive place that ached and tin-
gled all over again. She jerked, gasping, and Donovan
smiled quite devilishly.

"We've all night, Corie, remember?"

∽ Thirty-two ∾

Corisande blinked open her eyes, feeling as if she'd just awakened from some extraordinarily unsettling dream.

Of course, she and Donovan hadn't . . . No, no, no, she would never have allowed it, never have—

"But you did," she whispered to herself, suddenly afraid to move, afraid to shift even a baby toe as she watched bright patterns of sunlight play across the deep green rug. Which confirmed she wasn't in her room where the rug was cornflower-blue, but in Donovan's . . .

Oh, Lord. And it was morning, a brilliant morning, but how late she couldn't say. She scarcely remembered falling asleep, but everything else, everything else suddenly came flooding back to her, and her face began to burn. Her face, her body, as if Donovan were still kissing her, still touching her, still holding her.

Corisande squeezed her eyes shut as another memory drifted through her mind, this one very vague, hardly a memory at all because she'd been so exhausted, but more unsettling still than any of the others. Had Donovan really said that he loved . . .

Now Corisande did move, her heart racing as she raised her head from the pillow and glanced over her shoulder only to stare almost blindly at the empty space beside her. At the rumpled covers, tossed to the side but bunched against her in such a way that she had been almost certain Donovan was lying next to her, sleeping.

But she was alone.

She sat up, her gaze sweeping the silent room.

Of course she was alone. Damn him! Damn him! Just as she would be alone a few weeks from now when Donovan sailed away from Cornwall, away from Britain. The pain that cut through her heart was more excruciating than any she'd known.

And she could bear it no longer. Of course the man didn't love her! Had he said he wanted to stay with her? That he no longer wanted an annulment? She had no vague memories of that, no, none at all, and even if he had said those things, it didn't matter. It wasn't as if she loved him too!

Corisande threw back the covers, her throat tightening not so much at her nakedness or the scarlet splotches of blood staining the white sheets as at the bald-faced lie she had just told herself. She vaulted from the bed and ran for her room, swiping away the ridiculous tears that had sprung to her eyes.

Oh, yes, she had to end this madness and end it now; she could no longer stay under this roof. She would just have to think of some other way to help the tinners. She hastily poured water into the basin and began to splash herself, making as much of a mess and even more than had Donovan, washing his smell from her, washing all traces of last night from her body and then quickly toweling herself dry.

At the wardrobe, she skipped over all the lightweight colorful dresses Rose Polkinghorne had made for her and grabbed one of her own, donning the familiar gray cloth garment as a sudden commotion of carriages pulling onto the drive carried to her from outside. Tugging on a white stocking, she hopped on one foot to the window, her eyes widening as Arundale footmen came out of the house to meet the half dozen carriages while others began carrying trunks down the wide steps.

Oh, no, Nigel and Charlotte couldn't be leaving already! Not when she planned to use them if need be to—

"Good morning."

Corisande spun, dropping the other stocking as she stared at Donovan, stared at how handsome he looked plainly dressed in a full-sleeved white shirt, black breeches, and riding boots, her senses suddenly gone wild.

"You don't have to rush so, Corie. Nigel and Charlotte are at breakfast, plenty of time yet to say good-bye. I didn't want you to miss them so I came upstairs to wake you."

His voice was so low and husky, his gaze wandering over her so intimately, that it was all she could do to keep her presence of mind. She bent to retrieve her stocking and then turned away from him to tug it on, seeing out of the corner of her eye that Donovan had raised a jet-black brow, a teasing smile on his face.

"I don't really see that such modesty is necessary—"

"No, of course you wouldn't, but I don't bloody care what you think!" Her voice had caught, but that said, Corisande felt much emboldened as she went back to the wardrobe to get her shoes. She wasn't surprised to find that Donovan's smile was gone when she whirled to face him again, his expression sober, his eyes grown very dark.

"Your greeting isn't exactly what I expected, Corie."

"Oh? And what did you expect? After you—you seduced me? Took advantage of me when I was distraught, overwrought, hardly myself—"

"Good God, woman, are we back to this nonsense again? Of course I didn't seduce you!"

He'd shouted, and Corisande jumped, backing up against the door as he sighed heavily and came toward her, his tone much more restrained.

"What's wrong, Corie? Why are you acting like this?"

"Acting? Oh, yes, that's exactly the point here, isn't it, my lord? Well, I'm not going to act anymore, no, not another day, not another hour, not another moment. Our agreement is finished, Donovan. Over! I want an annulment and as quickly as you can arrange one, your bloody inheritance be damned!"

Corisande turned and grabbed for the doorknob as Donovan's voice suddenly grew very low behind her.

"Woman, you're not going anywhere until we have this thing out—"

"I *am* going—to my father's house, which I should never have left in the first place, and don't you dare try to stop me! If you do, I swear I've a very entertaining story I'm sure your brother would love to hear— Oh!"

Donovan had reached above her head and slammed the door back into place, then spun Corisande around so roughly that she felt a moment's fear. His face had grown as swarthy as she'd seen it, though his eyes held a trace of desperation.

"I suggest you consider very carefully before leaving this house or revealing anything to my brother, if you care at all about the welfare of your friends. I doubt Captain Oliver Trelawny would relish time in prison if his smuggling activities became known to the king's excisemen. Or any of his crew."

Corisande gaped at him, wholly stunned, while Donovan felt his gut twisting at her incredulous silence, which was a telling sign of what his warning might just have cost him.

Hell and damnation, this wasn't how he had imagined the morning would be! He hadn't come up here to threaten her friends but to wake her with a kiss and to tell her again that he loved her. Corisande had been so sleepy last night when he finally revealed what lay in his heart that he doubted she had even heard him. Now she would probably never believe him; dammit, why couldn't he have thought of some other way to prevent her from leaving him?

"So . . . so you followed me the other night to the cove?"

"What did you expect me to do?" Donovan's gut twisted all the more when he saw her stiffen. "Good God, you'd just been nearly strangled on the heath! I couldn't believe it when I overheard you asking Peggy Robberts to pretend her babe was coming so you could ride out again to God-knows-where; then, to discover you're a smuggler—"

"Fair trading is what we call it here!" Corisande countered hotly, so hurt, so indignant, so furious she didn't know what to do. Donovan, love her? Ha! She must have been dreaming to have come up with such a preposterous thought! "And it's what has kept this parish from starving, my lord, long before you ever set a foot in Cornwall!"

She turned around and flung open the door this time before Donovan could stop her, but he soon caught up with her, grabbing her arm to pull her to face him.

"Corie—"

"Don't fear, Donovan, I took note of your threat. I'm not going to ruin things for you with your brother," she half whispered through her teeth lest any servants were near. "I'm sure he and Charlotte are growing quite impatient to bid us farewell. We should go."

"Yes, but we're going to talk of this later, Corie, do you understand me? We *will* talk later."

She didn't answer, glancing away as tears suddenly leapt to her eyes—Lord help her, she was a mess. She started when she felt Donovan's fingers at her chin; he obviously wished for her to look at him, but to see her sniffling and crying was the last thing she wanted right now. She wrenched herself away and ran down the hall, scarcely hearing his ragged sigh.

*   *   *

Yet further discussion was not to be, at least not that morning or into the afternoon. No more than a few moments after the Duke of Arundale and his duchess—whining already about the length of the journey in front of them —and their entourage rolled away in their big black carriages, Henry Gilbert came galloping down the drive with news that one of the mine shafts was flooded from last night's storm. No men had been injured, thankfully enough, but Donovan should come straightaway to survey the damage.

So Donovan had gone, not to Corisande's surprise, although she was taken aback when he ordered Henry Gilbert to stay at the house to ensure that she would not be left alone for the day. Left alone? Ha! More likely to keep an eye on her! She had at once gone upstairs to her room, having no wish to share company with the man, and now here she stood at her window. The sun was already beginning to set in a blaze of orange and crimson fire, and still Donovan had not returned.

Which was fine with her. She hoped he would be gone through the night, and then they wouldn't have to talk, but she hadn't enjoyed being left with only her roiling thoughts to occupy her either.

She had already decided she wasn't going to meet the *Fair Betty* tonight no matter if the signal came; if Donovan did come home and find her gone, he might guess her destination and try to disrupt the landing. Better that she didn't go there at all. Oliver would have to manage on his own.

But thinking about those three men—now *that* had plagued her. That they might soon be enjoying the hearth fire and eating supper at the Trelawnys' inn was almost too much for her to bear. They might even be plotting to kill her.

She had only to think of that ominous warning . . . *"Now you know when you hear from me again, madame, you will not doubt that my words are true!"* . . . and it was like reliving once more the horror she'd known on the beach. Just to recall how close she had come to drowning left her shaking and yet growing angrier by the moment. Those bastards! Why should she be wondering when they might strike again when she knew exactly where they were staying?

Finally Corisande could stand the endless pacing in her room no longer. Her mind was made up. But she couldn't just go there and confront them. They would laugh in her face. But they wouldn't dare laugh at her if she . . .

Corisande's heart was racing before she got to Donovan's room; the vivid memories she had tried so hard to hold at bay hit her with full force as soon as she saw his bed. A bed that must have been made hours ago—Lord, she could just imagine what Ellen Biddle must have wondered upon seeing the blood. Two deflowerings?

Shoving the thought away, Corisande concentrated upon her search, and it didn't take her long. She found Donovan's pistol easily in the bottom wardrobe drawer, a shiver coursing through her when she traced her fingers over the smooth barrel, wondering how many men he might have shot—

"Oh, Lord." She didn't muse any further on that score; Donovan was an army officer after all. Instead she hid the pistol beneath her cloak and quickly went downstairs, deciding she would leave through the front door and let everyone wonder. She should have guessed Henry Gilbert might be watching for her. The agent rushed from the drawing room, his huge Adam's apple bobbing nervously.

"I'm going out for a stroll, Gilbert," she began, only to see that the scrawny fellow had the audacity to step in front of her.

"F-forgive me, Lady Donovan, but Lord Donovan asked that if you go out anywhere, I should accompany you."

"I only plan a short stroll, there's no need to trouble yourself—"

"But it's no trouble, my lady, truly. And if I don't, I'm sure you understand that His Lordship will be most displeased with me."

"Henry."

"Y-yes, my lady?"

Corisande drew out the pistol and leveled it at the man's stomach, and Henry Gilbert's eyes nearly popped from his head. "I strongly suggest you go back into the drawing room and have yourself a nice brandy. Are we understood?"

She didn't have to say another word as the agent slipped and slid across the polished floor in his haste to oblige her. And when Corisande turned back to the front door, she saw that the footman had disappeared too.

Lord help her, now if things would only go this smoothly with those Frenchmen.

∞ Thirty-three ∞

"Why, they're not here, Corie. Left in the wee hours of the morning, they did, half knocking down my door to tell me they were going on their way. Pah! Good riddance, I say! An' do 'ee think they left me an extra pence or two for how well my Oliver and I treated them?"

Corisande jumped at how hard Rebecca Trelawny slapped the wet cloth upon the trestle table, the woman clearly disgruntled as she scrubbed vigorously.

"An' that's not the worst of it! A fine new fishing boat was taken during the night, can 'ee believe that? Slipped out of the harbor without a soul giving any notice at all—which is no surprise! After that gale an' the shipwreck, why, everyone was exhausted and snug in their beds, giving no heed that there might be thieves among us."

"You think those men took it, then?" Corisande had scarcely asked before Rebecca hit the table with another resounding whack, causing several old fishermen to lift their heads from their ale with some apprehension.

"Ais, so I do! I told Oliver from the very first when those three came round asking for rooms that they had a mean, harsh look about them, but he laughed an' gave me no mind. I told that to the constable, too, just this morning, but there's nothing to be done now. The boat's gone, they're gone—" Rebecca paused, straightening from the table to study Corisande. "Why would 'ee be asking for them, Corie? Aw, no, don't tell me they stole from the church!"

"No, no, nothing like that," Corisande hastened to assure her, although she didn't quite know how to explain why she was looking for them. She certainly couldn't tell the truth; Rebecca would worry, and with Oliver still being out at sea . . . "Um, well—"

"Ah, Corie dear, give me a moment, will 'ee?" Rebecca threw the cloth over her shoulder and rushed across the smoky room to the hearth. "I've got a leek an' pork pie cooking—my Oliver's favorite—an' he'll have a fit if the crust is scorched."

More than grateful that she'd been spared from struggling for an explanation, Corisande called out, "That's all right, Rebecca, I must run! Take care now."

She was gone out the door before the woman had turned from the oven. The pistol Corisande held beneath her cloak was clasped so tightly in her hand that her fingers had begun to cramp. With dusk quickly fading into darkness, she leaned with a sigh against a wall, filled with as much relief as fury that her attackers had apparently left Porthleven.

So what had that French bastard meant, then? When she heard from him again? Obviously they wouldn't dare to return to the village now, not after stealing a fishing boat if, indeed, they had been the ones to commit the crime. But who else would have done such a foul—

Corisande gasped, her thoughts scattering, as a thunderous cannon shot shattered the peaceful stillness and a huge explosion of water burst high into the air only a hundred yards from the end of the quay. In shock she looked farther out to sea where a ship under full sail was making directly for the harbor while behind her another ship, much larger, bore down in hot pursuit.

Oh, God, a revenue cruiser giving chase, she was certain of it, while in front . . . in front . . .

As shouts went up throughout the village, people spilled from their homes and rushed down to the harbor. Corisande began to run along the quay as more cannon boomed, the shots clearly intended as a direct warning for the *Fair Betty* to heave to and allow herself to be boarded. For now Corisande was convinced the hapless cutter was Oliver's; she watched in horror as another roaring blast sent up a great plume of water so near to starboard that she feared the cannon fire might have struck the ship.

"Lord help us, oh, no, oh, no, 'tes my Oliver! My Oliver!" Rebecca Trelawny's hoarse cries rent the air, the woman at once grabbed by neighbors as she nearly toppled from the quay in her desperate frenzy.

Corisande had never felt so helpless as she watched the *Fair Betty,* so close now to harbor, finally slacken her speed and give way to the king's cruiser. A hue of such outrage—whistles and curses and catcalls, boos and hisses—arose from the village that she had no doubt Oliver and his crew would hear it and take heart that their neighbors and friends were with them in spirit.

She added her own voice to the wild melee, shaking her fist, shaking the pistol as an eight-oared galley filled with armed excisemen was launched from the cruiser, and she gave no heed that she was squeezing upon the trigger. She was knocked to her knees when the weapon suddenly fired, her ears ringing so loudly from the deafening crack as she struggled to rise that she didn't hear Donovan shouting until he was almost upon her.

"Good God, Corie, put that damned thing down! Will you have them think someone's firing out there and start a battle?"

Flushing with chagrin, she dropped the pistol as if it were a live snake, and Donovan grabbed up the weapon and shoved it into his belt.

"I—I'm sorry," she began, only to stiffen when he hauled

her to her feet, deep indignation filling her. "For heaven's sake, why am I apologizing to you? You had a hand in this, didn't you? Somehow you found out about Oliver returning tonight and you alerted the king's men! I should have known you'd be here to watch—"

"I'm here because once again, woman, I had to come looking for you!" Donovan pulled her along with him to where he'd left Samson. "And thank God I did too. Come, we've got to hurry."

"Hurry? Are you mad?" Corisande tried to wrest herself free, but Donovan's grip upon her arm was like a steel vise. "I can't go, I have to stay here! God knows what they're going to do to Oliver—"

"You can't help him, Corie. His fate is in the Crown's hands now. But your father needs you and Frances too!"

She stopped struggling, noticing for the first time how grim Donovan looked, his face etched deeply with worry.

"My father? What's wrong? What's happened?"

He didn't readily answer, lifting her onto Samson's back and then vaulting up behind her.

"Donovan?"

"Your sisters are gone, Corie. They were taken from their beds sometime during the night."

"Taken?"

His grave nod left Corisande cold, so cold that she could only stare blindly ahead of them as Donovan guided Samson from the crowded quay and onto the road where he kicked the animal into a gallop. As villagers scattered out of their way, it seemed they had reached the parsonage in an instant, the place eerily dark and silent but for a light burning in the kitchen window.

"After what you spouted earlier about wanting to go home, I came here first to look for you and found Frances and your father instead," Donovan said, lifting her down. "Then I heard the cannon and— Hell, that doesn't matter.

Your father was tied to a chair when I found him, Corie. He's been badly beaten, but he'll—Corie?"

She'd fled inside, not waiting for Donovan as she careened through the parlor and down the hall.

"Papa? Papa!"

She burst into the kitchen, coming up short in front of the high-backed settle as her father lifted his head from his hands to look at her. One of his eyes was swollen shut, his face puffy and covered with ugly bruises, a line of dried blood trailing down the corner of his mouth. Splotches of dull brown blood stained his shirt.

"Oh, Papa . . ." Tears blinding her, Corisande looked up at Donovan, whose arm had gone round her waist. "Frances?"

"I carried her upstairs, put her to bed. I found her down here lying on the floor—she must have been baking."

"Yes, yes, she likes to bake bread late at night," Corisande said numbly. "Is she all right?"

"Groggy, can hardly open her eyes, but I think she'll be fine. She doesn't remember much more than that they forced her to drink brandy laced with laudanum."

"They?" Corisande whispered, ice-cold intuition clutching at her heart. Donovan didn't answer, nodding to the piece of paper that had been skewered to the kitchen table with a knife. But Corisande went instead to her father; she sank down next to him and laid her hand on his arm, her throat so tight she could hardly speak. "Papa? What happened?"

A tear running down his swollen cheek, Joseph Easton shook his head in despair. "I tried to find it, Corie. I tried so hard to find it but I couldn't remember . . ."

"Corie."

Starting, she looked up as Donovan handed her the letter he'd just removed from the table.

"I know you don't like knives."

His voice was so huskily soft, his eyes so full of concern, she couldn't help but be touched. But her hands were shaking so badly she couldn't focus upon the writing, and she handed it back to Donovan. "Please . . ."

"They've taken the girls to France," he said without looking at the letter, obviously having already read its grim contents. "To Brittany—Roscoff—where they'll wait only until Monday morning, barely three days from now. If they don't have what they want by then, Marguerite, Linette, and Estelle will be given over to Moroccan pirates who still trade with the French no matter the war—"

"But what could they want?" Corisande cut him off hoarsely, desperate tears clouding her eyes. "We don't have anything! My father is a vicar—we've no money!"

"Corie, whoever wrote this letter says your family has a cache of jewelry that belongs to him."

"Jewelry?"

"He says, too, that he's the one who pushed over those barrels, who attacked you on the heath, who rode after you that one night—"

"One night?" Momentarily confused, Corisande had only to glance at Donovan to know that he must have followed her back to the Robbertses' that night of the landing. But she didn't press it further as he went on, his voice becoming angry.

"And he was the one who gave you a warning last night on the beach. Good God, woman, you never told me that he spoke to you!"

"I did! I said he claimed he hadn't brought me there to kill me and then I tried to tell you the rest, but you said we would speak of it tomorrow—" Corisande fell silent, her face burning as she looked down at her hands. "He told me that when I heard from him again, I wouldn't doubt that he spoke the truth. I didn't understand . . . it made no sense until now."

"But I knew. God forgive me, I knew all along . . ."

Corisande glanced at her father, his voice despondent. "Knew what, Papa?"

"That Louis had done those terrible things. He came here at night, sometimes during the day at my window. He would tell me— Ah, but there was nothing I could do! He swore he would kill you if I said a word to anyone!"

"The window," Corisande murmured, recalling the day she had brought Donovan to meet her family, and a window in the study had been open for the first time in years. Her father had been in the garden, looking so distressed, and then at her wedding, after the barrels, she'd never seen him so upset—oh, God. Heartsick that she hadn't recognized his torment, she prodded gently, "You said Louis, Papa. Who is he? Why would he be doing this to us? If you know, you must tell—"

"He's one of the devil's own. A murderer!" Joseph turned from her to stare into the cold hearth, his face ashen beneath the bruises. "I knew nothing of him until he came here—two weeks ago, no more! He knew your mother when she was a girl—he knew your grandmother Véronique, too, and hated her. Hated her for the wealth his father, the Marquis de LaCroix, had squandered upon his mistress—"

"His mistress, Papa?" Corisande blurted out, as stunned by what he had just said as that his hoarse words had spilled forth in a lucid flood she'd only heard before in his sermons. She glanced at Donovan, who stood listening silently, then back to her father when he gave a broken sigh.

"Adele told me about her mother before we were wed— how she escaped from Paris at the height of the Revolution, de LaCroix already imprisoned and facing execution, and fled to Brittany to the country house that he had provided for Adele no matter she was not his child. Ah, God, she wept so when she told me how a wild mob set upon the house, screaming that they were going to kill the monarchist's whore. Véronique made Adele change into a servant's clothes and entrusted her care to their beloved maid Laurette, then she secreted them both from the house just as the mob shattered the front door. That was the last time Adele saw her mother; the house was in flames by the time she and Laurette reached the hills."

A heavy silence fell in the kitchen, but it did not last long as Joseph went on, rocking himself forward and back as tears began to stream down his battered face.

"She didn't tell me about the jewelry until a week after you were born, Corisande. I think she'd known it might cause an impasse between us, and said nothing until Laurette decided she wished to return home out of concern for her parents. The woman would take no payment for all her pains, but Adele insisted she have one of her mother's rings, a ring such as I'd never seen before, gold with a heart-shaped blue sapphire surrounded by diamonds. And there was more, too, rings and necklaces and brooches and pearls and . . . and I demanded it all be thrown into the sea."

"The sea, Papa? But why?"

"Because I was a fool and didn't understand how much it meant to your mother! A leather packet filled with those things had been pressed into her hands just before she and Laurette had fled. Because Véronique had been a man's mistress, not his wife! It was the only time we ever raised our voices to each other, your mother crying that the jewelry should one day belong to our children while I wanted nothing more than to be rid of it. But when she swore she would leave me, I said no more. We never spoke about it again until she fell sick—"

Joseph's voice broke, and Corisande jumped up to sit beside him. But he seemed determined to continue, turning his ravaged face to hers.

"She was dying, she knew it, and she made me promise that I keep the jewelry safe for you and your sisters. I found a small chest, and the night she . . . she left us, I remember walking outside and digging a hole, but nothing after that—nothing! God help me, I tried to find it—while Louis came here almost every day telling me what he would do to you and your sisters if I didn't. He murdered Laurette! He showed me the ring! He's been an émigré in Germany all these years until he finally went back to France to see if there was anything left of his father's estate. That's how he found us! He came upon poor Laurette in the village where Véronique's country house . . ."

His voice had grown so choked that he clearly couldn't go on while Corisande sat there stunned, feeling as if the blood had drained from her face.

"Corie?"

She met Donovan's gaze, her voice no more than a whisper. "I know. I think I know where my father buried that chest."

∽ Thirty-four ∞

Incredulous, Donovan had already been planning what they might be able to do to help Corisande's sisters—had been since he'd seen the letter—but now he stared at her while her father appeared dumbstruck as well.

"That night . . . that night my mother died, I followed Papa onto the heath. It was raining, a terrible storm like last night's, and he was weeping so hard, I feared he might become lost. So I followed him and watched as he buried a small wooden box, but I never thought to ask him what had been inside. It seemed a private thing—"

"Good God, woman, then let's not sit here!" Donovan shouted vehemently. "We've got to find that chest and get ourselves a ship, though with that revenue cruiser in the bay it might be difficult . . . hell, we'll think of that later. Do you have shovels?"

"Yes, in the stable." Corisande was astonished at how quickly Donovan had taken charge. Yet she was nearly knocked to the floor as her father lunged to his feet so suddenly that the wooden settle tipped forward. Donovan reached out to catch it just in time. Breathing her thanks, she rushed after her father, grabbing his arm as he headed down the hall.

"Papa, Donovan and I can do this! You're hurt—you should lie down—"

"No, I will help!"

Her father's tone as determined as she'd ever heard it, she said no more, but instead ran back to the kitchen to grab one of the oil lamps while Donovan went after her father.

"I'll meet you in the garden!" Corisande started to the kitchen door, but then decided she should check on Frances. She took the steps two at a time, holding the lamp high as she went into the housekeeper's room.

"Corie?"

Scarcely recognizing the weak-sounding voice, Corisande sank down onto the bed. "Yes, it's me."

"My girls, Corie, my poor girls. I heard them weepen, so scared—"

"They'll be fine, Frances, I promise. Donovan and I will find them. He knows what to do. We'll find them."

The words were out before she realized she'd said them, but Corisande didn't linger to dwell upon how much she was depending on Donovan. She pressed a kiss to the housekeeper's forehead and then left the room, almost ready to head down the stairs when a faint whimpering made her move to the room shared by Estelle and Linette.

Tears burned her eyes at the signs of struggle, bedclothes twisted and lying upon the floor, a lost slipper, Linette's collection of seashells that she kept beside her bed crushed into fragments beneath a heavy foot. And lying forlornly across Estelle's pillow was Luther, his scruffy head tucked between his tiny paws, his tail wagging halfheartedly for an instant before it fell still altogether as he began again to whimper.

"I know, Luther, I know," Corisande murmured, swiping at her eyes. "I want Estelle home too."

She couldn't stand it, fleeing down the stairs and rushing outside to find her father and Donovan waiting for her by the garden wall.

"I'm sorry. I had to check on Frances." She lifted her

lamp and led the way through the metal gate and out onto the heath. "Careful, there are holes dug everywhere."

"So I discovered," came Donovan's wry reply, making her smile in spite of herself.

But she sobered as she searched around her for landmarks, not wanting to remember that terrible night eight years ago but forcing herself to remember, forcing herself to retrace painful steps taken when she was only twelve years old. When her father had wept so wretchedly she thought he might become ill. She had feared for him then, and followed him into the pouring rain.

She had almost gone to him when he stumbled, her own silent sobs tearing at her as she watched him pull himself to his feet though he was nearly doubled over with grief. Finally he had stopped only a few yards from an old stunted tree she'd used to climb and begun to shovel . . .

"Over here! By the tree, but not too close."

Donovan was there first and immediately threw off his coat to begin digging at the spot where Corisande had shoved the toe of her shoe into the damp earth. The hole was soon several feet deep before she realized from studying the positioning of the tree that she'd misguided them.

"Donovan? Papa? I'm sorry, but I think it was closer over this way." She was grateful that neither complained. Donovan's strong steady strokes with the shovel more than overshadowed her father's efforts, who did his best to keep up.

And even when her father had to pause to catch his breath, Donovan continued on, sweat soaking him, his white shirt becoming almost transparent and clinging to his powerful body. She swallowed and looked down instead at the deepening hole, gasping aloud when Donovan's shovel suddenly scraped against something hard.

She went down on her knees beside him, all of them digging with their hands to clear away the dirt from what she could see as her breath caught was a sturdy wooden

chest. She nearly fell forward face first in her haste to retrieve it from the hole, but Donovan caught her shoulder
and threw her a glance that clearly said he was the one to
try.

While she and her father looked on, he leaned into the
crater and hauled out the chest. Corisande thought that it
appeared much smaller than she remembered, no bigger
than Donovan could clutch easily under his arm. But she
had been a child when last she'd seen it. She held up the
lamp when he set the dirt-caked chest in front of her father,
whose hands shook as he slowly opened the lid.

For a moment Corisande felt as if she could hardly focus
her eyes for the sparkle and glitter that seemed to burst
forth from the chest. Her breath snagged again as she gazed
down upon a dazzling tumble of pearls and brilliant jewels,
silver, and gold. But what caught her attention lay half buried in one corner, and she glanced up at her father.

"May I, Papa?"

"It's yours, Corie. Yours and your sisters'—"

He choked on the words, and Corisande's heart went out
to him; she knew they couldn't tarry, Donovan already having risen to his feet and thrown on his coat. But she had to
see . . . it looked like a portrait . . .

She slowly drew in her breath as she lifted with trembling
fingers a diamond-framed miniature of a woman wearing
large pearl-drop earrings—the same lustrous earrings she
could see gleaming in the chest—and with rich auburn hair
. . . a gently smiling young woman who looked much like
her.

"Véronique," came her father's hoarse voice. "Your
mother was holding that medallion when she died."

"She was lovely," Corisande murmured almost to herself,
tracing a finger over the portrait.

"Like you, Corie. Just as I've always said."

She glanced up to find Donovan staring at her with such

intensity that she quickly dropped her gaze again, her hands trembling even worse now as she replaced the miniature and closed the lid. "We—we should go . . . see about a ship, I mean."

She rose to her feet, ignoring Donovan's proffered hand and hoping her father hadn't noticed. But he was occupied with the chest, although it was clear he barely had the strength left to lift it. As Donovan went at once to help him, irrational anger filled her to see that her father could trust him so.

The man was a bloody informer! she ranted to herself as they walked back to the house, Donovan carrying the chest tucked under one arm while supporting her father with the other. He'd brought the king's excisemen down upon Oliver and the *Fair Betty,* she was certain of it!

Yet even as she nursed her mutinous thoughts, she knew they rang as false as the glaring lie she'd told herself earlier, which only made her hold on to them all the more desperately.

Donovan helped her father to a chair and then set the chest upon the kitchen table. Her father broke down and began to sob, the strain of the past two weeks, the strain of painful memories aroused, finally proving too much for him. She could only kneel beside him and clutch his hands. Her father had become once again the wretched shell he had been since her mother died . . . his misery making her throat tighten and cold, paralyzing fear burrow all the deeper into her heart.

"I'll fetch the doctor and see what we can do about finding a ship," Donovan told her, but she refused to look at him, his low curse lost to the anguished sobs echoing in the room.

"Ais, Corie, 'ee can imagine my Rebecca was none too pleased to see me heading back to sea. But when Lord

Donovan found me at the inn an' told me what had happened to your poor family, I was ready to sail in a blink. Now all we must do is keep a good look out for that damned revenue cruiser, but it's so dark I'd wager a pocketful of guineas they've gone home to their fires. Ais, gone home to their fires and to cry into their beer that the *Fair Betty* was clean as virgin snow, not a barrel of brandy on her!"

As Oliver Trelawny's delighted laughter swelled around her, Corisande couldn't help smiling either, more than relieved that he and his ship had survived their close call. Survived it and triumphed, apparently, in only ten minutes' time, the disgruntled excisemen heading back to their cruiser after a fruitless search that was done before darkness had fully fallen.

Yet her smile quickly faded as she thought of Donovan below deck in Oliver's cabin, where the captain had told him he could help himself to a bracing bit of rum brought aboard to bolster them all during the long Channel crossing. And she had no plans whatsoever to go near that cabin but to stay aft with Oliver—

"Lord, Corie, I'm sorry to be laughing at such a terrible time for 'ee." The captain's gruff apology broke into her thoughts. "You say Dr. Philcup had a good look at your father an' Frances?"

"Yes, they'll be fine. It was hard to make my father stay in bed—he wanted to come with us to Roscoff—but the doctor said it would be too much of a strain for him. He'll be staying there through the night to keep an eye on them both."

"Ais, good man, Philcup. Charges a mite too high a price if 'ee ask me, but a competent fellow all the same." Oliver gave a grunt, searching Corisande's face in the lantern light. "As for feeling well or not feeling well, why don't you go join your husband? You're looking pale, Corie, agitated, jumpy as a cat—"

"I'm not jumpy!"

Oliver grunted again, louder this time. "No? Then what was that testy outburst? A hiccough? I don't blame 'ee now, given 'ee must be worried sick for your sisters, but you'd best get some rest an' maybe help yourself to a dram of rum too. I've offered my cabin to 'ee, it's yours and your husband's for the night—"

"And what of you?"

"Ha! If I get tired, I'll sleep up here under the stars. An' I've a crew taking shifts who'll help me, so don't think 'ee have to stay here to keep me awake. Now go below an' join that fine husband of yours! He's as worried about the girls as you, Corie, in case 'ee haven't noticed."

"Of course I know he's worried!" Corisande blurted out, not liking the censure in Oliver's tone. "Why would you say—"

"Just popped to my tongue, is all. He offered to pay me a king's ransom to sail back to Roscoff, did 'ee know that too?"

Corisande shook her head, chewing her lower lip.

"I thanked him kindly an' turned down his money. You're like family to me after all, but oh, ais, he's worried just the same as you—"

"All right, all right!" Corisande left him, not because she wanted to join Donovan but because she'd had quite enough of Oliver's lecturing. There wasn't anything left to see anyway; the lights of Porthleven were already swallowed up by darkness as the *Fair Betty* headed out of Mount's Bay and southward into the Channel on a journey that would get them to the Brittany port well before dawn.

Yet as she stormed below deck, she swore she could hear a faint chuckle trailing after her. Her face growing red, she burst into Oliver's cabin, coming up short at the sight of Donovan sitting on the bed with his back against the wall, one arm resting on a raised knee and a near-empty glass of rum in his hand.

"Ah, so gracious of you to join me finally, wife."

As much stung as startled by his sarcasm—she hadn't heard it in days—Corisande wondered nervously if she should maybe leave the door open. But Donovan took that decision out of her hands as he rose and came toward her. Corisande sidestepped him and then whirled around with a gasp as he slammed the door shut.

Yet when he turned upon her, his expression to her surprise wasn't angry or sarcastic, just very serious. That unnerved her even more than she would have thought, and she edged backward, coming up with a start against the bed.

"Sit down."

She did, his low voice brooking no argument, although she bristled, glaring at him. He seemed not to notice, moving to Oliver's mahogany desk to pour himself another glass of rum; the ship's rolling motion apparently wasn't bothering him either, for he stood so squarely, his lean, muscled legs planted so firmly, that he looked as if he had been born to the sea.

"Captain Trelawny has done quite well for himself—I've seen few cabins so well appointed. A crystal decanter, glasses, brass fittings, polished wood—"

"Yes, he's done well, and I'm grateful it wasn't all lost to him today, no thanks to you."

Corisande heard the glancing ring of the decanter hitting a glass, but Donovan didn't look at her although she could see that he had visibly tensed. He seemed so tense that she began to feel quite unsettled again; the cabin suddenly felt quite small and close around her as she quickly sought to change the subject.

"Were things very bad at the mine? The flooding?"

"Bad enough, but the pumps did the job. Do you want some rum?"

As Donovan's brusque voice sent nervous chills plummeting down her spine, she gave a slight shake of her head. "No, no, thank you." But now her heart began to pound fiercely when he finally turned from the desk, his eyes jet-black in the lamplight and trained full upon her.

"Henry Gilbert is well, too, in case you were wondering. A bit shaken from having a pistol pointed at his gut, but he'll live. You never cease to amaze me, Corie—"

"So you've often said."

The biting words were out before she had even realized she'd spoken them and she wished she hadn't when a look of such pain crossed Donovan's face that she felt it almost as strongly as if it were her own. And what his pain could mean, ah, Lord, she didn't even want to think of it!

With a strangled cry, she flew across the cabin to the door, but Donovan was already there, catching her in his arms and hauling her against him. She struggled wildly but in vain, even in her desperation her strength no match for his. Within an instant he had pinned her flailing arms behind her with one hand, his other thrust through her hair to pull her head back to face him, holding her so tightly her scalp stung.

"We're going to talk, Corie, *now, here,* and have this thing out!"

"No, I've nothing to say to you!" she cried, her only escape to sink deeper and deeper into lies. "You're an informer and I despise you! I don't know why you're here— my sisters' welfare has nothing to do with you! What do you care if they come to harm? Why put yourself in danger? Once you have your bloody inheritance, you'll be gone from our lives forever!"

"I've already won my inheritance, woman, and I've not left you! God help me, I've not left you!"

∞ Thirty-five ∞

Corisande went still, staring into Donovan's anguished eyes.

"As for your sisters, I know what it's like to have someone you love taken from you. I've a young daughter, Corie, only two years old, and I don't know if she's alive or dead! I've been searching for Paloma for months—her mother, Nina, was murdered by French troops, and I was so far away fighting near Madrid that it was weeks before I found out. By the time I returned to the village where they'd lived, a nursemaid had long since taken my daughter and fled. No one could tell me where. That's why I needed my inheritance! If not for Paloma, I would have told Nigel to hell with my father's will. But I couldn't. I needed the money—"

"Needed the money . . ." Corisande echoed in a whisper, stunned by everything he'd just told her.

"Yes, to pay the men I hired at the start to help me search. They'd risked their lives time and again to cross enemy lines with me, and I couldn't reward them generously enough. Yet it didn't take long for what money I had to be gone."

"So that's why you tricked me into marrying you," she said almost under her breath as Donovan looked at her in confusion. "I overheard you talking with Morton Robberts —you were already going to help the tinners, you'd already fired Jack Pascoe, and then I came along looking for Henry—"

"Would you have helped me if I'd told you the truth, given who I was, given what you thought of me? I doubted you'd believe anything I said—maybe still don't believe . . ."

His embrace had tightened once more, though he'd loosed his fingers from her hair to cradle her face, his thumb softly stroking her cheek. "Corie, I didn't tell you that Nigel had brought word of my inheritance because I didn't want you to leave me—especially when you were in such danger. I wanted more time to try to find out who was attacking you. And this morning—"

"This morning your true nature came through!" Corisande cut him off, desperately trying to close her ears and her heart to what she sensed he was about to say. "You're right! I don't believe anything you— Oh!"

Donovan had jerked her against him so abruptly that she felt she couldn't breathe. He held her so tight, his dark eyes burning into hers. "No, I think you do believe me, Corie. Just as you believed me last night when I said I wouldn't hurt you, when I asked that you trust me. If you hadn't, you wouldn't have let me touch you, you wouldn't have given yourself to me so completely, wouldn't have kissed me as you did—"

"And I told you that you seduced me!"

"Seduced, woman? Am I seducing you now?"

She gasped as his mouth captured hers, his kiss so wildly possessive, so hot, so hungry that she felt herself rise on tiptoes to be closer to him, her hands suddenly clutching at his shirt.

"Am I enticing you against your will, Corie?" she heard him demand raggedly against her lips just before his tongue plunged into her mouth, his deepening kiss arousing a response in her that was nothing less than carnal, her own tongue swirling and playing with his. She heard him groan, felt him dragging her skirt above her thighs and lifting her, then suddenly she was the one with her back to the door, her legs hoisted around his waist.

"Tell me you want me to stop," Donovan taunted her as he kissed her eyelids, her lips, her throat, his rum-scented breath like a scorching heat upon her skin. "If I'm seducing you, tell me you want me to stop!"

His lips found hers at the same moment she felt his fingers slide into her body, and when he pressed against that soft aching place with his palm, she gave no more thought to making him stop than even remembering what he had said. Suddenly it was just Donovan kissing her and his fingers moving inside her, slipping out only to enter again while she began to moan brokenly against his lips.

But he silenced her cries, filling her mouth with his tongue as he withdrew his fingers to fill her with his body— not slowly but fiercely, Corisande gripping at his massive shoulders as he thrust deep, deep inside her. She began to shake and writhe against him, her release coming as fast and as furiously as a wave crashing over her head, and she was drowning in the wildness of it, the incredible wonder of it, her blood surging in her ears.

From some distant place she felt Donovan crush her against him, felt his body quake and shudder and then collapse against her, but she had no fear that she would fall. He held her as close to him as if they were one, so close that she could feel his heart pounding against her breast . . . then gradually it slowed, long moments passing before she had the strength to lift her head from his shoulder.

And when she did, Donovan was staring into her eyes as he eased his body from hers, his hand going between them to his breeches as her dress fell back around her ankles. Yet still he kept her backed up firmly against the door, their bodies still pressed so closely together that she could feel the heat of him through her clothes. But that couldn't match the heat in his eyes, not carnal, but something so much deeper burning there.

"I love you, Corie. I didn't want to, I fought it—God knows I never wanted marriage, never wanted a wife. But I love you! I've never said that to any woman before."

"Not even the one who gave you a child?"

Corisande scarcely realized she'd asked him such a thing before Donovan was shaking his head, his voice almost a whisper.

"Nina was my mistress for a time, but she didn't love me, or I her. I'm holding the only woman I've ever loved and all I ask from you, Corie, is that you tell me you believe me. It would be enough . . . for now. Please tell me that you believe me."

She believed, ah, she believed—could see it in his eyes, hear it in his voice, feel it in how he held her. Just as she felt a terrible anguish welling inside her, too, ice-cold fear swallowing her joy. He had a daughter, and he would surely go back to Spain to find her, which was only right, but behind enemy lines—he had said so! And if she gave herself over to him now and something should happen—oh, God . . .

"No, no, you ask too much of me!" she cried out hoarsely, pushing against him, trying to wrest herself free. "I—I can't give you what you want! I could never give you what you want! I'm sorry! I'm sorry! Please let me go! Please!"

She nearly fell when Donovan suddenly moved away from her, her eyes so blinded with tears as she clutched wildly at the wall to regain her balance that she didn't see him open the door. But she heard it slam and she knew she was alone.

Wretchedly, utterly alone.

* * *

"Ais, now, the tavern where that bastard said 'ee could leave word for him is straight down the dock. The White Hart, isn't that what the letter said, my lord?"

Donovan nodded, while Oliver tugged worriedly at his beard.

"Lord, I want to have me an' my men come with 'ee, I don't like that the two of 'ee are going there alone, but I can't help thinking if the man sees the whole lot of us, he might panic an' do God knows what—"

"I agree, it's best this way," Donovan interrupted, anxious to be on their way. It was still a few hours before dawn, but the dock was already coming to life, and they were on French soil. The only good thing was that Roscoff was a well-known smuggling port, and their arrival had caused little stir; two dozen or more ships of all sizes lay berthed along the wharf.

Most of them were probably English, Donovan thought darkly with a glance in Corisande's direction. She wasn't looking at him but at Oliver as the captain made her lift her hood over her hair.

"There's nothing down here but whores an' tavern wenches, an' I'll not have 'ee drawing attention to yourself with that pretty auburn hair, Corie. Now stay good and close to your husband."

Stay good and close? Donovan swallowed hard at Oliver's low command but steeled himself grimly against thinking about anything other than the task that lay ahead. Yet it was almost impossible when Corisande moved next to him, though she'd remained silent. He hadn't heard her speak at all since last— Hell and damnation, enough!

"We'll be waiting here if you've need of us," Oliver said to him, thankfully distracting Donovan's thoughts. "One shot into the air an' we'll come a-running to help, my lord, our pistols at the ready."

Donovan nodded again, ensuring that his own pistol was

tucked securely in his belt and yet hidden under his coat.
Oliver Trelawny left them and headed back to the large
rowboat where ten of his crew sat silent and armed, the *Fair
Betty* anchored farther out in the harbor. Which left Donovan and Corisande standing alone on the wharf, well, not
fully alone as a bedraggled pair of sailors reeled drunkenly
past them, one of the men casting a bleary-eyed glance at
Corisande.

"Stay close." Donovan repeated Oliver's order, his voice
harsh. But maybe then she would heed him with their
bloody lives at stake. "Remember, Corie, under no circumstances do you hand over that chest until we know your
sisters are safe—if we end up having to hand it over at all.
It's the only thing we have to guarantee we're going to make
it back in one piece to the ship. Do you understand?"

Corisande felt stung that he had spoken so gruffly to her,
but what had she expected? She gave him a small nod,
gripping the wooden chest under her arm as he set off at
such a hard pace that she had to hurry to keep up with him,
despite her long legs.

He must be angry, he must be . . . Ah, but she couldn't
think right now about how angry Donovan must be, how
deeply hurt—she had no idea where he'd spent the night
while she'd hardly slept at all in Oliver's cabin. Anxiously
she wondered if her sisters might be bound and gagged and
held captive in any one of these shabby two-story buildings
flanking the harbor. And the few sputtering lanterns hanging here and there did little to dispel the wharf's sinister
look.

She could hear voices and raucous laughter, shrill female
laughter, too, spilling out onto the dock from the several
lighted taverns they passed, which illustrated fully that Roscoff was a place that never grew quiet. She jumped when a
sailor suddenly careened out of a door to fall to his knees in
the adjoining alley and start retching; she moved closer to

Donovan when a trio of men followed after him, laughing and jeering.

"I—I don't like this place."

Donovan didn't respond, but Corisande could see that his hand had moved under his coat to his pistol, which gave her some comfort. Yet she felt nothing but an icy chill slice down her spine when a voice suddenly carried to them from the shadows, a harsh accented voice that she knew so well.

"Ah, madame, monsieur, you've come to Roscoff and so quickly. I saw the ship enter the harbor and wondered perhaps if it might be you."

She spun, but Donovan caught her arm, demanding in a sharp whisper, "Do what I say. Do nothing but what I say."

"And I say you both move over here where we will talk," the voice barked in a low command.

Corisande saw that Louis, the Marquis de LaCroix, had stepped farther into a dark alley next to a tavern bearing in English the name The White Hart, no doubt for the benefit of its smuggler patrons.

"No, we'll talk out here on the dock," Donovan answered for them, but Corisande was suddenly overwhelmed by such fury and outrage at what that bastard had done to terrorize her and her family that she couldn't restrain herself.

"Yes, out here in the light, and we'll not say a word to you until we see that my sisters are safe! You fiend! Coward! I've the jewelry, de LaCroix, do you hear me? We found the chest, and I swear you won't see a single pearl until I know my sisters are safe—"

"Good God, woman, will you wake the entire port?"

Donovan had seized her arm and drawn her back against him, but Corisande gave him little heed as she saw Louis moving out of the shadows toward them, her vehement outburst clearly having worked. He was not as big as Donovan but powerfully built, his moustached face hardened with bitterness and— Oh, Lord. She stiffened in fear when she saw that Louis held a pistol leveled right at Donovan's chest. Suddenly she wished desperately that she had kept silent.

"*Oui*, madame, you resemble my father's whore Véronique, and for that alone I could have killed you. But now I see it was wise for me to let you live. Keep very still, madame, and you"—the marquis shifted his glittering gaze to Donovan—"draw your hand away from your weapon. Good, now raise both your hands slowly . . ."

Louis suddenly gave a low whistle and his two compatriots rushed from the alley, one wresting Donovan's pistol from his hand while the other reached out to grab the chest from beneath Corisande's arm. But all she could think of was her sisters and how Donovan had said the jewelry was their only guarantee; with a fierce cry, she swung her fist with all her might and cracked her attacker in the face before fleeing to the edge of the dock, her breath tearing from her lungs as she ripped open the lid and held the chest out over the water.

"No, I will see my sisters! Bring them out here at once, or I'll empty this whole thing into the sea!"

Corisande saw Louis's eyes flare, his face stricken with rage, his pistol still pointed so ominously at Donovan that she began to pray, hard. But in the next instant, immense relief swept through her as the marquis nodded to his men.

"Go. Do as she says."

They disappeared at once into the alley, and she saw light spilling from a door near the back of the building, but she wasn't through with Louis yet, oh, no. "Hand your pistol over to my husband. Now!"

The marquis stared at her as if she were insane, but when she plunged her hand into the chest and pulled out a brilliant diamond necklace, throwing back her arm to fling it out into the darkness of the sea, he lowered his pistol, and Donovan was there in an instant to take it from him.

"Good God, Corie . . ." was all she heard him say before muted weeping carried to them from the alley. The pitiful sound grew louder as Louis's two accomplices brought forth her sisters half stumbling in their dirty, crumpled nightgowns—Marguerite, her eyes red-rimmed and swollen from crying, carrying Estelle who had her arms flung around her older sister's neck, while Linette trailed behind, clutching Marguerite's sleeve.

"Tell your men to stand away from my sisters and toss away their weapons!" Again Corisande held out the necklace, and Louis, his face gone chalk-white from fury, could do naught but comply.

"Do as she says!"

Donovan felt his heart lurch when he saw that Corisande was teetering perilously close to the edge of the dock, but he forced himself to focus upon the three dangerous men in front of him, retrieving his own pistol as weapons were dropped and hurling the rest with a low curse into the sea. Then he beckoned to Marguerite, who was trembling from head to foot as she glanced from him to Corisande. All three girls were clearly so terrified that they hadn't budged an inch.

"Marguerite, listen to me," he said to her firmly, her wide, frightened eyes jumping to his. "Take Linette's hand, that's right, now come over here and stand behind me. Everything's going to be fine. Everything's—"

"Donovan!"

Corisande's cry split the night, but he saw the danger too late. Louis had pulled a knife from the back of his belt and grabbed Linette by the hair to yank her against him before there was anything Donovan or Corisande could do.

"*Oui,* put the chest down on the dock, madame, or the girl dies, do not doubt me!"

∞ *Thirty-six* ∞

As Linette burst into terrified tears, the long knife blade pressed to her throat, Corisande was so stunned she simply stood there, frozen.

"I said put the chest down in front of you! *Maintenant!*"

She obeyed him, shaking so violently as she returned the diamond necklace and closed the lid that she feared her knees might give way when she set the chest upon the dock with a loud *thunk*. But when she straightened she froze again, her eyes widening to see a man wearing only breeches creep up behind Louis, creep up so silently that no one was aware of him, not even Donovan, as everyone focused their attention on her . . . until the cock of a pistol made her jump, the weapon suddenly pressed to Louis's temple.

"Harm the girl, man, and *you* die."

As Louis swore vehemently, everyone else now stared at the handsome dark-blond stranger, who appeared nearly as tall and strapping as Donovan, and at the other men who suddenly emerged from the shadows with wicked-looking cutlasses and pistols drawn. Corisande's gaze flew to Linette, her heart thudding painfully in her throat. Dear God, why wasn't Louis dropping the knife? Why wasn't he—

She gasped as an enraged bellow rent the air. Louis had shoved Linette away from him and was lunging straight for her, straight for the chest—at the same moment Donovan dove for Louis and both men crashed to the dock amidst the high-pitched screams of her sisters. Suddenly everything was confusion, Corisande crying out, too, when she saw Louis raise his knife in the air to strike.

"Donovan! Oh, God, Donovan!"

She nearly tripped over the chest in her haste to reach him only to be grabbed round the waist and swung out of the way as a shot exploded, then another almost simultaneously, Louis's knife spinning in a spray of blood across the dock as he slumped onto Donovan. The next thing she knew she'd been released, the blond stranger lowering his pistol as Donovan flung off Louis's limp body—his right hand, his pistol, the front of his white shirt bloodied from a gaping hole in the marquis's chest.

It was then that Corisande saw Donovan had been cut, bright red blood oozing through a gash in the upper sleeve of his coat, and she started to run to him but was suddenly encircled by Marguerite, Linette, and Estelle, her sisters falling upon her tearfully. Her eyes brimming, too, she sank to her knees to embrace them; when she looked up again, Donovan was surrounded by Oliver and his crew, who must have come running at the sound of pistols firing. The handsome stranger who had helped them, an Englishman she was certain of it, and the other men had vanished just as mysteriously as they had come.

Louis's compatriots had disappeared, too, no doubt taking one look at his bloody corpse and deciding no amount of jewelry was worth dying so hideously for. It was a sickening sight, the marquis's right hand shattered by a bullet that must have been fired by the stranger just as the knife was descending, saving Donovan's life and giving him the split second he needed to fire his own pistol. And she hadn't even had the chance to thank the man . . .

"Corie, girls, come, we must go!" Oliver cried as he hurried over to them, shepherding everyone in front of him. "Soldiers might have heard—the last thing we need are questions! Go!"

Corisande grabbed up the chest, and Oliver grabbed up Estelle, while Linette and Marguerite lifted their nightgowns and ran barefoot alongside them. The crew of the *Fair Betty* and Donovan had their pistols lowered and at the ready as they all headed back to the eight-oared rowboat. And none too soon, as people began to pour onto the dock, a crowd gathering around the body they had left behind.

The commotion only grew worse as they rowed out to the *Fair Betty,* but very quickly they were all safely aboard and the anchor hoisted. Corisande tried to push the horror of Roscoff from her mind as she herded her sisters below deck and into Oliver's cabin. The pitching motion of the ship was a wondrously encouraging sign that they were well on their way. Another blessing was her sisters assuring her that they hadn't been hurt, especially Marguerite. Dear God, if those men had touched her . . .

"I'm hungry, Corie!"

That from Estelle, and Corisande was only too glad to pull out for them from Oliver's private larder what was left of the pork and leek pie Rebecca had baked, and an untouched plate of buttermilk cake. She wasn't hungry, though, content just to watch her sisters eat heartily and begin to smile again, and giggle when Estelle took a spoon and tried to balance it upon her nose.

But suddenly Estelle grew still, tears filling her eyes. Corisande knew at once her sister was thinking about Luther; Estelle had always performed that silly trick with him before.

"Luther's fine, Estelle. He was lying upon your pillow when I found him. He'll be so happy to see you—"

"But they tried to kick him, Corie, tried to stomp him until he went to hide under the bed."

Sighing, Corisande brushed the buttermilk cake crumbs from Estelle's mouth as she drew her close to give her a hug. "We won't think of that anymore, all right? Marguerite, Linette? We're all safe and sound and together and we won't think of that anymore. Now I want you to wash up and then try to get some sleep—"

"But what about the chest?" Marguerite broke in excitedly. "Can't we have a peek inside?"

Corisande sighed again; she had wanted to see them quickly settled so she might find Donovan. He had been cut, his wound would need tending—

"Please, Corie?"

"Very well, but only a peek. Then I want you to get some rest. We'll talk about all of this when we're home."

As she lifted the wooden chest to Oliver's bed where they were all sitting, Corisande should have known waiting to explain everything that had happened would be impossible. The moment she opened the lid, she was bombarded with questions peppered with girlish oohs and aahs, and she resigned herself to telling them as much of the story behind the jewelry as she could, given that Estelle was only nine. The full truth of it she would tell Marguerite and Linette later.

"Oh, Corie, this was our grandmother?"

Corisande nodded at Marguerite, who held up the diamond-framed miniature of Véronique for her younger sisters to see.

"She looks like you, Corie—a bit like Mama, too," Linette said very softly.

"Yes, and all of this is a gift from Mama to us," Corisande murmured as she returned the beautiful portrait medallion to the chest and closed the lid. "Now lie down, all of you. This bed is certainly big enough that you'll have plenty of room."

She was pleased that there was little complaint. The covers were soon tucked in snugly, the lamp turned down, and Corisande had almost reached the door when Estelle's sleepy voice drifted to her.

"Isn't Donovan going to come and tell us good night?"

"I—I'll go see," Corisande fumbled, not knowing what else to say.

He wasn't below deck, that she soon realized after a quick search of the first mate's cabin; the crew's berths were empty, too, all of the men probably at their posts until they were farther out into the Channel. She climbed the narrow stairs, a balmy breeze stirring her hair as she stepped onto the deck. She saw Donovan at once, standing far to the prow, standing so tall and straight that her throat closed tightly as she remembered how close that knife had come— Dear God, she loved him so much.

She loved him so very much!

Corisande was astounded, for the first time not denying to herself the truth of what lay in her heart. For the first time not wishing for it to go away or that she didn't want it . . . for the first time not feeling afraid. She felt only one thing, that she wanted desperately to be with him. She must have flown across the deck, for in the next instant she was standing just behind him . . .

"Donovan?"

He spun, and her stomach sank to her shoes at the hardness of his expression, the tension in his body.

"Donovan, I—"

"What, Corie? Come to tell me you can't wait for us to reach Porthleven so you can formally lay your charges against me?"

His voice was a low growl, and she shivered. "Charges?"

"I'm an informer, remember? At least according to you."

"No, no, I wanted to thank you for helping me find my sisters," she blurted out, realizing with a sick feeling that Donovan was clearly in no mood to talk to her. She stammered, her thoughts suddenly in a jumble. "I—I would have liked to thank that other man too—"

"And his American friends?"

She stared at him, wholly confused as he gave a hollow laugh.

"An Englishman with American friends in a French port, and we're at bloody war with both of them."

"You—you think those other men were American?"

Donovan shrugged. "I heard them talking among themselves when Oliver and his crew came running—and it wasn't the king's English. Hell, it doesn't matter."

He turned abruptly back to the railing, and Corisande felt as if she had been dismissed, Donovan's broad back still stiff with tension.

"I . . . I was wondering how your wound—"

"A scratch. Already seen to, thank you. One of the crew kindly loaned me a clean shirt."

He said no more, and Corisande didn't have the heart to press things further. Now was not the time. He was obviously furious with her. But hopefully tomorrow—

"Your sisters. They're well?"

She started, suddenly encouraged that his tone had grown softer. "Yes, yes, fine. Estelle, in fact, was asking for you. She wanted to tell you good night—"

"You tell them for me. You should get some rest yourself. Bloody big day for you."

His sarcasm hitting her like a fierce blow, Corisande turned away, scarcely able to see for the tears burning her eyes as she fled across deck. She didn't stop until she had reached Oliver's cabin, fumbling with the door in an attempt to close it quietly.

"Corie?"

"Go to sleep, Estelle, go to sleep," she said hoarsely, grabbing an extra blanket and throwing it around her shoulders before settling herself in a stuffed wing chair bolted to the floor. "Donovan said he would see you when you wake up, all right?"

Corisande got no answer; gentle sounds of sleeping came from the bed while she could but stare blindly into the darkness.

"Corie, will 'ee wake up? You girls have slept right through the docking, 'ee have!"

Corisande blinked open her eyes, squinting at the daylight streaming in the door. "What . . . ?"

"It's Oliver, Corie! An' I'm telling 'ee, Frances is damned an' determined to climb up the gangplank herself if you an' your sisters don't show yourselves to her an' quick! Can't ee hear her bellowing? Like a cow she sounds, bawling for her calves!"

Corisande started from the chair, suddenly feeling dizzy from standing up too quickly. She was so groggy she could but mumble a hoarse thank-you to Oliver as she went to the bed to shake her sisters awake. Then she heard it, carrying down the stairs from outside, Frances's voice loud enough to shake the very timbers of the ship.

"Marguerite, Linette, and Estelle Easton, I'll not be waiten another minute! I don't want to come aboard the ship—I like to feel the good, steady land beneath me, but I will! An' that goes for you, too, Corie Véronique! Come out here this very instant so I can see all my girls are safe!"

"Well, did you hear her?" Corisande blurted out to her sisters, who looked like rumpled ragamuffins as they yawned and stretched, while Estelle was already clambering from the bed. "Up with you and go give Frances a hug!"

Estelle and Linette needed no second urging but skittered from the cabin, as Oliver followed after them, shaking his head. But Marguerite stood looking at her doubtfully.

"I can't go out there like this, Corie," she said, glancing

down at her dirty flannel nightgown. "And my hair isn't brushed—"

"I'm sorry but I can't do anything for your hair," Corisande said wryly as she took off her cloak. "Here, put this on. It'll do until you get home."

Smiling gratefully, Marguerite whisked the cloak around her shoulders and darted from the cabin, leaving Corisande to pick up the chest and fit it snugly under her arm. Wondering if poor Oliver had had to awaken Donovan, too, she hastened up the steps, smiling at the brilliant sunny day that greeted her, smiling in anticipation of seeing him.

Her eyes swept the deck, but he wasn't there. She imagined he must have joined the noisy crowd milling on the dock. It appeared much of the parish had turned out to welcome them home, no doubt everyone having heard of her sisters' plight.

She could see Frances beaming from ear to ear, laughing and crying at the same time as she hugged first Estelle, then Linette and Marguerite, then all three at once. And there was her father, beaming as broadly as Frances and surprising Corisande that he would have braved such a crowd. But she still didn't see Donovan—

"Corie."

She spun, her eyes meeting Oliver's, and at once her smile faded as she saw his somber face, his perplexed eyes.

"Lord Donovan left the moment we docked, maybe a half hour ago now. Didn't say much except to thank me an' that he had things to do at home. I know 'tesn't my business, but did 'ee have a quarrel with the man— Corie?"

She'd fled, barreling down the gangplank nearly straight into Frances, taking only an instant to give the housekeeper a hug before she thrust the chest into her arms.

"Take that home, Frances, and help Papa find a safe place for it—one we won't forget!"

Frances looked from her to the wooden chest, sputtering

in confusion, but Corisande had already moved on to her father. He was surrounded by her sisters, so she could only throw him a kiss, then she was ducking her way through the crowd, praying that Pete was still where she'd left him in the Trelawnys' stable.

⤭ *Thirty-seven* ⤭

"Y-you're leaving, my lord?"

"Yes, for London," Donovan said tersely to Henry Gilbert, whose large Adam's apple bobbed up and down as he swallowed in surprise. "I'll send word to you as to what needs to be done as soon as—"

"Needs to be done, my lord? Forgive me for interrupting, but I don't understand."

"You will, Gilbert, you will," Donovan said cryptically almost to himself, striding into the library. He had hoped not to encounter anyone, pack a few things and be on his way, but damned if Henry hadn't just been setting out for Porthleven, having heard that the *Fair Betty* had returned.

It seemed the agent had hired a fisherman to watch for the ship and then let him know as soon as it was sighted— Gilbert's loyalty amazed him. But better he be loyal to look after Arundale's Kitchen and the tinners' welfare when Donovan was gone. Just because he wouldn't be returning to Cornwall didn't mean he wasn't going to honor his part of the agreement.

"Brandy?" he asked, and Henry looked even more confused although he nodded. Donovan poured two brimming drinks and handed one to the agent, then lifted his glass and half emptied it in a swallow while Henry sipped his cautiously, no doubt recalling well the time he had nearly choked. As Donovan remembered it, they had just made a toast to his marriage . . .

"Will Lady Donovan be accompanying you?"

Donovan didn't readily answer, tossing down the last of his brandy.

"M-my lord?"

"No, Gilbert, she will not be accompanying me." He set down the glass with a hard thunk on the desk, his gaze falling upon a small stack of letters. "These arrive today?"

"No, yesterday evening, my lord, but you'd already gone to Porthleven. I heard some news at the mine today, though, that I think might interest you. About Jack Pascoe."

Donovan looked up, his scrutiny so intense that Henry appeared suddenly quite uncomfortable.

"If . . . if you care to hear it, my lord. You seem in quite a hurry—"

"What news, man? Of course I'm bloody well interested!"

"Well, my lord, Jack Pascoe's dead. An accident at Great Work mine, or so they're saying. It seems he'd been drinking before he came to work his core late last night and he started boasting that he'd brought the king's excisemen down upon Oliver Trelawny and that one day they'd catch him red-handed and your wife, too, my lord, please forgive me for saying so. I heard all this from Jonathan Knill, whose brother works at Great Work and—"

"So what happened to the bastard?" Donovan broke in with impatience, making Henry Gilbert jump.

"H-he slipped, my lord, slipped and tumbled down the main shaft. At least that's what the tinners said when the accident was reported. But I think—well, they've no love for informers around here—"

"So I've discovered," Donovan muttered, the pain suddenly so fierce inside him that he suddenly wanted nothing more than to escape it. To hell with packing! He could buy what he needed along the way and in London. The sooner he was out of this house, out of Cornwall, the better. "Help yourself to the brandy, Gilbert," he said tightly, thrusting the letters into his coat pocket. "A pity that such fine stuff should go to waste."

He stormed from the library, and Henry Gilbert hastened after him.

"But—but, my lord, some of those letters I believe are bills. If you're going to London, shouldn't I see to—"

"Take them all, man!" Donovan spun so suddenly that Henry knocked into his arm, causing the letters to scatter to the floor.

Cursing, he sank to his haunches to help the agent retrieve them, noticing that one of letters was water-stained, the original writing upon it nearly faded, although more recent writing clearly indicated it had been forwarded from Arundale Hall. His heart seemed to stop when he saw that the letter had come from Lisbon, his fingers trembling as he tore it open and began to read.

"This one is addressed to you, my lord . . . from Miss Lindsay Somerset."

"What?" Donovan's voice was so hoarse—God help him, his daughter had been found! She was safe in Lisbon!—that he could barely speak.

"From Lindsay Somerset, my lord."

"Are you sure it isn't for my wife?" Donovan took the letter, hardly able to focus upon the feminine scrawl for the emotion clouding his eyes while Henry Gilbert could only stare at him. "What are you looking at, man? Didn't you say you had bills to pay?"

"Yes, yes, my lord, I do. I most certainly do." Henry fled with a handful of letters back into the library, leaving Donovan standing alone in the entry hall.

Hell and damnation, what could Corisande's friend want with him? He pocketed the letter about Paloma and angrily ripped open Lindsay's, cursing when the top half tore off in his hand and fluttered to the floor. He swept it up, deciding he wasn't even going to read the damned thing. Why should he? He had other things to think about . . . his daughter to think about . . . yet he began to read anyway almost in spite of himself . . .

I hope you don't think it too forward of me to write to you, my lord, but it is only because I so dearly love Corie and want the best for her. I've heard only the most wonderful things about you here in London, and I told Corie so in my last letter—ah, but it's not my purpose here to recount all of that. I wanted you to know how wonderful Corie is, too— though I truly hope you've already discerned that for yourself —but she has such a fearsome temper at times that I felt I must write to you and explain—

"Fearsome temper?" Donovan said with a snort, reading on.

. . . explain that, well, Corie would never admit it, no, not even to me, but she's very afraid, you know. I wondered a long time why she seemed so set upon scaring away any young man who came near her, but when you look at her father—what became of the poor man after her mother died—

Donovan glanced at the other torn half of the letter in his hand, but he had no stomach to read further. No stomach because suddenly he was so furious with himself that he didn't know what to do.

Damn him for a fool, how could he not have seen it? That time last week when he had tried to kiss Corisande and she had panicked, then cried herself to sleep? How she had tried so desperately to run from him the other night—even attempting to jump from the balcony—and he had demanded why she was afraid of him? But maybe she hadn't been running from him as much as from something else . . . maybe feelings that frightened her so . . . feelings he had sensed all along ran as deep and as fierce as his own . . .

Cursing his blindness, cursing himself for having spoken to her so callously last night on the ship when she had come to thank him, Donovan stuffed the torn letter in his pocket and sprinted outside, his heart thundering in his ears as he headed for the stable.

"What do you mean he's not here?" Corisande began to think she would have to shake an answer from Henry Gilbert, who was gaping at her so fearfully, his Adam's apple bouncing. "I've no pistol, Henry! I'm not going to shoot you! I just want to know where Donovan—"

"Th-the stable, I think. A few moments ago—I imagine to get his horse. He . . . he said he was going to London."

"Oh, Lord."

She fled back outside, wondering wildly if she had missed him. Henry Gilbert had been so engrossed in his work when she burst into the library, who could say if it had been a few moments ago or maybe a quarter hour ago that Donovan had left? She must have frightened the poor man to death, too, papers flying into the air as he dropped to his knees and ducked behind a chair. It had been so comical she might have laughed, but she didn't feel at all like laughing.

She'd never ridden so hard, exhausting poor Pete. He would never make it any farther, not to Helston, and certainly not to London. She ran to the stable, her lungs hurting, already so out of breath.

She couldn't believe Donovan would leave her without even saying good-bye—ah, yes, she could, and she couldn't blame him. Yet it still made her angry all the same and—and, oh, please, please, may he still be in the—

Corisande gasped, spinning so crazily out of the way as a horse and rider galloped through the stable doors that she lost her balance and fell flat on her face, the wind knocked from her. For a moment she could only lie there, coughing at the dust and bits of hay settling around her, but suddenly she was hauled to her feet, coming face to face with Donovan.

"Corie? Good God, woman, are you all right?"

She stared up at him, so grateful that she'd caught him in time, so giddily happy that he hadn't left yet for London, so . . . so angry that he was going to leave without saying good-bye!

"You . . . you cad! Scoundrel! Reckless horseman!"

"Reckless horseman?"

"You could have killed me! *Killed me!* And I came all this way to find you!"

"You came to find me?"

"Yes, that's only fair, isn't it? After all the times you had to come after me? But then Gilbert said you were going to London and—and without even a good-bye and . . . and you're going to annul me, aren't you?"

"Actually," he said huskily, drawing her into his arms, "I'd annul you just for the chance to start over with you again as my bride, Corie, if I thought it might help me win your love."

As tears filled her eyes, Corisande plucked at Donovan's coat; she had suddenly grown so flustered. "I . . . I don't think that will be necessary, my lord."

"No?"

She shook her head, swallowing hard so that she might continue to speak. "I think I've been quite won over already . . . quite won over. I'm just so sorry, Donovan, that it took me so—"

She didn't have to finish. Donovan's kiss was so warm, so tender, that she felt her heart filling with unimaginable joy. And when he finally pulled away from her, long, long moments later, he had the funniest, wryest smile on his lips.

"I wasn't going to London, you know."

"No?"

He shrugged. "No. Couldn't leave you. That's all there is to it. I guess you're stuck with me, woman, for better or worse, informer or not—"

"Oh, no, Donovan, I never believed you were an informer! I only said that because—"

Again Donovan silenced her, this time with a finger placed gently to her lips. Later, he thought, later he would tell her about Jack Pascoe, but not now. Not now.

"That's all behind us, Corie. Are we agreed?"

She nodded, and he drew her close, hugging her fiercely to him as he murmured against her hair, "And no more fair trading, are we agreed? After seeing that revenue cruiser, I can't bear the thought that—"

"Agreed."

She'd answered so hoarsely that he drew back to look into her face, only to discover tears coursing down her cheeks.

"Corie?"

"I want you to find your daughter, Donovan, I truly do, and I'll do anything I can to help you. I'll love her as if she were my very own. But for you to go behind enemy lines—"

"There won't be any enemy lines, not in Lisbon," he said softly, watching surprise light her face. "Paloma's been found. My daughter's been found. We have only to go get her, Corie. Will you come with me to bring my little girl home?"

Corisande reached up to cradle his face, her lips sweetly, so sweetly touching his, and Donovan knew that he needn't have asked. But he couldn't help himself from asking for one final agreement when she drew away from him a moment later, her beautiful eyes shining.

"One last thing, Corie. Would you promise here and now that you'll never call me lambkins?"

"Only if you promise never to call me a shrew."

"Oh, you're no shrew, woman." Donovan hugged her against him, his smile as teasing as her own. "Just lively. And I wouldn't want you any other way."

If you enjoyed this book, take advantage of this special offer. Subscribe now and...

Get a Historical

No Obligation

If you enjoy reading the very best in historical romantic fiction...romances that set back the hands of time to those by-gone days with strong virile heros and passionate heroines ...then you'll want to subscribe to the True Value Historical Romance Home Subscription Service. Now that you have read one of the best historical romances around today, we're sure you'll want more of the same fiery passion, intimate romance and historical settings that set these books apart from all others.

Each month the editors of True Value select the four *very best* novels from America's leading publishers of romantic fiction. We have made arrangements for you to preview them in your home *Free* for 10 days. And with the first four books you

receive, we'll send you a FREE book as our introductory gift. No Obligation!

FREE HOME DELIVERY

We will send you the four best and newest historical romances as soon as they are published to preview FREE for 10 days (in many cases you may even get them before they arrive in the book stores). If for any reason you decide not to keep them, just return them and owe nothing. But if you like them as much as we think you will, you'll pay just $4.00 each and save at *least* $.50 each off the cover price. (Your savings are *guaranteed* to be at least $2.00 each month.) There is NO postage and handling—or other hidden charges. There are no minimum number of books to buy and you may cancel at any time.

FREE Romance

(a $4.50 value)

Send in the Coupon Below

To get your FREE historical romance and start saving, fill out the coupon below and mail it today. As soon as we receive it we'll send you your FREE Book along with your first month's selections.

Mail To: **True Value Home Subscription Services, Inc. P.O. Box 5235
120 Brighton Road, Clifton, New Jersey 07015-5235**

YES! I want to start previewing the very best historical romances being published today. Send me my FREE book along with the first month's selections. I understand that I may look them over FREE for 10 days. If I'm not absolutely delighted I may return them and owe nothing. Otherwise I will pay the low price of just $4.00 each: a total $16.00 (at *least* an $18.00 value) and save at least $2.00. Then each month I will receive four brand new novels to preview as soon as they are published for the same low price. I can always return a shipment and I may cancel this subscription at any time with no obligation to buy even a single book. In any event the FREE book is mine to keep regardless.

Name

Street Address   Apt. No.

City   State   Zip Code

Telephone

Signature
(if under 18 parent or guardian must sign)

Terms and prices subject to change. Orders subject
to acceptance by True Value Home Subscription
Services. Inc.   11726-9

Nationally Bestselling Author
MIRIAM MINGER

"A gifted writer whose books belong on every romance reader's shelves."
—Romantic Times

__SECRETS OF MIDNIGHT
0-515-11726-9/$5.50

Corisande Easton has spent her entire life struggling to help the underprivileged of Cornwall. So when she meets Lord Donovan, owner of the tin mill, she confronts him about overworking the tinners. Corisande finds her temper flaring—until Donovan softens her fury with his gentle ways, to become her newest, most passionate cause.

__WILD ANGEL   0-515-11247-X/$4.99

The fierce Irish warrior, Ronan, takes a deathbed oath to protect a chieftain's rebellious daughter. Triona is a hellion of a woman, defying Ronan's every command. So he plans to marry her off, to be rid of the wild lass forever. But then Ronan realizes the fiery passion of this beautiful woman is something he wants for himself.

Payable in U.S. funds. No cash orders accepted. Postage & handling: $1.75 for one book, 75¢ for each additional. Maximum postage $5.50. Prices, postage and handling charges may change without notice. Visa, Amex, MasterCard call 1-800-788-6262, ext. 1, refer to ad # 466

Or, check above books and send this order form to:	Bill my: ☐ Visa ☐ MasterCard ☐ Amex	(expires)
The Berkley Publishing Group 390 Murray Hill Pkwy., Dept. B East Rutherford, NJ 07073	Card#_____	($15 minimum)
Please allow 6 weeks for delivery.	Signature_____ Or enclosed is my: ☐ check ☐ money order	
Name_____	Book Total	$_____
Address_____	Postage & Handling	$_____
City_____	Applicable Sales Tax	$_____
State/ZIP_____	(NY, NJ, PA, CA, GST Can.) Total Amount Due	$_____